GW00480530

A FINE YOUNG MAN

Sharon Mulrooney

Norman,

Remembering those
Cross words and
drives out to
Roundstone!   x Shar

This book is a work of fiction. Names, characters, places, and incidents either are products of the author's imagination or are used fictitiously. Any resemblance to actual persons, living or dead, events, or locales is entirely coincidental.

Sharon Mulrooney

Printed in the United Kingdom

First Printing: May 2018

ISBN-978-1-9996070-1-2

To three generations of Inas
and all the strong women behind the stories of men.

PROLOGUE

He did turn in his grave, as his great granddaughter predicted.
But it was the slow, luxuriant stretching turn of someone under an eiderdown on a Saturday in Spring with no good reason to get up yet. It was the sleepy, toe-curling turn of a man who has earned his rest, savouring the warmth and comfort, the birdsong outside the window, the anticipation of tea and toast and marmalade, a bit later on.

Every time the story was told, it came out a little bit different.
How would it be, this time?

Sharon Mulrooney

St Margaret's
Taylor's Hill
Galway

August 1939

Dear Michael

I am writing this letter because I don't know if I will have the opportunity, or maybe even the courage, to see you ever again.
You know that I have admired you since I was a boy. Your Finn Mac Cúmhail stories gave me a good idea of what it takes to be a hero. You have spent nearly your whole life serving the dream of a Republic and along the way you have sacrificed your family, your friendships and your own comfort and safety.
Earlier today I avoided meeting your eye, not because I was ashamed but because I didn't want to see hatred or disappointment there. I share your dream for our beloved country, but I have chosen a different road and today I took one of the most difficult steps along it.

In eternal friendship
Bert

Sharon Mulrooney

BERT'S JOURNEY
1912–1916

Sharon Mulrooney

CHAPTER 1

August 1914

A thunderstorm had finally broken the sweltering heat of the day. Bert ran home, an hour late for his tea. His shorts and thin cotton shirt were no protection from the downpour, and his left boot leaked where the sole was peeling away from the upper. He danced a jig over the cobblestones, avoiding the puddles. He had delayed as long as possible the moment when his Mama would see his split lip and black eye. He turned into the alley and ritually touched eight gates with his fingertips before lifting the rusty latch and leaning his shoulder against their own green one. He paused in the yard for a moment, took a deep breath and made a futile attempt to tame his wiry hair. He was hungry but expected to be banished to his room without any tea. He briefly considered pilfering some bread from the scullery and stuffing it into his pocket to eat later. The family was still sitting at the kitchen table. They stopped talking when he walked in. His cheeks burned. Resorting to fisticuffs was a sign of weakness. He dared not meet his father's eye. The legs of Papa's chair squealed on the linoleum floor as he stood up.

"We were just thinking of sending out a search party for you, Bert," he said in a surprisingly neutral tone.

Bert quickly glanced at his mother.

"Sorry, Mama."

He did not see the expected flash of annoyance in her green eyes. She just nodded. Papa told him to wash his hands and find something dry to wear. In the scullery on the wooden drainer, a pile of dirty dishes waited for his sister Eileen, and the empty coal bucket stood reproachfully by the door, waiting for him. He scrubbed his hands vigorously, trying to blend the new scratches into the red swelling of his knuckles. Had someone died?

The smell of cabbage lingered, and his stomach rumbled. His mouth ached at the thought of luscious, pink, fatty bacon. He went upstairs to change. There was no sign of his eldest sister Louise, who often walked out with Alfie in the evening, whatever the weather. Bert liked Alfie. He was always in good humour and some of it was rubbing off on Louise, who could be very serious. If she went off and got married, there would be a bit more room in the house. His food was on the plate when he got downstairs, and he sat down and mumbled a quick Grace before meals. That was one Protestant formality his mother insisted on.

"Thank you, Mama," he said, and she smiled, just a tight little grimace.

They were all sitting there staring at him. The news must be very bad, but his stomach couldn't wait.

"So, what happened to you?" demanded Leo.

Bert shot his older brother a dagger look across the table and chewed his food very slowly and carefully. Leo followed his brother's sideways glance at the wooden cradle by the fire, where Papa was rocking it absent-mindedly with his outstretched foot.

"Well, Bert, there are greater battles afoot than your own."

Leo's chair creaked as he tipped it on to the two back legs. Mama frowned at him.

"Ah Mam, I'm sure it will all blow over very quickly," Leo said, the chair legs banging down on the floor as he leaned towards Bert, with a gleam in his eye.

He held up the newspaper for Bert to see.

'We could not stand aside! Britain will not allow Germany's fleet to batter France's undefended coast," it read.

Bert choked on a lump of bacon and had to gulp down some water.

"What does it mean?" he said, stupidly, looking at his father, who had explained all about the ultimatum and what would happen if Germany didn't back down.

Papa was pulling agitatedly on the pipe. "Britain is at war with Germany."

Conor stirred in the cradle and cried. He was the only one of the O' Briens born on the wrong side of the Irish sea. Bert had never dared to ask if that made him English. Eileen stood up.

"I'll bring him to you, Mammy."

Their mother quickly took the last sip of her tea.

"That's the first time he had the good manners to wait until you were finished your tea," Papa muttered.

Bert wasn't sure what being 'at war' really meant, but he didn't want to draw any more attention to himself by asking, so he sidled out to pick up the coal bucket in the scullery. Eileen was already clattering the dishes in the sink. The empty pail swung against his leg as he crossed the yard to the bunker, darkening the permanent bruise there. He staggered under the weight on the return journey, his knuckles shining white on the cold curved handle. He made it a matter of pride to get all the coal in one go, rather than half-filling the bucket twice. He added coal to the kitchen fire and put some lumps into the brass scuttle for the parlour.

Papa leaned across and looked at his eye. He spoke very quietly.

"What happened?"

"I got into a fight."

Bert stood up straight, ready to face the consequences, but he could feel the annoying blush rising up from his neck. Papa lifted one grey eyebrow, but he didn't reach for the cane straight away.

"Jeremy Audley was casting aspersions about Conor," Bert said stoutly.

His father's moustache twitched but he didn't make his usual joke about Bert swallowing the dictionary.

"And you had to stand up for your brother, I suppose."

Bert's tongue kept running over his swollen lip. Did it look as big as it felt?

"Yes, Papa."

Audley had called his baby brother a Mongoloid.

"They don't live for long. They were never meant to be born. It's nature's way."

The way he said it sounded as if Audley had overheard it from an adult, so it must be true. Bert punched him so hard he heard his knuckles cracking. He wanted a little brother to teach how to tie flies and go fishing with, to play football with, to cheer at sports day and Audley had snatched it all away.

His father's stern look was still resting on him. Bert squirmed and looked up at the Sacred Heart of Jesus, hanging above the mantelpiece. He was hoping his father wouldn't make him repeat those words. Jesus held out one hand, palm upwards, and his piercing blue eyes stared back as Bert waited for judgement to fall.

"I'm proud of you, Bert. You should always stand up for what you believe in."

IIis lip started to bleed again when he smiled.

Even after the thunderstorm, the air in the bedroom was stultifying. Bert couldn't sleep. He whispered across the narrow space between the beds.

"Leo? Are you awake?"

Unlike his brother, Leo took after their mother, with his smooth, mousy brown hair and aquiline nose. His eyebrows were always cocked as if he was waiting for someone to laugh at his jokes. Bert would watch the girls' heads turning as the family went up to Communion. Papa stepped out of the pew and stood with his hands folded across the front of his Sunday suit while the family filed out in front of him, led by Mama. A flick of curls to the left, or a twitch of lace to the right would mark Leo's progress up to the altar. They looked at him from under their eyelashes while they were standing on the church steps after shaking Father Murphy's hand. Leo never gave them any attention.

"Yes, I am awake. I can't get to sleep with you tossing and turning and groaning every five minutes," Leo sighed.

"What do you think will happen, with this war?" Bert asked.

"The newspapers are saying it will all be over by Christmas," Leo said. "Bad luck for me."

"What do you mean?"

Bert sat up, his night shirt twisted around the tops of his legs.

"I would join up tomorrow. I'd make a great soldier." said Leo, sitting up too.

"Join the British army?"

"Next year, I could sign up and they would never guess my age. I'm tall, and I'm strong. They...

"Well, then I'm glad it will be all over by Christmas," Bert said. "You could get killed. Do you know how many men died in the Boer war?"

"No, but what has that got to do with anything?"

Leo was lying with his hands behind his head staring at the bedroom ceiling, wondering how many miles it was to Berlin on his imaginary map of Europe.

"Twenty *thousand*." Bert said, knowing Leo wasn't really listening.

"For Empire and for gold. Why do you want to go and fight the Germans for invading Belgium? Because of a diplomatic alliance? I can think of lots of better ways to spend my life."

"Doing what?" Leo challenged. "Someone has to stand up for the underdog. And what is the point of a treaty if you're not prepared to defend your allies?"

Leo always used his fists to make a point, even when he risked taking a beating from Papa for fighting. Bert preferred to win with words. The fight with Audley was not one he would repeat in a hurry. Compared to Leo's heroic declarations, Bert's dream of going to university seemed cowardly and selfish.

"I would like to be an international diplomat."

He waited for Leo's snort of ridicule, but it didn't come. Bert's scholarship to St Cuthbert's would give him opportunities that his father and brother had never had. On Leo's first day at school, Papa had given him his very own new slate. He sat on the scullery step after school each day, teaching Bert how to hold the chalk, and how to write his name. By the age of eight his younger brother had overtaken him and was writing words that Leo couldn't spell. He was jealous when Papa praised Bert and when he turned fourteen, he was glad to leave school and take a job as a messenger boy on eight shillings a week working for Guinness, like his father and grandfather before him.

After a year, he got itchy feet and told Bert he was secretly saving money to escape to London, or even to New York. The war would give him the perfect opportunity to get away.

Bert was watching a fat black spider tentatively start to cross the ceiling and then retreat into a corner.

"Leo?"

"Mmmm?" he murmured, not even opening his eyes this time.

"Will Conor die young?"

"I don't know, Bertie. I suppose he is in God's hands."

"But we are all in God's hands."

Bert wondered if the spider had any sense of how big the ceiling was, stretching all around him. Had it instinctively sought the safety of the corner, or stumbled there by accident?

"Go to sleep now." Leo's voice had dropped to a whisper.

Bert turned on his side to face the wall and shut out the view of the solitary spider.

In the fortnight following the declaration of war, time weighed heavily. The weather continued hot, and Papa's temper was short as Leo repeatedly dropped hints about running away to join up. Bert was waiting impatiently for his fourteenth birthday. He didn't know what to expect, but he was sure that something would change. He woke every morning to the sound of Leo's grumbling preparations for work. Leo only came alive in the evening. Unlike Bert, the morning sun was anathema to him. Bert jumped out of bed and followed Leo downstairs, a whole day stretching out in front of him. Sometimes his mother sent him to get the messages or gave him little jobs to do and then he was free. He took bread and dripping in a newspaper parcel and cycled further and further afield every day, exploring the pools of the river Don, the Team and the Derwent, even following the Tyne upstream almost as far as Hexham, looking for the elusive treasure trove of trout. One day he wanted to come home with enough fish in his basket to feed the whole family.

As he cycled, the muscles of his legs getting stronger every day, he went over the new words that were teeming inside his head, trying to capture the sing-song inflection that Michael Power brought to them. Sometimes on a lonely stretch of road with hawthorn hedges on either side, the blue sky above, Bert would try saying them out loud, rolling his tongue around the strangeness of them. They didn't follow rules like Latin words or sound musical like French words, but there was some secret magic in them that he couldn't explain.

"Gorramahagat."

When he tried out the words with only the birds to hear, he felt the master of them. Later, in the Powers' cottage when he stood with his hands behind his back reciting his new words, they sounded guttural, like freestanding sounds without a meaning. Michael reassured him that the music of the Irish would come, if he just let himself go, and stopped trying so hard. Bert fought back tears of frustration. He was used to being a good student. If only he could ask for Papa's help.

"It's inside in your head, and in your heart, Bert. Let it come out."

Bert could feel a tight band across his chest. Some of it was fear, he knew. Papa would disapprove of Michael and his friends, and stop Bert from visiting the cottage. Keeping the secret from Papa was a small price to pay for this special friendship.

CHAPTER 2

The encounter that would change his life happened on a hot July day when the twelve-year old Bert was passing through Elswick, disappointed that he had only two fish in his catch for the day. A boy and a girl aged about seven or eight were playing in the dirt outside a row of dilapidated cottages. Bert knew who lived here. The itinerant Irish labourers his father scorned for helping to break the coal strike. The ragged children looked up as he passed, silently surveying his clothes and his bicycle. An idea came to him. He dismounted and leaned the bicycle handlebars against the whitewashed cottage wall.

"Where are your parents?" he asked the children.

They looked at each other and shrugged. Bert lifted two fish from the basket on the front of his bicycle and held them up. He raised his eyebrow and the little girl pointed with a grimy finger towards the door of the nearest cottage. He managed to hold the slippery fish in one hand and knock on the open half-door with the other. A waft of smoke and fresh sweat preceded the appearance of a tall man, drips of water tracking through the black coal dust on his face. He had bright blue eyes, a wide brow and a dimpled chin.

"Sorry," the man said, wiping his forehead with a beefy hand and adding another layer of sooty blackness.

He seemed friendly, despite having his ablutions interrupted.

"I caught these fish this afternoon and wondered if perhaps you would like them."

Bert felt a little foolish and hoped the big man wouldn't take offence. The man looked bemused but took the fish.

"There's a grand tall boy out here, after giving me two trout," he said, over his shoulder.

A woman stepped out of the gloom and took the fish. She nodded shyly at Bert.

"Will you take a drop of water? You look hot."

The man opened the bottom half of the door, pushing it out so that Bert had to take a step back.

"No thank you, I really ought to go home now. Mama will wonder where I am."

"And will Mammy wonder where her fish is?"

That was the first time Bert heard Michael laugh; a gurgle from deep in his barrel of a chest.

"No, I'll simply tell her I had no luck today," Bert said, and he sounded pompous even to himself.

The children came and stood at their father's legs, holding onto his grey canvas trousers with slender fingers. The girl's eyes were round and curious, and the boy was quietly taking everything in.

"Well, it's us that had the luck today, isn't it?" the man said, resting his huge hand on his daughter's dark curls. She smiled up at him with adoring indigo eyes and murmured something that Bert didn't catch.

"If you're passing another evening, come and see us. I'll tell you a story about a fish," he called after Bert as he cycled off.

For three days, Bert tried to put them out of his mind, but something drew him back. Perhaps it was the promise of a story. Perhaps it was the tantalising knowledge that his father would not approve. On Friday, he cycled through the settlement in the morning, but it was deserted. The children were not playing outside, and there was no smoke rising from the chimney of the cottage. Bert did not want to arrive unannounced. It seemed polite to wait for another invitation. Perhaps they had moved on. Papa said this kind of people were unreliable. On his way home later that day, Bert nearly cycled past the cottages without stopping. He heard a shout, and the big man came out onto the road.

"We were looking out for you!"

Bert stopped, delighted. The man held out his hand.

"My name is Michael Power." Bert's hand was dwarfed by his.

"Bert."

"Short for Herbert, is it?"

The man pumped Bert's arm and looked at him expectantly, as if something amazing might come out of his mouth.

"Herbert Vincent O'Brien."

Every time he spoke to Michael in those early days, he blushed like a girl. Michael laughed his big round laugh.

"That's a fine name for a fine young man, isn't it, *a ghrá*?"

His wife held out her hand. It was tiny and rough, like a bird's claw. Her red-brown hair was pulled back from a high forehead and tied in a bun, and she had hazel green eyes and freckles across the Bridge of her nose. Her wide mouth made a big smile.

"Annie," she said, shaking his hand.

The children had run out and were jumping up and down with excitement beside the front basket of the bicycle.

"*A ceathair, a ceathair!*" they shouted, grinning.

Annie frowned at them, and lifted her apron to shoo them away, speaking quickly. Bert didn't understand a word she said to them. He turned to the bicycle.

"I brought four today."

"So the children tell me."

"Michael?" Annie nudged him.

"We couldn't take them off you," he said.

Bert sensed that it was Annie who was uncomfortable with taking charity.

"But I caught them for you," he said, holding them out to her.

"What will your Mammy think - another day with no fish?"

"She doesn't know I've been fishing."

"And what does she think her young *spalpeen* has been doing all day long?"

Bert shrugged, embarrassed. By the age of twelve, these children would probably be down the mine.

"Well, we'll take the fish only if you'll come in and have a sup of tea and listen to a story of mine," said Michael.

Annie took the fish.

"*Gorilla maggot,*" Bert thought she said.

The clay floor was spread with dried reeds; the only furniture a table and four wooden stools and two straw pallets on the floor. The sparse room gave no sign of the heights and depths that Bert would reach within its walls. Hanging over the fire was a blackened kettle and to one side, a matching pot stood empty. A bowl of steaming potatoes in their skins sat on the table, a generous lump of lard melting down between them. The children ran to sit cross legged on the nearest mattress and waited expectantly.

Annie chopped the heads and tails neatly off the fish and threw them into the empty pot. She made tea in a tin teapot and stood it on the table to draw. There were only four tin mugs on the shelf above the table. Michael stoked the fire and smacked his lips. She poured him some tea and he took a gulp. The children leaned forward eagerly. Michael cleared his throat, leaned his elbows on his knees and began to speak in a sing-song voice that belied his size.

"Demne was the son of Cúmhail mac Art, a man who had been a great warrior. He was killed by his enemies before Demne was even born out of his mother. As soon as Demne was old enough, his mother sent him away to another house to learn how to be a hunter. And sure

enough, after a few years wasn't he a great hunter. After that, his mother said to him, "You need to become a great warrior, like your father."

So off he went and learned all the skills of a great warrior. His father's enemies were all the time trying to kill him. And his mother was all the time trying to make him into a class of a fighter. But Demne had grown into a man of peace and he knew what he wanted. More than anything else in the world he wanted to become a poet. He took up his studies with a poet named Finegas, who lived near the River Boyne.

Now the River Boyne was home to a magical salmon that ate nuts from a hazel tree and was known as 'an Breadán Feasa,' or the Salmon of Knowledge. A druid had foretold that whoever ate first of the flesh of that magical salmon would have knowledge of all things. For many years, Finegas had been watching that salmon, waiting for his chance to become the wisest man in all of Ireland. Until one time he finally caught it after a day and a night of fighting it on his fishing line, up and down the banks of the river. At the end of it all he was so exhausted that he only wanted to sleep so he took the fish to Demne and told him to cook it. And then he said...

Michael looked towards the children.

They said together, *"But whatever you do, don't eat the flesh of the salmon."*

The trout were sizzling on the griddle now, and one of the children's stomachs rumbled. The girl, Niamh, gripped her arms tightly around her waist and giggled. She had inherited her father's infectious laugh.

"Now a hunter and a warrior Demne might have been, but that did not stop him from burning his thumb while the salmon was cooking. So, didn't he suck his thumb to ease the pain, not thinking what he was doing."

Little Tomás obliged with an indrawn breath.

"He had tasted the salmon. When the boy brought the cooked salmon to his master, Finegas looked into his eyes, and he knew that something had changed. His heart was broken because he had a dream of himself being the wisest man in all Ireland. When he asked the boy had he tasted the salmon of knowledge, Demne told Finegas what had happened. Finegas sighed to himself and he knew that the young Demne was the one intended to eat the salmon. He changed the boy's name to Finn and from that day forward, he was known as Finn mac Cúmhail. He received three gifts that would make him a great poet: magic, insight, and the power of words."

The children clapped and immediately jumped up to look into the griddle pan.

"Did you like the story?" asked Michael.

"Yes, I liked it very much."

"Is it one you've heard before?"

"No, but I have heard of Finn Mac Cúmhail." Bert was afraid that Michael would think he knew nothing.

"May I ask you something?" Bert asked as he stood up to go.

The children were clamouring for their food, and he didn't want to intrude any further.

"Of course, and you after bringing us our dinner," Michael said.

"What does *gorilla maggot* mean?"

Michael looked over at the children, rolling his eyes, and they giggled.

"*Go raibh míle maith agat*," Michael said. "It means *may a thousand good things be upon you.*"

It seemed a very long-winded way of saying thank you.

"Do you not speak Irish in your own house, and you with a fine name like O'Brien?"

"No."

Bert looked at the floor. Papa never spoke a word of Irish. Mama had never learned to speak it.

"You talk like an Englishman. But you'll always carry your name with you, Herbert Vincent O'Brien, so be proud of it."

On the way home that evening, Bert was thoughtful. Months before, Leo had made an idle threat to go and work down the mines when he finished school. Papa got very angry and said that no son of his would work as a miner.

"Do you realise what those men have suffered over the last six weeks, with no money, no roof over their heads, and scab labour brought over from Ireland of all places, to keep the mines open? What would a Connemara man know about coal mining? It's not the same as saving turf by any manner or means. But these fellas from the west of Ireland are divils - they'll do anything for a few bob. They'd even take another man's job of work off of him."

Bert knew he would have to keep his lovely new words and his new friends to himself for now. Every night when he filled the coal bucket, Bert looked at the black lumps and wondered if they had been hacked out of the ground by Michael. He didn't mind carrying the heavy bucket any more, and even the bruises on his shins didn't bother him.

CHAPTER 3

His long-awaited fourteenth birthday finally came. Bert was sitting on the river bank, daydreaming about bringing home at least six trout, when a tug on the fishing line told him a large fish was fighting on the end of it. He fought the instinctive urge to reel it in too quickly, and finally after tiring it out he eased his net underneath the fish and lifted it carefully onto the bank. Bright droplets of water flicked from the writhing tail, and he felt like Finegas. Bert had read all the Irish myths and legends he could find in the library. He had even found some Irish books that Papa kept in a cardboard box under the bed and sneaked them out one by one to read them. The large trout joined five others. A heron stood on the opposite bank, its one-legged pose oddly restful. Bert had learned that when he was still, he could pass into another dimension of nature, his senses tuned to every twitch of grass, every whisper of wings. But today was not for tranquillity.

Today, he would show his mother that he was a real man. He might even manage to wipe away the sad look that had been on Mama's face for the last two months since Conor was born. Before, she was always full of good humour and energy. In the evening she would tell the family all the gossip from the baker's shop, or stories about her childhood in County Cork. Bert thought that Papa, who was so serious about everything, had fallen in love with Mama because she made him laugh. But she never laughed any more.

When the baby had started to show, Bert noticed the neighbours gossiping behind their hands. There was a 'knowingness' to their nods and smiles after Mass. Mama often went upstairs to lie down in the afternoons while she carried Conor. Papa said that everyone in the family had to mind her. Sometimes, when Bert got home from school, the fire was low, and the water in the kettle was cold. When Mama did come downstairs she was pale and tired. Bert made her a cup of tea and then somehow, she would find the energy to make their tea. Once, Bert tried to peel the potatoes, but he didn't do a very good job and Mama said that he could help in other ways. By June the bump seemed to be an unbearable burden for her to carry. Her ankles swelled up and even her face had changed shape.

"Don't worry Bertie, Mama will be fine once the baby comes," Louise reassured him one evening, when she caught him anxiously watching Mama. "All these changes are normal, when a woman is expecting a baby."

He blushed, hoping she was not going to share any more details. In some ways, Louise was right. A few weeks after Conor came into the world, Mama's ankles were back to normal and she didn't need to hold her lower back when she stood up from her chair. But she still was still wearing loose dresses, and her soft wispy hair was all tangled, because she never took the time to brush it. She looked older, more like Bert's friend Gerald's mother. Now Conor was nearly two months old and Mama was still not quite herself.

He raced home on the bicycle, the breeze in his hair cooling his hot scalp. There was a long hill to climb, and the blood was pounding in his eardrums when he reached the top, breathless. He freewheeled down the other side, reaching a frightening speed just as he negotiated the curve at the bottom. No carts or other vehicles blocked his way, and he exhaled in breathy relief. He felt so tall, it seemed as if everyone must notice. Old Mr Frith sat on a stool outside his front door, soaking up the late afternoon sun. He raised his hand to hail Bert as he passed down Saltwell Road.

He shouted at the top of his voice, "I can't stop, Mr Frith, I have our tea in the basket!"

The clock on the church struck five as he pushed the bicycle through the back gate. The fish were lightly coated in dust from the road. He went into the scullery for a jug of water to throw over them. He carried the dripping basket into the house. Mama was standing there, wiping her hands, smiling at him.

"What have you got there, young man?" she asked, looking into the basket. "Oh my goodness, what a surprise!" For just a moment her eyes lit up in the old way.

"I caught them all myself." he said, and she hugged him.

"Thank you, Bert, you are a good boy. I'll keep the gammon for tomorrow's tea, and tonight, we'll have a birthday feast on these!"

A wail from Conor distracted her. Bert lifted him out of the cradle.

"I'm glad you're not old enough to eat fish, or I would still be there, trying to catch one more," he said, and Conor smiled his lopsided smile, and dribbled.

From the scullery Bert heard a sound that he hadn't heard for a long time. Mama was humming.

"You are a clever boy," she said, as she snipped off the tails with a kitchen scissors. Bert wished she would call him 'young man' again. He stood beside her to wash his hands.

She smelt of flour and soap and lavender water, and she suddenly exclaimed as he stood there, "My goodness, I do believe you are taller than me!"

Bert blurted out the first thing that came into his head.

"You'll have a few years before Conor catches up with you."

"I think I'll still have my little Conor with me, after you've all flown from the nest."

Her face had closed over again. Suddenly Louise came in through the back door, her hair everywhere, her cheeks flushed. Her fingers were tightly clenched around a handkerchief, and her eyes were red and swollen. Mama nudged Bert with her elbow. He ran upstairs. but then he slipped quietly down again, his back pressed flat against the passage wall, to listen. Alfie was going to war. He had volunteered, along with some of his mates from the ironworks, and he was due to go to a training camp at the end of the week.

"He's so proud of himself, Mam. How can he do this?"

Mama clattered pots and pans.

"He thinks he is being a brave hero."

"But Mam, they have all got carried away and talked themselves into it. Iron will be even more important now to build ships and weapons for the war. It said so in the newspaper. Why can't he stay and forge iron? Why does fighting always have to be the answer?"

Mama hugged her. Bert had been reading the newspapers. They were full of calls for volunteers to join the army. Alfie could work at the foundry all his life and never have this chance of adventure again.

"Has he asked to speak to Papa?" Mama gently brushed loose wisps of hair from Louise's face.

Louise shook her head. Another fountain of tears erupted.

"I love him, Mam."

Bert stepped away from the wall and tried to climb the stairs without making the third step creak. It didn't seem fair to listen any more. He was torn between admiring Alfie and hating him for hurting Louise. When Leo heard the news, he would be even more eager to run away. Bert put his hand under his pillow and pulled out the brown leather-bound diary Louise had given him that morning, and the black fountain pen that had been his parents' gift. Although the pages had nothing written on them yet, he had still hidden it while he was out of the house. He sat down on his creaking chair and filled the pen to write his name carefully on the flyleaf.

Herbert Vincent O' Brien, 24th August 1914.

The birthday meal was a very solemn affair. Louise, with red rimmed eyes, bravely tried to eat the fish.

"These are fine trout, Bertie," she said, pushing hers around on the plate

Mama was distracted. Even Leo was subdued. He kept quiet until the brothers were alone in the bedroom later.

"I am sorry for Louise, but everything will be different when Alfie comes back as a war hero and proposes to her. She can tell their children how proud she felt when their Papa marched down the street in his uniform."

"What if he doesn't come back?" Bert asked. "Isn't that the reason why she's crying so much?"

"I think it's wounded pride. Louise has been expecting Alfie to talk to Papa for a few months. She has only just realised that Alfie has room in his head for more than thoughts of marriage. Women can't see beyond their own noses."

Having no experience of the fairer sex, Bert did not feel qualified to reply. He started to get undressed.

"Happy Birthday," Leo said, holding out a brown paper parcel.

Bert hadn't expected anything from his forgetful brother. He opened the parcel and found a smooth, carved wooden figure. The grain of the cherry wood followed the sinuous curves of a leaping, twisting salmon that seemed alive.

"I remembered the story you told me about the Salmon of Knowledge."

Bert smiled and stroked its smooth length with his index finger. A tiny flick in the tail said that the creature would never be subdued.

"It's beautifully carved, thank you."

Leo looked down. "I sometimes wish I could be clever, like you."

"I sometimes wish I could be carefree, like you."

CHAPTER 4

Bert was coming back from the playing fields slightly ahead of his classmates. The September sun was cheering after a week of rain, and he was looking forward to the next lesson. Jeremy Audley stood in the corner of the changing room, washing his hands at the sink, looking furtively over his shoulder as Bert came in. He left quickly. Later Bert found his Latin comprehension Prep. spoiled with black ink. Such a low-down trick seemed beneath an older boy, but Bert could not help feeling suspicious. That evening, Bert sat at his desk, sucking his pen and burning precious paraffin until after midnight. Leo grumbled about the light, so he dimmed it and Leo then told him he would go blind if he kept on working in such gloom.

"I have to hand it in tomorrow," Bert said, when Leo sighed loudly again.

"What possessed you to leave it until now?" Leo asked.

"Audley poured ink all over my work," Bert muttered.

"I'll go up and meet him at the school gates, and teach him a lesson he won't forget," Leo said, sitting up in bed.

"He's not worth it." Bert scratched his head and tried to remember a particular phrase he had used the first time around.

"Bert, you don't understand. You broke all the rules and punched an older boy and Audley won't stop until he gets you back where it really hurts."

Bert looked across at Leo. "What does it matter to you?"

"It matters because Conor is *my* brother too," Leo turned his back and pulled the blanket up to his ears.

Bert and Gerald Grimes had naturally gravitated towards each other in the first week at St Cuthbert's. In walking through those gates they may as well have embarked on a voyage to a foreign land. Bert thrived on it and Gerald struggled. He was bullied by the boys who had never known a pang of hunger in their lives. They poked him between his jutting shoulder blades, bent his wire framed spectacles and mocked the stammer which only afflicted him when he was in their company.

Gerald's mother had hand-sewn his grey twill trousers and the fourth form boys were not deceived by her attempts to match the style of the trousers on sale in Borthwick's, the appointed merchandiser of school uniform. Mrs Grimes had pawned her departed mother's wedding ring to buy the crested blazer, which was too much of a challenge even for her talented fingers. For all the facts and figures that had won him the scholarship, Gerald didn't have the nimble wit to navigate this new world. Bert quickly picked up the language and manners of the Preparatory school boys, but he could walk home with Gerald looking forward to his tea and not have to remember to call it dinner. Bert's tan and sun-bleached hair could just as easily have been acquired on a beach in the south of France as from a summer of fishing and cycling in Northumbria. Gerald had worked in the mill for the summer months and his pasty face and anxious squint seemed to attract every cruel behaviour the other boys could think up and Bert couldn't always be there to protect him.

The day after burning the midnight oil with Latin, Bert had a history lesson first.

Master Brown waxed lyrical about the colonies and how they enriched the Empire and Bert couldn't resist asking how Master Brown thought the people of Australia, India and Africa would record the history of their settlement and civilisation. The master was disparaging in his dismissal of Bert's question and the other boys sniggered.

The master collected the boys' essays on 'The Rise and Fall of the Tudors." Bert was expecting a good mark. He had written that the Tudor plantations were a rude awakening for the people of Ireland. They were the beginning of a programme of deliberate and consistent exploitation of the Irish land and the Irish people. Bert secretly hoped that they might debate the topic in class, so that he could show off all the reading he had done.

Gerald was quiet for the rest of the day and Bert wondered if the older boys had discovered a new form of torture for him. He seemed to accept his vile treatment as his lot in life, which incensed Bert.

"There is no point in fighting them," Gerald had said. "There are people like them and people like me. The healthy litter rejects the runt. It's nature."

Bert protested. "You shouldn't accept that, Gerald. You're twice as clever as most of them."

"Inside my head I go to a place where I just don't hear their voices. It seems to work. Otherwise, I would go completely mad."

Bert was worried that the boys had found a way of getting through Gerald's defences.

"Are you well?" he asked as they left school that afternoon.

"Yes, thank you," Gerald replied.

"I could help your mother this evening if you're sick."

Gerald's mother worked as a char lady in some of the grand houses in Gosforth, and on Thursdays, Gerald helped her.

"I am not sick, thank you."

The tremor in his voice gave him away. Bert could not persuade him, so they parted at the corner of Saltwell Road, and Gerald continued the walk to his home on the other side of Bensham. The next morning, they met as usual to walk to school together.

"Did you go with your mother, last evening?" Bert asked, thinking he still looked ill.

"We pretended to go to a Ball," Gerald smiled. "It's a game we've played since I was little. Mam loves it."

The Scottish landowners only visited the big house occasionally at weekends but they paid Mrs Grimes to always have it ready.

"I stand at the top of the stairs and announce Lady Grimes in a posh voice and then I take her arm and we walk down the stairs smiling and nodding at the Chinese vases."

He looked more like himself for a few minutes and then he was reflective again.

"My Mam wants me to be a doctor or a lawyer and have lots of money, so I can live in Gosforth and she can be my housekeeper. I just need to do well at school and then get a scholarship to University. One step at a time, I can do it if I try."

Bert thought that Gerald wiped the corner of his eye just before Master Brown hailed them from the top of the steps as they passed through the main school gate. With his thumbs hooked into his lapels, he tried to look like the master of all he surveyed despite the short stature and wide girth that told the world how sedentary and self-indulgent he was in his appetites. Gerald gasped and went pale.

Brown grabbed each boy by an ear. Bert took some tiny satisfaction from the master's difficulty in reaching up to his ear, but he inflicted more pain in the twist as a result. They were marched silently to the headmaster's office. The polished parquet floors squeaked and the sniggers of the other boys followed them. At the Headmaster's door, Master Brown released Gerald's ear to knock and then dragged Bert in first.

"Good morning."

Mr Frost leaned across his mahogany desk, his dark brown eyes looking over the half moon of his spectacles. The only other time that Bert had set foot in this inner sanctum was on his first day, when Mr Frost had given him a patronising lecture about the standards of behaviour expected of a public school boy.

"Good morning, Sir."

He pulled back his shoulders and tilted his chin, his ear burning as the blood flowed back into it.

"What explanation can you possibly have for this?"

The headmaster threw Bert's history notebook down on the desk. Bert shrugged, unsure of the nature of the accusation. His silence seemed to incense the headmaster even further.

"The *arrogance*. The *presumption*. This is a downright *insult* to your teacher's intelligence."

Mr Frost was alternately prodding the pages of the notebook and pointing at Bert with his outstretched finger. Surely his essay did not warrant this level of vituperation? Bert waited for another cue as to what was expected.

"Do you have anything to say?"

Bert shook his head.

"Let us see what your friend Grimes has to say about it then, shall we?"

Mr Brown stepped to the door and summoned Gerald.

"What do you have to say about this?"

The headmaster threw Gerald's notebook down beside the other one. Gerald gulped and seemed confused.

"Grimes, why did you give your essay to your *friend* to copy? What incentive or coercion did O'Brien use to persuade you? Perhaps he offered to give you his Latin comprehension in exchange? What stupidity led you to think that Master Brown would not notice the distinct similarity between these pieces of work?"

Bert's wounded academic pride hurt more than Gerald's inexplicable betrayal. History was Gerald's strongest subject, but he could never have written the beautifully provocative analysis of Anglo-Irish history that Bert had crafted over many hours.

Bert looked at his friend's trembling lip, his red rimmed eyes. St Cuthbert's was only bearable for Gerald as long as the masters held him in high esteem. Even the most condescending of them could see that he was an asset to the school, despite his humble social standing. The bottom would fall out of Mrs Grimes's world if Gerald was accused of cheating.

"I am sorry," Bert said with just enough humility to be taken as remorse.

Gerald's head whipped around, and in his pale grey eyes, Bert saw a fleeting temptation to tell the truth. Then the long sandy lashes blinked once behind the thick lenses of his spectacles, and Gerald turned away. A flush crept over the worn collar of his shirt.

"You will both be punished as cheats, but the severity will reflect the relative seriousness of your roles in this shameful little episode."

The headmaster dismissed them with a wave, not looking up from his papers as they turned and left. Gerald grabbed his arm as soon as the door closed behind them but Bert pushed him away. He was afraid that Master Brown would shortly follow them out.

The other boys had dispersed at the sound of the bell, so there was no cat calling or jeering as they went to their own classrooms. Bert spent the day wondering what had possessed Gerald. It was as though common sense and intelligence had simultaneously abandoned him.

"I had no idea it was yours." Gerald said quietly as they walked home together.

How could this matter get any more ridiculous?

"My name is on the front of the notebook. How could you *not* know it was mine?"

"The really awful thing is, I thought it was Audley's essay. I thought it rather well written, for him, I must admit."

Now Bert was really confused. "Audley gave it to you, to copy?"

"Yes, he caught me stupidly crying in the changing room when I had lost my essay and offered to help. He said the history master had changed, and nobody would know it was his essay from last year. He had written it out on a foolscap page."

Bert took a deep breath. The sting of the cane had not compared to the sting of Mr Frost's words as Bert had left his rooms after his caning that afternoon.

"I had thought you would make something of yourself, young man, and I find myself thoroughly disappointed. I very much doubt that this school will be able to shape you into something resembling honourable manhood, with this poor start."

The long red welts across the palms of his hands would be difficult to hide. The ordeal of explaining to his father would be the final humiliation.

"We will not let Audley win," he said emphatically.

"But surely he has, already?" said Gerald.

Bert simply shook his head, and they continued the journey home.

CHAPTER 5

The Powers' cottage was humming. Michael had just read out the headline from the Newcastle Daily Chronicle - 'IRISHMEN FOR THE BATTLE LINE.'

Michael's friend Seán from Galway was sitting in one corner, looking thoughtful. Around the fire was a group of men Bert had not met before. The air was thick with pipe smoke. The children were lying down pretending to be asleep. Bert winked at Niamh when she caught his eye. Tomás had his eyes tightly shut.

Michael asked Bert to read the article aloud.

"I love the way you roll your tongue around the English words."

Bert knew that most of the others couldn't read.

"*The greatest fighting men of our time are Irishmen – Kitchener, French, Smith-Dorrien, and Roberts,*" Bert read.

The men cheered.

"*These men appeal to all Irishmen on Tyneside to join the Tyneside Irish battalion now being formed.*"

Seán groaned. The quote from Lord Kitchener went on,

'*I feel sure that all Irishmen on Tyneside will respond willingly to this appeal to defend the Empire.*'

Michael was sucking so hard on his pipe that it gurgled. Niamh was giggling under the blanket. Her father was too distracted to give out to her.

'Keep going, Bert, will you?'

"*Lord Kitchener's call is to every man who is fit. For every Irishman the path of duty is clear. If you would preserve your nationality, you must fight for it. Germany, the belly of the nations, must be defeated if free nations are to exist. Irishmen must take part in this great struggle. It means risk and sacrifice, but it also means honour, and comradeship and courage. The cause is worthy and the opportunity great.*"

"Never mind that opportunity," shouted a coarse faced man from Wexford called Patrick. "Wouldn't we be better off fighting for our own freedom while their backs are turned, and they're worrying about the big fellas on the continent?"

Michael Power hushed him with a wave of his hand. 'Let the *garsun* finish reading it out first, Patrick."

"*Those who are inspired by that love of freedom dominant in the Irish race and which is threatened by Germany's lust for power, should enrol themselves now in the Tyneside Irish Battalion and preserve for themselves and for their children that glorious liberty so dear to the heart of every Irishman.*"

Michael sat back on his wooden chair with his hands on his knees as if nothing more needed to be said. Seán was unusually silent. Bert wondered if he was tempted to take the King's shilling. He struggled to feed and clothe a wife and five children.

"Poor Catholic Belgium," Annie said under her breath.

The men talked around her. Nobody acknowledged her comment, and she seemed unsurprised.

"The only fighting I'll be doing is for my own native soil. The big fellas are only interested in themselves. Belgium is only important all of a sudden because the Germans can go through it into France. If the English didn't need us to go and die for them, would they be humouring Redmond with their promises of Home Rule? The politicians have had their chance, and they failed. We have to fight now, while the English have their backs turned."

Michael's eyes were dancing, listening to Patrick.

"They say it will all be over by Christmas," Bert said.

Perhaps just because he was still holding the newspaper, or because his newly broken voice had some authority, all the eyes turned to him. He leaned close to the fire to hide his blush. He had nothing wise to add.

"There would never be time to organise," muttered Seán.

"The Volunteers are ready and waiting. We just need more men," Patrick said.

"Aren't we much better off getting Home Rule, instead of thinking we can overthrow one of the greatest empires the world has ever seen?" said Seán.

He looked into the bottom of his tin mug. "What makes you think that we'll succeed where others have failed before us?"

"They will be far too busy in the Parliament now to be worrying about a Home Rule Bill. We have to strike at their heel while they're fighting the bigger enemy."

The eyes of the other men shone in the firelight at Patrick's words. Michael was nodding furiously. Seán stood up and shook the last droplets of tea into the fire, making it sizzle briefly.

"I'm away to my own house," he said. "One sure thing is we won't solve the world's problems sitting around the fire."

"That's for sure." Michael patted him on the back. "See you in the morning, so," he said very casually.

Seán nodded goodnight and stepped out the door, his shoulders slumped, letting in a little breeze that cleared the smoke for a moment. That was the last they ever saw of him. After he was gone, the talk started up again. Bert looked at his watch. It was late. He would need to cycle at top speed to be home before ten o'clock. As he pulled on his overcoat, Michael waved a crinkled magazine at him.

"We're finished with this if you want to do a bit of practising during the week," he said. Bert folded it in half and hid it in the waistband of his trousers, under his shirt.

"*Slán agus beannacht libh.*"

"*Slán abhaile,*"

The words of blessing followed him as he rode down dark laneways towards the glow of gaslight on the wider streets. His palms throbbed from the caning, an uncomfortable reminder that he was not yet the grown man he pretended to be on his visits to the cottage. He lifted the latch on the back door, pulled off his boots and tiptoed through the scullery in stockinged feet. Papa was sitting staring at the last embers of the fire.

"Very late, young man," Papa murmured, not sounding particularly perturbed.

"Yes, Papa. We got into quite a serious discussion."

Bert nudged the edge of the dull brass fender with his toe. Mama would ask him to polish it soon. He stuck his hands deep into his pockets.

"About anything in particular?" his father asked.

Bert racked his memory for the details of his made-up story about helping Gerald with his Latin Prep.

"The war." he replied.

"Yes?"

Bert had a rush of inspiration.

"The Newcastle Evening Chronicle is calling all Irishmen to join up."

"It was the only thing being talked about at work today. Did your brother say anything to you?"

Bert shook his head. Leo's day dreams of going off to war were as vague as ever.

"I'm worried that Leo will get a notion to go off and sign up. He is so cocky, he might even get away with it," Papa said, leaning forward and tapping his pipe gently on the hearth to dislodge the last dried remnants of tobacco.

Bert said nothing.

"There was a letter from your school today."

There was no change in Papa's tone. He pulled the letter from underneath the cushion on his chair.

"The headmaster, Mr Frost, says here that you were found cheating."

"Do you believe him?" Bert asked, taking his reddened, puffy hands out of his trouser pockets.

"Indeed I do not. But why did you let them accuse you of something you didn't do?"

"Gerald was tricked into copying my essay. He didn't deserve to be punished."

"That boy, Audley, again?"

Bert nodded.

"Poor young Conor doesn't even know his own name yet and people are fighting over him."

Papa sounded sad.

"I can take it," Bert said, feeling braver.

"Yes, we can all take it, son. For as long as he needs us."

Papa reached across to the single paraffin lamp that stood on the mantelpiece. As he followed his son up the narrow wooden stairs, their black shadows danced grotesquely on the wall ahead of them. Leo was snoring. Bert slid the folded newspaper under his mattress, looking forward to a leisurely read after school the next day. He lay flat on his back for a few moments, breathing deeply. It had been a very long day and sleep was not long in coming.

CHAPTER 6

It was the middle of November. Christmas was too far away. The low grey skies hung pregnant with overdue rainfall. Bert's school days began and ended in the dark. His father suffered badly in damp weather. A chesty cough rattled his whole frame. Even a chronic illness would not keep his father away from work so the morning routine continued unchanged. Conor's cries woke everyone. Mama tiptoed to the basket where he slept to soothe him. Within an hour, the house was full of bustle. Louise was training as a nurse and Eileen was working at the mill and walking out with a young man named Joe. As Papa passed the door of the boys' room he knocked, and Leo groaned. He sat and stretched and moaned about the prospect of the day ahead.

In later years, Bert wondered if Leo remembered fondly the comfort of that small room, the warmth of their mingled night-time breath, a memory to go back to when he was waking up in strange places with strange men around him, without the prospect of a bowl of steaming, sugared porridge to lure him to get up and splash his face with water.

After breakfast, Bert played with Conor in the cradle for a little while before taking his satchel from the hook in the passage and kissing his mother goodbye. Conor's favourite game was to grab Bert's two thumbs firmly in his little fists and pull himself into a sitting position with a big smile on his round face.

Today before leaving the house Bert glanced quickly at the latest copy of the Irish newspaper, *An Claidheamh Soluis* – The Sword of Light. The pages were worn through on the folds, having been passed from hand to hand. Bert was always the last in the chain, but he felt honoured to be included. His spoken Irish was coming along quite well but he struggled to read it. More than ever, he wished that he could share the paper with Papa. But that would mean admitting to two years of wilful deceit. At first, Bert had only wanted to avoid an argument about the strike breaking. But the secret of his visits to the Powers' cottage had grown with every month that passed, until it was too big to share. Now Niamh and Tomás spoke to Bert in Irish and they only sometimes laughed at his mumbled replies.

Bert wanted to make his father proud, to justify Papa's sacrifice in leaving everything behind and coming over to England to give his children better prospects. Papa thought that Irish was the language of peasants and paupers. He would despise Bert for associating with tinkers from the west of Ireland instead of hobnobbing with his posh English school friends.

Leo continued to chafe at the drudgery of life. He had learned to say very little at meal times, to avoid being reprimanded by his father for his table manners, his flippancy, or some other imagined misdemeanour. At night he told Bert about the pranks that he and his fellow messengers played at work. Bert sometimes laughed so hard he had to duck under the blankets. Leo said he would run away to war just to stop seeing the words 'Son of Employee' stamped across his clocking-in card as he came and went every morning and every evening.

"I want to be my own man, not to spend my life in someone else's shadow."

"Papa is well respected at the Brewery, isn't he?" Bert asked.

"Yes, of course he is, but how am I ever going to make my own mark? They expect me to be just like him, so if I am, they won't be surprised. Where is the merit in that?"

"Do you think it's better to lie about your age and run away to war?" Bert asked.

"Yes, I do," said Leo sullenly and turned his back, pulling his blankets over his shoulder.

After school, Bert sneaked up to the bedroom to continue reading the worn magazine. He lit the lamp, feeling guilty for using the paraffin intended for his studying. He laid the paper out on the desk, determined to read it from cover to cover. He struggled with some of the words and tried saying them out loud. Perhaps he had misunderstood something. How could too many country dances be destroying the Irish language, as it seemed the priests were claiming? He scratched his head and followed the words with the tip of his finger like a six year old. Although his feet were getting cold and hunger pangs were nagging he had no sense of time passing. The sound of Leo's boots on the stairs startled him. He quickly folded the paper and tried to slip it under his school books. His father stood there.

"Bert, your mother has been worried. She didn't hear you coming in from school."

"Sorry, Papa, I was doing some...work."

"What are you hiding there?"

Bert's hand froze. Then he held out the newspaper.

"*An Claidheamh Soluis*?"

Bert simply nodded. Relief of a kind flooded through him.

"Come down and wash your hands. Everyone is waiting for their tea."

Papa left the room. Bert snuffed the wick on the lamp and followed him downstairs.

He kissed his mother on the cheek as she stood at the stove.

"Sorry Mama, I didn't notice the time passing."

"I was just worried about you," she said.

Bert resisted the urge to flinch when she reached up and ruffled his hair.

"Usually I could set the clock by your comings and goings."

Conor was gabbling in his cot, and Eileen was laying the table. Leo was standing by the fire, rubbing his hands together.

"It's beginning to freeze," he said. "I could see the horses' breath when I was passing the Brewery stables. I don't envy them tomorrow morning, trying to pull carts on those slippery roads."

They all sat down and Mama murmured the Grace.

"Why the long face?" Leo asked Bert, punching his arm. "Did you get a bad mark in a test?"

Bert shook his head, not daring to catch Papa's eye.

"Is Audley at it again? Just tell me. I'll teach him a lesson he won't forget. I know which way he walks home. No one would see a thing..."

"Leo!" Mama shot him a silencing glare.

"Bert doesn't need you getting involved and making things worse. A pity you wouldn't have some of that fire in your belly for your duties at work," Papa said quietly.

The mealtime passed, and the girls cleared up while Mama fed the baby. Papa summoned him to the fireside.

"Are you able to read the Irish?" Papa asked.

"I have a confession to make."

"It certainly seems as if you do."

"I have some friends. One in particular, Michael Power. He teaches me."

"And where did you get these friends from?" Papa was routing his pipe and tapping the old shreds of tobacco into the fire. "Not from your fancy school, that's for sure."

Bert told him everything. He gabbled.

"I've wanted to tell you for so long, but I was afraid you would forbid me to go there. I deceived you, but only because I didn't want to disobey you."

"What made you think I would stop you?"

"Do you remember how angry you were with Leo when he talked about going down the mines?"

Papa laughed. "He only said that to make me cross. The mine owners should never have brought in Irish fellas to break the strike, but those Connemara men were

33

only working to put bread in their children's mouths. I would never judge a man for doing that."

"*Ar mhaith leat labhair as Gaeilge?* Do you want to speak in Irish?"

His father's grey eyebrows relaxed. They talked in a world that stretched only as far as the shadows cast by the flickering fire. The clattering from the pantry and the murmur of conversation from the parlour were miles away.

"Why on God's earth did you keep this a secret for so long?" Papa asked.

"I thought you wouldn't approve. You've never spoken any Irish to us. I thought you were ashamed of it."

Papa stared into the fire for a long time.

"It's very complicated," he said.

"When the Guinness crowd asked me to go over to England for them, I was horrified, to begin with. Your grandparents were old and your mother was worried she might never see them again. We were hardly youngsters ourselves. We had to take Louise and Eileen out of their school, and you boys were still very small. But the job on offer was a promotion. You know what it's like in Guinness. You can only go up the ladder by filling dead men's shoes, and I never would have done so well if I had stayed in Dublin. Being in England gives you better chances too – look at the schooling you're getting."

"I understand that, but why not hold onto the Irish?" Bert asked.

"Your mother never learned Irish. Why would she, in a well-off Protestant Cork family? They don't teach Irish in the National Schools. You learn it at home. Granny and Granddad O'Brien used to speak Irish around the house when we were small, and that's where I learned it."

"So why didn't you pass it on to us?"

"It will only hold you back. Poor people speak Irish. Look at your friend Michael Power. I'm not saying anything against him, but he's a manual labourer, no more and no less."

"But if educated people never bother to learn it, the language will be lost completely," Bert said indignantly.

His father smiled.

"Do you see, Bert, you won't find the likes of Redmond or any of those fellas, the educated ones who are going to change the world, sitting around speaking Irish. It won't open any doors for you. If you want to fill your mind with a dead language, pick a useful one like Latin, or even better, learn French, so's you can talk to the lawyers and the diplomats. Don't be wasting your time on the Irish."

"I wanted you to be proud of me."

Papa put his hand on Bert's knee.

"I am proud of you, son. You have a good brain inside that hard head of yours. But my advice would still be the same. Irish is a dead language, and not even a useful one. Don't waste your time on it."

Afterwards, when he was lying in bed, Bert held up the logic of his father's advice against the tug of his emotions. His father hadn't told him to stop visiting Michael Power. Provided Bert could keep on top of his school work, he could see no reason to drop the Irish.

As spring warmed the ground, and they slipped back into the routine of lessons every day, Bert noticed that Patrick Leahy had stopped visiting the Powers' cottage. There were lots of heated arguments around the fire, and Bert was glad Seán wasn't there to hear some of the things that were being said about the Irishmen who joined up. Michael was the peacemaker when emotions ran high. Bert wondered if Patrick had overstepped the mark and was no longer welcome.

"They're only traitors, there's no other word for them," spat one man, when he heard the news that another Irish miner had signed up.

Michael sat back from the fire, his long legs stretched out straight in front of him, the heels of his boots resting on the warm hearth.

"Ah now, that's a bit harsh. There's always been Irishmen in the British Army, in Napoleon's time, in ... in ...

"But as Patrick said before he went, this is our moment in history, our one little chance, to fight back – what was it he said? 'Like a snake that bites the ankle of the foot that stood on it.'"

"And what are you doing, so?" Michael provoked, and the man subsided into silent contemplation of the fire.

"We can't be judging others if we're not prepared to do it ourselves," Michael said.

"We didn't go home with Patrick because we have to earn a crust to feed our families. They come first, even before our beloved Ireland. That's why Seán went off and did what he did. Not for love of the English, but for love of his children."

"I want my children to be free."

"So do I, in the name of God. But there's no good being free if they have no food in their bellies."

The wave of his arm took in Niamh and Tomás, sitting in their usual positions, wide-eyed and quiet.

"So, have you given up on Independence already?"

"Indeed and I have not. We all have our part to play and ours will come soon enough."

It was Niamh who whispered to Bert that Patrick had gone home to join the Volunteers. Annie had started taking in sewing, so she always sat slightly apart from the men, either at the window, snatching the last moments of the light, or huddled up to the lamp, squinting over her work. Bert could never get a sense from her which side of the fence she sat on.

Even after twelve hours down the mine, Michael had endless patience for teaching Bert night after night. During the day Bert was translating the adventures of Odysseus and Hercules. At night Michael took him into the world of *Cú Chulainn* and the *Fianna*. Bert's dreams were full of brave warriors banishing tyranny, far removed from the gruesome reality that was descending on Europe.

Louise sometimes talked about the men she was nursing. Some of them couldn't even speak, and she said they just waved their arms around if anyone asked them questions about what had happened to them. She said their eyes were blank, as if they had pulled down the blind on a train carriage. Her vivid descriptions of injuries, amputations and 'shell shock' had no effect whatsoever on Leo. He was just counting the weeks until his birthday.

After months of long heart-to-heart conversations, Papa had given up trying to change Leo's mind. Later, he would wonder if he had given up too easily and Mama would remind him that those spring days of 1915 had been the most peaceful in the house, even if it was only on the surface.

Michael was passing "*An Claidheamh Soluis*" to Bert before he gave it to some of the others now, and he truly felt part of a golden circle. '*The revival of the language is an important statement of national identity,*' one article declared. The Irish people had been too complacent, themselves perpetuating the myth that Irish speakers were lower class citizens, and that English was the language of aspiration and of success in the world.

The decline of the language had meant the loss of many cultural reference points, and thus a loss of identity. '*Reviving the Irish language is a vital step in restoring a sense of entitlement in Irish citizens to declare themselves a people, an independent nation.*'

Bert showed the article to his father, convinced that the veil would fall from his eyes. Instead he shook his head sadly.

"As long as the landowners and the lawyers and the doctors are at the top of the pile, with their Trinity College educations and their fine ways that everyone else wants to copy, nothing will change. It's in nobody's interest to change the order of things. Sometimes I even think there's a part of every Irishman that wants to feel oppressed, so he can blame somebody else for his ill fortune and not feel responsible for doing anything about it."

Bert struggled to reconcile his father's attitude with the passionate republicanism of Michael and his cronies. One night, Michael read out a letter from

Seán. Bert only just managed to hold back his tears. Seán's family had gone back to Connemara, and he was in the trenches in France, 'up to his knees in mud.'

"When I stare at the sky above my head, I paint pictures on it. I see my beautiful little Róisín, with her red cheeks, and the cheeky smile on Aidan. I know they're going to bed with their stomachs full, and that tides me over for another day."

"Every man has to do what is right by him, and by his family," Michael said, after he finished reading it out.

Annie was crying discreetly into her sewing, and even Niamh and Tomás had picked up on the sombreness of the moment. The same night, Bert saw Leo marking something on a piece of paper before climbing into bed.

"What are you doing?"

"Counting the weeks to my birthday."

"You'll only be seventeen." Bert knew it was futile, but he had to keep trying.

"Bert, I can't wait until I am eighteen, so that Guinness can call me a 'lad' instead of a 'boy' and then wait until I am twenty one, so they can call me a 'man.' I'm ready to do a man's work now. And it is a man's duty to fight for his country."

"It's not even your country," Bert said rudely.

"And which one is yours? What do you even remember about Ireland? You were three years of age when we came here. I was five."

"There's much more to it than that."

"There might be for you, Bert, with your Irish revival nonsense, but it means nothing to me. The place where I was born shouldn't stop me from doing what I want to do."

Later, Bert had a dream. He was holding one end of a long, long rope. Leo was standing far away holding the other end of the rope. There was no barrier between them, just a line drawn in the dust with a pointed stick. Open ground stretched between their feet. In vain, Bert tried to pull his brother across the line. Leo held firm, smiling at Bert across the widening distance between them, the rope seeming to stretch to elastic infinity. Leo didn't move. He just held on and kept smiling.

CHAPTER 7

Bert tapped on the cottage door as usual, pushing it open at the same time. Something felt different. He could see the children sitting on the floor, arms hugging their knees, watchful as always. As he stepped inside, Bert was confronted by eight men, almost filling the entire room, standing to attention in two rows, their serious faces turned towards Patrick Leahy, also standing to attention. A stiff khaki canvas tunic and what looked like new boots gave him an air of authority despite his shabby trousers and roughly trimmed hair. It was the first time Bert had seen Patrick clean shaven, and when he turned to face the door his eyes narrowed and Bert felt afraid. Michael stood in the centre of the front row seeming even taller than usual, with his shoulders straight and his chest puffed out. Bert glanced around, looking for Annie as he put down his satchel. Michael indicated with a nod that he should stand at the end of the front line, so Bert squeezed in beside the wall, doing his best to imitate their military postures.

"The Volunteers are looking for men in England. We need eyes and ears everywhere, and we need money, and arms."

Patrick's Wexford accent sounded stronger after his few months at home. The men were all nodding and Bert felt the pulse of their excitement. The door opened, and Annie was standing there, bringing a breath of fresh air into the sweaty masculine space. Patrick's mouth twitched with irritation, but he didn't speak. Annie silently summoned the children, including Bert in her gesture. The little ones scrambled to their feet. Bert took a step forward, hesitated, and then caught the look Annie directed at Michael and followed her out. She gave the children two apples from her basket, and they sat against the cottage wall, happily munching them.

Annie looked at Bert. "You're too young, Bert. You have your whole life ahead of you. Don't be wasting your life on the dreams of deluded men."

Bert had never seen her like this before. Her shawl was askew, and her auburn curls had fallen down from the bun on her head and hung around her face. Her green eyes were flashing. She held his gaze, one hand firmly gripping his arm, forcing him to listen. Bert was torn between resentment and relief. She had taken him outside with the children, humiliating him in front of the men, but he knew he wasn't ready to go back in there.

"You have everything going for you, here, Bert. A grand education and a family and a sound roof over your head. Don't be getting yourself into trouble when there's no need."

Bert didn't answer. He just took his bicycle and left. He sped along the twisting lanes, steering blindly around the familiar potholes, his legs going like pistons, his breath catching in the night air. Everything was different now. Paddy's green tunic had woken something in the men. Bert had felt its power. He had felt it inside himself – an unfamiliar, fizzing restlessness that was somewhere between the nerves before an examination and the excitement of visiting a new place. But he had allowed himself to be ushered outside with the children, and it would take more than a basketful of trout to prove his manhood in that cottage. He would have to find a way to prove himself worthy. Annie would be the most difficult to convince. In answer to the niggling voice saying that his father would never forgive him if he joined the Volunteers, Bert told himself that every hero starts his journey with an act of rebellion.

He hardly slept. The next day he was reprimanded twice at school for day dreaming. He had made up his mind. He would leave home and live in the cottage with the Powers, fishing and running errands to earn his keep. He could pass on secret messages, and coded letters, calling the Volunteers to meetings. He would go home for his tea every few days so they wouldn't miss him too much. It was time for him to grow up and do something useful. Leo was right - school could only take you so far. Leo had been earning eight shillings a week since he turned fourteen and now he was ready to go off to France to prove he was a man. Bert could do the same here, and in the name of a worthier cause. He rehearsed how he would break the news to Papa. He would say that radical change requires sacrifices. He would be giving up his dream of going to university but that would be nothing compared to the sacrifices great men had already made to win Irish freedom. Lying on his bed he stared at the cold full moon hanging in the black sky and prayed for inspiration. First, he would have to make himself useful to the cause. When they asked him to join the Volunteers, everything else would follow.

The next evening his fretful prayers were answered. The lane to the cottage was unusually quiet. The moon cast a glare on the walls, freshening the tired whitewash and deepening the shadows. It was the first time Bert had seen the shutters closed. The place looked strange and unnatural. He pressed his cheek to a narrow chink in the nearest shutter, which stood slightly ajar. The gloomy cottage was crowded with men bending over and between their legs he could just see a trapdoor standing upright in the mud floor. The edge of a long, wooden crate was being lowered into a hole beneath. He held his breath, not wanting to make a sound in the crisp silence of the lane. The damp thud of the trapdoor being shut carried outside, and he heard the rasping of the straw mattress being dragged across the floor. Suddenly there was noise everywhere. Niamh and Tomás came skipping down the lane from another cottage. Inside, someone cleared their throat, and Annie asked who wanted tea. Bert said hello to the children and Niamh took his hand and led him in the door.

"Look who I found outside," she said, smiling.

Bert noticed the quick glance that passed between Patrick Leahy and her father before they said '*Dia Dhuit,*' and asked him how he was.

"Will you have some tea, Bert? You're just in time for it," said Annie politely and for the first time ever he felt like an unwelcome intruder in Michael's home. She handed him the mug of tea and pointed at a three-legged stool. A few of the men said their *Sláns* and shuffled out the door. Patrick shook his head and frowned at Michael, who took out a pack of cards, and dealt everyone in. Niamh sat on the floor, curled up between Bert's legs and looked at his hand of cards, and every so often she twisted around, cupped her hands around her mouth, and breathed into his ear what he should do. Her hair smelt of smoky fires and fresh air in equal parts. He could feel the heat of her little body against his calves. Her lisping whisper tickled his ear. Tomás sat across the room with his thumb in his mouth, his round grey-blue eyes moving from one player to the next, picking up all the nuances. They played a few hands before even a word was spoken.

"How are your studies going?" Michael asked respectfully.

"They are going well, thank you," Bert said, and paused, not sure if this was the moment.

"But I am thinking of finishing with school very soon and doing something more useful."

"And what might that be, my fine young man?" Michael hadn't used the pet name for a while.

"I could carry messages. I know the woods and the countryside around here like the back of my hand. The nooks and crannies, and even a cave or two," Bert said.

Michael tried to hide a smile.

"And how would you propose to make a living out of such knowledge?"

"I can catch fish every day, and pick berries when they're in season, and I know from Eileen how to make bread."

Annie said, laughing, "Is it my job you're wanting to do?"

"I know some good hiding places." Bert nodded towards the children's mattress.

"That might be useful, all right," Michael said, ignoring Patrick's frown.

Now Annie was shaking her head.

"I can take you tomorrow," Bert said eagerly.

"Can I come?" Niamh beseeched her father with her hands folded as if in prayer.

"Niamh! Behave yourself!" Annie said fiercely and turned to Bert.

"It will be too dark by the time you get home from school."

"That's the reason why I have to give up school," Bert said conclusively.

"Tomorrow is Friday," Michael said. "We can wait one day. Be here on Saturday at two o'clock. We finish work in the mine at twelve. We'll do it then."

"In the daylight?" Patrick asked, and Michael rolled his eyes.

"We have to see the place first, to make sure it's right. We won't be moving anything in the daylight."

Patrick dealt another hand, and nobody spoke again for a while. Bert avoided catching Annie's eye. Niamh was a wiry bundle between his knees, and Tomás continued to watch him sombrely, his lips pursed in concentration. After half an hour, Michael stretched like a cat leaving the fire.

"*Come out here with me,*" he said in Irish and Bert followed him outside.

He put one arm around Bert's shoulders and his meaty, soot-ingrained hand came around and rested on Bert's chest, dwarfing him as it had on that very first day.

"Don't be giving up school," he said. "You might be quite useful to us now as a pair of hands, and a pair of eyes, but think of the future. Ireland has lots of pairs of eyes and pairs of hands, but we need more brains as well. Fill yours up with book learning, and the wisdom of the great men who have travelled the road before us and you will be ten times more use to us."

"But the war will not last forever. This might be our only chance."

"If there's one thing we've learned from the likes of Wolftone, it is this - we'll have to strike more than a few blows, Bertie, before we win our independence."

Bert's chest was suddenly full and he wasn't sure whether to laugh or cry.

On Saturday afternoon, Patrick winked at Bert when he appeared carrying his fishing tackle.

"I like the way you're thinking," he said, "You look like a fine sample of a poacher."

They approved of the cave. It was high and dry but could only be reached by climbing down a steep bank and crossing a shallow pebbly beach in the curve of the river that did not hold footprints. Later, Bert watched the men disappearing into the darkness with the crate, annoyed that he had been told to stay with Annie and the children. He was tempted to sneak after them, but Annie took his sleeve.

"Follow your orders like a man. Everyone has a job to do, and you have done yours. Go home now, and we'll see you again."

He spent another sleepless night. He watched the waning moon and imagined Patrick coming back to the cottage with Michael, maybe the two of them having a little drop of poitín to celebrate the night's achievements. Papa had asked at tea time why he was looking so distracted these days, and Bert had made up a story about imminent examinations. The lying and the excitement were taking their toll on his stomach and his mother had noticed.

"Don't waste your food. Think about all the men in the war with not enough to eat."

Bert scoured the countryside for more hiding places and Michael said he was a great Scout, but he never told Bert if he had used his secret hideouts. Patrick had stopped coming to the cottage and there seemed to be fewer visitors. Weeks would go by without Bert seeing Michael Power. Annie said he was working longer hours down the mine, or that he had to go and meet someone. She had lots of excuses for his absence. Bert could only reach one conclusion. Michael must have decided he wasn't man enough to be a Volunteer. He had left the kitchen and gone out with Annie and the children that first day, instead of standing up for himself like a man. He had no-one to talk to. Gerald wouldn't understand. His father would just roll his eyes and say that Michael Power was feckless, like all his kind. Bert resigned himself to this slow and painful weaning process and did lots of reading and writing essays, hoping that one day he would have an one accepted by "*An Claidheamh Soluis.*" His marks at school improved and there was talk of entering him for a scholarship to Oxford.

So it was that on St Patrick's day, when Bert arrived at the cottage, expecting a hoolie, and he found the place deserted, he was not as devastated as he might have been only a few months before. A letter arrived a two days later, delivered care of his father at the Brewery.

* * *

16th March 1916

Dear Herbert Vincent O'Brien

We are going home on the boat tomorrow. It has been a very long few years since we came over here and I am not sorry to be leaving English shores.
I will miss you, and so will Annie and the children. Thank you for your friendship and keep up the Irish.
Your friend
Michael Power

CHAPTER 8

April 1916

They called it the 'Rebellion' in England and there wasn't much fuss about it. The newspaper reports were scanty and derisory. Bert searched between the lines for clues, wondering where Michael Power might have been. Were Annie and Niamh and Tomás safe? Were they all dead, or on the run? There was no way of knowing. Every few days Bert cycled past the cottage, in the vain hope that the Powers might miraculously return, or that Patrick would reinstate it as a meeting place for the Volunteers. But the dust settled, and the grimy windows declared that Annie's nurturing hand was gone for good.

"Do you see, Bert, the uprising failed because no-body joined in, apart from the Dublin crowd. There is no appetite for it. People are so used to being under English rule that they don't even think about it anymore."

Papa was always looking for opportunities to undermine Bert's opinion of what he called his *misguided Irish friends.* As if his father wanted to deny his own heritage, his own roots. They were sitting having their tea. Bert kept his eyes firmly fixed on his plate. They would never agree. He had an inkling of how Leo must feel most of the time. Silence was the best response. Mama got very agitated when they argued, even if it was amicably, about the 'Irish situation,' as she called it.

"If the English wanted to pretend it was an insignificant rebellion, they shouldn't have executed Pearse and the other leaders," Bert mumbled.

"There I do agree with you," his father said, pointing his fork at Bert.

Mama frowned at his table manners.

Papa continued to speak with his mouth full, "They made martyrs out of those men, when they should have just let them stay in gaol."

The tension in the house was building as Leo's birthday came closer. Nobody was talking about it and the unspoken knowledge lay like a heavy blanket over every conversation, every reference to the summer, to the future. The boys could hear their mother and father whispering as they climbed the stairs to bed, and the murmuring often went on into the night. Bert guessed that Papa was consoling her, trying to persuade her to accept the inevitable. Every night he looked across at his brother's shape under the blankets, and he tried to imagine what life would be like if that bed were empty, and Leo gone.

Bert missed the Powers more than ever, during those late spring months. The cottage, the family and the Irish lessons had been a part of his life for so long that Bert no longer felt whole without them. Michael didn't even write to let him know that they were alive and safe.

As the hawthorn blossoms emerged and the days got longer, Bert cycled past the newly inhabited cottage, just to remind himself of those halcyon days. The strangers living there didn't acknowledge his wave, so he kept going. It finally dawned on him that he might never see Michael Power again.

On the 12th of June 1916, Leo Philip O'Brien, son of employee, clocked out of the Guinness building for the last time, clutching his final wage packet. That evening, Bert watched Papa fighting with himself, not wanting the words on his heart to reach his lips. Nobody knew what to talk about. Mama was white and tense, trying to keep smiling for Conor, who had just turned two years of age, and noticed every smile and frown in the house. Leo was wise enough not to show his glee when he went out to the public house for a last drink with his friends

"Why don't you just report him as under age?" Bert asked his father.

"He's old enough to decide for himself at this stage, Bert. I tried to reason with him, and I tried to persuade him. But there's a time in every man's life when he has to stand on his own two feet. Leo wants to go. I can't stop him."

His voice cracked and he turned his face away.

Mama cried when Leo came home in his uniform. He looked taller, wider, more muscular; his shape defined by the boots and belt. Bert wondered if his new deference to his brother came just from Leo putting on the uniform, or had he actually changed in some less visible way?

Leo twirled in the kitchen, and Conor shouted, "Again, again!"

His army boots squeaked on the linoleum. Conor clapped. They laughed; Conor's babyish mumbles mixing with Leo's baritone. Mama chopped onions in the scullery and when he caught her stifled sob Bert vowed inside his head to make her proud of her middle son. Bert leaned against the door frame of the kitchen. On one side, his two brothers played peek-a-boo. On the other, the stooped shoulders of his brave mother shook with her sobs.

They saw Leo once more, before he was sent to the Front. Three months of hard training had changed him. By the time Bert had got used to seeing his brother's bulk under the blankets in the other bed, and to the smell of his boots where they stood by the door, Leo was gone again. Bert had been looking forward to bed time on the first night of Leo's embarkation leave, expecting to hear lots of stories about Leo's misadventures with his fellow volunteers. But Leo had no funny stories to tell. He just shrugged when Bert asked him questions. The man who shared his room now was a stranger.

They had read the newspaper reports of the 'big push' in July. Although he would never admit it, Leo must have had some doubts. He had never really thought about death as one possible outcome of his adventure. He just thought that going to war was the quickest way to grow up and get away from home.

Conor found a stick, taller than himself, and marched up and down the back yard with it on his shoulder, shouting "Eff-ri, eff-ri," and turning smartly when he reached the wall. He held his stout little body to attention and his gentle round face was set in a stern frown of concentration. He refused to be distracted, even when Bert offered to kick a ball to him.

"No, Eff-ri, li' Leo," he said crossly, and turned away.

Bert glanced at the scullery window and his mother was standing there, leaning against the sink, watching them. He took the bicycle from the shed and went out the back gate. He had to get away, into the fresh air and far from the walls and alleys. He cycled past the old cottage, and on and on into the countryside. Out there in the hills he could forget about everything. His father wanted him to study book keeping. There would be a job at Guinness if he put in a good word for Bert. Papa seemed to want to replace one 'son of employee' with another as a token of good faith to his employers. The school masters were pushing him to sit for the Oxford entrance exam. Bert finally understood Leo's need to get away. He did not want his life to be laid down in front of him like tram lines, with no possibility for deviation.

On the river bank, Bert sat as still as a stone and watched the comings and goings of hordes of ants, and a kingfisher shot out of the reeds like an arrow. The water slowly meandered past, leaves and small branches twirling, catching, moving on. It helped.

Sharon Mulrooney

LEO'S JOURNEY
1916–1918

Sharon Mulrooney

CHAPTER 9

I 'm making this little brown book into my Pandora's box, a safe place to put my thoughts, and I hope that the lid will always stay on it.

13th October 1916

The sound of artillery fire is booming in my head. Earlier on when I peeled away my socks, my heels were bleeding and leaking yellow pus. Every bone in my body is aching or burning. Every dawn that creeps across the sky might be my last. I feel like a hunted animal, huddled at bay in a shallow hole.

The sky is like a pale grey blanket. Out there is the great, wide unknown. I dread the order to move from my familiar hole, although sometimes I just want to stand up and run towards the enemy, to end it all quickly instead of dragging it out. These sand bags are my prison as well as my hiding place.

How can I be lonely? I eat, sleep and relieve myself about two feet away from men on every side. At the start I was afraid to make friends in case they died. Then one day I talked to Eddie, and I liked him. He has read a lot of books. I asked him if he was afraid to make friends out here and he said some lines from a poem that Bertie would know – I can't remember the name, something about it being better to love someone and lose them than never knowing what it's like to love someone.

Since then we share the odd cigarette and talk about home, but only in the dark. If someone saw me crying I might have to admit to myself how awful it is here.

15th October 1916

I think I might have liked France. The stone walls are higher and they look more solid than the ones I remember from Ireland, as if they would stand up for hundreds of years. The tall barns and the farm houses with the shuttered windows would look very homely, if the fields around them were green instead of muddy brown. We sometimes get local bread with our rations and once we had cheese. It tasted nothing like ours at home. I didn't even know it was cheese. Maybe some fine day I'll come back and taste French food on a plate and try a glass of wine with it like the French people do. When I hear them doling out the rations, I imagine Mama standing in the pantry, humming. I see the evening sun shining through the window and glowing in her hair. I can hear the swish of her skirts on the flags as she turns to take the carrots off the rack and I breathe in the fresh smell of the green carrot top as she chops it off. I can feel the cold fresh water as she pumps it into the sink.

Then I clench my eyes tight and hunch my ears into my shoulders to shut out the other sights and sounds. I chew the cold stew in my tin dish and tell myself it doesn't taste of rotten horse meat and sawdust.

19th October 1916

I often think of the horses at the brewery, snorting in the early morning air, waiting to deliver their barrels, shifting in their traces and grateful for a rub on the muzzle and a slap on the neck. Here, they flinch from any human touch, even though they have learned not to rear away from rotting cadavers, or smoking shell holes. They expect to be beaten by men who do not understand them. Their rolling eyes say more than words about his hell we are sharing.

Eddie got a parcel from home today with a cake from his mother. It took so long to reach him that it was blue around the edges, but we ate it anyway. Even the mouldy cake could not hide the oily taste of the tea.

***

19th October 1916

Dearest Mama, Papa, Louise, Eileen, Bertie and Conor

The weather continues to hold, with no rain for three days now, which is a blessing, because the trenches get very muddy when there is too much rain. We have been quiet for a while now, and I have been teaching some of the men how to play chess. Sometimes it is difficult to remember which stones are which pieces, and Eddie said why not just play draughts with them, but I enjoy trying to remember where my pieces are!

We had a three day rest in the rear trenches, and it was nice to walk around standing up straight. The discipline is not so strict, but the food is the same. It doesn't taste very good but there is plenty of it. Mama, I am sorry I ever complained about stew for tea. We shared a cake from Eddie's mother today, which was a nice change.

The light is fading now, so I will stop here. My loving thoughts are with you all. Give Conor a kiss for me. I wonder will he remember me when I come back?

Your loving son and brother Leo

25th October 1916

I can't write home. It would be too hard to pretend. I haven't slept since Wednesday last, or maybe it was Sunday. Every day is the same. Trench repairs, patrols, four hour watches on the fire-step, try to sleep, eat, shave. The sun was just going down and we were trying to finish a game of cards. I was due on the first night watch. The Captain gave us the orders for dawn. One of the men laughed, the kind of laugh that you don't know is coming until it's out of your mouth. Eddie looked across at me and he was scared. He must have seen the same on my face. I wanted to say goodbye, just in case, but he shook his head. The Padre came to our trench and said some prayers. I really listened to the words for the first time ever in my life even though I must have said the Our Father hundreds of times. "Thy will be done, on earth as it is in heaven." How could this be His will? I was down on my knees in the mud, praying like a mad man. Until that moment it hadn't really sunk in that I could just end up dead in one of these muddy fields. Then it was dark. The sun goes down quicker in France. I spent the whole night thinking, thinking, about Mama and Papa, Bertie and the girls. I was worrying about Conor growing up, and then I started worrying that he probably won't grow up. I felt sorry for hurting Papa, for laughing at him and ignoring his advice. How would I let him know that I am sorry, if I'm dead? I was thinking about clever Bertie and his way with words, and I had a picture in my head of him sitting at his desk in the bedroom, working away there. And brave Mam waving from the door, smiling at me even though I broke her heart. I did a lot of praying. God must have heard a lot of prayers from the lost sheep in this particular valley of death. Now I know why old people go to Mass every day. Praying for a welcome at the pearly gates is one thing. But I started thinking even worse things. What if there is nothing after death, and my life on earth has been completely wasted? I could die in a muddy hole and disappear into nothingness. I prayed for another chance to prove myself.

There is only room for grey thoughts in your head, in the hours before dawn. When you're worrying about dying, they go very dark grey. I was trying to remember Conor's funny little laugh and the smell of Papa's pipe smoke to push away the sound of the coughs and smell of the mud as the sun came up over the horizon, bringing my dying one step closer. The Captain, who hardly ever comes out of his bunker after the sun goes down, found me. I didn't try to hide that I was crying. He put his hand on my shoulder and gave me a lit cigarette, the last comfort of the condemned man. He didn't say a word.

When the sky was almost light, the men took their positions. The clicking of bayonets and boots squelching through mud were the only sounds. Nobody was talking.

My legs were tight and my ears were buzzing, waiting for the signal. The command cracked through the air like a pistol shot. "Go!"

I scrambled over the sandbags, went flat on my stomach, and suddenly the sky looked very big and wide and I felt free and it was alright. I crouched and ran across the mud to the first shell hole. I pulled myself out and used my elbows as levers, like a legless cripple, left, right, left, right. I dragged myself across the wasteland. My trousers ripped on the shredded metal of a shell that was stuck in the ground, but I felt all around it with my finger and my skin was still whole. I slid along on my belly like a serpent, and I felt as if I was a part of the earth. Nothing could touch me. No sounds, no pain. No wild thoughts. I was just an animal looking for shelter. The next hiding place was ahead of me. I coiled up and sprang into a hole that was not much bigger than the man who was already crouched in there. He had blue eyes and a round mouth and his eyebrows were the yellow of a candle, like his hair. I stuck my bayonet into his neck, deep, deep into his neck. His last mortal sound was a little quiet gasp that somehow unblocked my ears. Suddenly my head was full of roaring, chattering gun fire. The vibration of it went through me and I could feel the blood flowing inside every inch of my body. A machine gun strafed the ground in front of me and three men fell down like string puppets. I ducked back into the hole and the back of my hand touched his cheek. It was still warm and soft. He had just shaved. The bullets chattered above my head and I curled up into a tight ball, holding my knees to my chest, staring at the buttons on his tunic with their helmet and pike. A loose thread was dangling from one of his buttons.

I stretched my neck up a tiny bit and looked over the edge of the hole. The second wave of our Company was just climbing out of the trench. They crouched and ran and slithered, like I had, across the mud. They fell, and they fell, and they fell, one after another. The machine gun sounded like it was laughing at them. Ha ha ha ha ha, and they were falling down like children playing a game. Was I being a coward, hiding in that hole? I don't know why but I had to touch his face again. Now it was cold like a stone lifted out of the river. He was staring at me, so I closed his eyes. His eyelashes were very long.

I could see a boy on a bicycle, his breath steaming, stopping to knock on a shiny black door. A woman with golden hair opened it. She wiped her hands on a red apron, and she shook her head, with her soft curls swinging from side to side. She stepped away from him but he reached out his arm straight with his head down. He waited until she took the telegram and clutched it to her heart, then he nodded and turned back to his bike.

I was lying there for a long time, just breathing in the woolly smell of his tunic, and the soap on his face and for a while, I couldn't even smell the mud or the stink of my own fear. I was looking at the grey weave of the material and I could hear the clacking of the loom like they have in the place where Eileen works. I saw the pattern cutter laying out the pieces and I could even hear the seamstress singing. She couldn't hold a tune, but she was smiling as she pulled the threads tight.

His blood went a darker shade of red and settled in the crevices of his ear, a streak of it crusty on the smooth lobe.

When I woke up it was getting dark. I could hear moans, but no machine gun clatter. I looked over the edge of the crater. Men were crawling through the mud, dragging others behind them. I tried to move but I was trapped. His knees had gone stiff and pinned my legs against the side of the hole. I pushed him away and slid my leg out. I didn't want to leave him on his own. I blessed myself - it was all I could think of doing. A hiss made me turn and the Captain was signalling me to follow him.

Our trench was full of injured men. Eddie was there. He nodded over at me, two survivors in the face of certain death. Well, my body survived. These last seven or eight days I've been calling out to God, and He doesn't answer. Maybe my soul is gone somewhere else already; up to heaven with the other one I sent off to its final resting place, or down to hell. I don't know any more.

* * *

28th October 1916

Dearest Mama, Papa, brothers and sisters,

We were just in a terrible battle. God was with me, my shield and my strength. Keep praying – He must be listening. So many others were not as lucky. We were sent to the rear for a rest and we had baths in a big barn with the haystacks all around us. The farm women washed our undershirts and hung them out to dry and they gave us onion soup and lovely bread. We felt much better after that. Eddie is getting very good at chess now. With all the practice I'm getting I might even beat you Bertie, when I come home!

They will be collecting the letters soon. I hope this one reaches you quicker than the last one.

My thoughts are with you all, and I hope that this letter finds you well.

Your loving son and brother,
Leo

1st November 1916

Yesterday Captain Brightwell got shot by a sniper when he was helping to replace the sand bags around the fire step. He wasn't supposed to be there. He should have left it to the men. But none of us are where we're supposed to be. Only half of our Company is left alive. We're mixed in now with the Northumbrian Fusiliers. It's good to hear the voices from home, but I got a bit of a shock when Audley turned up as a First Lieutenant with the Company that was relieving us in the trenches. I don't think he would know me to see, but I am not planning to tell him who I am.

But hearing him reminded me that there is a normal life waiting at home. This is not real and won't go on forever. Some days I want to just climb over the sandbags and run and run until they shoot me down in a hail of bullets. At least that way I would know when my end was coming.

* * *

8th November 1916

Dearest family

We have had a very quiet few days with every day the same. It's getting dark earlier and earlier and it's hard to keep busy sometimes. That might sound a bit strange but there is a lot of waiting in between the fighting. We play cards and draughts and tell the odd ghost story. I darned all the holes in my other socks today, so that shows you how bored I was! Thank you, Mam for the food parcel, the lads always love your cake.

Thinking about you all, my best wishes

Love Leo

28th November 1916

Today I was on trench repairs. The new Captain ordered us to make another passing place for the stretcher bearers. It is very hard for them to pass down the trench during a battle, carrying injured men. I was hacking into the clay – it is worse than window putty, how it clings to the tools and slows you down. I knew it was going to take five or six hours to do the work. I was sweating inside my coat even though my breath was coming out white. One of the men was humming 'Onward Christian Soldiers," or another one of those Methodist hymns. My feet were slipping all over the place and I split the blisters that were just healed after we marched back from the rear trenches. The lice must have woken up with the heat in my scalp so they were marching up and down and having a great time sucking my blood. Even though the spade started off new, with a fine sharp blade on it, after the first stroke, it could just as well have been blunt and rusty. The clay clogged it all up and made it twice as heavy. Then it started raining. Well, it was half sleet. It was coming in gusts like a sheet that escaped off the washing line, whipping at my face. I just threw off my helmet and started scratching my head like a madman with my nails digging into me. One of the men just handed me the helmet back, but he said nothing. I crammed it back on my head and grabbed the spade again, so I burst the new blister that was coming up on my hand.

I was raging. I stuck the spade into the clay, levered out a rectangular lump and threw it onto the tarpaulin. It landed with a big wet thump and the Lieutenant muttered "Good lad" at me, as if I was six years of age and I was making a mud pie. I hacked again at the wall in front of me, and my rage was making me stronger with every stroke. Then the spade sliced cleanly through, and the sudden lightness of it made my arms fly up, and the load flew through the air and landed on the heap so easily. Only when I turned back to the wall did I see what I was after doing. I cut the arm off a corpse. It was buried so deep in the mud it was part of the trench wall protecting us. I screamed and threw down the spade. I went over to the pile and picked up the severed part. His sleeve was hanging limp and his hand was clenched – I could see every knuckle clearly, as if the hand was angry with me. The other men stopped digging. Eddie blessed himself and said a Hail Mary. I went down on my knees in that stinking, wet hole and I was holding up the arm like some kind of barbarian sacrifice.

"I'm sorry, I'm sorry," I kept shouting. I didn't know who I was shouting at, and I still don't know. The Lieutenant relieved me from duty. He wouldn't let me help the others to get the body out. The Captain found the identity tags. He said the soldier would get a decent Christian burial. His words did nothing for me. He just made me think that I might end up in an unknown grave.

I was smoking and staring up at the sky and wondering if the man I stabbed in the neck would have a Christian burial or if he would stay in that hole until he rotted away to nothing. His wife, his mother, his sisters and brother might be wondering forever if he was coming home. My arms kept twitching. It was as if the muscles were remembering how easy it was to slice through human flesh instead of this evil Flanders clay.

When that last spade load was flying through the air I was happy for that one moment, thinking I suddenly got stronger. Not just a lad any more. I was still alive, and this war had made me as strong as any other man. But you don't need to be very strong to slice the arm off a dead man, with his flesh rotting from the bones. Not strong at all.

30th November 1916

The passing place is made. We stuck wooden stakes deep into the clay - that will set around them as hard as rock, and then we nailed big sheets of metal on to the stakes. The dead man is already forgotten. We won't talk about him, because we all might suffer the same fate. An invisible merging with the earth. The Captain will write a letter of condolence to the family. He won't mention that the man had been dead for weeks and was only found by accident. Or that their son was buried with his arm laid in beside him, chopped off his body by one of his comrades. The Captain might put something in his daily diary. They must keep track of us all somehow. I wonder what date will they give to my armless friend's passing? He probably died in the height of the Summer but they might not want to tell his Mam. She will want to remember him as a boy running across the fields with the skylarks up above. If they give him a September date his lassie could look at the autumn leaves and remember him that way. Or will they give him the drizzling November date when we resurrected him from the mud and gave him a burial place that will be marked with a cross? In fifty years from now, when his grandchildren come and huddle around that cross, will they be canny Northerners, or savvy Londoners? Will they be rich or poor, tall or short, nasty or nice? It doesn't matter. They will stand on that spot, where someone of their flesh and blood gave up his life, fighting for something important. Or maybe they will never be born at all and his legacy will end in this wormy French soil. That is what I'm afraid of. That I'll die here and no-one will remember me or know why I died.

* * *

15th December 1916

Dearest Mama, Papa and brothers and sisters,

I am writing from a new place. It is strange to see houses and shops after so long out in the flat fields. I think it must have been quite pretty here before the war, with cobbled squares, and big old buildings. The Town Hall and the Cathedral are destroyed, but I can see that it must have been as big as York Minster.
The people of the town keep their food in the cellars. I tasted olives. They are the size of a cherry, with a stone, and they are black! The beer is a nice change after months of oily tea. It is good to be busy. I am sure you are looking forward to Christmas – it feels strange to be away from home for another one. We all thought it would be over by now. I sometimes think I have been here forever.
I send you my best wishes for the season. I think we might have snow here soon. The air has that heavy feel of snow, but we are under a roof so that's grand.

Sent with all my loving thoughts.

Leo

22nd December 1916
The fancy stone work and the shutters on the houses that are still standing make them look like fairy tale houses even though they are dark and empty – nearly everyone has been evacuated. A few civilians stayed, and they scuttle across the streets and squares like ants when you lift a stone, desperate to get back into the safety of the darkness.

We are working in the dark too. Underneath the Cathedral there is a labyrinth of tunnels that they dug out hundreds of years ago to make a chalk quarry. The cellars underneath the houses are all joined up by these tunnels, and the people store their wine and food down here. When we got here I was very glad to be out of the wind. It howls across the land for miles, it's so flat here.

I like it better under a roof than out in the trenches, but these cold yellow drops go down our necks and the walls and floors of the tunnels are very wet there is no-where to settle down in comfort. We can stand up straight in some of the main tunnels, but most of the time we have to bend down and shuffle through big long stretches of tunnel to get to the workings. The miners say they've never seen anything like it. They are a surly lot, and they haven't much to say for themselves.

They think they're doing all the hard work, but I wouldn't mind having a go at the pick axing as a change from pushing the cart along miles of tunnels with my neck bent in half.

I'm not afraid of shrapnel or snipers or mortars exploding on top of me anymore. I'm only afraid of getting buried alive in one of these tunnels. I keep on dreaming that I'm stuck in a hole under tonnes of earth, shouting but no-one hears. I wonder if they have the Christmas tree up yet, at home.

The roof of this cave is always dripping. Sometimes the vibrations of exploding shells go right through the chalky clay, and I feel like a mole, hidden from the world, twitching through another day, or another night. We don't know which is which down here.

24th December 1916

For Christmas Eve we were above ground for a change, in the ruins of the Cathedral, some of us on watch, and some playing cards. The sky was clear after weeks of snow and there was a full moon. Eddie and I climbed up the bell tower, against orders. There was a blanket of snow stretched all around us for miles, hiding all the sharp edges and the black roofs on the broken buildings and the churned mud. The cold pure air was lovely after the underground air that sits like a lead weight in your lungs and takes away your breath. We were lying on our backs on the cold stone and looking for the Christmas star. Eddie told me about his Christmases growing up in Leeds and they sounded like my own. Eight o' clock Mass on Christmas morning, rushing home after it to open presents beside the fire. Turkey or goose for Christmas dinner and mince pies and always more than you could eat. He turned his head and smiled at me and his hair flopped over his forehead. He looked like a little boy, with his broken front tooth and his nostrils flaring in the cold. I asked him if he thought we would still be friends after the war.

Eddie sat up and lit a cigarette and blew a smoke ring. I don't know what he was going to say. One minute he was there, smiling, his eyes following the smoke into the dark sky and the next minute he was gone. His body stayed up for a moment and then it just keeled over towards me. That's how they found us – me holding his shoulders so that he wouldn't slip down and bang his head while we waited for help. Help came, but the back of his head was gone. Sergeant Downes ordered two men to carry him down the steps. There was blood spattered on the snow around the rim of the parapet. When the snow melts, his blood will be on the stone and he'll have the tower as his monument. Some of his blood dried into my tunic so he is part of me now, too. The Sergeant was shouting but I couldn't hear him. My ears were full of a noise like a waterfall going over a cliff. I stood up and I was shaking my head to clear the sound, but it would not go away. The Sergeant grabbed me and pulled me down just as another bullet whined past and lodged in the wooden post at the top of the steps. We crawled to the edge of the parapet. Down below the people were coming out of their houses and going across the square to the Cathedral. They came from every corner and every side and their footprints made a star shape in the snow. The Sergeant pulled me down the steps.

"There's going to be a service at midnight."

"For Eddie?"

He must have thought I was stupid.

"For Christmas, lad, for Christmas."

Somehow the people had found a priest and brought him there. We had midnight Mass in the ruins. They did all the hymns and prayers in French, but most of the time I knew where we were. I offered it up for Eddie. After Mass we had a kind of midnight feast and a wake for Eddie, and I kept on wondering what the Captain would put in the letter to Eddie's family. I'll write and tell them that he died smiling with his head full of happy childhood memories, while he was looking for the Christmas star. We must keep believing that star is still out there somewhere, otherwise everything is hopeless.

Just in case I die, I want this little book to tell anyone who comes after me why I am still fighting. It's for ordinary people like the ones I broke bread with tonight, the shop keepers and the priests and the shoemakers, the mothers and their children, the ones who can't fight for themselves

* * *

28th December 1916

Dearest Mama, Papa brothers and sisters

I have some sad news. My friend Eddie from Leeds was killed by a sniper on Christmas Eve. We had midnight mass in the Cathedral (well, the ruins). The French celebrate Christmas on Christmas Eve so they gave us food and wine. Lots of them came back in secret to be in their own houses for that special night.

I feel a bit lost without him to talk to. The others won't play chess with me. They prefer draughts. I might be rusty again when I get back home, Bertie.

I hope you are all well. Bertie, make sure you keep up with your books, and mind Conor. Audley's company is coming to relieve us in three days so I will try and keep out of his way so I won't be tempted to punch him on the nose for you!

Your loving son and brother

Leo

* * *

15th January 1917

Dearest Mama, Papa and family

Mam, thank you so much for the food. It went down very well with all the lads. The local people are running low on food now so they have to be careful with their rations. Eileen and Louise, thank you for knitting the socks. Thick socks are a great blessing. My heels are full of blisters since the other ones got completely worn through.

The new year is not very different to the old one, except for missing Eddie. I wrote to his Mam and Dad but could you to write to them as well, just in case my letter doesn't get through? You can tell them he was a generous, good friend, with a great sense of humour, and that he was a great help to me. He was talking about home when he died, and he had a big smile on his face. At least he didn't have a lass to be heart-broken as well as a family.
I hope all goes well with you,

Your loving son and brother

Leo

23rd January 1917
Audley found me. I ducked behind a wall the first time I spotted him and he was talking to the Sergeant so he didn't see me. Then we got the order to form ranks so I went quickly to the mustering place and I didn't see him coming up behind me.
Then I hear his voice like a snake hissing in my ear, "I heard your name mentioned, and wondered if you came from the illustrious O'Brien family of Saltwell Road?"
I just look straight ahead and say, "Yes, Sir."
"Another insolent upstart, I can see." he says and then he steps away so quietly I'm not sure if he's still standing there behind me.

We had three days in the rear trenches. We just go from tunnel to trench and back again. Our teeth and our feet are just rotting away, and we're digging and digging but getting nowhere. It will take us years to get behind the German lines. I'm sure when we get closer, they'll hear us and come down the tunnels like ferrets after rabbits.

If I had my way, I would die like Eddie – quick while I'm thinking happy thoughts. The only problem with that is I don't know where I might find a few happy thoughts from.

30th January 1917
Tomorrow might be the big day.

2nd February 1917
I'm still alive. Am I supposed to feel like a hero for surviving? I keep seeing the blue eyes and the yellow eyebrows of the man I killed. His face is printed on the inside of my eyelids so there is no escaping it. I see it in the sky, and in the puddles. I do not want to kill any more men for wearing a different uniform. They take out their photographs at night and kiss the faces of the ones they love, just like we do.

We attacked. The Captain said we were creating a diversion so that further up the lines, the Canadians could break through. We lost a third of our Company. The Northumbrian Fusiliers lost half of their men. Audley got a field promotion. He is going to be our Commanding Officer. Someone said he kept going out to bring wounded men back to our trench.

I went over in the third wave, and we took a section of the German trench and held on to it for a good few hours. The men who went before us did most of the hard work and we rolled into the trench onto a pile of German bodies. I climbed across them to get into position. I left my boot prints on their backs, walked on top of them, pushed them over. Dead men. Dead people. We were beaten back, and tonight we are in our own trenches, and we are celebrating our 'victory'.
If I ever get home safely, I will burn this little brown book and all its dangerous thoughts.

17th May 1917
It has been a while since I wrote anything down because there is nothing new. We're bored stiff and the only battles these days are with the rats and fleas. Audley is itching for some action. He comes down and inspects the tunnels every two hours and gives us jobs to do. I was on night watch last evening, glad to be above ground even though it's cold for May. Maybe even the seasons have stopped and here we are, stuck between the winter and the hope of spring. I was standing there smelling at the air like a dog, trying to get any smell of spring, and then suddenly Audley was there beside me. I don't know how he does it, but he manages to look clean when the rest of us are covered in muck from head to toe, scratching away at our flea bites. He didn't even look tired. He lit up a cigarette and held it out to me. I can't smoke since Eddie died. Even the sight of the red tip made me want to bend over and vomit on Audley's boots.

"Go on, take it, O'Brien," he said, jabbing it at me in the dark. I was holding my hand up to my face and he could see I was shaking. He didn't say a word, he just took a big puff out of the cigarette. The night was so quiet I could hear the tip sizzling and then the huff of his breath. I didn't dare to look over at him.
"I need three brave men I can trust," he said.
I only wondered for a second why he would pick me out and then I quickly said, "Yessir."
I wasn't going to give him a chance to say I'm a coward. Then he says,
"It's not an order but a request for volunteers. It's dangerous."
I was waiting for him to tell me more, but that was it. He shook my hand.

I am going tonight.

BERT'S JOURNEY
1918 - 1924

Sharon Mulrooney

CHAPTER 10

25th May 1918

From the moment the telegram boy appeared on his bicycle at the top of the road, time slowed and Bert felt a huge weight settling across his shoulders. He had sitting at the window day dreaming about his upcoming visit to Oxford, instead of studying as he should have been for the entrance examination. He looked down at the book on his lap to give the boy a chance to stop outside another house. But he was still pedalling closer, reading the numbers on the doors, like an angel of the Apocalypse. Bert leaned on his desk, the legs creaking as they took his weight, and bent his neck to follow the boy's progress. There was only one more house left before the O' Briens' with an absent son.

"God, forgive me, but let him stop at the Garvey's house."

He kept coming and passed underneath Bert's line of sight. Bert held his breath. He looked up at the cold blue May sky beyond the chimneys. There was a brief pause before the rat-a-tat of the brass knocker that Mama polished every Friday afternoon before the rent man called. Bert ran to the stairs to stop Mama opening the door. She was already standing in the passage with the piece of paper in her hand as he tumbled down the narrow stairs. She turned around and held it up and he sat down on the step. They both stared at it until her hand started shaking and a single tear rolled down her cheek. He stood up. He had not stood so close to her since that afternoon in the scullery when she noticed how tall he was. The familiar lavender scent, her tousled hair, the swish of her dark skirt on the floor were all the same, but she was different with him now. He made her tea.

They sat with the telegram on the table between them. Bert would go to Papa's office to break the news. The girls would be home soon, and Mama would be there to tell them. When Bert went upstairs to fetch his boots he picked up his scattered books from Leo's bed and put them in a neat pile on the floor, in his own part of the room. He moved his socks from Leo's top drawer back to their rightful place in the third drawer. When he came back down Mama was sitting at the kitchen table, staring into space.

They still didn't speak.

"Leo is gone, Papa" he said to his father, as soon as he saw him. His mouth was dry.

His father looked surprised. Papa must have known as he walked through the warren of corridors in response to a summons from the office that it could only be to hear terrible news. Conor had started escaping out the back gate, to go exploring. Sometimes Mama was not quick enough to catch him and once he had ventured as far as the main road before she caught up with him. Papa had put a new bolt on the back gate, high up out of Conor's reach. Perhaps Papa had been expecting to hear that Conor had broken his leg falling off the fence. Papa's face turned grey and he grabbed his chest, and Bert reached out for him. For just a moment Bert was holding him. Then Papa stood up and pushed Bert gently away. He nodded to the secretary sitting behind the desk.

"Could you let Mr Hathaway know that I respectfully requested to leave early today?" She nodded.

"Certainly, Mr O'Brien. My condolences to you and your family."

She stood and shook his hand, and discreetly straightened her skirt before walking towards the closed door of the manager's office.

They walked home together, very slowly.

Papa said quietly just before they got to the gate, "I wish I hadn't let him go."

He braced his shoulders ready to step through the gate and see his wife.

"It was his choice to go, Papa." Bert said.

"I should have stopped him, somehow. I just wasn't clever enough to think of a way."

A week later Conor found Bert in his room staring blankly at the pages of a text book. Conor climbed up onto Leo's bed, his round bottom wiggling in the baby's napkin he still wore at the age of four.

"Where's Leo gone?" Conor asked, shrugging his shoulders and holding out his hands, palm upwards.

Bert stood up and held both of his little brother's hands and supported him while he bounced on the bed with all his might.

"He's gone to see Jesus and Mary and the angels in heaven," Bert said.

Conor smiled. "I want ' go," he said breathlessly, tugging Bert's hand as if to lead him.

"We'll all go there, one day," said Bert, forcing himself to return his brother's lopsided grin.

"Pay fu 'ball?" Conor asked, with the beseeching look that Bert could never resist.

"Yes, come on. Those books are boring, anyhow."

Papa had organised a job for Bert in Guinness over the summer holidays since the Oxford University bursary would not cover all his expenses. Nobody mentioned Bert's 18th birthday coming up in August. The newspapers were reporting daily that conscription was on the way. In bed that night, Bert broke out in a cold sweat. He threw off the blanket and paced up and down the bedroom floor, talking to Leo.

"Where are you, Leo? Was it painful, at the end? What is it like to be dead?"

He used to talk to Leo when he was in France, inside his head, like a prayer. And just like with his prayers, he never heard any answers. Perhaps Leo could hear him better now that his soul was floating free from his body. He looked at the bed and saw Leo's laughing face, his shadowy moustache, the wild hair that Papa was always threatening to cut off with a shears spread across the pillow, his fingers linked behind his head.

He looked over at Bert and said, "I'll always be here. Don't worry about me. I'm fine, now."

But as soon as Bert climbed into bed and closed his eyes all he could see was the blocky telegram letters spelling out 'DIED OF WOUNDS'. His mouth was full of soil and blood and he couldn't breathe. When he turned to ask Leo, he was gone.

Conor was banging his spoon on his mug and chatting away.

"Try and sit up straight, love," his mother said gently, touching the sticky fingers that were spread like a chubby starfish on the table.

He slouched and rested his chin on the table, his long dark fringe drooping over his high forehead, rolling his eyes. The first time he had done it weeks before, Bert laughed and now it was a nightly ritual. After tea they played football in the dusk, up and down the back lane. When he was the goalie Conor threw himself on top of the ball with great enthusiasm as if the object of the game was to smother it. When he was a striker, he ran three steps, stopped dead in front of the ball, and tried to give it an almighty kick. Sometimes he made the ball roll a few feet and Bert would pick him up, swing him in the air and cheer as if he had scored the winning goal at a Cup Final. Afterwards, they would tramp noisily back into the house before being hushed by their mother. Bert wanted to spend as much time as he could with his small brother before he went away to Oxford, leaving Conor with no male company but Papa. He had never been a playful man, and he had become like a shadow moving silently between work and home. He wouldn't talk about the war, or work, or anything at all. Bert tried to reach him with the Irish, reading out an article in *An Claidheamh Soluis*.

"They're looking for Irish teachers, Papa, to teach the National Schoolteachers themselves!"

"Nothing has changed, son. Pearce and Connolly and all the others, martyred in 1916 and the country is no better off than it was before, only that we've lost some fine men. There's nobody with any appetite for change. The ordinary man in the field only wants to put food in his children's bellies. He's not thinking all these high-flown thoughts about them speaking Irish and finding their national identity. Home Rule will come in after the English finish fighting this war in Europe. They'll be well rid of Ireland, and all its troubles. They'll have enough on their plate."

It was the most animated Papa had been about anything in weeks. Most of the time he sat staring into the fire saying nothing. Sometimes he didn't even seem to have the energy to take a drag out of his pipe. Louise said that the men she was nursing in the hospital were just the same.

"Does he think he's the only one who is grieving?" Bert hissed across the kitchen table one evening, when their father had left the room. "He didn't even go fighting like the men you're talking about."

"He feels guilty, Bert, for letting Leo go." Louise touched his hand.

"He couldn't have stopped him."

"I know, and so does he, deep down, but he is blaming himself that Leo is gone."

"What will it be like when I am away too?" Bert asked, and Louise shrugged.

"Time is the greatest healer," she said, and grunted as Conor barrelled into her stomach, having raced through the back door and the scullery at full speed.

"Hello, my little man," she said. "Where were you when I came home from the hospital?"

"Ou' wi' Mama," he said indistinctly, pointing behind him where their mother was silhouetted in the doorway, removing the pin from her hat and wiping her feet.

Louise sat down to hug Conor and he climbed into her lap, sucking his thumb, another habit his mother had been unable to break in him. Louise stroked his fine dark hair and tickled his ears.

"Hello, Mama, where have you been?" Louise asked.

"We went across the road to have a cup of tea with Eileen," she replied, smiling. "Joe has made a great job of the wallpapering."

"Poor Joe," said Bert. "He only had four days' leave, and he spent two of them up a ladder with a paste brush. I'm sure that wasn't what he had in mind when he was thinking about coming home from the Front for a few days."

"He was very happy to do it, I'll have you know. He says he likes making the house nicer, ready for when he comes home for good. Eileen was helping him too."

"I'm sure she was. Otherwise she wouldn't see much of him before he has to go back on the train on Friday."

"Each to their own," said Louise softly, continuing to stroke Conor's head.

He had dozed off in her lap and was snoring gently. Alfie had not survived even a year in the trenches. Louise had been very brave when she heard the news. She threw herself into her work at the hospital and for the last three years she had worked long hours, coming home exhausted, her hands chapped and her hair hanging in straggling loops. She never showed any resentment about Eileen finding a husband before her and she was like a second mother to Conor.

All summer long, Bert dutifully added columns of numbers and noted them neatly in ledgers; sub-totals and totals of bottles, of gallons, of pounds, shillings and pence. He could not help wondering who was counting all the men who had died. There must be offices full of clerks filling ledgers with numbers, each one a life lost, leaving grieving mothers and brotherless brothers. He clocked into work at eight each morning, and worked until five in the evening, without rest or respite. He took no tea breaks, no dinner break. As long as he sat at the desk with a ledger open flat in front of him, he did not have to think. He transferred numbers, sharpened his pencil, neatly corrected his errors, filled every minute. Mr Hathaway was pleased with him and had asked if he would think about staying after the summer instead of going to University. Everyone was pretending that in August he would have a choice, that his life was his own.

One night in July they were sitting at the dead fire just before going up to bed when his father turned to Bert and said, "I only wish we had stayed in Dublin. Leo would still be with us, and the Army wouldn't be able to get their hands on you in August."

Conscription didn't yet stretch across the Irish Sea but there was talk that it might be introduced.

"I can't get around it."

"You could be a conscientious objector," his father said, not looking at him. "You'll be at Oxford. A lot of those intellectual types have gone down that road."

Bert bit his lip.

Every night he could hear Leo in the other bed chanting, "Cowardy, cowardy custard, stick your head in mustard."

"I couldn't do that, Papa. But I have an idea."

If he volunteered for the Royal Naval Reserves he would avoid conscription to the infantry. Unlike the infantrymen, who were sent to the trenches almost immediately, the naval training went on for months. Perhaps the war would be won by the time he had to lift a weapon.

The coming of age birthday breakfast felt more like the last meal of a condemned man. Bert woke to the smell of rashers frying. Conor came tumbling into his room, his eyebrows puckered as he tried to remember the words of the happy birthday song. He bounced on the bed and Bert grabbed him and tickled him under the armpits.

The official papers sat on his desk under the window. Yesterday there had been no lines of men jostling and joking while they waited to sign up. Bert's boots squeaked when he stepped forward to give his name. The medical examination took place in a small white room that was surprisingly chill, even though the sun was baking the cobblestones outside. The doctor prodded him.

"Slight pigeon chest. Nothing we can't sort out. Bit of drill will soon have you ship shape. Fine teeth."

Bert could smell brandy on his breath as he shone a light into Bert's eyes and directed him to look up, then down. He nodded curtly and made notes, peering at the printed form over the rim of his half spectacles. Bert stood shivering in his underwear.

The doctor looked up.

"Still here, old boy? Off you go. You're right as rain."

Bert scrambled into his trousers and grabbed his shirt. How easy it had been, in the end, to hand himself over. Now he had three days before he would board a train south, not to the dreaming spires of Oxford, but to a training camp outside London.

"Come on!" shouted Conor, racing down the stairs and laughing hysterically as Bert tumbled after him, roaring like a dragon.

"Boys, boys, you are so noisy!"

"And you're not even a boy anymore," Mama said, looking at Bert.

He ducked through the doorway to the scullery and hugged her. She brushed back a wisp of her hair and smiled sadly.

"Happy Birthday, son."

Bert thanked Louise for the breakfast.

"We have to send you off in style," she said. "One of my nursing friends is a farmer's daughter."

Conor turned his nose up at the bacon and eggs but ate two slices of fried bread.

"It's a shame that Papa is not here to enjoy it," Louise said, and her mother nodded.

He had left for work without even taking a cup of tea. He said losing another son was no reason for celebration.

"My Grandad walked from Newcastle to see this when it was first opened in Hyde Park, you know," a short, stout man declared to Bert, as they strode towards the towering glass and steel structure. "Six days, it took him. Said it was worth every blister."

Bert craned his neck. Glass panes glittered gold in the late afternoon sunlight. The men ahead were slowly shuffling inside, as if they were attending a state service in a magical, fairy cathedral. The great doors swallowed them up.

"I thought it burned down, after the Great Exhibition?" Bert said.

They joined the straggling line of men. Bert's new boots squeaked.

"They rebuilt it here. They call it the Crystal Palace."

"Why are we here?"

"Training camp. This is it."

Then Bert noticed the men drill marching on a flat, raised terrace, framed by a low stone balustrade. A tall pole stood in the centre of it. The man waved towards a set of steps leading down to a wide grassy area.

"The water."

He pointed to the terrace.

"The Quarterdeck."

Bert laughed. The man was serious. He frowned. They shuffled forward and stepped through the wide doors. Bert gasped. Beyond a row of palm trees lay a vast central courtyard marked out with white lines that looked like a playing pitch for an unknown giant game. Various rooms led off the central area and everywhere, men in blue serge were shouting, pushing and shoving. Even the overwhelming odour of sweat and the condensation of a thousand breaths on the glass panes could not chase away the feeling that he was walking into a fairy castle.

They reported to a Lieutenant sitting behind a scarred wooden table, who checked a list and barked orders to fall in for briefing on the main deck at 1700 hours.

"Fifteen minutes to stow your kit. Berth deck astern."

Bert hesitated. The Lieutenant jerked his chin slightly to the left. Bert stood aside to let the next man through to the front of the queue. How was he supposed to find the main deck and the berth deck in this great big greenhouse? His companion had disappeared down a glass walled corridor. He quickly followed, glancing through various doorways as he passed. They led to long galleries full of white shrouded shapes. He looked over his shoulder and stepped into one gallery. He lifted the corner of a shroud and glimpsed a gold encrusted casing of some kind. Men were passing up and down the corridor, talking or looking straight ahead. No-one paid him any attention. He lifted the shroud with both hands above his head and gasped. He was looking at a golden sarcophagus, engraved with Egyptian hieroglyphs over every inch of it, even on the soles of the feet. Dark, kohl rimmed eyes stared dolefully at him. The hands were crossed over the chest, partly hiding a black eagle with spread wings. He dropped the sheet and stepped back.

This place was truly wonderful. Under every dust sheet lay ancient treasures from all over the world. The rooms were not even locked. He staggered back out into the corridor and followed a group of men who looked like new arrivals. Minutes later he was directed to a bunk in a glass dormitory. Steel girders stretched overhead, surprisingly elegant even in their functionality. He threw his kit bag on the bunk and followed the men back to the mustering point. The white lines in the central gallery turned out to be the markings of a battleship, mapped out on the floor.

"Welcome aboard HMS Victory," boomed a hidden baritone voice.

The sound of three hundred suppressed sniggers could not be ignored.

"All our vessels are on active service" their training officer said, stepping up onto a podium and scanning the men's faces for any hint of derision.

"Here, you will learn the basics of naval discipline, gunnery, signalling and navigation, before being sent for further training on one of the vessels of the Fleet."

Bert wondered how he planned to instil naval discipline into men who were eating, sleeping and training in a great big greenhouse full of ancient treasures.

CHAPTER 11

March 1919

The bitterly cold air seared Bert's lungs as he pedalled up the steep hill, the frame of the old black bicycle protesting at every push. Thick blue gloves saved his fingers from cleaving to the rusty iron handlebars. They were well travelled gloves. Louise had knit them for Leo, and they had come back in his black metal box with everything else. Bert sometimes made a pillow out of them at night, the scratchy wool oddly comforting against his cheek. The hummocky grass in the middle of the boreen forced him to cycle on one side or the other with the hawthorn bushes looming out of the mist and scratching his face before he had time to swerve. Dry stone walls stretched in every direction, defining the lane, drawing his eye to the low, grey horizon. He was looking out for a cross roads. Someone was supposed to meet him there. They would be frozen, standing exposed to the wind with no decent trees for shelter. He was late, he knew. He had underestimated the distance from Tuam. Without a map, he had asked for directions.

"How far is it to Dunmore?" he asked. They sized him up, his English accent, his short, military haircut.

"For a tall fella like yourself, it should only take you an hour," replied one.

"It's exactly seventeen and a half miles," said another, doffing his cap.

"If you go the back way, you'll save yourself a couple of miles," said a third, directing him cross country.

It had taken hours and he was hungry and tired. Even with the lightest burden, a bag containing a shirt and underwear, some pencils and his "Father O'Growney's Rules of Irish Grammar," his back was aching. The bicycle was well beyond its useful life, but it had been the only one left in the Stores. There was no money for new bikes. With a final surge, he crested the hill, and saw the cross roads ahead. He freewheeled down, spotting a dark figure silhouetted against the twilit field.

The figure stood as he approached, and a hat was waved in greeting.

"*Fáilte, Fáilte, Céad míle Fáilte. Dia Dhuit. Cén chaoi a bhfuil tú?*" Welcome, welcome, God be with you, how are you?

"*Dia 's Muire dhuit, tá mé go maith.* I'm well. I'm sorry to be so late. I thought you were closer to Tuam."

"Many's the fella that makes the same mistake. It's a good few miles, all right. Come on inside anyway and we'll get you some food and a drink to warm you up."

The man pointed down the right hand *boreen* and Bert saw a light gleaming through the deepening dusk. He turned the bicycle wheel and his stomach rumbled.

"*Pádraig Ó Conaile is ainm dom*" said the man, holding out his hand. "I'm Paddy Connolly."

"Bert O'Brien." Bert pulled off his glove.

The warmth of the man's huge work-calloused hand brought back the memory of Michael's, and he smiled. Paddy slapped him on the back just as Michael had been in the habit of doing and propelled him down the lane.

"We'll get you a big feed of potatoes first. A man can't work on an empty stomach. I told them not to come until later on, but they started coming an hour ago. Sure, you couldn't keep them away."

The cottage was long and low, with three tiny, deep-set windows facing onto the lane and a neat stack of turf against the end wall. Yellow light spilt from the open door onto a short stony path. A babble of voices and the tang of peat smoke greeted them as they stepped inside.

"He's here, I have him with me," shouted Paddy.

There was a clap of approval and suddenly Bert was overwhelmed with handshakes and smiles and more slapping on the back. He was manhandled to the best stool by the fire and a mug of tea was put in his hands. A ring of faces smiled benignly at him in the flickering light of the fire and one paraffin lamp, no-one speaking now, as if waiting for some great words of wisdom. A woman bustled forward, her very large bosom wrapped tightly in a shawl that crossed her chest, seeming to require its support to prevent her toppling over with the weight of it. Her cheeks had the high colour of the hostess of a propitious occasion. Her dark eyebrows seemed permanently raised in a question mark.

"You won't be getting anything out of him until he's had some dinner," she said.

She elbowed her way through them carrying a steaming plate of potatoes. Bert had imagined a classroom with a blackboard and chalk and an orderly row of chairs.

Perhaps these people were his welcoming committee rather than his students. He was so hungry he couldn't think straight, and it seemed that everyone was waiting with bated breath. He took a sip of tea. He bent to the task of peeling the crumbling, floury potatoes, the chipped enamel plate balanced on his knee, conscious that if he looked up, several pairs of curious eyes would meet his own. He fought down a blush, remembering the time at the Power's cottage when he had read out loud from the newspaper to the attentive ears of Michael and Patrick and Seán.

How much had changed in five years. His voice had settled into a proper baritone and didn't wobble any more. He had lost a brother, and sometimes he thought, a father. He had sacrificed the hallowed halls of Oxford for the hedgerows of Connemara. Less than a month before he had been eating in the mess hall at HMS Victory waiting for his discharge orders from the Royal Naval Reserve. He didn't even catch sight of the sea before the war was declared over. If only Leo could have lived for a few more months, he would be at home now, looking forward to his life's adventures. Bert carried Leo's diary with him everywhere. As soon as he turned the last page, he knew he would never go to Oxford. He would never be a book keeper. He would not stay at home even to make his Mama happy. He owed it to Leo not to live an ordinary life. And here he was.

He gulped more tea, the dry flouriness of the potatoes unrelieved by gravy or butter.

"The goodness is in the skin," said the woman, pointing accusingly at the pile of skins he had pushed to one side of the plate.

"That's how we poor Irish survived this long on the humble potato," said Paddy.

The blush crept up the back of Bert's neck. He cut the skins into pieces and shovelled them into his mouth, gulping the sweet tea between each mouthful. He told himself that they were not intending to imply anything. Paddy and his wife were gracious hosts, and his welcome could not be faulted. They had put enough sugar in the tea to trot a mouse on it.

The curious glances from the others were hardly surprising. An Englishman, coming to teach them Irish. He would be the talk of the town and the countryside, Seán O'Farrell from the Gaelic League had warned him. He wanted to tell them he was born in Dublin, that an English accent didn't make him English. He wanted to tell them he was as much an Irishman as the next man. He would never tell these people he had marched down Whitehall, his starched white sailor's collar choking him, a coward and a cheat disguised as a Royal Naval Reserve Volunteer.

"Thank you, Mrs Connolly, that was delicious," he said, after swallowing the last mouthful.

He smiled at her, and she reached out her hand, and for a moment he thought she was going to ruffle his hair, newly tufty after being shorn for months. She took the plate and smiled back, inclining her head.

"Indeed, you're welcome. You can call me Noreen."

"Hasn't he lovely manners?" she said to no-one in particular.

With no further excuse for prevarication, there was a rustle of excitement. There must have been at least twenty, thought Bert, as he stood up, feeling at a disadvantage hunched on a stool when most of them were standing.

He wished he had taken up Seán O'Farrell's offer of a formal introduction. Bert had insisted that he could find his own way around and introduce himself. Seán had more important things to be doing. He had to cover the whole of the West of Ireland, from the Shannon to the sea, up to Sligo and Leitrim and down to Kerry. There were just not enough teachers. *Conradh na Gaeilge* was fighting a losing battle to grow more Irish speakers, even here in the west where there should be a good foundation. Bert cleared his throat.

"Good evening everyone, it is a great pleasure to be here, and thank you for the very warm welcome."

They clapped enthusiastically, Paddy Connolly beaming around the room as if Bert was his personal protégé.

"Seán O'Farrell has told me that there are quite a few of you interested in learning to speak Irish."

Bert was hoping to flush out his prospective students from any curious on-lookers, but every single one of them nodded and smiled expectantly.

"Can I ask if any of you have a few words already?"

Only three hands went up, and Bert was relieved. He would prefer to start with 'empty vessels', as Michael Power had called him.

"You might be wondering what qualifies me to be a *Timire*. I was taught Irish by a man called Michael Power from Carraroe, whom I met when I was twelve. He was over in Newcastle working as a miner, of all things."

There was a murmur of interest.

"He came home a few years ago and we lost touch, but he was a very inspirational man, and he gave me a love of the language that has never left me."

Paddy Connolly coughed discreetly.

"The same Michael Power went to National School with my cousins in Carraroe. We used to go over and save the turf with them every summer. I remember him as a big strapping fella, with a great smile on him."

Bert laughed.

"Yes, that sounds like him. Do you have any idea where he is these days?"

Paddy's face clouded.

"I heard he came back in '16. I don't know what happened him."

"Well, I'll be travelling around between here and Tuam, and across to Headford, and even over to Ballinasloe. I might meet him somewhere on the road."

"You never know where you might cross his path," said Paddy.

There was another impatient rustle among the standing crowd.

"Shall we start with the weather?" said Bert in a moment of inspiration.

They spent the next hour talking about rain, wind and sun, clouds, snow, and storms. Bert had nowhere to write up the words, but then Michael had never taught him that way. At about ten o'clock one woman stood up to go and by ten past the hour everyone was gone. They all shook his hand as they went out the door, like guests at a wedding. Noreen appeared with another mug of tea and she and Paddy joined Bert at the fire.

"That was a great success, altogether," said Paddy.

"Did you think so?" asked Bert.

He was wondering if he could really make any progress with a group that big when they were all standing around without a pencil or paper between them or a blackboard for himself.

"I did," said Noreen. "You had some of the best National School teachers in the county there, all in one room together. Some of them travelled twenty miles to come and see you."

"How will they get home at this time of night?" Bert asked.

"Don't worry your head about that, they'll be grand. There's various carts and donkeys going in all directions. A few of them have bicycles, like yourself. No-one will be left walking all the way home."

"Did you see Noel Sheehan?" said Noreen.

"I did, *a ghrá*, and he looked very well, considering."

Noreen turned to Bert.

"He's a terrible man for the drink. Only last year the priest told him he wasn't fit to be teaching and put another teacher into the school at Kilkerrin Cross. It was the kind of a wake up call that he needed. He hasn't touched a drop since, and Father Grogan said if he stays off it until next September, he'll give him back the job."

Bert nodded, not sure if he was supposed to say anything. He wondered what time they went to bed. It had been a long day.

"Ina Feeney was there too, did you see? Quiet as a mouse, as always. But sure she's only been teaching a couple of years. She's not a day over twenty, is she?"

Paddy turned to his wife for confirmation.

"Fair dues to her. Her father is a great GAA man, if you know what I mean," said Noreen, touching the side of her nose.

Bert seemed to only be expected to nod and look interested. After she had thoroughly deconstructed every single one of his future students Noreen yawned.

"You must be tired, after all your cycling and that. Come here and I'll show you your bed."

She stood up and threw the dregs of her tea onto the fire. The men followed suit.

A peaty cloud of smoke rose out of the glowing embers. Bert hesitated to follow straight after his broad beamed hostess up the vertical wooden ladder in the corner of the room. When she turned at the top and waved her arm, he took his courage in his hands and climbed after her. A thick mattress filled most of the space in the roughly boarded half loft, and as long as he stayed bent double, his head would not brush the underside of the thatch, bound neatly to the beams above. Noreen swept her arm to take in the pitcher of water and basin in one corner, and the thin towel draped over a wooden rail in the other.

"Thank you, Mrs. Connolly. I mean, Noreen. I think I will be very comfortable here."

There was not much room to manoeuvre and he had to sit on the mattress to let her pass.

She gradually disappeared down the ladder, puffing, "*Codladh sámh*. Sleep well."

Bert lay back briefly on top of the blanket, grateful to be horizontal, then had to sit up again. He looked around. His sparse eerie was bare of any other items so he had to climb down the ladder to answer the call of nature. He tiptoed towards the cottage door.

"I forgot to leave you this," said Noreen, bustling out of the only other room in the cottage.

Bert caught a glimpse of a long-johned Paddy kneeling by a high brass bed, his hands clasped and his head bowed. Noreen handed Bert a porcelain chamber pot.

"Thank you, Noreen," he murmured.

He carried it back up the ladder, challenged by the one handed vertical climb and sensing that she was standing there, watching to see him settled. He didn't look over his shoulder and finally he heard the door of the bedroom creaking shut. The silence was complete. The country darkness lay like velvet against the tiny window. He waited half an hour in agony before using the chamber pot, to give his hosts plenty of time to fall asleep. The heat from the fire had completely dissipated so he slept in his shirt and trousers, only taking his socks off for some semblance of undressing for bed.

CHAPTER 12

Bert had never heard a dawn chorus like it. The darkness had gone from velvet to coarse, black linen. He peered at his watch, a gift from his parents for his eighteenth birthday. It was only half past four. The starlings and blackbirds were having a party outside his window. His feet were freezing so he rubbed them briskly, pulled on his socks and rolled over, holding Leo's gloves against his cheek. He closed his eyes, pretending that if he opened them, Leo would be there waiting to throw a sock at him.

A cockerel crowed from far away. A dog barked. Downstairs, Bert could hear stirring, and quickly relieved himself before Noreen came out to tend the fire. He immediately regretted it. How was he going to carry the now brimming pot down that ladder?

He pulled on his boots and was climbing down, managing to keep his balance, when Noreen came out of the bedroom, humming.

"*An bhfuil ocras ort?*" Are you hungry?"

"Good morning Noreen, I'll just step outside a moment," he said, navigating around her and making his exit.

He nearly tripped over a black and white sheep dog lying across the door step. After lifting his nose hopefully, the dog sank back to rest his snout on his paws, his brown eyes watching solemnly as Bert dashed the contents of the pot into a ditch on the other side of the lane. He still didn't move when Bert stepped over him again. Noreen was mixing bread dough on the scrubbed table, and the fire was already glowing.

"I'll make us some tea, once the kettle is boiled," she said, grunting with the effort of kneading.

Bert sat on the stool and watched her.

"Paddy will take you over to the school house after you have a bite," said Noreen.

"The children will be in it until three o'clock and then it's all yours. The teachers will come over as soon as they're finished at their own schools."

"I could probably give a lesson from five o'clock to seven," said Bert, relieved at the prospect of a bit more structure.

"That sounds grand," said Noreen.

Paddy came out of the bedroom as the bread was cooling, and he nodded genially.

"I've a few messages to do in town today, Bert, after I show you the school house. You could come with me if you like and get used to the lie of the land."

"That would be lovely, thank you," said Bert.

Why did they smile like that every time he opened his mouth? He helped Noreen to clear the table, which caused further amusement.

"You were very well brought up, weren't you?" said Noreen.

He had just swept the crumbs from the table and thrown them on the fire.

"We all had our jobs to do at home," said Bert. "Mine was bringing in the coal, but in the absence of that, I'd like to help in whatever way I can."

Noreen sniggered behind her hand, then caught Bert's eye.

"Sorry, I don't mean to mock you, Bert. It's only that you're so well spoken. You sound like a County Councillor or a Justice of the Peace. We wouldn't be used to having them in our house."

"*I wander'd lonely as a cloud, that floats on high o'er vales and hills, when all at once, I saw a crowd, a host of golden daffodils.*"

Bert exaggerated every vowel and enunciated every consonant. Noreen laughed so much she bent over and held her ribs.

"Wordsworth! I loved that one at school!" she said.

Paddy was mortified. Why couldn't she just go along with the young man and his elocutioned ways instead of making such a fuss about it? He was a visitor, and he could talk whatever way he wanted, as far as Paddy was concerned.

"I won a scholarship to a private school. My friend Gerald and I had to learn how to 'speak properly' very quickly or else we would have been eaten for breakfast, metaphorically speaking."

Noreen nodded.

"And you speak the Irish as well as any I've heard," she said.

"I think you have an ear for it," said Paddy, taking his coat off the hook on the door.

"Are you ready to come and see the school house?"

Bert was delighted to escape the smoky cottage and the intensity of Noreen's attention.

"It's only a short step down the lane," said Paddy as Bert went to get his bicycle.

"I thought I could cycle around to get my bearings while you are running your errands," said Bert.

"Running my errands, indeed," repeated Paddy.

The Connolly's house sat in a shallow valley, and it was over the brow of the second hill that the school house stood, squat against the flat bog stretching out on all sides. Short furze bushes and the endless stone wall following the winding road by which Bert had arrived were the only relief from the dark expanse. The pools of black ditch water sucked in the light rather than reflecting it, and Bert could not help wondering why a school would be built here, in the middle of the wilderness, with not another house in sight. As they crested the hill, a rag tag line of children was coming along the road, some barefoot, some carrying lunch pails and others with single sods of turf. A desultory wisp of smoke rose from a single chimney on the school.

"What are the children carrying?" asked Bert.

"Turf. It's turf for the fire. That's how they pay for their schooling."

"All of them?"

"Only the ones without the money to pay for the books and slates," replied Paddy.

The men stood for a few moments, the wind lifting the tails of their jackets and carrying the sound of children's laughter as they sprinted the last few yards to the school gate. A slightly built woman with fair hair pulled back in a bun, a blue cardigan buttoned up to the neck and a tweed skirt swinging around shapely legs, was vigorously ringing the bell, greeting each child with a smile. She ushered the stragglers inside and closed the door.

"Ina Feeney, one of your students from last evening," said Paddy, striding ahead. Bert hurried to catch up.

"Is she a local woman?" he asked.

"Her father, Máirtín Feeney, is a big man in the GAA, a builder. He's doing all right for himself. Sent his three girls as well as his boys off to boarding school in Dublin. The two boys played for the County team. They say Máirtín Feeney paid Liam Foley in cash for the new GAA playing field."

The chanting of the "Hail Mary" stopped as soon as Paddy opened the door, straight into the large, bright classroom. The children, ranging from six to twelve years old, looked even more ragged, all sitting in rows, some with muddy knees sticking out underneath the scratched benches.

"Carry on please, children," said the teacher, frowning slightly.

Paddy bowed his head and clasped his hands in front of his buttoned jacket and the children started again as Bert followed suit.

"...blessed art thou amongst women and blessed is the fruit of thy womb, Jesus..."

"Sorry to disturb you, Miss Feeney," said Paddy when they had finished. "I just wanted to show our new *Timire* where he would be working."

"You're very welcome, Mr O'Brien. The school house will be at your disposal after three o'clock, and we'll keep the fire banked up, won't we, children?"

"Yes, Miss Feeney," they chanted, twisting around in their chairs to get a better view of the stranger.

He didn't look very English, they told their parents later, with his hair sticking up and the patches on his elbows.

Bert inclined his head and said, "I look forward to seeing you later."

The teacher smiled and quickly quelled the sniggers from the older children with a sharp instruction to open their history books at page forty seven.

Silence descended after a brief rustling. Paddy cleared his throat. Bert had been looking into her pale greyish eyes, noticing the slight flaring of her nostrils as she breathed, the pale pink flush rising on her cheeks, the nervous way she tucked a strand of hair behind her ear. The pearly nails on her long, slim fingers. He inclined his head again and followed Paddy outside, taking a deep breath of the cold morning air.

"You seem to be very taken with the lovely Miss Feeney," said Paddy out of the side of his mouth. "The father wouldn't take kindly to any inappropriate interest being taken, if you know what I mean."

"She seems to be a lovely lady, and a very competent teacher," said Bert.

"Her father is very protective." said Paddy.

"Rightfully so," said Bert.

"We might do things a little bit different here than you'd be used to over in England," said Paddy.

Bert nodded.

"Come on into town and I can introduce you to a few people."

They walked the five miles slowly, Bert wheeling the bicycle.

"Did you know Michael Power very well?" Paddy asked.

"I saw the Powers nearly every day for four years. They were like another family to me. Niamh used to sit at my feet when we played cards and tell me which cards to play. Tomás was full of mischief. I was teaching him how to fish when they went away."

"Did you know he spent time in Frognach?"

Paddy delivered the news like a man who takes pleasure in giving people a shock.

Bert stopped walking.

"When? How? He can't have been. He wasn't even in the country when they made those arrests."

"He went back to England in the summer of '16. After the Rising was a failure, himself and Patrick Leahy went back to England. They were going to London to raise money. They were on the boat train from Holyhead and as soon as they got off it they were arrested."

"All of them?"

"Patrick and Michael had stepped off the train to find a trolley for the bags. Annie and the children saw everything through the window."

Bert was remembering that lonely summer. He had often cycled past the Powers' cottage, consoling himself by imagining Tomás learning to fish in Lough Corrib and Niamh picking blackberries in August. It had never crossed his mind that Michael might be in prison.

"Annie stayed inside in the train with the children, and she had to watch Michael and Patrick being marched off down the platform, not knowing what was happening."

"How long was he interned?"

"Until the Christmas that same year. Annie took the children to Wales to be near him, but she was never allowed into the place. She had to beg on the streets. Eventually they found shelter with a family from Kilkenny who had settled in Wales."

"I had no idea," breathed Bert.

"It's probably just as well you didn't know. There was nothing you could have done except to worry."

"Was he harmed in any way?"

"No, but they say he came out a very bitter man. He wouldn't stay in England after that. He brought a few of the younger fellas back with him. I heard they're based around Limerick somewhere."

The silence was pierced suddenly by the shrill song of a lark as it rose over the bog. He wanted to jump on his bicycle and ride away fast, up and down the hills. When his mind was in turmoil it was the only remedy. Why had Annie not called on him to help? Why had Michael never written? Had they just left him behind, a nice boy who would never amount to much?

"Now, this is our *Dún Mór*, our big fort, that the town is called after," said Paddy, as proud as if he had built it himself. "It goes all the way back to 1235, seat of the O'Connor kings of Connaught before the Normans came and built their own big castle there beside the river."

The main street was crowded with women in dark shawls carrying baskets and men on bicycles, trousers tucked into their long socks and flat caps on their heads. A herd of cattle was being driven out of town after the fair, the farmer looking dour and dissatisfied with his day's dealings, a jet black dog skulking along at his heels, anticipating a kick at every step. Bert did not hear a single word of Irish being spoken. He hadn't expected it in Dublin, and even in Tuam he had not been surprised that everyone seemed to speak English. But he had hoped to find pockets of Irish in small towns like Dunmore. It seemed as though there was very little to build on.

"That's where the Feeneys are living," said Paddy as they reached the edge of the town, pointing to a large, stone, double-fronted house with a circular driveway and tall pillars, although there were no gates hanging from them. Hydrangea bushes huddled in the cold, and daffodil spikes were just emerging from the dark soil. The hedges were well-tended and the grass looked as though it had been cut with a scissors. A boy came around the corner at the back of the house, his arms like white branches sticking out of his navy blue *geansaí*, and pushed a delivery bicycle across the gravel. He mounted and rode off, whistling.

"They have their messages delivered," said Paddy as if that should confirm something to Bert.

He could imagine Miss Feeney sitting on the stone bench in the garden on a sunny day doing some embroidery or reading a book. She would look up and smile when she heard his footsteps crunching on the stones, put her work aside and pat the bench, inviting him to join her. He looked up and realised Paddy was walking on, still talking. He caught up, breathless.

"You're welcome to stay with us of course, on the days that you're teaching at our own school."

"Thank you, Paddy, I really appreciate it. Seán said there's a family just outside Ballinasloe who need a few bob, and they would give me dinner and a bed once a week."

Bert felt awkward. He didn't know whether he was supposed offer money to Paddy. He should have cleared up all those things with Seán O'Farrell before he left Ballinasloe, but everything over here seemed to happen by a tacit understanding. Ever since he had arrived in Ireland he had been swimming against invisible undercurrents without making any progress. He was a stranger in his own country. Just as he was about to bring up the subject of paying for his lodging, Paddy turned abruptly into a gateway and lifted the knocker on a peeling blue door in a grey walled cottage.

"There's someone in here I want you to meet," he said.

Bert tripped over a pail of water standing on the path, regained his balance and licked his hand to flatten down his hair. The door opened and a tiny woman, no taller than the middle button on his jacket, peered out, her blue eyes watering in the cold air. She blinked.

"Who is it?"

Paddy took the crabbed arthritic hand that was waving in front of his face and placed it on his cheek.

"It's only me, Mammy," he said soothingly.

She stepped back and swung the door open.

"*A Phádraig, a ghrá*, what are you doing out on the step? *Tar isteach*. Come in."

Bert wiped his wet feet on the mat and followed Paddy inside. He could feel his pupils expanding in the gloom.

"I brought you our new *Timire*," said Paddy, presenting Bert with a flourish that was lost on the old woman, who was bent over plumping embroidered cushions on the two chairs by the fire.

"Well, well, isn't that grand," she said, turning and holding out her hand to shake Bert's.

Her fingers felt like the shafts of feathers, light and brittle.

"Hello, I'm Herbert O'Brien. I am very pleased to meet you," he said.

"Herbert!" roared Paddy. "I thought you would be a Robert."

"*A Phádraig*, there's no need to be so rude!" exclaimed his mother.

He looked suitably crestfallen.

"*Caitlín Uí Chonghaile is ainm dom*," she said, putting her hand against her chest as if communicating with a pygmy from the forests of New Guinea.

"*Tá fíor áthas orm a bheith anseo. Tá mé ag tnúth go mór le mo chuid oibre a thosú anocht.* I'm delighted to be here, and I'm looking forward to starting my work tonight," said Bert and was gratified when she looked surprised.

"That's fine Connaught Irish you have there. Is that what they've settled on?" asked the old woman.

"I think there are so few teachers, Mrs Connolly, that the Gaelic League will take whomever they can find."

"Beggars can't be choosers, that's for certain," she said, adjusting the angle of one of the chairs. "There's no point in arguing about which style of Irish people should be learning, when they should just be getting on with it."

Bert was standing in the middle of the room.

"Sit down here, young man, don't be standing there with one arm longer than the other," the old woman said irritably.

"So, how do you feel, being a fugitive and all?" She said it like 'fudge-a-teave.'

"Well, I'm not really one yet, Mrs Connolly. They'll have to find out about me first!"

"True enough."

She stroked her chin which had a fine growth of grey hair adorning it.

"But you're belonging to an illegal organisation."

"I don't really think of it that way, myself, Mrs Connolly," said Bert. "They banned the Gaelic League for sedition and incitement to violence without a shred of evidence against the members. They're just playing it safe."

"We didn't fight this long – I'm in *Conradh na Gaeilge* myself since the autumn of 1893, before you were even a twinkle in your father's eye – to let them stop us now, just when the people have finally awoken to the call."

"When the priests had to celebrate Mass on the rocks, the faith of the people grew even stronger. A bit of oppression works wonders."

"Haven't we been oppressed all the time, for seven hundred years, and we still managed to drive our own native language to the very far edges of the west coast where they're nearly falling into the sea. It wasn't the English that killed it off, it was ourselves. Too busy aping their fine ways to think about what was happening to us."

She hung the kettle over the fire.

"Pádraig Pearce was right, God rest his soul. We have to teach the children that speaking Irish is a part of who we are as a nation. We need more schools like Scoil Éanna, so they grow up with it," said Bert fervently.

"It's funny to hear those words from a fella like yourself," she said, scratching her hairy chin again.

"I was born in Dublin," he said, quietly.

"A *Jackeen*, to boot!" she said, slapping her aproned knees.

Bert counted silently to ten.

"Do you know what Pádraig Pearse had inscribed over the door to *Scoil Éanna*?" he asked.

"No, indeed I don't."

"I care not, though I were to live but one day and one night, if only my fame and my deeds live after me."

"Cúchulainn, was it?"

"Yes."

"So, you're the great warrior, protecting us from the invader, is it?" she cackled and rattled the kettle on its hook.

"She's only teasing you, Bert," said Paddy, his hand on Bert's shoulder.

Bert stood up.

"I won't interrupt your family time together," he said, holding out his hand. "Mrs Connolly, it has been a pleasure to meet you."

"You didn't stay for a cup of tea," she wailed. "The kettle is just coming to the boil."

"Thank you, Mrs Connolly, but I won't. Paddy, if it is all right with you, I'll see you back at your house, later?"

"Of course, if that's what you want to do," said Paddy, briefly standing until Bert left.

Bert stood on the step. Should he try to refill the pail, to save the old lady doing it? No, he would probably end up dropping it down the well and he didn't want to give them any more cause for laughing at him. He cycled slowly around Dunmore, wondering if the stares were because he was a stranger or because they were curious to see the Irish speaking Englishman. There was no warmth in them and the loneliness he had been fighting for two weeks now suddenly overwhelmed him.

CHAPTER 13

What grand notion had he had, that he would come here and be welcomed as a kindred spirit, finally belonging somewhere? The Dublin cousins had met him from the boat and given him a bed for his first night on Irish soil in sixteen years. He had expected some feeling of familiarity, to feel the blood connection that flowed between them, as children of a brother and sister. There was nothing. His aunt Evelyn, Papa's elder sister, had passed away years ago and two of the cousins, Grace and Regina, now lived in the tiny red-bricked cottage in Ballsbridge where Bert had been born. The place held nothing for him either. No early memories flooded back. He was a well-treated visitor, with fresh linen on the bed and a clean towel. No impolite questions were asked about how long he would stay but when he said he was going to *Conradh na Gaeilege* to see if there was a teaching job available, he saw the look of relief between the sisters. The General Secretary of the Gaelic League had arranged for him to return to Bridge Street a few days later and he was interviewed in Irish by a panel of three. They sat behind a long polished mahogany table in a high-ceilinged room. Bright sunlight was streaming through the tall Georgian windows behind them and bits of dust danced in front of Bert's eyes as he squinted at his interrogators. Even though he stumbled over some of the formalities, they seemed happy with his performance.

"We'll send you down to Ballinasloe to meet Seán O' Farrell. He organises the West. He has only seventeen *Timirí* at the moment, and he'll be delighted with you. Have you a bicycle of your own?"

Bert shook his head. He had had to sell his bicycle to contribute towards the boat fare. His father had flatly refused to pay, hoping it would stop him from going. His mother had discreetly handed over what he needed, saying she had been saving it for a rainy day.

"There's one left down in the store, I think. You can take that one. You are responsible for maintaining it and returning it in the condition you find it, if you please," said the chair of the panel, his chin wobbling as he scribbled directions on a pad of paper.

"May I take it on the train?" asked Bert.

"You certainly may, young man," said the chair of the panel, standing up to shake his hand, and looking sideways at his colleagues.

"You've a lot to learn, but I think you'll go a long way. "*Go n-eiri an bóthar leat agus go raibh cóir na gaoithe ar do dhroim i gcónaí.* May the road rise before you and the wind always be at your back."

"*Slán agus beannacht,*" said one of the others.

"*Go raibh maith agaibh.* Thank you," said Bert.

When he stood up he had to stop himself from saluting.

Grace, the elder cousin, congratulated him and Regina said she would make him sandwiches for the long train journey west. They settled down for an evening by the fire and they told him lots of stories about growing up in Dublin, more at ease with him now that he was leaving.

"When we were small, we knew it was nearly Christmas when the big hamper from England arrived," said Grace.

Regina smiled. "You know the story about the streets of London being paved with gold? I had a picture inside my head of you all living in a new castle, eating goose for your Sunday dinner and fancy English goodies every day, and I thought you would be too grand for the likes of us."

"Mammy always said to us that Uncle Philip was giving you a better life in England, so it's strange to see you here," said Grace, not lifting her eyes from her darning.

"I suppose it depends on what is important to you," said Bert, remembering Christmases with no goose, and Mama saying they were having a baked ham, pretending it was just for a change.

"Maybe England is not such a great place now with all those men killed and the ones who did come back with no jobs to go to," said Regina.

"*Regina,*" hissed her sister, and then said to Bert, "We were very sad to hear about Leo."

"Yes," was all that Bert could muster.

"Did you ever find out...?"

"How he died? No, only that he died of wounds. That was hard for Mama because we don't know how long he suffered. If she knew he had gone quickly, that might have made it a little bit easier for her."

"What possessed him to go and fight for the English?" asked Regina.

Her sister shot her another venomous glance.

"I couldn't understand it at first either," said Bert. "But I understand better now."

89

"He wasn't even of age, was he, when he went?" said Regina.

"No."

"And your father let him go?"

"Leo had made up his mind. What could Papa do, short of locking him up?"

"Would he not stay out of respect, if his own father asked him to?"

Bert shook his head.

"I was supposed to study at Oxford. Papa wanted that life for me more than anything else, and instead, here I am. We were both a disappointment to him in our different ways."

"Oxford. You must be clever." Regina said.

Before Regina could take a breath and commit another indiscretion, Grace lifted her head.

"And what are you hoping for?"

"I'm hoping to be as brave as Leo, fighting for what I believe in," said Bert.

The cousins immediately gave great attention to their needles. Bert wasn't quite sure where he stood with his father now. He would write a letter home as soon as he was settled. Perhaps Papa would relent once he knew that Bert had a real job. After all, that was all Papa had ever hoped for Leo.

Kingsbridge station was chaotic. Men strode across the black and white tiled floor that was slick with rain. Women huddled in their shawls, concealing bundles that could be goods and chattels or children staying close for warmth. A cold wind was howling in along the tracks and swirling around everyone's ankles. On platform one a train pulled in with a billow of steam and screeching of brakes. Bert stood in the queue at the ticket booth feeling completely foreign. People were speaking English. He could read all the station signs. The grey clouds and biting wind could have been Northumbrian, but even when he briefly closed his eyes he felt like a stranger. The odour of brewing malt from the Guinness Brewery across the road combined with a country smell coming off the heavy coats and woollen waistcoats of the people around him. Bert watched as barrels were clattered off a cart, the great solid horse snorting impatiently as two broad shouldered men rolled the kegs towards the train. The queue moved forward and Bert stepped up and put his head close to the grille, to ask for his ticket to Ballinasloe.

"You're a bit late, aren't you?" the ticket master muttered sullenly.

"Am I?" Bert looked at his watch, then wished he hadn't, as the man raised an eyebrow scornfully.

"The train doesn't leave until eleven, is that correct?" Bert asked.

Perhaps he had misunderstood the timetable.

"The rest of them were here a half an hour ago. They're gone to *have a cuppa.*"

"The rest of them?"

"Eight or ten of them."

Bert took his ticket and change, and touched his cap, hoping not to look too stupid. The man behind him looked him up and down, unabashedly staring him in the eye before taking his place at the grille. Bert discreetly felt the buttons on his trousers and lifted his tie to look for stains. His boot laces were tied, his cap was on straight. He patted his pockets and picked up his suitcase and walked towards the train.

He walked almost the full length of the train before seeing a carriage that might have a seat. He climbed up and was met by the smell of wet coats and sweat and damp hair. He stowed his suitcase on the grey metal rack overhead and sat in a window seat. Uniformed porters pushed trolleys past, shouting to one another and waving their arms. Sacks of letters and brown paper parcels were hoisted onto the baggage carriage where the hand of an unseen man dragged them inside. Directly beneath Bert's window a family of three was standing awkwardly. The mother was simultaneously dabbing her cheek with a lacy handkerchief and patting the chest of a young man who seemed desperate to escape her embrace and board the train. The father shook the young man's hand and slapped him on the shoulder and he turned and climbed up the three metal steps. Bert could see the relief in his face. He sat opposite Bert, exhaled and waved three fingers at his parents. His mother was now waving her handkerchief at him and bouncing up and down.

He caught Bert's eye and muttered between barely open lips, still smiling down at them, "I am never, ever, letting them come with me to the station, ever again."

Bert laughed.

"Not long now."

He held out his watch below the level of the window, so the young man could read the time, just as a shrill whistle erupted.

A guard marched down the platform, shouting, "Stand clear, now, stand clear."

He slammed the doors in quick succession. Finally, they were moving and the young man sat back, blowing out his cheeks.

"I'm Bert O'Brien."

Bert stretched out his hand and the young man shook it firmly.

"Hello, how are you, I'm Danny Donovan," he said.

He took off his cap and ruffled his gingery hair, disturbing a neatly combed parting. The faint, soft sideburns and the innocent but hungry look in his blue eyes gave away his age. He leaned forward, elbows on his knees, turning his cap between his hands.

"Why the tearful farewell?" Bert asked.

The man looked out the window.

"I'm sorry, I didn't mean to intrude."

Bert looked out the window on the opposite side of the train to save any further embarrassment. Phoenix Park stretched out to the right, magnificent budding oak trees framing a dark imposing obelisk that stood against the paler grey of the sky.

"What monument is that?" Bert asked.

Danny followed his gaze.

"It's to the Duke of Wellington. One of your own. Commemorating the battle of Waterloo."

His tone was even and polite.

"What do you mean, one of my own?" Bert asked, "I'm not English, you know. I was born in Dublin."

"So was yer man, Wellington. But as he said himself, *being born in a stable doesn't make one a horse.*"

"*Tá mé ar mo bhealach go Béal Átha na Slúaighe,*" I am on my way to Ballinasloe ... to start teaching Irish with the Gaelic League," Bert said conversationally.

His eyes flickered as he watched the passing countryside through the window.

"*An bhfuil Gaeilge agat?* Do you speak Irish?"

He looked across and Danny shook his head, eyes lowered.

"Did you say Ballinasloe? I'm going there too."

He craned his neck to look down the carriage before leaning across and whispering.

"My cousin is in the Volunteers. Mammy would only let me go because he promised to mind me."

"Why are we whispering?" Bert whispered back.

"There's a load of RIC men on the train. Fresh over from England."

The door crashed open at the other end of the carriage and Bert and Danny sat up like guilty schoolboys. Three men with short hair passed through to the next carriage, joking and pushing at each other. Every single passenger stared out the nearest window, not even talking amongst themselves.

An hour later, Bert could feel Danny watching him intently as he unwrapped the careful parcel his cousin had made.

"Mammy tried to make me take something, but I didn't want to be like a young fella, going off with his sandwiches, you know?"

Bert had his mouth full of boiled ham and bread and thick salty butter. He handed over a sandwich. Danny sank his teeth into it.

"Did you bring them all the way from England?" Danny asked when he tasted the fresh bread.

"I stayed with my cousins in Dublin for a few days."

"Have you any other family over here?"

Bert shook his head, his mouth full again.

"That must be easier, I think," said Danny as he gulped down the last mouthful.

"You can do what you want without everyone looking at you and judging you."

"There is something to be said for that," said Bert.

"I can't wait until I start doing my training," said Danny.

"You don't get a gun straight away. There's not enough of them to go around. We'll be using sticks for doing the drills."

He pretended to shoulder a gun and dropped his voice to a conspiratorial whisper again.

"How did you learn the Irish, so?" Danny asked, as if their earlier conversation hadn't been interrupted.

"A Connemara man called Michael Power taught me," said Bert.

He was using a match stick to pick a stringy piece of ham from between his front teeth. Had he been this irritating as a boy? Michael must have had the patience of a saint.

"I'd like to learn, but it's hard enough," said Danny.

"I'm planning to have a class in Ballinasloe if you would like to join," said Bert.

"Would I have to pay you money?"

"No, not at all," said Bert.

"How would I find you?"

"I don't know yet where I'll be living but I'm going to see a man called Seán O'Farrell and he will soon tell me."

"Grand, I'll ask him so, once I'm settled. My cousin will know him, if he lives in the town."

The journey passed quickly and soon they were pulling into Athlone station. There was a great commotion as the uniformed men disembarked, shouting to one another and hoisting their kit bags onto their shoulders. The people on the platform stood tight lipped, watching the new arrivals through narrow eyes.

"It's a Barracks town," said Danny, pointing to the high granite walls looming above the station.

Then they were slowly moving off again, across the wide blue expanse of the Shannon, the sunlight glittering on the water. Bert wondered if he would get a chance to do some fishing.

"How far is it to Ballinasloe?" he asked.

"Not far on the train now. We should be there in less than half an hour," said Danny.

Bert took out his notebook, wondering if he should write a letter home now, or wait until he had some more definite news. He had no idea how long it would take for a letter to reach home. The rattling vibration of the train made his decision for him. He glanced across at Danny.

"Would you like to learn a few words of Irish now?"

He was willing to try anything to avert that hungry, curious gaze.

"I would," said Danny.

"*Dia dhuit*"

"*Dia 's Muire dhuit* ...sure I know that already. Everybody knows how to say hello."

"Sorry," said Bert.

"It's all right. How would I say, 'the sun is shining'?" Danny pointed out the window.

"*Tá an grian ag taithneamh*"

Danny repeated it and they worked until the train slowed for Ballinasloe station.

"That was grand, thanks a million," said Danny.

He took Bert's hand and shook it enthusiastically.

"I enjoyed it too. Be sure to get in touch about the classes. I'll probably spend a few days getting the lie of the land and start teaching next week."

Danny tipped his cap and nodded distractedly. He was already scanning the platform for a sight of his cousin and spotted a similarly built young man who was waving a flat cap.

"I'll see you, so," he said.

He stepped down and started running as soon as his feet touched the ground. Bert was reminded of Leo's mercurial enthusiasms and great energy. He fought off a wave of loneliness. He swung his battered brown suitcase down off the rack and stepped out into his new life. Immediately, a short portly man with neatly combed and oiled hair stepped forward, his shoes highly polished and his dress considerably smarter than the other people on the station.

"*Dia dhuit, Seán O'Fearail is ainm dom*," he said, firmly shaking Bert's hand.

He took the suitcase with the other, in one fluid movement.

"*Dia 's Muire dhuit. Bert O'Brien*," he replied.

He had to trot to keep up with the much shorter man as he led him through the station, clearing the way through crowds of people, crates of chickens and bicycles.

"*Mo rothar!*" shouted Bert, turning quickly towards the baggage carriage.

He raised his arm to catch the train guard's attention as he was just about to slam the door having handed down the last trunk.

"My bicycle please!" Bert shouted, holding up the ticket.

The guard lowered the bicycle towards him.

"There you are Sir, no bother at all."

"*Go raibh míle maith agat*," said Bert and was met with a blank stare.

"Thank you."

"As I say, Sir, no bother at all."

He reached out his arm and slammed the door just as the whistle blew. Seán was standing there with the case.

"You can see why we need you," he said.

Bert followed him through the almost empty station, the crowds having quickly dispersed. A pony and trap stood tied up outside, and Seán hefted the bicycle into the trap, and invited Bert to join him on the seat with the suitcase on his knee.

"I thought you could spend the night with us and then I would take you on a tour tomorrow to the various places. You'll have a triangle, you could say, between Ballinasloe, and Dunmore and Tuam. We just had to split the *Craobh* in two."

"That sounds fine, thank you very much," said Bert.

"Vera has cooked us a nice bit of lamb for the dinner," said Seán.

He was proud to have secured a leg of spring lamb when everything was scarce. The new *Timire* was probably used to eating well, judging by his accent and Seán would never want anyone to think he offered less than the finest hospitality. Not that he would want the new man to think he'd be fed with lamb every night. Far from it. Seán was salivating at the thought of the tender juicy meat, and on a Wednesday too.

"*An raibh turas maith agat?*" he asked.

"It was a great journey, thank you. I met a young lad who was very excited about joining the Volunteers."

He lowered his voice and checked over his shoulder, as they had drawn up outside a small grocery shop in the wide main street.

"Ciaran Quinn's cousin, is it?" Seán replied.

"I didn't learn the cousin's name. His was Danny Donovan."

"Yes, his mother's brother is Frankie Quinn, the father of the same Ciaran. There's two of them in it, with not an ounce of sense between them. But they can't be faulted for their enthusiasm, anyway."

He swung down from the seat of the trap.

"Just wait there a minute, will you Bert, while I go in here."

Bert had a good bird's eye view of the town. The houses were solid and well built and a tall grey church spire dominated the skyline. Two young boys in tattered brown shorts went running past, barefoot, grabbing at each other's caps. A hand shot out from a doorway, bringing one of them to a sharp halt. The other boy tripped over his feet and stopped too. The face of the woman couldn't be seen but her scolding voice carried out into the street. The first boy stood shamefaced, muttered something and then was gone like the wind, laughing again with his friend as they climbed the hill. Seán came out of the shop with a cauliflower and handed it to Bert.

"Our own has black spots all over it and lamb isn't the same without the bit of cauliflower, in Vera's opinion, anyway," he said.

They meandered through the town and up a steep hill and finally the pony stopped outside a small terraced cottage and Seán jumped down.

"If you get down and take the bicycle off, I will introduce you to Vera and then I have to take the horse back."

Bert clambered down with the suitcase and cauliflower just as the front door opened.

"You're very welcome, Sir," said a slight, pale woman who was rubbing her hands on her apron.

A smile lit her narrow, heart shaped face, and she pushed back a wisp of sandy coloured hair before holding out her hand. He had to put down the suitcase, swap the cauliflower into the other hand, and finally, he took her hand, inclined his head.

"Thank you very much, Mrs O' Farrell."

"Indeed, call me Vera, it's short for Veronica," she said, all in one breath.

Bert handed over the vegetable, kicking himself for not bringing a gift for his hostess.

"Thanks, come away in out of the cold," she said, "The bicycle will be grand there, against the front wall, so it will."

Seán waved and shook the reins and the pony ambled off.

"We got a loan of the horse and cart off the priest," she said with a laugh in her voice.

"I hope Seán doesn't have to go too far with it and then walk all the way back."

"Not at all, no bother to him. Will you have a cup of tea, after your journey?"

She had swung the kettle over the fire before he had even answered.

CHAPTER 14

Bert's ride around Dunmore had taken him back to Castle Street. After only a hundred yards he passed the last gloomy granite town house and felt the breeze coming from the open fields. He followed the sound of a river running over stones, left the bicycle and crossed a boggy field, resisting the urge to jump over the clumps of reed grass. He was within sight of the town's upper storey windows and he was sure that at least one pair of curious eyes would still be following him. He reached the river bank and hunkered down, soothed by the shrill song of a courting blackbird. He sat on a boulder, his elbows resting on his knees, and allowed his eyes to drift unfocussed across the surface of the water. The breeze rustled through long scutch grass. On the gently sloping opposite bank, muddy cattle prints formed tiny dark pools, and water boatmen skimmed the surface. At his elbow, pale green fern buds tipped with purple were beginning to unfurl. In full summer this place would be lush and cool. He would come back and sit on this same spot on Leo's anniversary, and remember him. Now the wind was rising so he stood and shook out his trousers and stretched. Thick clouds were scudding across the sky and the blackbird was silent. His boot sank into a boggy hole and he tugged it out, the serenity of the moment lost in the realisation that he would probably be drenched before he finished the five mile cycle back to Paddy's house.

He rode along, whistling. This evening he would give his first proper lesson in the school. He wondered how many of his students would come if the weather turned as nasty as the sky promised. There was a good chance Miss Feeney would come, even if it rained, since she didn't have far to travel. Up ahead he thought he recognised the last hill before the cross roads, grateful that the rain was still holding off. He took deep breaths to ease the stitch in his right side. A piercing pain shot through him and he stopped and got off the bicycle, holding his side which seemed to make the pain worse. He felt as though a pitchfork had been driven into his abdomen, and he doubled over, gasping for breath. The rain came suddenly on a gust of cold wind sweeping down the hill. In seconds he was soaked and he abandoned the bicycle and staggered up the slope, leaning to the left to ease the pain. His hat was swept off his head and he turned and watched it tumbling down the road, unable to summon the energy to follow it.

Half an hour later he was still on the road, climbing another hill, his teeth chattering now and the pain so intense he thought he might be dying. At the top he stood, taking a deep breath, fully expecting to see the final cross roads below him. Instead, a small cottage huddled in the lee of the slope. He stumbled towards it, completely unconcerned that he must look a very pitiable sight, his hair plastered to his head, one boot still coated in mud, his trousers and jacket creased. He knocked loudly on the door, stepped back and supported himself against a drystone pillar. The door opened only a crack and a woman's narrow face peered out. Bert could barely lift his head.

"*Dia dhuit. Tá pian uafásach agam i mo bholg,*" he gasped. "I have a terrible pain in my stomach."

She looked blankly at him, her foot jammed behind the door to stop him from forcing his way inside. He took a deep breath and looked at her properly.

"I need a doctor, I think. Is there one in Dunmore?"

She opened the door, calling over her shoulder, and stepped forward to help him.

"Why didn't you say it was yourself that was in it?" she said, "You looked the worse for drink and I have enough trouble with that in my own house already without asking for more."

She put her hand under his elbow and steered him through the door.

"Mammy, will you send one of the children for the doctor?"

She took him to the fire where a stout woman was stirring a pot. The older woman looked closely at him, a wisp of grey hair escaping from a loose bun on the top of her head.

"It's on the right side, the pain, is it?" she asked and he nodded.

"Probly th'appendix, so," she said, handing him a tin mug of buttermilk.

"Catríona, come down here, will you?" the other woman shouted up a ladder in the corner.

A skinny pale girl's face peered through a rectangular hole in the ceiling. The bright blue eyes widened when she saw the stranger on the stool in front of the fire. She clambered down the ladder, her bare feet barely skimming the rungs and stood in front of her mother.

"Run into town for me, there's a good girl, and knock on Doctor Mulraney's door. Tell him it's an emergency. The new *Timire* is in a bad way."

The girl grabbed a red shawl off a hook on the inside of the front door and wrapped it around her head and shoulders.

"Will I tell him to bring the cart?" she asked, looking at Bert anxiously.

He felt like a strange Victorian exhibit, the subject of concerned discussion but not included in the conversation. He didn't have the energy to care.

"Do. He might have to go to the hostiple."

For politeness he sipped the buttermilk, which was turning, and made him retch.

"When did the pain start?" the old woman asked.

She had one hand on his shoulder and the other feeling his forehead with the dispassionate touch of one familiar with nursing.

"About an hour ago. When it started, I thought it was just a stitch. Now it's much worse, and it feels like I have a knife in my stomach, on this side."

"Your temperature is up, I'd say. Will I send the young lad to Paddy and Noreen to let them know you're here?"

Bert agreed and another child was summoned from the loft.

"Could someone pick up my bicycle from the ditch? Bert asked.

"Of course they can," said the grandmother, stirring the soup in the pot. "Is it about a mile back the way?"

Bert nodded.

"Pick up the bicycle and bring it over to Paddy Connolly's and tell him the *Timire* is with us and we're going for the doctor," she said to the lad and he disappeared out into the rain.

"My name is Bert O'Brien," he said when the pain eased for a moment.

"We heard all about you," she said, forgetting to tell him her own name.

"Geraldine Donnellan," said her daughter, shaking Bert's hand.

His palm was soft against her callouses and dirt ingrained knuckles.

"Would you feel more comfortable lying down?"

She supported him as he stood and led him to a wooden box bed in the corner, under a small, deep window.

"Thank you for your help. I didn't feel able to walk up another hill," he gasped, lying back.

Straw rustled under a rough brown blanket.

"Not a bother in the world," said Geraldine, tucking another blanket around him.

He winced as she brushed against the pain.

"I've a son about your own age, gone to America this twelve month and I hope that someone would do the same for him."

The old woman tutted over the fire, and Geraldine rolled her eyes.

"He was the apple of his granny's eye. She didn't want him to go."

"Indeed I did not, with no-one worth speaking of around the place to do the man's work," the old woman muttered.

"We talked about it long and hard, Mammy, before he went. Dara wanted to make his own way in the world, instead of scrabbling around here or going digging spuds in England."

"Indeed, if his own father lifted a finger every so often and did a biteen of work we wouldn't be so badly off."

"Shush now, Mammy, young Mister O'Brien doesn't want to be troubled with our family affairs, and he practically on his death bed."

Geraldine fussed around, putting a cushion under Bert's head. The pain had spread but felt less intense now, and he could breathe without wincing. It seemed like hours before the doctor came, with Bert drifting in and out of sleep, waking to the gentle bickering of the women, the door opening when the boy returned from Paddy's house, the gale building outside with every minute. Finally, the door burst open, the young girl holding it against the wind, her cheeks damp and reddened by the rain and wind, and her hair straggling out from under the shawl.

"Joan Cahill's baby came early and the doctor is with her, and he says he'll come as soon as she's settled," she gasped out the news as she flung off the sodden shawl.

"You poor thing, you didn't even get a lift back in the cart."

Her grandmother roughly dried her hair and gave her a bowl of soup and a lump of soda bread.

"Can I have some?" the boy's voice wheedled from the loft.

"Come down out of that. We'll all have some in a minute," his grandmother said, doling out bowls of soup at the table.

Bert dozed off again, to try to escape the pain. He wondered how far away the hospital was. He heard the deep voice as he emerged from a dream about Leo losing his legs to a shell, his green eyes widening when he looked down and they were gone. Bert opened his own eyes as the doctor handed a heavy black coat to Geraldine, and then removed a shabby jacket and rolled up his shirt sleeves. Geraldine added them to the hunchback pile of garments hanging on the inside of the front door.

"Now, young man, what is it that's ailing you?" said the doctor briskly, leaning over Bert's bed, and pulling back the blanket.

He prodded gently around Bert's abdomen, nodding and muttering each time Bert inhaled sharply, trying not to yelp.

"This is quite serious. You'll have to go to the hospital. We'll do what we can make you comfortable in the cart."

"Is it th'appendix?" the old woman asked, as she handed the doctor a delicate china tea cup and saucer.

"I think it is, Mrs Foley. It will have to come out." He sipped the tea. "That's a lovely cup of tea." He perched on the edge of a stool as if he was about to take flight any second. "I haven't sat down since I got up this morning."

Bert heard a knock at the door, and a timid cough.

"The cart is here for you Doctor, whenever you're ready."

A round faced man stood there, greasy strings of hair flying in the wind when he lifted his cap to the women.

"Come in out of the wind, Packy. Don't be standing out there."

Geraldine Donnellan closed the door behind him when he stepped inside.

He stood, rotating his cap in his two hands, looking down at shabby black boots that had seen better days. Long gingery sideburns accentuated the lack of hair on his head.

"How's your mother?" the old woman asked.

"She's doing a bit better, thank you, Mrs Foley," he said. "She got to Mass on Sunday instead of the priest coming out to give her Communion, and it was a great comfort to her, although she was in a lot of pain after it."

"God love her, she's a martyr to those legs. Give her my regards and say she's in my prayers."

"Thanks, Mrs Foley, I will. How are you, yourself?" he asked shyly.

His feet were fidgeting. Bert was wondering how long the doctor would take to drink his tea. He grunted with the effort of sitting up. He would prefer to walk to the cart if he could. The doctor immediately put down his cup and stood.

"Come on, so, Packy. We've a customer for the hospital in Ballinasloe. Can we borrow that blanket please, Mrs Donnellan and I will be sure it gets safely back to you?"

"Of course, and welcome," she draped it over Bert's shoulders as he shuffled across the room, each step sending a shooting pain through him.

"Thank you very much for everything," Bert said as they left.

"You're more than welcome, young man."

The whole family came to the door to wave, as if he was going off to be married rather than to go under the surgeon's knife. He wished he had written a cheerful letter home, days ago, and posted it, so that his mother's first news of him wouldn't be this.

A sheet of freezing rain hit his face as the cart turned into the wind. He ducked under the blanket and tried to find a comfortable position as they jolted along the road.

"You won't be doing any teaching for a little while, that's for sure," a strident voice advised him through the mist of pain.

A nurse was tucking in the sheets on his bed, her florid, white-cowled face close to his as she lifted the edge of the mattress. He caught the sickly sweet odour of alcohol on her breath. He closed his eyes again, hoping she would go away. How did every single person he met in Ireland seem to know who he was? He opened one eye when he sensed her leaving. Her dark nun's habit swept the floor as she bustled through the ward, stopping occasionally to remonstrate with a patient.

"She is in charge, let there be no doubt about that," said a voice from his left, and Bert turned to see a man with his head bandaged and his leg suspended from a frame above the bed.

"Welcome to St Francis ward, young sir. I'm glad to see you awake. I was going mad with no-one to talk to."

The bed on his right was vacant, but Bert looked down the ward, counting eight other occupied beds.

"What's wrong with them?" he whispered.

"They're all bed-bound, like myself, and sure you can't be shouting across the ward, or Sister Demonata comes rushing in and tells us all to be quiet."

"Sister Demonata?" Bert raised an eyebrow.

"That's only my name for her. I couldn't tell you her real name. But that one suits her, anyway."

"What happened to you?" asked Bert, nodding towards the leg.

"I jumped out of an upstairs window," he replied, "and the cart of hay that was supposed to be there was gone."

"Why on earth...?"

The man glanced towards the door and put his hand up to shield his mouth as he leaned towards Bert.

"There was an RIC man knocking on the front door, and let's just say that I didn't want to be the one answering it."

"I see," said Bert, surprised the man trusted him without even knowing his name.

"Seán was in to see me a little while ago, while you were still asleep."

The man winked and touched the side of his nose.

"*An bhfuil Gaeilge agat?* Do you speak Irish?" asked Bert hopefully.

"*Tá, go leor. Eamonn O'Farrell is ainm dom.*"

"Are you related to Seán?"

"I'm his little brother. He's four years older than me."

Bert laughed and then regretted it as the stitches in his abdomen stretched.

"I'd shake your hand, only I can't reach you," said Eamonn.

He winced as he shifted his weight in the bed.

"Did the RIC men catch you?" asked Bert.

"Well if they did have, I wouldn't be here. They broke down the door and everything, but my lady wife is not a woman to be crossed easily, and she did a fine job of distracting them while Jimmy O'Leary carried me on his shoulder to his own house across the way, and I lay low until they were gone. I was in agony, and I couldn't make a sound in case they'd hear me. Mairéad didn't know where I was or what had become of me. I heard the scream when she came out and saw the cart gone and the blood on the ground."

He waved towards his head.

"Split open, it was, and the blood was something terrible."

A hush had settled on the ward, while everyone tried to listen to their conversation, but they were talking so fast in Irish that no-one else could keep up.

"Do you know who took the cart?" asked Bert.

"I have an idea, and he'll regret it, that's for sure."

They fell silent when the nun returned, and she worked her way up the ward, removing a bed pan, tucking in a trailing sheet, taking a temperature. Everything was done with tutting disapproval, as though her patients were recalcitrant children.

"So, you're awake now, are you," she said accusingly to Bert when she got to his bed, and she looked on his chart.

She stuck a fever thermometer under his tongue and pointedly looked at her watch while a whole minute ticked by. She made a note and tucked in the perfectly tight sheet around him. Eamonn was winking and nodding from behind her back and the only thing that stopped Bert from laughing was the pain from the stitches.

"Don't be associating with men like this, if you want my advice," the nun said acerbically, pointing over her shoulder with one thumb. "You'll only find yourself getting into trouble."

Bert put on his most charming smile.

"Sister, I wonder if it would be possible to have some paper and a pen and ink? I would like to write to my parents."

Her face lit up.

"Certainly, I will ask one of the orderlies to bring you some. The post goes into town in the late afternoon, if you have it ready by then."

"Thank you, Sister, I really appreciate that," said Bert.

Eamonn snorted. The nun didn't even glance in his direction but swept majestically out of the ward, her shoes squeaking slightly on the highly polished floor.

"Well, you certainly have a way with the words," said Eamonn, *"Thank you, Sister, I really appreciate that!* She won't lift a finger for me, except to do the bare minimum to keep me alive and healthy so they can discharge me as soon as possible."

* * *

19th March 1919

Dear Papa and Mama, Louie, Eileen and Conor

I am writing to let you know that I am generally well, although at the moment I am in hospital in Ballinasloe, having had my appendix removed in an emergency operation last evening. The surgeon said it had almost ruptured, which might have been fatal, so I should thank God. I had a very uncomfortable ride in a pony and cart to reach the hospital and as I have only a partial memory of the journey, I suspect I may have been unconscious for some miles of it, which was probably a blessing.

Regina and Grace were very kind and looked after me well for the first few days in Dublin. I have secured employment with the Gaelic League, as a teacher of Irish.
I will be teaching the National Schoolteachers themselves, so that they may pass on the learning to their pupils. I have briefly met one group of future students, but unfortunately, I have not been able to teach them yet, due to my current indisposition.

On the whole everyone I have met has been friendly, although I sense a certain initial wariness from people who don't know me. Sadly, my English accent is a barrier which I must work hard to overcome. Fortunately, Michael's Connemara Irish has stood me in good stead among the people who matter most.

I will probably have to stay in hospital for ten days. I am being looked after by a very ferocious nun, whose real name I have not yet established, but who has been dubbed 'Sister Demonata' by my bed neighbour. I hope I don't accidentally use that name to her face, or she might take her revenge on her bed-bound patient!
My neighbour is Eamonn O' Farrell, and in one of those coincidences seem to be so common place in Ireland, he is the brother of Seán O'Farrell, the Organiser for the Gaelic League in the Western area, or *Craobh*, which means branch. We have been chatting in Irish which I have enjoyed most thoroughly.
The Gaelic League people have given me the use of their last bicycle, and I can see why it has been lying unused in the store. The front wheel is buckled, so I must constantly compensate by steering slightly to the right, just to go forward in a

straight line. The brakes are inadequate, and I should imagine that on a wet road they will be worse than useless. I shall spend some time trying to fix these faults as soon as I am discharged from hospital.

My teaching area will cover the east of Galway County and I will be cycling for hundreds of miles every week, going between Ballinasloe, Headford and Tuam. It's not surprising they find it difficult to recruit '*Timire*', as I am called, when there are such large areas to cover. The wages for the job cover my living expenses. All the money in the Gaelic League comes from voluntary contributions and it is encouraging to think that there are people who put their hands into their pockets week in and week out to contribute to saving our beautiful language.

I miss you, and hope that you are all in good health. I will use the Tuam Post Office as my correspondence address, should you wish to write.

Your loving son

Bert

CHAPTER 16

Bert fervently wished that he had carried out the repairs on the bicycle before leaving Paddy Connolly's house. The constant morning drizzle had made the road slippery. At the bottom of every hill he took his life in his hands, hoping he would not turn a corner to career into a herd of sheep or cattle.

Seán O'Farrell had promised to give him the front wheel from a bicycle which was lying idle in his yard, already missing the saddle and the back wheel, so Bert had decided to make the journey to Ballinasloe, teach his first lesson there, and then fix the bicycle. The gently undulating countryside stretched out, sweet smelling after the rain, the hedgerows along the road starred with dandelions, and the steel grey sky hanging over the fields. Cattle stood huddled under hawthorn bushes, not convinced the rain would stay away, and a blackbird hopped up and down at the edge of a field trying to convince the worms that it was still raining.

The corner of his Irish grammar book dug into his back through the fabric of the bag he had slung over his shoulder, so Bert stopped and leaned the bicycle against a gate to adjust his load. The rest of the journey should take him no more than an hour and he was looking forward to eating the soda bread with gooseberry jam that Noreen Connolly had given him, wrapped in a cloth. He couldn't resist putting his fingers in and breaking off a piece of the bread before remounting. He whistled, remembering his youthful summers cycling in Northumbria, the sun on his face and the north easterly wind in his hair. He was beginning to wonder if the sun ever shone in Ireland when he looked up to see a rainbow, spanning almost the whole of the dark sky in front of him. He had never seen one so complete, with each colour clearly delineated rather than misting into the next. With that positive omen above, he sped along, ignoring the twist in the wheel, and the potential danger of each bend in the road, confident that he was destined to arrive in one piece.

Three men sat on a row of desks which had been turned to face the back wall, their feet on the benches. The more petite women could slide in to sit at the desks, and they occupied the front two rows like overgrown school girls. There was some coughing and shuffling, but on the whole they sat still, eagerly awaiting the beginning of the lesson. Most of these people were ten years older than Bert, experienced teachers who could surely see that he didn't need to shave every day and must wonder at his audacity. Bert remembered his first day at St Cuthbert's, his knees trembling at the thought of someone declaring him a fraud. The relief he had felt at the end of that first day would surely be repeated here. All he had to do was begin. He cleared his throat and introduced himself, and before he knew it, Seán was catching his eye and tapping the silver watch that hung on a chain from his generous midriff. Bert blinked as he realised that two hours had passed.

"Well, ladies and gentlemen, I think we have done very well today. I look forward to seeing you all again next week."

It took a full fifteen minutes for the class to disperse, each person determined to shake his hand or slap him on the back.

Seán was the last person left.

"Well, Bert, you're a great teacher, altogether. I'm very glad I sat in to your class. I must confess I had some doubts with you being so young and everything. But I am in no doubt whatsoever that you will be a great success."

He shook Bert's hand vigorously throughout and finally released him at the end of his speech. Bert exhaled.

"I was a somewhat nervous myself, Seán," he said. "But I think that was a good lesson. I will be delighted if they all come back for more."

"Now, I'll do it for you this week, but when you're here on your own, you need to lock the door of the school, and hand the key in to the priest's house. The teacher can pick it up then in the morning. It's the easiest way to manage the locking up, I think."

"That's fine with me," said Bert, packing away his book and chalk.

"Did you find your accommodation satisfactory?" Seán asked as they walked towards the priest's house together.

"Very pleasant, thank you. The family was very friendly, and the lady of the house said I can leave some things in the room, to save me carrying everything with me all the time."

"That's grand, so. I am away off to my bed now, and no doubt we will see each other again soon."

"How is Eamonn? I've been meaning to go and visit him in hospital," said Bert.

He hadn't yet summoned the courage to face the terrible Sister Demonata.

"He got out yesterday. He's recuperating at home, so you could go and see him. He's going out of his mind with boredom."

Bert could relate to that. While cycling from place to place took several hours each day, his students were only available to teach in the afternoon, after their own charges had gone home. He was an early riser and liked to arrive in plenty of time for each of his lessons, with the result that he often had the hours between noon and four o'clock to himself. The next day he called into Eamonn's house in Ballinasloe before leaving for Tuam.

"Is it yourself that's in it?" Eamonn shouted down from his bed when he heard Bert's voice at the front door.

Eamonn's wife Mairéad held the door wide, smiling a welcome although she didn't know him from Adam. Bert took off his hat and ducked under the lintel, remembering this was the same front door that had been smashed in by the RIC only a few weeks before. He hesitated to speak, knowing that his accent might refresh uncomfortable memories for Eamonn's wife.

"*Dia dhuit*," he said, and she held out her hand to shake his.

"You're very welcome, Master O'Brien," she said.

"Call me Bert, please," he said, conscious that he towered over this tiny woman.

Her hour-glass figure was in no way concealed by her floury apron, and her blue eyes were bright and intelligent under copious auburn curls. She seemed to be smiling even when her face was at rest, and she ushered him upstairs to the bedroom, shushing Eamonn when he urged her to hurry.

"You're an awful impatient man, altogether," she said, fluffing up his pillows.

Eamonn winked at Bert and she caught him, and continued, "Well, it was impatience and nothing else that got you the way you are now."

She pointed at his leg which was still swathed in plaster.

"How do you make that out?" Eamonn asked, his tone humouring rather than curious.

"Well, if you'd waited another day for the RIC to clear out of the station, instead of going in there, all full of business, they wouldn't have been chasing after you and you wouldn't have had to jump out the window."

She turned to Bert, holding out her hands in supplication.

"Need I say more?"

Bert shook his head. She was obviously not a woman to be crossed.

"I'll bring you a cup of milk in a minute," she said.

She picked up a *Freeman's Journal* off the floor and tutted as she folded the pages neatly and placed it on the bedside table. Eamonn rolled his eyes as she went out.

"No better woman in the world," he said loud enough for her to hear.

She tutted again.

"Are they still after you?" Bert asked.

Eamonn seemed very relaxed.

"Those particular ones got sent to Limerick, I think. The new ones haven't got around to coming after me yet. They've more to be doing with themselves."

"Is there much Volunteer activity around here?"

"A fair bit. That young lad you were telling me about, Danny, from the train, has joined up, and by all accounts he's a bit of a firebrand. He wants to be doing things all the time – putting a torch to the Barracks, and the like. The officers are having a hard time slowing him and his cousin down, and of course you know what young fellas are like – they need to prove that they're better than the next man, so they're all at it. No discipline, that's the problem. If you want to have any kind of organised resistance, you need discipline."

Bert stayed quiet. Eamonn, trapped in his bed, probably just wanted to vent his spleen.

"How did you find your lesson yesterday?"

Eamonn offered him a butterscotch sweet from a tin. The sugar coating melted on Bert's tongue, reminding him of Christmas stocking treats.

"They were very interested, and they got involved in the discussions. I really enjoyed myself."

"You're wise beyond your years, young man, but at the same time there's a kind of innocence about you. Hang on to that because I think it will get you through some difficult situations."

"What do you mean?" asked Bert.

"We're in troubled times, is all I'm saying, Bert. The RIC are being chased out of most of the small towns and villages now. They are too frightened to stay. People don't trust them anymore. It's just the same as a teacher and the children. If forty children in a classroom don't want to sit down and learn, the teacher can't force them. He might as well give up and go home."

"Are they giving up?"

"They're starting to give up, alright. Dublin Castle has a challenge on their hands. They used to be able to put local men into those jobs, albeit Protestants, for the most part. There was an uneasy peace to the arrangement. With the shortage, they're bringing in men from England, who have no notion how to talk to people, your good self excluded, of course..."

"I'm not English," said Bert.

"Of course you're not. Well that explains it," said Eamonn.

"And the tension is mounting, you could say. It's a bit unfair that they all get tarred with the same brush but the local fellas who grew up in these communities get treated the same as the new fellas. You have to see the uniform first, and then the person inside it. It's the only way to fight a war."

"Is it a war?"

"It's a war and let there be no mistake about it. We've declared our own government, and the English are still here. They're an occupying force, no better or worse."

"I didn't really see it that way," said Bert, fiddling with a tassel on the edge of the embroidered eiderdown.

"I put the little bit of money I had saved up into that Dáil loan scheme," said Eamonn. "They made a film of it, with Collins himself appealing to the nation. Sure, you couldn't turn him down with him sitting behind the very block where Robert Emmet lost his head."

Bert shivered.

"That's what happened to me when I saw it. I came straight home and took out the tin. Freedom doesn't come without a cost and we're as close to freedom as we've been for hundreds of years."

He held up his thumb and forefinger, an inch apart. Mairéad came bustling in.

"Here's a drink for you. You'll dry out with all that talking."

"Thank you love," said Eamonn.

He threw his buttermilk at the back of his throat and seemed to swallow it in one gulp. Bert hadn't got used to the taste of buttermilk. Why didn't they drink tea?

He sipped politely at the thin, slightly sour liquid, not finding it in the least refreshing.

"I'd better be off," he said, standing up. "I'm teaching in Kilkeely this evening, and I want to call in to thank Mrs Donnellan for being so kind when I was taken ill."

He held up a paper wrapped parcel.

"I bought some sausages for them this morning."

Eamonn sent him off with an imperious wave from the bed, declaring he would be standing on his own two feet the next time Bert laid eyes on him.

"I look forward to that," said Bert, shaking Mairéad's hand.

He climbed on his bicycle, tensing his shoulders to compensate for the wobbly wheel. Then he remembered he had Seán's new wheel and sailed happily along the road with a strong wind behind him almost pushing him up the hills.

The summer months passed quickly, and Bert was twice as busy now that the children were on their school holidays. His students were eager, and the size of his classes grew week by week. Now he was shaving every day and the new bristles grew fair against his wind-browned cheeks. His mother wrote often, her letters laced with admonitions to keep himself safe and not get involved with anything dangerous.

The newspapers in England were full of reports of Volunteer atrocities and army reprisals. His father never wrote. He didn't even add a line at the bottom of Mama's letters and Bert wondered if she was writing without Papa's knowledge.

Amidst the fields and along the remote lanes he used as short cuts between the towns, Bert cycled through a land of seeming peace and plenty. Hens pecked the parched earth outside cottages, endlessly hopeful of finding a stray kernel of corn. Cows lowed as they meandered across the fields to milking sheds, urged by young lads with sticks and loping black and white dogs. The turf was cut and footed, the pyramids casting tiny shadows in the evening sunlight as Bert glided past. His load was still light. He only carried a spare shirt and underwear, a razor and soap. His book of Irish grammar, with chalky fingerprints on the cover and thickened, well-thumbed pages, was the heaviest burden in his bag. Sometimes his contentedness with this new life swelled to inexplicable elation. As he cycled west from Ballinasloe, he looked forward to seeing the lovely Ina Feeney. Her gentle, understated strength of character reminded him of his mother. She didn't let Bert take himself too seriously although she always listened attentively when he was teaching. Once he had offered to walk her home after the evening class.

"Thank you so much, but my father promised to pick me up at ten o'clock. He likes to have a reason for coming out in his new motor car."

She tied a scarf around her head and smiled at him. Bert had not summoned the courage to ask again. He would rather live in hope than take the chance of being turned down a second time. He agonised every week, not knowing if he was being a pragmatist, a fool or a coward.

CHAPTER 17

The lesson had finished, and Bert was convinced that Ina was deliberately taking a long time to pick up her books. He turned his back to her and vigorously rubbed the chalk off the blackboard.

Then, worried that he might seem rude, he said, "The weather has been fine, lately. I did wonder for a while if the sun ever shone in the west of Ireland."

Her laugh was like her voice, soft and musical.

"Indeed, we have been lucky for several weeks. The children will be as brown as berries when they come back to school next week."

He turned around, and she laughed again. Flustered, he brushed his clothes down, leaving a chalky trail on his waistcoat. He clapped his hands to rid them of the chalk and tried again, making it even worse.

"You need a clothes brush," she said.

"Yes, I'm afraid that's a luxury I don't carry in my bag. I like to travel light."

He could taste chalk on his lips and realised that was why she had laughed. He rubbed his sleeve across his mouth.

"Sorry. You must think me such an oaf."

He averted his eyes and fumbled with his bag.

"Not at all," she said. "Quite the contrary," and then she seemed flustered.

"I can hear Father's motor outside. Thank you so much for the lesson, and we'll see each other next week?"

"Yes, I look forward to it. Enjoy the last few days of your holidays."

The school room seemed very empty after she'd left. He watched her through the wind-grimed window, bending to talk to her father before climbing into the motor car beside him. She lifted her arms to tie her brightly coloured headscarf around her hair before the motor swept off. Bert locked the door and put the key under the whitewashed stone outside, the pungent odour of a potted red geranium dispelling the last of her rosewater scent from the air. He walked to Paddy Connolly's house, looking forward to one of Noreen's scones. No matter how late he came back she always had a cup of tea and a scone ready for him.

"You'll come back on Friday for the *Céilidh*, I take it?" said Paddy as they shared a pipe by the fire. This was a habit that Bert was determined to master although at present he couldn't see the attraction of either the taste or the sensation of the smoke swirling in his mouth.

"I didn't know there was going to be a *Céilidh*," he answered, wincing at the thought of exposing his lack of dancing skill to anyone, but in particular to Ina Feeney.

"Oh, yes, it's the high point of the summer. We clear out all the desks in the school house, and we have a great band that comes over from Tuam to play for us. The ladies cook a few hams and of course we have a barrel of stout on the go, too."

The week passed quickly, with Bert alternately looking forward to a social occasion where he may be able to speak more freely to Ina Feeney and then dreading the prospect of embarrassing himself.

Eamonn laughed when he shared his dilemma. "If only I was on my feet, I'd teach you a few steps," he said, and then raised his hand before he had even finished the sentence. "Mairéad will help you!"

Bert didn't even have time to reply before Eamonn bellowed, "Mairéad, come in here to me, *a ghrá*, we have a fella who needs some dancing lessons!"

She came with alacrity, laughing and taking off her apron. She took his hand and dragged him downstairs into the kitchen.

"Have you any steps at all?" she asked.

She was gripping his arms and steering him into position, facing her.

"No, sadly not. Michael Power tried to teach me years ago, but I never seemed to get the hang of it," said Bert.

"Every young man needs to know a few steps. How else will you be able to ask a girl to dance?"

From the bedroom came Eamonn's deep baritone, "Da da, da da, da da, diddle diddle da da..."

"Just follow what I do."

Mairéad straightened her back, her arms dead straight down her sides, her chin tilted up as she launched into a reel, laughing as Eamonn paused to take a breath and lost time with the music. Bert tried to follow the intricate steps, his eyes on her feet, his forehead furrowed. He stopped.

"It's hopeless. I'm just not a natural dancer," he said, gasping for breath.

"You don't have to be. Nobody will be looking at your feet. You just need to know which direction to be going in, so you're not tripping over everybody else. Let's start with a "Siege of Ennis.""

"I didn't know there was a siege of Venice," he said, confused.

"Ennis, the Siege of Ennis. They always play that one at a *Céilidh*. If you learn that one, the Walls of Limerick and all the others will follow. Come on, stand over here and we'll start again."

Eamonn resumed the music, beating time with spoons on his knee. When Bert next looked up, there was Eamonn, leaning against the door frame of the kitchen.

"Are you fit to stand?" he asked, losing his step and glad of a reason to stop.

"I try to stand up a few minutes every day. To build up the strength in the legs. Today I managed to get down the stairs. You're doing great, there. Mairéad is a good teacher, isn't she?"

"She is a great teacher, but I'm afraid I am not such a good pupil," he said, sitting on a stool.

"When you go to the *Céilidh* you can just watch the first few dances until you get the hang of it, and then join in after a little while," said Mairéad.

She patted him on the shoulder.

"I think we'll leave it at that, for now."

The school room was full of people Bert had never seen before, and the chatter of excited conversation and the musicians tuning up their instruments was almost deafening. A fug of pipe smoke and warm bodies added to his claustrophobia as he tried to make his way towards the wobbly table under the blackboard where the drinks were laid out. Noreen was there keeping a watchful eye on the young lads in particular to make sure they didn't imbibe of the stout. She smiled at him, amused at the expression on his face.

"I saw Ina Feeney going out to get a breath of fresh air," she muttered, nodding towards the door.

She had her hand over her mouth as if the room were full of lip reading spies. Bert had deliberately arrived an hour late, hoping that the dancing would be well under way and he could escape notice. Everyone was so busy talking he wondered if they intended to do any dancing at all. He elbowed his way out through the crowd again, smiling at the few people he recognised, and finally emerged and took a deep breath of the mild evening air. It was still almost daylight at ten o'clock, a west of Ireland phenomenon that continued to surprise him even as his first summer drew to a close.

With a clear view up and down the road, there was no sign of Ina, so he walked around the school house in search of her. She was sitting with her back to the rear wall of the school house, a white finely crocheted shawl spread beneath her on a grassy hummock, her eyes closed and her narrow shoulders relaxed as she breathed in the scent of the woodbine that trailed along the top of the stone wall bounding the nearby fields. He stood for a moment, taking in the sight of her, hands clasped in her lap, shapely ankles showing beneath her moss green tweed skirt, a light breeze lifting her feathery fair hair. He hesitated to interrupt her solitude but could not turn away from this golden opportunity.

He tentatively cleared his throat and her eyes shot open and then crinkled into a smile.

"Hello. I found it too hot and noisy in there."

"May I join you?" he asked, gesturing to the ground beside her.

"Of course."

She tried to stretch the shawl out, then realised that if he were to sit on it, they would be very close together, and stopped.

"Don't worry, I'll just sit here."

He perched like a cat on a stone several feet away from her. The fields, empty of livestock and crops, stretched before them like a green patchwork quilt, seamed by dark hedges and undulating as if concealing the contours of a sleeping giant. After several minutes of companionably listening to the evening chorus of birdsong, Bert thought that social decorum probably demanded some pleasantry of him. The hairs on his arms were standing straight up, alive to her proximity. He turned and glanced quickly at her. She blinked in reaction to the sudden movement of his head.

"Thank you for sharing this with me," he said, unable to think of anything more interesting.

"I've enjoyed your company," she said, without a hint of irony.

The band suddenly struck up a reel, and he exhaled.

"I am not a very good _Céilidh_ dancer, but would you like to dance with me?"

She laughed.

"I'm hiding out here because I'm not a very good dancer."

"I suppose we have a choice of dancing badly together, or not dancing at all," he said, raising an eyebrow.

"That's a poetic way of putting it."

She held out her hand so that he could help her to stand.

"Which shall it be?" he asked, one palm held out.

She put her soft sweet white fingers in his. Her eyes were the pale blue of an ebbing dawn tide as she returned his gaze. She allowed him to tuck her hand into the crook of his arm. As they reached the front of the school house, she gently withdrew her hand, smiling apologetically. They danced clumsily, crossing arms, going under arches, moving in and out in the lines of the Siege of Ennis, the Walls of Limerick, the Bridge of Athlone.

Bert was intoxicated by the heat and smoke, the swirling, unrelenting music, the chanting and clapping. Smiling faces loomed closer and retreated in an impenetrable pattern, and occasionally, he would catch a glimpse of her dress, the green skirt twirling above her slim calves, her hair a golden halo, her smile a beacon he constantly sought amidst the chaos of the flowing dance.

"Well, you had the look on your face of a fella who was having a great time, last night," said Noreen in the morning, when he came down the creaking ladder from his bed.

"I had a lovely time, thank you, Noreen."

He tried to edge past her to empty the chamber pot.

"What time was it when you finally came in?" she asked, standing stoutly in front of him. Her bosom thrusted out as if to dare him to pass without answering satisfactorily.

"I should think it was about one o'clock," he said.

"And since when does it take two hours to walk from the school house to here?" she asked, "Didn't the dancing finish at eleven o'clock? I'm sure Father Grogan wouldn't have let it go on any longer. He doesn't approve of dancing anyway."

"It did finish at eleven. I escorted Miss Feeney home."

"Home to Dunmore, is it? Where was her father, and what did he think of such shenanigans?"

"A message came to say that his motor car had broken down. I offered to escort her home and there appeared to be no objection."

"No objection, indeed!"

Noreen stood aside, impressed that Bert had penetrated Máirtín Feeney's defences so thoroughly. To her knowledge, his precious daughter had never been escorted anywhere except by her dear father, he was that protective. Bert stepped outside. He stood in the lane, breathing in the morning air. The world looked different. The sky was higher and brighter and the yellow of the gorse had a new intensity. He was glad he hadn't lied to Noreen. She was like a second mother to him, fussing over him when he arrived wet, in bad weather, wrapping up extra food for him in case he got hungry before his next meal, and now, taking an unhealthy interest in his romantic attachment to Miss Feeney, or Ina, as he now felt entitled to call her.

They had crept away from the dancing before it finished and collected his bicycle from the Connolly's yard. Ina sat side-saddle on the cross bar, holding tightly onto the middle of the handlebars, occasionally letting go with one hand to hold down the skirt of her dress when it lifted too high in the breeze. The soft curls of her hair brushed the underside of his chin, his arms bracing her on both sides occasionally feeling the fine lambswool of her shawl, as he swerved around a bend and she leaned to adjust her balance. Her delicate scent joined with the heady honey suckle and woodbine along the hedgerows and chased out the remnants of smoke and sweat from the school room. He felt a pure, white joy. He pedalled hard to the tops of the hills, and they swept down the other side, laughing at the speed and the danger and the being together. When they reached the edge of the town, she touched the rigid muscle of his forearm, and asked him to stop.

"Could we walk for the last part of the journey?" she asked, and they had dismounted.

There were still lights shining in some of the bedroom windows. They walked sedately down Castle Street and turned into Main Street and he wanted it to stretch forever. Her house was in darkness, but for one window on the ground floor, and a lantern in the grand porch. Behind the curtains, her father's silhouette stood and moved towards the door, and before they had reached it, the door opened, and he held out his arms. She ran forward, and he embraced her briefly.

"Safely home, thank God," he said, looking up and smiling his thank you, expecting to see the priest or some older, married couple from the town as her escort.

Bert hung back in the darkness of the path beyond the lantern's reach.

"Who's that?" Máirtín Feeney asked brusquely.

He sensed from the tension in his daughter's body that this was no familiar neighbour. His high freckled forehead creased into an anxious frown.

Bert stepped forward, holding out his hand.

"Herbert O'Brien, *Timire*."

He was hoping the title would confer some respectability and cast away any doubts about his motives and morality. Máirtín Feeney shook his hand, but there was no warmth in his grip.

"Thank you, sir, for escorting my daughter home. I hope you were not unduly inconvenienced."

"Not at all, it was my pleasure," said Bert, smiling at Ina.

He immediately realised his mistake as Máirtín Feeney's blue eyes narrowed under their bushy eyebrows. In Ina's glowing cheeks, the pulse at the base of her throat and Bert's loose, ejitty grin, he could not miss what was hanging in the air like another source of light, radiant in the stillness of the night.

"Well, good night, and thank you again," said Máirtín Feeney bluntly.

He took down the lantern and ushered Ina inside with one plump hand on the small of her back then closed the wide black door firmly. Bert could hear the bolt being shot and a chain rattling. Moments later the light inside was extinguished and the gloom deepened. As soon as he cleared the edge of the town, he whistled all the way back to the Connolly's house, replaying every moment of the evening in minute detail, while the miles flew past unnoticed.

In the morning Bert felt no urgency to travel back to Eamonn and Mairéad's house in Ballinasloe. After his first few weeks in Ballinasloe they had insisted that he stay with them and he had left the comfortable but impersonal lodgings. This morning he stared across the flat brown peat bog behind the Connolly's house, the empty chamber pot hanging from his hand. He savoured again the memory of speeding through the darkness with his arms around the soft, warm form of a beautiful, gentle woman. Then he recalled Máirtín Feeney's expression changing in a flash from wary acceptance to suspicion. He would just have to woo the father. When Máirtín Feeney came in his motor car to take Ina home after the next Irish lesson, Bert would ask for a few moments of his time. He would respectfully reassure Mr Feeney of his chivalrous intentions towards his daughter. The man could see that Bert was penniless. There was no point in pretending otherwise. Bert would impress on him that this was just a temporary state of affairs. He was young and resourceful, and, he would modestly assert, intelligent enough to be offered a place at Oxford. Noreen's voice penetrated his reverie.

"Come in out of that, Bert, and have some breakfast before you faint with the hunger."

CHAPTER 18

Very few of the children had returned to school on the appointed day. The continuing good weather was at fault. There was plenty of work on the farms in England, and the men were making the most of it, earning an extra week's wages over there before coming back home. The older children were saving the turf and the hay, so that everything was in good order for the onset of the autumn. There was a festive atmosphere in the school room that evening, as the teachers exchanged their summer anecdotes, but Bert could not engage in the conversation.

There was no sign of Ina by five o' clock when the lesson was due to start. She had never been late before. Her habit had been to arrive early, welcoming Bert to her schoolroom and asking if he had everything he needed. They rarely had more than a few minutes together before the other scholars arrived, but Bert had grown used to that quiet oasis in the week, watching her moving gracefully around school room, laying out the slates on the desks, stretching up to open or close a window, sliding behind one of the children's desks to sit for the lesson, her skirt lifting briefly from her ankles. He realised with a start that the group was getting restless. He cleared his throat and began. Their passion for the Irish fed his own. He came alive when he was with this particular group in a way that didn't happen with his other groups. Even without Ina among them, they were his favourite class. He would have to find some more books for them and wondered if *Conradh na Gaeilge* would have the money to provide them.

Paddy Connolly, who had joined the group this evening, clapped him on the back as the last student left.

"You're a great teacher, altogether," he said. "You have them lapping it up. If they can only be as enthusiastic with the children, we'll have them all speaking Irish in no time!"

"Ina... I mean, Miss Feeney, is hoping to start the older children with some Irish this term," said Bert.

"Is she now?" said Paddy with more interest in Bert's use of her first name than in her teaching prowess. "I wonder where she was, tonight?"

"Perhaps her father's motor car is still out of commission, and she was unable to come," said Bert, deliberately not catching Paddy's eye.

He locked the door and placed the key under the stone. His plan to leave a note with the key so she would find it in the morning was frustrated by Paddy lingering to walk home with him.

"Or maybe he forbade her from coming?" said Paddy, putting his hands in his pockets and strolling casually down the road.

"Why would he do that?" Bert ran to catch up.

"You know he has a reputation for being very protective, don't you?" asked Paddy, pausing in the road and facing Bert.

"Noreen mentioned something," said Bert, trying to sound disinterested, his heart pounding.

Surely Mr Feeney would not prevent Ina from learning Irish just to stop them from seeing each other?

"Did you know that her three sisters went off to be nuns, one of them a Carmellite, and the two brothers are studying for the priesthood?"

Bert shook his head.

"With his only sons going off to the missions in Africa, and three of his daughters in convents, this is a man who might be worrying about who will mind him when he gets old." said Paddy.

He held up the fingers of his left hand and pointed to the first of them. For once, Bert was not irritated by one of Paddy's little speeches. Pointing to the next finger, Paddy elaborated further.

"This is a man who wouldn't be familiar with the courting rituals, when it's over thirty years since he did it himself."

Bert nodded, already somewhat overwhelmed by the challenge but with a sinking feeling that there was more to come. The third finger was held up.

"Ina Feeney considered joining the Carmellites herself, at one time."

Paddy took a deep breath.

"And last but not least," he held up the fourth finger, and waggled it emphatically, "he thinks you are a strange English man."

Bert stopped walking but before he could say anything, Paddy continued.

"I know you're not, you know you're not, she knows you're not, but you can't blame him for thinking you are. You might speak beautiful Connaught Irish, but when you go about your daily business, you can't escape it, you sound like a Protestant."

"A Protestant?"

Bert's fists clenched by his side.

Paddy was surprised at the naivety of this young man. What else was anybody going to think, with the fancy English manner of speaking he had about him? He reminded Paddy of the landlord's agent who used to come to collect the rent off his father when he was a young lad, although he suspected Bert was an educational cut above the same Mister Porter.

"Not that that would be the worst thing in the world. I know some very nice Protestants. The Hemphills, over towards ..."

"What can I do?" Bert felt as though the wall he had to scale had suddenly tripled in height.

"I think you'll have to take it slow and steady."

"I wasn't planning to rush her down the aisle next month," said Bert, in despair.

"If you wanted to stay with us the odd weekend, instead of going off to Ballinasloe, and you were seen at Mass in Dunmore, that might help," said Paddy.

Bert had the horrible feeling that he and Noreen had discussed all this at great length and that Paddy had been despatched to join the class this evening for the very purpose of having this conversation. Bert was a pawn in some great chess game, unable to see what any of the other pieces were doing. He waited. There was more.

"It wouldn't do any harm to maybe get in touch with Michael Power."

"What on earth would Michael Power have to do with any of this? I haven't seen him for nearly four years. I have no idea where he is."

"I'm sure if we put our minds to it, and we have a word in a few ears, we can find out where he is," said Paddy.

Bert was temporarily distracted by the prospect of seeing his old friend.

"Really? Why haven't you said so before? I would love to see them all again."

"Leave that with me, so," said Paddy, and Bert could not induce him to say any more on the subject.

They arrived at Paddy's house and Bert couldn't face the prospect of sitting at the fire with them, eating scones and drinking tea and revisiting the whole discussion. He took the bicycle and pushed it into the lane.

"I need to do some thinking," he said.

Paddy waved through the half door, smiling at the look of bewilderment on Bert's face. "Don't worry too much about it, you are a fine young man and that is what will shine through. You might just have to be a bit patient."

Bert bit his lip, swung his leg over the saddle, and cycled towards the road, thoughts roiling in his head. Would they all be shocked if they knew his mother was born a Protestant? Why did his accent matter? What if they knew that Leo had joined the British Army? Why did other people's histories and actions have to define him? Why was it not good enough that he was born in Dublin, that he believed in Irish independence, that he loved the Irish language, that he had given up the chance to go to Oxford to come and teach Irish here in the back of beyond? Who were these petty people, to judge him? He cycled along the familiar road towards Dunmore, but he stopped before he reached her house. The only thing he could do there was moon about like a tragic Shakespearean hero denied his heart's true love, which would do nothing for his credibility with Mr Feeney. He remembered the place on the riverbank he had visited on his first day in Dunmore and left the bicycle and crossed the tussocky field at the same place as before. The sun was casting a butterscotch glow across the ferns, and he sank down at the edge of the water, his heart still pounding from the pedalling and the feeling of being trapped. He took off his boots and socks and rolled up his trousers, wanting feel the soothing flow of the water rather than just watching it. The cold shock of it was good. He wiggled his toes which were only half visible in the brown depths.

None of the barriers were insurmountable. Paddy and Noreen would help him to tiptoe through this new territory. He would happily go to Mass in Dunmore, especially if it gave him another glimpse of Ina every week. But what did Michael Power have to do with it all? He might not even recognise Bert now, without his school uniform and cap and knobbly knees sticking out of his grey shorts. The boy who found hiding places for guns and loved standing to attention in the kitchen was gone. Bert was probably the same height as Michael Power now, even though his shoulders would never be as broad.

Down in the rippled surface of the water Bert saw Leo's frowning face. He had changed as soon as he signed up. He was gruff with Mama when she asked what he needed for the training camp and completely dismissed Louise's worries whenever she said anything. He didn't lie on the bed anymore with his hands behind his head, telling Bert funny stories. At the time, Bert was hurt. He didn't know what Leo was trying to do by pushing them all away. He stared at the water and conjured up the old Leo, full of mischief, optimistic, always looking for adventure.

Bert's feet had gone completely numb so he lifted them out of the water and rubbed them vigorously with his socks. His toes were white and wrinkled like dead flesh and they reminded Bert of Leo's diary entry about chopping off the soldier's arm with his spade. Angry bile rose in his throat and he spat into the water and watched the phlegm float for a moment, then sink into the weeds. He cleared his throat and startled a kingfisher which shot like a blue arrow over the water and perched further downstream. Bert stood up, still feeling unsettled but much calmer. He was glad to find that Noreen and Paddy were already in bed when he got back to the house. He climbed quietly up onto his mattress and lay staring at the rafters and the thatch wondering how he could possibly talk to Ina if her father had taken a dislike to him and she wasn't allowed to attend his classes.

Two months had gone by and there was no word of Michael Power's whereabouts. Paddy insisted that their patience would be rewarded. He had still not been explicit about what role Michael could possibly play in Bert's courtship of Ina Feeney. Bert had seen her briefly several times after Mass, but her father whisked her away quickly before he had a chance to talk to her. One Sunday, as they trotted out through the church gate she looked back over her shoulder and smiled. The weather had turned bitterly cold and the numbers in his classes dropped, with some students unwilling to face the bicycle journey on icy roads. Bert followed a new routine, starting the week in Ballinasloe, and ending it in Kilkeely, so he could go to Mass in Dunmore with Paddy and Noreen on Sundays. Every week Mairéad discreetly enquired about his Kilkeely class and she was sympathetic when Bert told her that Ina had missed another lesson.

"What can I do? I can hardly pay a visit to the house and risk her father throwing me into the street?" he asked her one cold Tuesday night, as they sat at the fire.

Eamonn was gone visiting his brother Seán and he wasn't home yet.

Mairéad took her eyes off the flickering embers.

"Is there anything you could do to show him that you're the right kind of a man to be walking out with his daughter?" she asked.

"How do I know what kind of man he would find suitable?" he asked. "I was only just getting to know her, when he intervened."

"What do you know about him, himself?" she asked.

"He's a GAA supporter. He bought a field for them, and I believe he represents West Galway at the national council, or whatever they call it."

"Did he play hurling or the football, himself, in his younger days?"

"I don't know. Are you saying I need to learn hurling?" he asked.

She laughed.

"No, I'm just trying to get a picture of him in my head. I'm thinking that most fathers want someone like themselves to marry their daughter."

"We probably couldn't be more different," said Bert. "He made a lot of money as a builder, so he is probably very practical and down to earth and thinks I have my head in the clouds."

"That might be the way!" she said, jumping up.

Bert looked up from his stool.

"How do you mean?"

"Didn't you say to me that you did some little jobs for Michael Power, over in England?"

He nodded.

"Maybe if Mr Feeney knew that he would realise there's more to you than meets the eye."

"I didn't do very much," he said. "Hiding things, running errands. Once or twice I carried a letter to Patrick Leahy when he was on the run."

"You were only a boy at the time, sure, what else could you be expected to do? But you were supporting the Volunteers."

"Do you think that's why Paddy wants to find Michael?" asked Bert. "So he could vouch for my character?"

"You have a very funny way of putting things, but I think so, yes."

"Perhaps I should go to Limerick and see if I can find him."

"It wouldn't be a bad idea," she said.

Eamonn came in then, bringing a blast of cold air from outside.

"I was just with Seán. There's great reports of how well you're doing, and he's mighty pleased with you."

His limp was barely noticeable as he took off his heavy overcoat and hung it on the back of the door.

"Is there any tea left in that pot?" he asked, and Mairéad poured the thick dark liquid into a mug for him. Bert stood up.

"You come and sit by the fire and warm up. I'm going up to bed. Mairéad has given me some very interesting food for thought."

Upstairs, he could hear their voices and the occasional burst of laughter coming from the kitchen. They were probably laughing at him. He would go to see Seán the in the morning and ask for a few days off to go to Limerick and find Michael Power.

Seán was happy to give him a week off.

"Just let your students know so they're not traipsing across the countryside in this weather to find you gone."

Bert agreed to let each class know and then travel to Limerick at the beginning of December.

Paddy was delighted when he heard the plan.

"That's the way. Take matters into your own hands. I have no news about Michael, so I hope you find him well."

His preparations were scant. The contents of his travelling bag for the journey to Limerick were little different than they had been for months, the only addition being two pairs of long woollen socks Noreen had knitted for him. From Tuam it was easy to follow the road first to Galway, then south along the edge of the bay towards Limerick.

CHAPTER 19

The fields were flatter near the sea, gradually turning to rocky brown shore, awash with seaweed. He sniffed the saltiness of the air like a retriever and was reminded of the wide sandy beaches of Northumbria, majestic in their defiance of bitter North Sea gales. The weather was milder here on the Atlantic coast and there was no sign of the frost that rimed the inland roads. At Oranmore he stopped to rest. A rotund publican emerged from the half door of a thatched public house.

"How are you?" the man asked, rubbing his hands on a beer stained apron.

"*Tá me go maith, buíochas le Dia,*" said Bert. "I'm well, thanks be to God."

They chatted for a while and the publican refused to take any money for the pint of Guinness and the lump of soda bread and cheese Bert had gobbled down when he heard about his quest.

"Michael Power," he said, his voice full of awe.

"He's a great man, altogether. He passed through here a few months gone, on his way back to Limerick from Carraroe."

Bert was delighted to have such recent news of Michael's whereabouts.

"Would you have any idea of where in particular he was going?" he asked, swallowing the last mouthful of Guinness.

"No, I'm sorry, now. We were only talking for a short little while. He didn't look as if he was in the best of health, if I'm honest with you."

"Were the other members of his family with him?"

The publican shook his head, taking Bert's empty glass.

"He didn't say anything about them, so I don't know where they'd be."

Bert thanked him and asked if there was anywhere in the village where he could stay for the night. He ended up staying in the publican's own house and had to suffer the shrill, several times repeated advice of the publican's wife that he could have saved himself a few miles if he had come through Athenry and then over through Loughrea, but as it was, he may as well stay on this road and go down through Gort and Tulla.

In the morning he cycled off early, hoping to reach Limerick before nightfall. He was overly optimistic and found himself cycling without a light as the winter gloom settled into darkness at five o'clock. Lanterns and lamps were lit inside cottages. He caught glimpses of families gathered around their kitchen tables and occasionally he passed a man returning late from the fields, whistling and touching his cap as he went. Bert's breath trailed white behind him in the night air and he wished he had stopped at the last village instead of pushing on. He was looking for a dry outhouse in which to bed down when he arrived on the outskirts of a town. Even in the dark it seemed decrepit, with a large roofless building in the centre of the square which might once have been a market house, and a tall building resembling a mill that also looked deserted. He crossed a stone bridge, wondering if there was any life to be found, and spotted a lantern alight in the window of a wide town house. He knocked on the door.

"*Dia dhuit*," he started when the door opened, and then waited for a reaction from the young man who was staring blankly at him, before continuing in Irish.

"I was hoping to find a bed for the night," Bert said politely.

A frown crossed the man's high forehead, accentuated by his baldness and dark bushy eyebrows. Still, he didn't speak.

"Do you know of a place where I might stay?" asked Bert in English.

He put his hand through his hair, wondering why the man was staring so hard at him.

"No, sorry, I do not," said the man and closed the door in Bert's face.

He turned away. The derelict building might offer him some shelter. The door opened suddenly behind him, light spilling out onto the road, but he didn't turn, expecting an insult. A woman's voice hailed him.

"Sir, come back. You're welcome."

Bert turned towards her. She was urging him to come forward, her hands flapping in front of her long black skirt.

"I have money, to pay," he said.

"Not at all. My brother has a lack in his head. I don't usually let him answer the door, God love him. Come in out of the cold."

Bert did as he was told.

"I heard you speaking the Irish," she said, breathlessly.

She insisted on taking his bag and carrying it upstairs. He hesitated and then followed her. She opened the door of a room facing onto the street and held up the lantern to show a neatly made bed and a chest of drawers.

"This was my mother's room, God rest her soul, and if you're happy to sleep in it, you may."

Bert accepted the offer, and she invited him to come down for some food.

"It's only a bit of fatty bacon and cabbage," she said apologetically.

Bert passed the evening with the brother and sister. She told him the whole story. Their mother had passed away only a fortnight before and the brother, 'never the full shilling', was finding it difficult to get used to her being gone. He was always expecting to find his mother in the kitchen or the parlour or standing on the front step when he answered the door.

Bert wondered how Conor was getting on, being the only boy in the house. Mama was always a bit distracted. She didn't know how to react to his five year old adoration, especially now that he was getting stronger. He would throw himself at her legs to give her a hug, not realising that he could knock her down. Louise was working in the hospital all day, so she could only help in the evenings and by then Mama's patience was wearing thin.

"What has you on the road, at this time of the evening?" the woman asked him as they finished the meal.

He told her about the teaching but he wasn't sure whether he should tell her about Michael Power. Her family owned the draper's shop in the town, so she was probably a Protestant.

"You wouldn't stay another night and see the fair tomorrow? It's famous all around here."

Bert declined, explaining that he needed to go to Limerick to meet some people.

"So, you're going off to meet your fellow teachers, is it?" she asked.

He agreed, feeling only slightly guilty for lying when she had been so hospitable.

"Well, if you're passing this way again on your way home, call in and see us," she said.

The significance of her smiling glance was not lost on him. He thanked her, and said that he would certainly try to call in.

"It has been a very pleasant evening."

"Indeed, it has," she said, brushing imaginary lint off her knees.

He went upstairs, using the excuse of an early start for another day's travelling. She carried the lantern to his room, trimmed the wick and left it on the bedside table, telling him she would bring water for washing in the morning. She closed the door gently and he sighed, releasing the tension in his muscles and pulling off his boots before lying across the bed, wondering if he would ever want to stand up again.

Cold, bright sunlight greeted Bert the next morning and he left Six Mile Bridge in good spirits after a breakfast of porridge and soda bread. The road to Limerick was busy with people going the other way and they smiled and waved as they passed him. Cattle and sheep were being driven along the road and there was a festive air despite the cold. Young lads were shouting to each other and whistling to their dogs, and women were carrying covered baskets. Some of the children had bundles, but most of them were just skipping along, swishing the hedge with long sticks or chasing each other down the road.

Bert slowed down as he approached a grey stone bridge across a wide river he guessed must be the Shannon. The road was blocked by a pile of sandbags. A group of four soldiers who had been standing talking in loud voices turned to face in his direction and he braked.

"What's your business?" one Private asked, prodding Bert in the chest with the barrel of a rifle.

He was six inches shorter than Bert, so he had to tilt his chin to meet Bert's eye. The sneer on his face and his tight hold on the gun told Bert everything he needed to know. Another Private with dark, thickly oiled hair stood one step behind the first, with his broad shoulders squared so that his military jacket bulged across his chest. His khaki trousers were tucked into stout army boots. His weapon was a long truncheon which he smacked loudly into the palm of his hand, just waiting for an opportunity to use it.

"I'm going to visit a friend," Bert said, unable to think of anything more creative on the spot.

"'Wot you got in the bag, ven?" the second man asked with a strong Cockney accent.

"Just my personal toiletries and a spare shirt," Bert said, shrugging the bag off his shoulder. "Would you like to see?"

He rounded his vowels and tried to sound like Trenton, the St Cuthbert's head boy.

"S' all right, 'es one of us," the taller soldier muttered, turning away. He would have liked nothing better than to give this confident young man on the bike a good kicking as a warning to the other rebel scum who were causing so much trouble in the area.

The other man lowered the rifle.

"Where you from?"

The ingratiating smile was only slightly less repulsive than the sneer.

"Newcastle upon Tyne," said Bert.

He smiled and casually slung the bag back over his shoulder. The corner of the Irish grammar book dug into his shoulder blade.

"Who's the friend you're visiting?" the solider asked, needing to maintain the illusion of control.

"An old school friend, actually," said Bert even more affectedly. "He's surveying the roads in the area, and Limerick seemed a sensible place to meet."

"Watch yourself. Them Irish scum are vicious. Keep your mouth shut and your eyes open, that's my advice."

The soldier stepped aside to allow Bert to wheel the bicycle past the blockade.

"Don't venture saarf of English taan, across the bridge," muttered the bigger man.

"I appreciate the advice. Thank you, gentlemen," said Bert.

He took one hand off the handlebars to wave as he crossed the Bridge.

"Condescending blady officer class," muttered the soldier with the truncheon as they regrouped and resumed their idle conversation.

At the first opportunity Bert turned left off the main road to get out of their sight and dismounted to shake out his wobbly legs. He sat on a rounded, pockmarked milestone, his heart pounding. He could report to Eamonn, who was a sceptical as he, that the recent newspaper reports about the British Army terrorising people were true. Full military control of Limerick had only just been eased after a labour uprising in April, and these soldiers seemed to be just waiting to pounce and retaliate at the first opportunity. He would have to watch his step, but for once his accent had come to his rescue.

Looming over the head of the Bridge was a heavily fortified castle that looked as old as the one in Dunmore but much more palatial. Mills and factories lined the river bank and the streets were crowded with people. Bert had been naively thinking he would just walk around the town asking for Michael Power from Carraroe and eventually someone would direct him to Michael's lodgings. He wasn't the kind of man to go unnoticed in a place. But now he realised that Limerick was more like Newcastle upon Tyne than Ballinasloe, and he could spend days wandering around without making any progress. He found digs in a house on the edge of Irish town, having ignored the soldier's advice. The woman of the house was dressed in black and told him that she was mourning her husband. It seemed to Bert that he was destined to stay in houses of mourning wherever he went, but this time at least there was no doubt about where his hostess's allegiance lay.

"The soldiers are ferocious altogether," the woman said, her narrow face creased in distress.

"At the beginning of the year you couldn't go from one side of the town to the other without a special pass. The men went on strike over it and look at where that got us."

Her eyes filled with tears. Bert didn't like to ask for the details, but she told him everything. Her husband had been on strike from the biscuit factory, and 'fell in' with a crowd of Volunteers. They had some successes with raids on RIC barracks for guns, and it went to their heads.

"Whether it was what they intended, or whether it got out of hand, we'll never know," she said, warming up like a *Seanachaí*.

Bert resigned himself to the story unfolding in its own time even though he was itching to ask if her husband knew Michael Power.

"But they went to steal some guns from the Ennis barracks and they got caught."

"Were they imprisoned?"

"Put in jail? Are you joking me? Three of them got shot. Two of them shot in the back. My only small consolation is that my brave Seán would have seen his murderer, and I just hope he had a chance to look him in the eye and damn him to hell for all eternity before he died."

Bert shook his head. He couldn't bring himself to ask about Michael now.

"And how are you finding it in County Galway?" she asked.

"It seems to be quieter than here," said Bert.

"I am sorely grieving for my husband, but I'm not a bit sorry for what he did, and I'm glad he had the chance to die a hero."

She dabbed a tear from the corner of her eye with the edge of her sleeve and sniffed.

"I lost all my children to the influenza last year. Two beautiful girls and my small boy. Knowing that God takes the good ones young is my only consolation. Otherwise I would have nothing to live for at all, at all."

Bert had no idea what to say.

"Your few bob will tide me over for a while, and the union gives me a bit, even though they've very little left in the pot after the strike."

She seemed to talking to herself in a low voice, directed at the floor. Bert drank his buttermilk and looked into the fire.

"Who are you coming to Limerick to see, anyhow?" she asked, suddenly coming out of her reverie.

"I'm looking for Michael Power," he said.

The chair legs creaked as he sat up straight.

"Michael Power from Carraroe, is it?"

"The very man."

"And why are you looking for him?"

He wondered if there was still a hint of suspicion in her.

"I knew him years ago," he said airily.

"Years ago? Sure you're only a spalpeen yourself, aren't you?"

He bristled at her tone.

"He was my Irish teacher. I wouldn't even be over here if it wasn't for him. I want to pay the family a visit."

"You know them all?" she said, poking the fire, not looking at him, testing.

"Annie, and Niamh and little Tomás, yes, I know them well."

"Little Tomás is no longer little, I can tell you that!" she said.

"Does he have a big chest, like his father?"

She finally cracked.

"They stay around the corner, in Sackville Street."

Bert stood up and pushed the chair back, running his fingers through his hair.

"You can't go calling over to them now, it's way too late," she said. "Wait until after Mass in the morning and I'll bring you over."

"Thank you, Mrs O'Malley."

Her face fell.

"But I've sad news for you, too. Poor little Niamh was taken away by the angels, not long after my own, with the same influenza."

Bert's legs went and he sat down suddenly, his eyes stinging.

"The poor darling."

"Annie took it awful bad, all right. She's terry-fied that she'll lose them all, in the end, one way or another. At least she had the consolation of a daughter, and now, no more than myself, she hasn't even that..."

She was staring into the embers and absently rambling again, so Bert went up to bed without disturbing her.

CHAPTER 20

The church was full when Bert looked around from the front pew where Mrs O'Malley had insisted they should sit for early Mass. The congregation seemed to be made up of only elderly women and bent old men. They all stood as the altar boys passed up the centre aisle, followed by the priest. He was elderly too, and Bert could hardly understand a word of his sibilant greeting. The familiar rhythm of the Mass took over and Bert stood up, knelt down and sat in harmony with everyone around him but didn't listen to a word. He was frustrated not to be at the back of the church, so he could scan the faces and heads for Michael Power's. His scalp was prickling with the intensity of the curious stares from behind him. Mrs O'Malley's small smile told him she was basking in the mystery of him. Finally, when it was time for Communion Bert had an opportunity to look out for Michael as everyone came up to the front. There was no sign of him or Annie, although she was so tiny she could easily be missed in a crowd.

After Mass, Bert fidgeted on the steps while Mrs O'Malley introduced him to numerous people as the *Timire* for Galway East. He was shaking their hands and smiling and at the same time looking over their shoulders for any sign of Michael.

Mrs O'Malley was desperate to get the most out of her few minutes in the limelight.

"Don't be worrying. I'll bring you to his digs. Hold your whist."

Finally, the last Mass goer was gone and she was putting her hand in the crook of Bert's arm to steer him through the back streets towards Michael's lodgings. They turned left, then right, and she knocked on a peeling half door in a mean, low-roofed house. After a moment it creaked open and a pinched face framed by lank black curls peered out suspiciously. Bert stood back. He couldn't believe that the tiny woman in front of him was the generous, warm hearted Annie, who had welcomed him into her home, almost as a child of her own.

"Annie!" he declared.

She looked up and a smile broke across her grey, taut face, making her recognisable again. She came out the door and threw her arms around him, barely reaching to his chest, and laid her cheek against the buttons on his jacket.

"Bert O'Brien!" she said, half shouting back through the door.

There was a flurry inside and suddenly the doorway was full of Michael Power, who unlike his wife, was physically undiminished by the years. He grinned from ear to ear, and slapped Bert on the back.

"It's yourself that's in it!" he said, tugging Bert inside.

Mrs O'Malley followed him in without an invitation, delighted to be the guide of such a welcome guest. Bert hesitated just inside the door. Annie peered up, looking for a sign in his face that she knew and when their eyes met she nodded. He took both her hands in his.

"I am so sorry for your loss," he said. "*Ba í Niamh an cailín ba dheise sa domhan.* Niamh was the loveliest girl in the world."

Annie's eyes were on the floor, and Bert noticed the grey hairs in the crown of her head and felt the dry skin of her hands. Michael reached out to touch Bert's shoulder.

"She will always be in our hearts, Bert, and we can only thank God that He sent her to us, even though we only had her for a little while."

Bert squeezed Annie's hands before letting them go.

"Come on in and sit down here," she said.

"This is Mrs O'Malley. I am lodging at her house," said Bert, realising that she was still standing just behind his shoulder, staying very quiet.

"I've heard a lot about you," said Mrs O'Malley, when Michael greeted her.

Annie offered her the chair by the fire. Michael raised an eyebrow enquiringly.

"I'm Seán O'Malley's widow," she said, touching the black fabric of her dress where it draped her bony knee.

"Oh, I'm sorry for your troubles," said Annie straight away.

Between the influenza and the labour strikes and the fighting, Bert wondered if there was a single family left in Ireland that wasn't grieving.

"Bert, it's great to see you, altogether," said Michael brightly, declaring an end to the mutual condolences.

"You're not an easy man to find," Bert said, smiling.

"I have several friends who have tried to get a message to you with no luck. I've been in East Galway since the Spring, knowing that you couldn't be too far away, but with no way of getting in touch."

"We're not staying long in any one place, that's for sure," said Michael.

He looked across at Annie in the fond, conspiratorial way that Bert remembered from the old cottage.

"I heard about Frognach."

"We don't talk about that place, at all," Annie said, wringing her apron.

"There's a few fine lads I would never have known, but for the time I spent in there, all the same," said Michael in a low voice.

"*Cá bhfuil Tomás*?" Where's Tomás?" Bert asked.

"He went fishing straight after early Mass," said Michael.

"You were a good teacher. He has a bit of luck most times when he goes. The bailiffs are not so keen to be out catching poachers early on a Sunday morning, so it's the best time for him to go."

"He'll be delighted to see you," said Annie.

All the doubts Bert had harboured for years about the Powers' affections for him disappeared in those few moments. He could still remember the shock of finding the cottage empty and had to ask why they didn't leave a message for him.

"We had a tip-off that we were under the eyes of the authorities," said Michael.

"It was time to come home. I never did know where you were living but I sent a letter to your father. Did you ever get it?"

Bert nodded.

He could see now through their eyes what a one-way relationship it had been. Bringing the occasional trout and doing the odd job for them didn't really change the fact that he was doing most of the taking. They might have thought he was a well-off school boy with time on his hands who would just find something else to amuse him after they were gone.

"Paddy Connolly in Kilkeely remembers you fondly from Carraroe," said Bert.

"It was he who suggested I should try to find you."

"Paddy Connolly that used to come and save the turf with us when we were young ones?" said Michael incredulously.

"He remembers you very well from those days."

"Isn't it a small world, altogether," said Annie, handing them all mugs.

"He was a cousin of the Connollys down the road from us. He came every summer without fail." Michael explained.

"Tea, lovely," said Bert, just stopping himself from saying how much he hated buttermilk.

"We got used to the tea when we were in England. It's hard to do without it, now," said Annie, smiling.

"It's dear enough, though." said Mrs O'Malley tentatively, her first words since she had been introduced.

"It is that," said Michael, smacking his lips.

"But sometimes it's worth going without something else so that you can have what you really want."

The door swung open suddenly and a breathless young man stood there, his black hair sticking up all over his head, and his dark eyes wide. He paused for a moment with his mouth open when he saw the strangers. He closed the door and stood leaning against it, gasping for breath.

"What is it, Tomás?" asked Annie, rushing to his side.

"Is it the bailiffs, running after you?" said Michael with the old familiar laugh.

He knew that Tomás would never lead them back to the house if they had any chance of catching up with him. The young man shook his head, and still did not speak. Now that the heat of running was leaving his cheeks, a grey pallor crossed them, and he bent his head, and started sobbing, no more than a boy in that tall, well-built body. Annie stretched up to put her arms around his shoulders and usher him to a chair.

"What is it, *a ghrá*?" she asked, but he kept shaking his head.

She heaped a spoon with sugar and stirred it into her own mug of tea, handing it to him and wrapping his fingers around it.

"Drink that down, *a ghrá*, and take a few deep breaths."

Michael was standing over his son. The sack Tomás had dropped at his feet was flat, with no sign of an incriminating catch, should the bailiff suddenly start pounding on the door. There was no sign of a rod either, but Tomás may have jettisoned that along the way, to save his skin. Bert didn't know what to do, so he stayed silent, amazed by the height and breadth of the young man in front of him. He calculated that Tomás was no older than thirteen, but his chest was already broader than Bert's own, and he had grown almost to Bert's height in the four years since they had last seen each other. After gulping down the sweet tea, unable to settle in one place, Tomás agitatedly paced up and down the earthen floor.

"There was six of them. I was keeping an eye out for the bailiff and I saw them coming down the road, so I hid behind a gorse bush."

"Six of who?" demanded Michael.

"I don't know, Englishmen by their accents, but not Army."

Michael caught Annie's eye.

"Not Army?"

"No, they had RIC uniforms. They had guns. They battered down the door and pulled him out and..."

"What door? Who did they pull out?"

Michael took his son by the arm and looked into his eyes, forcing a gentleness into his voice that belied the urgency of his enquiry.

"The door of a house. I don't know whose it was. They were only in there a minute. They knew who they wanted and they dragged him out into the road."

"Where is the house, Tomás, *a ghrá*?" asked Annie.

"Out the Ennis road. I was going to the new fishing place I found, and there they were, as large as life, and I had to jump into the bush before they saw me."

"Good lad, you are quick in your head and quick on your feet, that's the way to be," said Michael soothingly.

"They made his mother come out, and she was holding her apron over her face. She was bawling her eyes out. They pulled it down, so she had to watch."

Tears ran down his freckled face and he dashed them away angrily with his sleeve, his lips trembling. Michael stroked his son's head, as he had when he was a little boy, tousling the hair that was just like his own. The electric silence was broken only by the boy's gasping breaths. No-one moved. Tomás wiped his nose one final time with a handkerchief his mother had put on the arm of the chair, holding the grubby grey cloth in front of his face as if to shield himself from his audience.

He took a huge shuddering breath and blurted out, "One man hit him with the butt of the rifle and when he fell the others kicked him there on the ground, except for the one holding his mother, with her arms up behind her back, and she screaming and screaming for them to stop."

He had to pause, his eyes rolling wildly.

"Mammy, there was blood all over the road."

He said it as a child would, sad and mystified after the killing of a favourite hen or a pet lamb for the pot.

She stepped forward and took him in her arms.

"It's all right, my brave *garsún*," she murmured and he seemed to shrink so that she was fully embracing him, although he was almost twice her size.

"I ran away, Daddy," he said, huge tears tracking down his dusty cheeks now.

"You did the right thing, Tomás," Michael said sombrely.

"It's never the right thing to run away," said Tomás.

"That's what you always say. If we run away from our troubles they only come following after us."

"This is different, son," said Michael, "This is very different."

His voice had diminished to a gravelly whisper. Bert looked around to find Mrs O'Malley tugging his sleeve. He caught Michael's eye and jerked his head towards the door. Michael nodded tersely, and Annie came to the door, and silently shook Bert's hand, nodding when he whispered that he would come back another time. Mrs O'Malley contained herself until they were inside her own front door, and then she broke down, sobbing uncontrollably as she hung up her shawl.

"Another young man's life lost, and what is it all for?" she wailed.

They sat in silence as the Angelus rang out from the church, an ominous tolling sound without any joy in it.

CHAPTER 21

Eileen looked up from kneading bread. "So, how was your journey?" she said as Bert came in.

Bert sat wearily on a stool, his whole body aching from the two solid days of hard cycling, with the wind against him all the way.

"I found him," he said.

"Well, that's great news, altogether!" said Noreen.

She didn't like to be a wet blanket, but she hadn't held out much hope for the success of Bert's quest.

"But then I lost him again."

"How did you manage to do that, and you're only gone a few days?" she asked.

"I was lucky enough to find digs with a lady called Mrs O'Malley, who knew Michael's family, and she brought me to see them on Sunday. But Tomás, their son, witnessed something terrible and they must have thought they were in danger themselves. When I went back to their digs on Monday, they were gone."

"But that's terrible. Was there no message left for you?"

"No," said Bert.

"It was just like the last time, when they left Northumbria. They disappeared in a puff of smoke and left not a trace behind."

"What about this landlady, would she have no idea where they might have gone?"

Bert shook his head.

"She didn't know them very well. Her husband was in the Volunteers with Michael, but he was killed a few months ago."

"Goodness gracious me, the world is going mad," said Noreen, making the sign of the cross on her ample bosom.

"I left your address with Mrs O'Malley, just in case Michael wants to write to me. I hope that was all right with you?"

"Of course it is, Bert. I hope you think of this house as your own home, even though I know you have a few of them!"

He smiled to please her but it didn't travel from his lips, and it didn't lift the lead weight on his chest. She scraped the scraps of dough and flour off the wooden table into one hand and threw them out the small window for the chickens pecking in the yard behind the cottage. As she leaned across to wipe the table top, she caught his eye.

"You didn't get a chance to talk about the lovely Ina Feeney to them, did you?" she asked gently.

"No, I'm afraid Tomás' story made me forget about her myself, for a little while," he said sadly.

"Was it RIC men?"

"Apparently. New recruits from England, I suspect. I had to pass an Army road block, on the outskirts of Limerick, too. I had to pretend I had a friend in the city to visit."

He did not recount his exchange with the men, not liking to admit even to himself that he had been glad of his accent. It might prove useful – like Perseus's cloak it would make him invisible to the eyes of his enemies.

He found it difficult to summon any enthusiasm for his class in Kilkeely that evening. Every bone in his body ached from the long bicycle ride, but his exhaustion went beyond the physical. Black doubts were weighing heavily on his mind. For as long as young men were being dragged out of their houses and battered to death in front of their own mothers, people were not going to worry too much about the notion of expressing themselves in their native language. These young men were being killed for actively resisting an occupation of their homeland while Bert was cycling from place to place, blithely indulging his desire to be a man of words, not a man of war. Perhaps Leo had been right all along and the only way for liberty and justice to prevail was through bloodshed and tears. Hundreds of thousands of men had lost their lives in the Russian Revolution, the French Revolution, and even the American Revolution. The intellectuals could stick to their high ideals but their dreams could only be fulfilled through the radical action and sacrifice of others. How could teaching Irish to a handful of National Schoolteachers make a difference?

His students were as keen as ever and delighted to have him back but the cold in the school house and the damp, clinging fog made him miserable. Was it the setting-in of the cold winter or the absence of Ina that made the place less appealing? Would he ever convince Máirtín Feeney of his worthiness to court Ina? He had pinned all his hopes on the meeting with Michael Power, without ever articulating to himself what might happen next. His boyhood memories of Michael were of a larger than life character, undeterred by his reduced circumstances, eternally optimistic and energetic. Now Bert had seen a new Michael, confronted by his son's proximity to death, running scared from the authorities, his bluff exterior worn slightly thin by years of living on a knife edge. Bert's assumption that Michael would somehow hold the answer to his dreams had been naïve. Now he was faced with an endless winter of cycling from place to place through drizzling rain and wind without any sense of purpose or prospect of relief.

Bert had resigned himself to this reality when a letter arrived at Paddy and Noreen's house, addressed to him. Noreen had only ever received one letter in her life, from an aunt who had trained as a nurse in Dublin and then emigrated to America. Her own sons never wrote to her. Noreen greeted Bert at the door with the letter in her hand. She smiled expectantly as if he was going to open it right there in front of her and read it out. He suppressed his irritation. The only peace and privacy he seemed to have these days was when he was on his bicycle.

"Thank you, Noreen." he said politely.

He was hoping she would disappear into the house to finish her work. Noreen did not budge. She stood in front of him waiting for him to open it, like a proud mother entitled to be the first to hear the good news about her son's examination results, or the offer of a job. Bert recognised Michael's wide, looping handwriting. His heart leapt. He used his index finger to slit open the seal and unfolded a single piece of crumpled paper.

* * *

8th December 1919

Dear Bert

It was very nice to see you today, and looking so well. I am sorry that you had to hear Tomás's terrible story, and that we didn't have the time to talk properly. We are hiding again, outside the city this time. We feel a bit safer in the fields and wide open spaces than within the talking walls of the town. I am writing to ask for your help.

Like an answer to his unspoken prayers, here was Bert's chance to repay all those years of generous hospitality and Michael's unstinting dedication to his learning.

I am so proud that they made you a Timire. For a young lad who hadn't a word of Irish a few years ago to be teaching the very National School Teachers of our country is a great achievement. I remember how you wanted to help the Volunteers when you were Tomás's age yourself. I am hoping that you still feel the same, now that you are a man. As a Timire, you are moving around the county of Galway all the time. With your bag on your back and that confident air you have about you, you would be a great man to carry messages from one place to another. If you want to help us, the man taking this letter to you will bring back your answer to me, and we would all be delighted with you.

Bert looked up to see Noreen still watching him, her head on one side like a blackbird listening for a worm underground.

"Who brought the letter, Noreen?" he asked.

"A fella called Brendan. You wouldn't know him. He came out on his bicycle from Dunmore this evening while you were teaching. He said if there was an answer he would come and get it from you in the morning."

Bert nodded and his eyes went back to finish the letter.

"He's a little bit simple in the head, but a hard worker, I hear. He breaks stones for Ina Feeney's father, of all people," she said coyly, looking sideways at him.

Bert's head jerked back up.

"Are you serious?"

Noreen turned away pretending indifference. If Bert didn't tell her what was in the letter she would just climb up the ladder when he was out of the house and have a read of it herself. She would prefer if he told her, because she was a slow enough reader, but if she had to do it, she would. She casually stirred the porridge in the big black pot that was bubbling over the fire to be ready for the morning. She liked to send Bert off with a full stomach when he had to go such a long way on the bicycle in this miserable weather.

You can trust the bearer with your life. I have known his employer for years and you can always count on him if you get into any troubles.

May God go with you,

Your old friend,

Michael

Noreen heard the rustling as he folded the letter and resisted the urge to turn around. Even though there had been no specific admonition to secrecy in the letter, Bert didn't feel inclined to share its contents with her. Noreen enjoyed a gossip as well as the next woman. She could hold back no longer.

"No news, so?"

"It was Michael, writing to tell me that he is safe and well and has moved to a new hiding place outside the city," said Bert casually.

"Nothing else? It was a long enough letter," she said, unable to modify her aggrieved tone.

"He says he is proud of my being appointed a *Timire*, since he taught me all the Irish I know," said Bert.

"I hope he would be. It's a great thing altogether," she said.

"You're very clever."

Flattery proved no more effective than a direct enquiry. Bert put the envelope inside his jacket pocket.

"I think I'll go off to bed now, Noreen. I'm still tired after that long journey."

"Good night, so," she said brightly.

There was always the morning, before he went off to Ballinasloe. Paddy might be able to get more out of him. Men sometimes opened up to another man. There was more to that letter than just a reassurance that Michael Power was well, and proud of his former pupil. It was well known that Máirtín Feeney was a great supporter of the Volunteers. He was generous with his money to them, not that he didn't have plenty of it, with no dowries to pay, and all his children off his hands, except for Ina, whom he was keeping at home to mind him in his old age. If all else failed, there was always Brendan. He was not the full shilling and might be persuaded to divulge all he knew about the matter. Paddy often came home from other houses with stories Brendan had told around the fire about burying wooden boxes and doing drills with long sticks pretending to be guns, in the fields up beyond.

If young Bert was going to get involved, she hoped he understood it was a dangerous business. She was only glad that Paddy was too old for it all, and they had no sons still on Irish soil to be worrying about. She was having dangerous thoughts lately that Bert was like one of her own. He was such a nice, polite and intelligent young fella with his whole life ahead of him. She hoped his head would not be filled with the nonsense that some of these Volunteers spouted.

Paddy came in about an hour later and Bert, still lying awake, knew that Noreen would be whispering the news about his letter and making wild guesses about what was in it. In the morning Paddy casually enquired if Bert was happy with the outcome of his journey.

"I enjoyed seeing the Powers again, but I was very sad to hear that poor little Niamh was taken by the influenza last year."

"How old was she, the poor craythur?" asked Noreen.

"I should think about fourteen years old," said Bert.

"And the apple of her father's eye, no doubt?"

Bert wondered if Noreen realised how transparent her conversational tactics were.

"Yes, and her mother's too," he said.

"I must have an early start this morning, because I want to call in to Seán before my lesson, to let him know that I'm back safely."

This was only a small white lie. Bert was planning to cycle through Dunmore this morning and go to the Feeney's house on the pretext of delivering his answer to Michael's letter. If he left Kilkeely early enough he should arrive before Brendan started out the road. He mounted the bicycle, his stomach full of porridge and bread, ignoring the sleety rain that was driving straight into his face all along the road to Dunmore. He pedalled hard up the first hill, feeling the iron strength in his calves, built up over the hundreds of miles he had cycled in the last six months.

Perhaps Ina would answer the big black door, when he knocked. A tiny smile from her would turn grey clouds to silver and raindrops to jewels. At the top of the steep hill, he exhaled, only then realising he had held his breath all the way up. The blood was roaring in his ears. He started down the other side, expanding his chest and relaxing his leg muscles. Then through the rain-misted gloom, he discerned the steady progress of another huddled shape on a bicycle, pedalling slowly up the hill towards him. He slowed. Who else would be abroad so early on such a miserable winter morning? The figure raised its head, seemed to recognise him, and waved one arm in greeting. Suddenly the other bicycle wobbled and skidded and the rider was thrown into the ditch beside the road. Bert braked and leaned his bicycle against the wall on the other side.

"Are you hurt?" he enquired.

He gently lifted the bicycle frame off the prone man who was lying awkwardly in the water-logged ditch. There was a groan, and the man put a hand to his hip. Bert had to reach one foot down into the ditch to get enough leverage to help him out, not wanting to dislocate the man's shoulder by just pulling on the arm that was easily accessible. A sodden tweed cap hid the man's face and his build was so slight that Bert felt as though he were man-handling a scarecrow. Bert got the man upright, having reassured himself that no bones were broken. The man tipped his cap to the back of his head and grinned toothlessly, reinforcing the scarecrow impression.

"Sorry," he said cheerfully.

"Are you hurt?" Bert asked again.

"Just a bit shook up, that's all. You saved me the rest of the hill, anyway," said the man, bending down to pick up his bicycle.

"How did I manage to do that?" asked Bert, wondering if the fellow was slightly simple.

The man suddenly took a step forward, looked all around, as if they were surrounded by curious on-lookers, cupped his mouth with his hands and whispered loudly, "I was coming to see if you had a letter for me."

Bert's urge to laugh overcame his annoyance that he wouldn't see Ina. He took the reply he had written to Michael out of his pocket and handed it over.

"I take it you are Brendan?"

The man opened his sodden jacket and placed the envelope reverentially in the inside pocket.

"I am your faithful servant," he said and bowed formally.

Bert wanted to laugh again.

"Do you have to take this all the way to Limerick?" he asked.

"Not at all. I take it to a man in O…"

Brendan looked around again, over his shoulder and up and down the road, put his finger to his lips and then talked through it.

"We are not supposed to talk about it."

"I see," said Bert.

"I was just worried that you would have a long way to cycle in this rain. You must have some bruises after your fall."

"I'm grand altog-hether."

Brendan brushed down his trousers, spreading the wet mud rather than removing it.

He held out his hand, oblivious to the mud that coated it, and said, "It has been a pleasure to meet you, Sir. I hope I can be of service."

Bert smiled. "Thank you, Brendan, it has been a pleasure to meet you, too. I look forward to working with you."

He shook the muddy hand, and then Brendan attempted something that resembled a salute, and mounted his bicycle. In seconds he had disappeared down the hill, and Bert was left with an unsatisfying feeling of emptiness in his pocket and in his heart.

Eamonn and Seán were standing in the front doorway when Bert cycled up and greeted him with smiles.

"We were only talking about you," said Eamonn cheerfully.

"How did it go? Did you find him?"

Bert shook their hands in turn.

"I did. Unfortunately. we only talked briefly, but I have since received a letter and replied, so we are in touch with each other."

"And is there any other news?" asked Eamonn, winking.

"No progress, I'm afraid," said Bert, shaking his head.

"Just give him time, Bert. Máirtín Feeney will see you're a grand fella, after a while, and you'll soon be courting her with his blessing."

Eamonn was nudging his brother in the ribs with his elbow and Bert could not help feeling embarrassed.

"Vera says will you spend Christmas with us?" said Seán, seeing Bert's discomfiture.

"That would be delightful, thank you," said Bert, who had given the matter very little thought, even though it was less than a week away.

He had a sudden pang of guilt. He had not written a letter home for several weeks and his mother would surely expect a letter for Christmas.

"What's wrong with you? Is it that you'd prefer to be looking at the back of Miss Feeney's head in the church on Christmas day than sitting with us?" teased Seán.

"No, I've left it too late to write a letter home and Mama will be upset," Bert said, reverting to the childhood term in his distress.

"Not to worry," said Seán.

"Come in here with me."

He looked up and down the street before pulling Bert into the narrow, gloomy passage. Eamonn followed and closed the front door. Seán opened a concealed triangular panel in the wooden panelling under the stairs, and nodded to Bert to bend down and look in. His head jerked in surprise at the rich, metallic smell of freshly killed meat and it banged against the frame of the secret door. He took a step back.

"What is it?"

What possible connection there could be with his earlier comment?

Seán grinned proudly.

"I have three big fat turkeys in there and you can have one of them to send home on the boat train."

"I couldn't take one," Bert said.

Seán and Vera had very limited means, and however they had acquired these birds, he was sure they had other plans for them.

"Hasn't one of them got your name on it?" said Seán.

"We'll take it over to the station this afternoon. It'll be up in Dublin by nightfall and on the boat to England first thing in the morning."

Bert was just standing there with his mouth hanging open.

"Now, write your Mammy a nice Christmas letter about how grand everything is in Ireland, and I'll get Vera to wrap this fella up very well for his journey."

Seán touched each of the parcels with the toe of his boot.

"One for ourselves and one for the priest's house," he said, his fingertip touching the side of his nose.

Bert could not help smiling.

"They won't be eating turkeys in many houses in England this Christmas," boasted Eamonn, his thumbs tucked into the waistband of his trousers as if he had made the grand gesture himself.

"True enough. But the O' Briens deserve to eat well, for all the hard work this fine young man is doing," said Seán.

Bert shook his hand.

"Thank you, Seán."

"You're more than welcome," Seán replied.

He ushered them all into the kitchen just as Vera called out that she had a cup of tea ready for them.

CHAPTER 22

Clumps of primroses and occasional cowslips splashed yellow on the damp verges as Bert cycled, whistling, along the now familiar route to Kilkeely, oblivious to the misty rain that softly bathed his face. He wondered how long the blooms would last if he picked a bunch of them to make a posy. Wilted ones wouldn't be any good to him. Ina Feeney had sent him a note saying that she would be coming to the Irish class this week. A heron glided over the field, the long, lazy strokes of his grey wings taking Bert back to another river bank, another life, when catching the sixth trout had been the unattainable goal.

His gaze came back to the road and his knuckles whitened on the handlebars. Around the curve just ahead was a group of men in the middle of the road, fortunately with their backs turned, pre-occupied with the passengers in a halted motor car which had been travelling towards him. He slid off the bicycle, removed the oilskin wrapped bundle from his bag and hid it in a gap where the stone wall was broken by a gatepost. A large dock leaf plant provided a convenient camouflage. He remounted and resumed his whistling, cycling fast around the corner as if he was oblivious to the road block.

"Oh, dear," he said, squealing the brakes and adopting his St Cuthbert's manner, smiling affably at the men who had turned towards him.

The sun was reflecting off the windscreen so Bert could not see the faces of the passengers in the motor car and did not want to show too much interest. The men were untidily uniformed in dark jackets and khaki trousers tucked into Army issue boots. They were delighted by this further distraction. The area was supposed to be full of rebels, but so far they had met only with herds of cows and half-witted farmer's children. Two vehicles, however mundane, provided a brief respite from the boredom of the last few days.

"Get off!" shouted one of the men at Bert.

He swung his leg off the bicycle and stood passively while one of them grabbed his bag and tipped out the contents onto the wet road. His freshly washed and ironed shirt was muddied as the man shuffled through his meagre belongings with the toe of his high laced boot, too lazy to bend down to look. Bert had long since acquired a second copy of the Irish grammar book and now he kept one in the school room in Kilkeely and the other at Eamonn's house in Ballinasloe. A piece of chalk crushed unnoticed under the heel of the exploratory boot was the only evidence of his profession.

"Where are you going?" the man demanded after finding nothing of interest.

"I am a teacher," said Bert, and the man picked up his accent.

"What do these ignorant peasant farmers need to learn? How to count their rows of potatoes?" asked the man, guffawing, and being joined by his fellows.

"I have a private arrangement as a language tutor," said Bert grandly.

The man looked for a sign from his sergeant, who could not be sure if Bert was someone to be reckoned with. This well-spoken man could be from Dublin Castle and the Sergeant didn't want to draw too much attention to himself and his men. They got this posting after burning down a house in Headford and killing a family who wouldn't give up the whereabouts of their conniving rebel son, a known Volunteer. This far West it did nothing but rain and there was nowhere to spend their 10 shillings a day. The house where they were billeted was run by two narrow faced, slitty-eyed sisters who cooked plain food, nothing like the well fleshed French country women who had welcomed them with open arms and fed them like royalty when they were in the Army. So, they had to keep their heads down for a while in the hope of a better posting in a decent sized town with some chance of getting a drink in a public house without being spat at. The Sergeant nodded and the Constable pointed to the muddy pile.

"You can take your belongings, now," he said.

They returned their attentions to the people in the motor car. The Sergeant was sure they were guilty of something, but the hole at the back for the bags had already been searched and the driver just kept on saying that he had been employed to drive this young lady and elderly gent to Ballinasloe and he could tell them nothing more. A cloud crossed over the sun and Bert glanced into the motor car and realised that the pale faced driver was Brendan. A burly, red-whiskered Constable was making the passengers get out of the motor car, and Bert was faced with Ina Feeney and her father, who carefully masked their expressions. He was suddenly inspired and spoke to them in Irish. There was a slim chance of these rough men having learned any languages at all.

"*Ná bíodh blas imní oraibh. Labhróidh mé le na fir seo.*" Don't worry, let me speak to these men."

"Why, these are my Latin pupils, the Hemphills!"

Bert put on a falsetto laugh.

"Latin?" the sergeant asked, not convinced that what he had heard wasn't Irish.

"Me sine prima manu temptare pericule belli." said Bert, turning towards the Feeneys, grinning.

Michael looked to his daughter to show the fruits of her Loreto convent education. She smiled radiantly.

"I would agree, Mr O'Brien."

She gracefully inclined her head and her father felt again the air between them charged with something he did not understand. His own courtship had been a sedate, sensible one, with neither excitement nor disappointment, and he had been happily married for thirty two years before his lovely Eilís had succumbed to the TB. If Ina was going to be the only daughter not going into the Convent, he wanted to find her a husband who would provide for her, make her happy and father a big family of healthy grandchildren. This young man was handsome there was no doubt and to give him his due, he had been a very reliable courier in the last few months.

The satisfactory completion of Bert's most recent assignment; to carry a handgun between two safe houses, had yet to be reported to him, but Máirtín Feeney was beginning to think that young Bert O'Brien might just be worthy of his daughter's attentions. He had just given her permission to go back to the Irish classes and he would be keeping a close eye on the young *Timire* to make sure that no inappropriate advances were made.

The Sergeant was confused, and not being a man who liked ambiguity, he settled on the safe option and gave the order for the barrier to be lifted.

"Let them through!" he shouted gruffly.

He held the door for the young lady and touched his cap to the old gent, to show them that they were not the only ones with fine manners. Brendan cranked the engine and the car drove off. Bert climbed on his bicycle and calmly cycled in the opposite direction, wondering when he would have a chance to reclaim the oil skin parcel, not more than fifty yards behind him.

There was a buzz of conversation as he entered the school room at Kilkeely that evening. It was unusual for him to find the school open when he arrived, but of course, Ina must have come early and unlocked the door. He found her smiling modestly at the centre of a huddle of admirers. She looked up and caught his eye. Everyone turned to face him. Within the four walls of the school room, protocol demanded that he treat all his students with equal courtesy and interest, so he had to be very careful. There was a whistle of admiration and someone started clapping. He coughed, and his students scurried and sat quietly at their desks, like models of the children they had been teaching all day. He was reminded of Niamh and Tomás sitting cross legged on their mattress, hanging on their father's every word as he retold their favourite stories.

"Is it Latin or Irish we're learning this evening?" one of the men asked, and there was great laughter.

All evening Bert could feel the warmth of these people as well as the enthusiasm they always brought to the lessons. As they were leaving each of them shook his hand, touched his shoulder or smiled in a way that was palpably different to their usual polite thanks. The sound of the motor car engine outside reminded him that he would only have a brief moment to talk to Ina. The others left with diplomatic speed, so they were soon alone in the classroom.

"News travels quickly," he said, not meeting her eye as he tidied up.

"Father was telling everyone in the town, this afternoon," she said, hoping that Bert didn't think she had been seeking all this attention.

"I had to leave the parcel hidden in a hole in the wall," he muttered, looking out the window.

Her father was sitting in the motor car, pointedly looking in the opposite direction.

"Did you have it with you today?" she asked, her voice rising.

He nodded.

"You did well to hide it before they saw you."

"It was a close run thing," he said, finally looking at her.

"Do you think that perhaps your father might allow me to escort you home from the lesson some time?"

She nodded quickly.

"He's very impressed with you at the moment. He asked me what the Latin meant. I had to admit I had no idea."

Her eyes were wide, the pupils dark pools, and her long, pale lashes barely brushed her cheek when she blinked.

His arm was aching with wanting to lift his hand and touch that velvet skin with the tip of his finger.

"It's from the Aeneid. Camilla asks Turnus to be allowed to be the first to go into hand to hand combat with the Trojans."

A movement caught his eye. Mr Feeney was climbing out of the car, noisily clearing his throat. Ina's lips twitched into a tiny wry smile.

"I think we have had our few minutes alone," she said, and stood up.

"Thank you for the lesson. I really enjoyed being back."

"Thank you for coming back," said Bert, half bowing.

She ran to the door, like a young girl, and looked back.

"I look forward to seeing you next week," she said, and was gone.

He watched her father open the passenger door and help her to sit. Mr Feeney raised a hand in greeting before getting inside himself, and then they were moving off, even before Ina had finished tying the scarf over her hair. Bert was relieved that he hadn't been required to explain the whereabouts of the gun. Had he been wise to even tell Ina?

The roadblock was about ten miles outside Tuam. It was just after ten o'clock now. He could be there and back in less than three hours, allowing for time to find the exact spot. The patrols would not be abroad at this hour of the night, and it seemed the only way to safely carry out his duty. He quickly locked up and strode back to Paddy and Noreen's house to retrieve his bicycle. The glow of the lamp inside told him they were still up but he didn't want to be delayed so he ducked under the window and cycled off into the darkness. The road took on a different character at night, without any of the familiar landmarks. In the darkness it was difficult to judge the distance he had travelled, but at his usual speed he could expect to arrive within an hour. The wheels swished a wet accompaniment to his whistling and the pale yellow disc of his bicycle lamp danced ahead of him like a tame full moon. A fox paused on the roadside, a front paw raised warily, before dashing across in front of him, causing him to swerve. He sped through the silent countryside for miles without seeing the glow of a cottage lamp or other sign of human habitation. A slight wind gave him added impetus and a very gradual downwardly sloping tilt to the countryside meant he would have a double battle on the return journey. He didn't care. For the first time since his arrival over a year ago, he felt as if he belonged to this place he loved so deeply. He swept down a long hill, anticipating the bend in the road and taking it without braking. Unless a badger or another fox were unlucky enough to be crossing, there was no danger. The road ahead was clear and he used the momentum of the hill, pumping his legs hard to keep up his speed along a straight stretch. Then he saw sandbags stacked at the roadside, and the long branch that had served as a makeshift barrier. There was no other sign of the patrol, and he sailed past, then slowed for the curve and stopped at the gateway.

Breathless, he plunged his hand into the space beside the gatepost, feeling for the edge of the oilskin parcel. His fingers met stone and mud. He knelt down properly, thinking he had misjudged the spot in the dark, and systematically felt around the base of the post. Then he unhooked his bicycle lamp and shone it directly at the dark hole. The dock leaf stem had been snapped, and it lay like a wounded sentry on the long grass. There was nothing in the hole. There was no mistake. He sat back on his heels and groaned, running his hands through his hair and streaking it with mud. Desperately, he searched the ground all around, then the base of the other gatepost, and he even climbed over the gate to look on the other side. There was nothing. His stomach heaving, bile rose in his throat and he remounted the bicycle, lost for any idea about what to do next.

All his dreams crashed around him. He had failed in his first serious mission. Carrying letters from Ballinasloe to Tuam and even once to Ballina had not been onerous, but he had been reliable and trustworthy. Now, as soon as they trusted him with something dangerous and incriminating he had failed. He was not worthy of Ina, not worthy of the admiration of his students, not worthy of belonging. The long hill defeated him and he dismounted, and pushed the bicycle miserably to the top, his head hanging, staring at his boots as they took each step.

The rain hardened into cold stinging drops that drove into his face when he remounted, and his misery was complete when a gust of wind snatched his cap. After twenty minutes of searching in the ditches he still had not found it and gave up. Two hours later, he finally arrived at Paddy's house and staggered inside and up the ladder, too tired to make the effort to be quiet. In the morning, Noreen was uncharacteristically quiet. She put a bowl of porridge in front of him almost begrudgingly and was completely lacking in her usual garrulous curiosity about his comings and goings.

"I'm sorry if I disturbed you last night," he said humbly, spooning in his porridge.

His nocturnal expedition had left him ravenous.

"This morning, you mean, don't you?" she said frostily.

For the first time Bert wondered about those emigrant sons, and how eagerly they might have left home. The 'where were you?' hung in the air between them, unasked. Even if Noreen had known about his work for the Volunteers he couldn't tell her where he had been before he found a way of breaking the news to Mr Feeney that he had lost the gun.

Noreen had looked him up and down when he climbed down the ladder, noticing the mud stained knees of his trousers and the streaks in his hair. Her hands went to her hips, but she resisted tutting, merely turning back to stir the pot of porridge. There was no sign of Paddy.

"He's gone to see his mother, early. She wasn't well last night and he was worried about her," Noreen volunteered.

"I hope it's not too serious," Bert said.

He pulled out his chair and quickly blessed himself before picking up the spoon to eat. His apology was the only other conversation that passed between them until he was ready to go and absent-mindedly cast around looking for his cap.

"Did you lose that, as well?" she asked, irritated.

"How did you...?" escaped his lips before he realised she couldn't possibly know about the gun.

He could see the gleam of victory in her eye. She was a clever woman.

"It blew off in the wind and I couldn't find it in the dark," he said, absentmindedly rubbing his hair so that flakes of dried mud fell onto his shoulders.

"Off with you!"

She harried him out the door with a broom, handing him a wrapped parcel of bread.

"Thank you, Noreen. I will see you later in the week," he muttered.

He went around the back of the cottage to get his bicycle. She had the bottom of the door open and was vigorously sweeping the floor when he passed her again. She waved and he felt forgiven by her smile. He would have to go to Dunmore first and face the music, however unpleasant.

The black shiny door was even more daunting than usual. The hollow echo of the lion door knocker reverberated inside. Bert cleared his throat and nervously brushed back his hair, hoping that the last flakes of mud were gone. Bríd the maid answered the door, her eyes bright with curiosity. She had peered out through a crack in the drawing room curtains wondering who could be calling at such an early hour. She was delighted to see Bert. She was curious to see the man who had Miss Ina's famously level head so distracted. Bert greeted her and asked if Mr Feeney was available.

"I'm sorry it's so early, but I wanted to call on him before leaving for Ballinasloe," he said, gruff with embarrassment.

"Indeed, it's not too early for this household!" she said, as if to say her employers might be well off, but they didn't get that way through indolence.

She went on, "I'm sorry to tell you that Mr Feeney is gone already, over to Galway. He's not expected back until tomorrow."

She gave him a curtsey, something she had been desperate to do since she started working as a maid, but the occasion had never arisen. This tall, well spoken English man seemed worthy of the effort.

"Thank you," he said, turning away, unable to think of a suitable message he could leave.

"Excuse me, Sir", she said timidly.

She glanced quickly over her shoulder and leaned forward conspiratorially.

"Miss Feeney is having her second cup of tea in the library."

Bert smiled.

"Could you ask her if I may have a moment of her time?"

She curtsied again.

"Certainly, Sir. I won't be a moment."

She almost ran across the hall, half wondering if she should have invited him inside instead of leaving him standing on the doorstep. A moment later Ina emerged and quickly crossed the black and white tiled floor.

"Bert! Come in, don't stand out in the cold," she said.

Bríd disappeared into the kitchen, full of herself, to tell the news to the delivery boy who had just knocked at the back door. Bert was very aware that their meeting must be brief. Even a few precious minutes snatched now could jeopardise his tenuous status if Máirtín Feeney found out.

"I was hoping to see your father," he said loud enough for the maid to hear through the kitchen door, as they stepped into the library.

She closed the big oak door behind them and couldn't help giggling. Bert's face was so serious, she stopped.

"Has something terrible happened?" she asked.

"The parcel was gone."

He started pacing up and down the scarlet red Axminster carpet in front of a wide mahogany desk.

"I went back last night to retrieve it, and it had disappeared."

Ina said nothing.

"Your father will be very disappointed and angry with me."

"There must be a rational explanation," she said, calmly.

Did she really understand how serious this was? There was not only the distinct possibility that he would be banned from seeing her again, as a feckless youth unable to carry out the simplest task, but if the RIC had somehow found the gun, they may well suspect him of concealing it, and he would not have such an easy time passing through the next road block.

"Maybe somebody saw you hiding it and then took it for safe keeping," Ina said.

"I don't know what to tell your father," he said, finally standing still.

"I told him last night on the way home that you had to hide it and he was impressed with your quick thinking," she said.

"We'll just have to hope he remembers that when he hears the gun is gone."

Bert looked at her open, gentle face, and for that moment he could believe that everything would be all right. By some miracle, the gun would reappear, and he would deliver it as planned, and he could continue to see Ina after the weekly classes, until...

"Would you like me to break the news?" she asked, watching him as he began his pacing again.

As tempting as her offer was, it would hardly raise Bert in her father's esteem. He told her he would come back on Saturday evening from Ballinasloe, and call on them at six o' clock.

"It might turn up before then, in which case there will be nothing to worry about," she said brightly, opening the library door to show him out.

They had been alone together for long enough, and Bríd would no doubt have her ears cocked for any sound. Sure enough, just as they crossed the hall, she came out of the kitchen and skittered across the tiles to open the front door. Ina smiled at the affected curtsey and waved goodbye to Bert, hoping that her cheeks were not too flushed which would give Bríd even more to gossip about.

The days until Saturday seemed endless and Eamonn's light hearted teasing about Bert's newly restored position as Ina's suitor rankled.

"You're not in the best of form for a fella who is courting the girl of his dreams," said Mairéad one evening when Eamonn was out as usual at Seán's house.

She wasn't looking at him, and her tone held no humour or malice.

"It might not last for much longer," Bert said miserably.

"What is the matter now?" Mairéad asked

She was exasperated, not with Bert but with the narrow-minded father who couldn't see what a fine man his daughter would be marrying.

"I can't tell you the details, but I failed to carry out an important mission and he will think I'm a complete idiot."

Bert's head was hanging almost between his knees as he stared at the hearth stones.

"You can't be successful at everything, *a ghrá*," she said, consolingly.

"There has to be times when things don't go as planned. Sure he wouldn't hold that against you."

"This is serious. We have little enough in the way of fi... in the way of essentials, without me losing things."

It was better for her not to know. The raids on houses were becoming more frequent, and the terrible things they were doing to people to make them talk didn't bear thinking about.

Mairéad patted his knee. "I'm sure it will all come right in the end."

They were finishing the dregs of their tea when the front door opened with a creak followed by muffled footsteps. Mairéad stepped out into the passage to see a pair of heels disappearing rapidly up the stairs. Eamonn shrugged off his coat.

"We've two extra mouths for breakfast in the morning," he said quietly, hushing her until they were in the kitchen again.

"There's muddy footprints all the way up the stairs."

Bert lifted his head, sensing the tension.

"Two lads from South Cork need a bed for the night." Eamonn said matter-of-factly. "They haven't had a roof over them these three nights."

Mairéad stoked the embers of the fire to get the kettle boiling.

"They'll need hot water, so," she said, humming.

Bert watched them following what must be a familiar routine. Eamonn made sure the curtains were tightly drawn and tested the bolt on the back door. Mairéad brewed a pot of tea and filled a pitcher with hot water.

"Would you ever carry that up the stairs for me?" she said to Bert, and he stood up, eager to help.

"They're in our room, above," said Eamonn casually.

"They could have mine," Bert protested. "I can sleep in this chair by the fire."

"Not at all, Bert. You need to keep your wits about you and get your sleep too. Don't worry about us, we will be very comfortable," said Mairéad, following him up the stairs.

Two men, no older than himself, lay prone across the candlewick bedspread in the front bedroom, and they jumped to their feet when they heard the footsteps. Mairéad put them at ease.

"Don't worry lads. Take your boots off you there and we'll dry them at the fire downstairs."

The tension in their faces eased slightly and one grinned, his teeth yellow and his face mottled with the cold and three days of patchy dark chin stubble. He could have been as young as sixteen.

"Will you have some bread and lard?" Mairéad asked.

She put the mugs of tea carefully on a bedside table adorned with white crocheted lace.

Bert had never been in this room which smelled faintly of femaleness and reminded him of his sisters' room at home. A Sacred Heart picture hung on the wall between the two narrow windows and a dark mahogany crucifix with a brass figure of Jesus hung over the bed. It was identical to the one in his parents' bedroom and he knew from childhood exploration that the front would slide off to reveal candles and holy water for the administration of the Last Rites. As a boy he had always wondered how well he would be able to sleep under such a sombre reminder of the inevitability of death.

The two men perched on the edge of the dark rose pink bedspread, hesitant to spoil it now the woman of the house was present. The younger one absent-mindedly stroked the palm of his hand across the knobbled surface, as if seeking reassurance from its familiar texture. The other one was the talker.

"Thanks very much, Missus, for taking us in. We're carrying orders to all the Brigades, and then up to HQ to report. We were nearly caught outside Clonmel, only that yer man here was so quick on his feet and jumped on the back of a wagon and pulled me in under the tarpaulin after him."

He patted his comrade on the arm. The boy, for now it was apparent that he was, grinned again but didn't say anything.

"He's my nephew, and he's a grand lad, altogether. His father will be looking down on him, God rest his soul, and he'll have a tear of pride in his eye."

The man blessed himself and then sipped his tea. The young man was looking at the floor. Mairéad nudged Bert, who was standing, simply staring at them. He wondered how the boy's father had met his end.

"With the help of God, and a few kind people like yourselves, we should be back home for Easter," said the talker, draining his tea.

"Would you ever go and cut some bread for me, Bert?" asked Mairéad, nudging him again.

Bert stumbled downstairs. Shouldn't he be doing more, like these men, risking their lives every day, rather than standing at the front of a classroom? He cut his finger in his haste to slice the bread and sucked the blood. He lathered the bread with lard from the pot and put six slices on a large plate. As he reached the top of the stairs he noticed a single red drop of blood had landed on the creamy smooth surface of the lard and glancing up to make sure he was not observed he quickly licked it off. The metallic, fatty taste conjured up an image of Leo slicing the arm off the buried corpse with his spade and Bert retched.

"Are you all right, there?" Mairéad asked, coming to the door of the bedroom.

He nodded and handed over the plate, turning into his own room.

"Goodnight," he mumbled, and closed the door behind him.

CHAPTER 23

June 1920

Bert woke early to a clear June sky after nearly a month of unrelenting rain. It would have been Leo's twenty second birthday. Which of his dreams would he be living now, if he were still alive? He might have started making his fortune in America, or joined the New York police force, or even travelled as far as New Zealand to work on a sheep farm. Bert was trying to live his life for both of them now. On the road, when he caught a glimpse of an RIC patrol, he called on Leo's wits and bravery, his mind became razor sharp and he felt ready for anything. Every time Bert passed through a road block unmolested he sent up a quick prayer of thanks and raised a mental cheer to Leo.

Some of his students had started teaching Irish to the children in their own classes, and Bert was delighted when two nine-year-olds from Ballinasloe took a piece of *buntús* to the *Feis* in Galway. Although he had fifteen regular students at Kilkeely, there was one he still sorely missed. Máirtín Feeney had taken the loss of the gun very badly. Ina's reminder of Bert's quick thinking and his attempt to retrieve the parcel in the middle of a stormy night had landed on deaf ears. Máirtín Feeney forbade her from attending the Irish lessons.

"You'll only be distracted. Teach the children what you've learned already. He's not a good prospect for a husband. He even says it himself; he's a man of words, not a man of action. Its action we need in the Volunteers, and its action you need from a husband to support you. Draw a line under it now, before you get a broken heart."

Bert was no longer even carrying messages. He asked Noreen for advice.

"Your chance will come along one day if you're patient," Noreen said. "Stick at what you're doing and you can't go far wrong."

"It's been months now."

Bert knew he sounded querulous. Noreen was like his own mother and he could let his guard down with her.

"How can I prove myself, if he doesn't trust me with carrying even the simplest message, any more?"

"Time works wonders," she said, "not only with healing wounds, but with fading the memory a little bit. Just let time take its time."

Bert sighed. Pat, the eldest son of Tomás O'Malley, a lifelong friend of Máirtín Feeney's who had a big farm outside Tuam, was rumoured to be interested in courting Ina. He was tall and handsome and would inherit the farm. At this rate, she would be married off to Pat while Bert waited for 'time to take its time.'

Leo's birthday might be his lucky day. He was planning to arrive in Dunmore in plenty of time to call at the big house before his evening lesson. The only thing that could go wrong would be if Máirtín Feeney wasn't there. Bert had a very important parcel to deliver. It would change everything. He cycled past the place where he had been stopped in March, for the first time in months not casting a second glance at the gatepost where he had hidden the gun. He swept around the bend and passed the location of the road block, enjoying the sensation of the extra weight on his back, knowing what was inside the bag. Then he seemed to hit a wall at twenty miles an hour.

Fifty yards further down the road was the now familiar array of tea chests and sandbags used by the Black and Tans for their road blocks. There was no-where to hide, and no option but to continue cycling straight towards them. The spit in his mouth dried up and his whistle with it. A hot flush swept across his shoulders and down his body and he was suddenly bathed in sweat. He tweaked his cap and lifted it in greeting as he glided to a stop, forcing himself to grin. This time there were six men and no distractions from any other vehicles or passers-by. Fields of hummocky grass stretched out on all sides, split by stone walls, without a shrub above six foot as far as the eye could see. An open backed lorry stood at the side of the road and three men leaned lazily against the wheels in the lee of the wind, passing a single cigarette between them. They didn't look up as Bert approached. A small smoky peat fire burned, with a billy can of water boiling up for the tea that promised to be the highlight of their day so far.

"A fine morning, gentlemen," said Bert, and they looked slightly taken aback.

This chap with the unruly hair and the patches on his elbows looked for all the world like a local but he spoke like an Oxford professor. One of the men instinctively touched his forelock, then pretended he had just been itching his eyebrow.

"What's your business?" asked one of the men, the routine question almost as familiar to Bert as to them.

He had to distract them so they didn't search his bag. He gave his usual answer about being a language tutor, while desperately racking his brain for something that would break the predictable pattern of events. One man would rifle through his bag while the other asked the questions. There was a chance this time it could be different, but he had to do something. Then he remembered the cake. Mairéad had made a barm brack for him to take to Noreen and Paddy for their wedding anniversary the following day. The extra weight in his bag was not just from the object wrapped in his spare shirt.

"Would you chaps like some cake to accompany that tea?" he asked, shrugging the bag off his shoulder.

Instinctively, his interrogator put his hand to his gun, then relaxed as the aroma of the richly fruited cake reached his nostrils. Bert presented it with a flourish.

"Baked only last evening by my landlady. I will say one thing for the Irish landlady. She bakes a very fine fruit cake."

The men looked at each other like children around a Christmas tree.

"Thanks very much, Sir," said the soldier standing closest to Bert, flamboyantly standing aside to let him pass.

"Have you forgotten your manners?" barked his Sergeant, and then turned to Bert. "Will you join us in a cup of tea?"

Bert shook his head.

"No thank you, I need to get on. I do hope you enjoy the cake."

The men saluted and he cycled off, hearing the men behind him mocking their Sergeant's invitation.

"Will you join us in a cup of tea?" they mimicked, their little fingers crooked.

Ina laughed when Bert told the story. They were sitting in the high-ceilinged drawing room, her father standing with his back to the newly lit fire, his face flushed with the celebratory whiskey the men had downed.

"Well, you've nerves of steel, I'll say that for you," Máirtín Feeney said.

Bert wished he would stand aside and let some heat out into the room. He felt honoured to be invited into the inner sanctum but even with a huge fire in the hearth, he could feel the chill of a room that was hardly used.

"You haven't told us yet how you got the gun back," said Ina, her eyes shining.

She was perched on the edge of a satin covered, spindly-legged chair, her feet placed neatly together, her hands in her lap. The warm whiskey reached his stomach and Bert sat back and crossed his legs, enjoying the attentive audience. Máirtín Feeney was starting to think that this fella maybe could be trusted to provide for his daughter and to mind her if times got tough. But Máirtín Feeney was a business man who liked a game of poker, and it never paid to show your cards too soon. He stood aloof, apparently not interested in hearing how the gun had suddenly reappeared after three months.

"My Ballinasloe class is at six o' clock on a Thursday, as you know," said Bert, and Ina nodded.

"Yesterday as usual I picked up the key from the priest's house and went to open up the school. The weather had been wet and there were puddles everywhere, so I was looking down, and treading very carefully through the school yard, to avoid getting wet feet.

I thought I saw some movement out of the side of my eye, over the wall, but when I looked properly there was nobody there, so I unlocked the door and went inside. There are often a few late stragglers to that class because they have to come a long way and they're worse when it's wet, so I wasn't surprised to have a smaller group than usual when I started at six."

"Are they on the same lesson as us?" Ina asked politely.

"Arragh, Ina, a *ghrá*, will you let the man tell his story," said her father, and she hid a smile behind her hand.

"At about quarter past six I heard the outer school door opening and assumed it was some of my latecomers, so I kept on talking. After a few moments they hadn't joined us so I stopped and went to open the classroom door. I didn't want them to miss the next part of the lesson, so I opened the door wide and said, "*Tar isteach, go gasta agus go ciúin, le do thoil.* Come in quickly and quietly please."

Outside the door were three bedraggled looking men, nudging each other to go in. They looked too young to be teachers, so I waited, holding the door open until one of them would get the courage to come in and the others might follow. The shortest one stepped forward and I led them into the classroom, only to see my students looking at me in horror. When I turned around the man was holding a gun above his head, waving it around.

He started shouting, "We need all the men in here, every hand we can get. There's a big Tan patrol coming through in an hour and we're chopping trees for an ambush!"

"In the name of God!" exclaimed Máirtín Feeney.

Ina's eyes widened but she didn't speak.

"I was speechless, as were my students. Then I told them we had more important things to be doing than cutting down trees. They ignored me, and suddenly all three of them were in the classroom, man-handling people to their feet. I shouted at them in Irish 'Off with you, and don't bother law- abiding citizens with your silly notions.'

Liam Breathnach was fidgeting and I thought he was nearly ready to join them, but I caught his eye and he sat down again. The lads were still calling for helpers.

'Do you call yourselves Irishmen sitting in here with the women, when there's man's work to be done outside?' one of them shouted.

I just asked him '*An bhfuil Gaeilge agat?* Do you speak Irish?'

He looked at me blankly so I must confess I shouted at them something like,

'Do you call yourselves Irishmen, and you can't even speak your own language, that gives us our identity, our heart and our soul inside us?' They were all very quiet after that. I looked at the third one, whose face I hadn't seen clearly before and recognised him.

'You! Danny Donovan. You said you would come to my classes and learn a few words, and now, the first time I see you, you are brandishing weapons and threatening my students, and terrifying the women! That is not the behaviour of a decent Volunteer.'

He was a young lad I had met on the train down from Dublin, full of himself that he was joining the Volunteers. Seán had mentioned that they were having trouble with a few of the young lads going off on their own, troublemaking.

'I'll have words to say to Eamonn O'Farrell about you!' I said and they all looked very shamefaced. 'Are the Volunteers handing out guns to the likes of you? What hope do we have, then?' I said, appealing to my students, and they all shook their heads, even Liam Breathnach. The three lads went off with their tails between their legs and I thought that would be the last of it."

"And it wasn't?" asked Ina breathlessly.

Her father was now leaning forward, hanging on every word.

"No. After the lesson, I locked up and I was just crossing the yard again, when someone vaulted over the wall and ran over to me. It was Danny. He handed me the parcel with the gun in it. He said he had found it and would I make sure it got to Eamonn.

'The funny thing is, I would have been too scared to pull the trigger anyhow, and it's better in someone else's hands,' he said, and I didn't have the heart to reprimand him any further. I was still curious about where he had found it, so I asked him.

'We were out on manoeuvres a few months gone, maybe in March, and you won't believe it but I went to relieve myself up against a gate post, and heard a strange noise, that wouldn't be from wet leaves, will we say, so I put my hand down into the grass, and there it was, all wrapped up in oilskin, as dry as a bone.'

"Well, well," said Máirtín Feeney, slapping his thigh, a smile splitting his face.

Bert couldn't help laughing.

"Best of all, he says he'll come to the class next week."

CHAPTER 24

The summer passed quickly. Eamonn told Bert he was the most useful courier in the West, traversing the counties of Galway and Roscommon several times a week, riding a new bicycle bought by Máirtín Feeney.

"You need a reliable bicycle, and you out in all weathers, doing such a grand job."

Bert had crossed into Mayo and gone up as far as Ballina carrying orders from Eamonn hidden in his sleeves or the soles of his boots. His clothes had never yet been searched, so believable was his alter ego as an eccentric down-at-heel Latin tutor going from one estate to another, teaching the children of the landed gentry. He was never tempted to read the contents of the sealed envelopes he was carrying. Occasionally on the long, lonely cycle rides with the wind lashing his face he wondered if he could really say he had nothing to do with shootings and arson attacks, when he might have been the courier of the orders to carry them out? There were certainly small groups of Volunteers like young Danny and his friends in Ballinasloe who were taking action as they saw fit instead of following Battalion orders but deep down he knew that he was deluding himself. His self-proclaimed commitment to the power of words over actions was being stretched to its limits.

The spurious authority granted by the English to the *Dáil* with the Government of Ireland Act in March had been nothing short of appeasement. The increasing numbers of RIC reinforcements were tangible evidence that the English had other plans for suppressing Irish resistance. Every issue of the *Freeman's Journal* overflowed with outrage. It seemed as if the British Government unofficially sanctioned the terror tactics and spontaneous reprisals of the Black and Tans. They were a law unto themselves. Many of Tans were survivors of the horrors that Leo had faced in France, no doubt fighting their demons the only way they knew how. Perhaps when these ill-disciplined, rough-spoken men stopped him on the roads, it was more than his upper class professorial patter that convinced them to let him pass. Could they sense that he found it difficult to completely condemn them; that he thought of them as victims as much as villains?

In August he was invited for Sunday dinner with Ina and her father at the big house. After the weekly class her father usually arrived in the car a few discreet minutes late to collect her and every Sunday they were allowed to talk to each other after Mass. Bert was in no hurry. He knew he had jumped only the first of many hurdles. Máirtín Feeney would not marry Ina off to a peripatetic, poverty-stricken Irish teacher no matter how much he admired Bert's courage. A huge roast of beef reclined on a silver platter at the head of the table and beside it a white china bowl patterned with nettle leaves was full of gently steaming potatoes. A matching gravy jug and vegetable dish sat on the mahogany sideboard.

"Bless us O Lord and these thy gifts which of thy bounty we are about to receive through Christ our Lord, Amen," Máirtín Feeney's sonorous voice boomed.

Bert bowed his head and closed his eyes. His own family would certainly not be eating this well. He had been neglecting his correspondence with home. Enclosed in the recent birthday card from his mother had been a crayoned scribble from Conor. His mother's faithful weekly letters full of mundane details of a life he had left behind rarely affected him, but that splash of colour without words crushed him with guilt. Had coming to Ireland changed him completely, or had he been slowly changing since that very first encounter with Michael Power? Bert had started off trying to impress Michael and now here he was trying to win over Máirtín Feeney when maybe he should be trying to live up to his Papa's expectations. Bert was really the only one left who could. Having thrown away his great education here he was, living on the bread line with no prospect of a roof over his head, courting a girl so far beyond his means that it was almost laughable. And risking life and limb every time he carried Volunteer orders, just to impress her father.

The prayer was over and Ina and Mr Feeney were looking at him expectantly.

"A penny for your thoughts?" Ina asked gently.

He must have kept his eyes closed a fraction too long.

"I was just thinking about home, and my family," he said quietly.

"This looks like a fine bit of beef," Máirtín Feeney said, audibly salivating.

"The O'Malleys always look after us well, on the meat side of things. Bert, would you carve for us?"

Was this a test in social etiquette, or a gesture of acceptance? His mother had always brought their food to the table already piled on the plates.

"I'm afraid I have little experience, although I'm willing to give it a try," he said, standing up to move to the other side of the table.

"Give it your best go, so," said Máirtín Feeney expansively.

His waistcoat buttons were straining as he leaned back in his chair to spectate. Ina looked nervously at Bert, who had taken up the carving knife and fork in the manner of a man who was about to start pruning a hedge. He lifted an eyebrow and smiled at her, sensing that he had passed the first test, of willingness. Ten minutes later he was sweating as he sat down, having completely carved the joint into thickish slices that lay like fallen dominoes on the platter, blood oozing from the central slices, the outer ones darker and drier.

"Pass over the plates, there, *a ghrá*," her father instructed Ina, and she filled them, serving herself last.

"This is delicious," Bert said, as they ate.

Food seemed to be the only thing that stopped Máirtín Feeney from talking. He grunted appreciatively. Bert had never tasted anything like the caramel drenched custards for dessert, and as he sipped red wine from a Waterford Crystal goblet, he was reminded how far from this lifestyle he had been raised.

"Happy Birthday," Ina said after they had finished eating, passing him a small parcel wrapped in tissue paper.

It was a white linen handkerchief, embroidered with his initials in the corner, in a vibrant blue thread.

"Thank you so much," he said, surprised that she knew the date.

"I'll use it every day and think of you."

She blushed, and her father cleared his throat. She nodded and slipped out of the room so suddenly that Bert was taken by surprise.

"What's the news from Tuam way?" Máirtín asked pointedly.

Bert had delivered an envelope the previous day.

"They're still in shock," Bert said quietly.

"The Town Hall is a just a black shell, and there were a number of buildings nearby that were seriously damaged too. They may have to be demolished."

"It's a very sad state of affairs," said Michael, shaking his head.

"I didn't stay long. They've brought reinforcements to the barracks. My every move was being watched. They'll be expecting more reprisals."

"Well they can't expect to burn down half the town and think that people will just sit back and accept it. You weren't seen going into the house?"

"I didn't go in. I cycled quickly past and then turned into the back lane. Someone waved at me from the yard and I left the message under a stone at the top of the lane."

"Good man. The lads won't be long following those orders, with the smoking ruins of the Town Hall there as a daily reminder of the evil occupation we are labouring under."

There was a quiet knock at the door and Ina came in with a tray laden with a teapot, cups and saucers and a plate of biscuits. They made conversation for another hour before Bert excused himself. Ina walked with him to the end of Castle Street and waved goodbye when he mounted his bicycle. The alcohol and the elation at being allowed to walk through the town with her sped his journey and he arrived breathless at Paddy's house. They had left a note saying they were visiting Paddy's mother and would not be home before dark. He brought out a wooden stool and sat on the front doorstep, watching white butterflies swooping over the hedge and listening to the chirping, rustling Sunday silence of his twentieth birthday.

When he woke the next morning after a restless night, his head was throbbing. Endless thoughts had circled him in the darkness like rooks sweeping around the crown of a tree in the twilight, vaguely threatening, their shapes difficult to define. Noreen's casual dismissal of his hangover reassured him that perhaps the unsettled feeling that remained in the morning was nothing more than his body's reaction to the wine.

"You look like a man who should stick to the stout," said Paddy in his jocular, know-it-all tone, and for once Bert found it easy to agree with him.

"You know where you stand with a pint of the black stuff," said Paddy, not satisfied until he could elaborate on his theory. "There's all kinds of strange things in wine that the French are probably used to, but it wouldn't suit the Irish blood, as a general rule."

Bert nodded agreeably.

"Was it in wine glasses you drank it? Waterford Crystal, I've no doubt."

Paddy interrogated him for a few more minutes about the inside of the Feeney's house and what they had for their dinner, before Bert stood up and thanked Noreen for breakfast. He climbed the ladder to get his bag ready for travelling. The handkerchief was lying on his pillow where he had held it close to his face all night, inhaling the almost imaginary scent of Ina. He folded it carefully and put it in his trouser pocket.

CHAPTER 25

Wisps of Mairéad's dark curly hair framed her face, having escaped from the bun that was usually tightly bound at the back of her head.

"Did you see the paper?" she asked, as Bert came in the back door, his breath pluming in front of him, having parked his bicycle outside.

Even the roaring fire she had built up against the cold November wind brought no colour to her white, high-boned cheeks. Her mouth, usually round and generous with laughter and smiles, was a tight, wrinkled line.

"No, what is it?" asked Bert.

"Murder and mayhem up in Dublin."

She handed him the *Freeman's Journal*. Fourteen people had been shot by the RIC at a football match in Croke Park.

"...the spectators were startled by a volley of shots fired from inside the turnstile entrances. Armed and uniformed men were seen entering the field, and immediately after the firing broke out scenes of the wildest confusion took place. The spectators made a rush for the far side of Croke Park and shots were fired over their heads and into the crowd."

"Why did they do it?" Bert asked, scanning the article quickly.

"Michael Collins' squad killed fourteen British spies in their beds in the early hours of Sunday morning," Mairéad said.

Bert nodded, continuing to read.

"They weren't long deciding what to do about it," she went on bitterly. "Two young fellas, only ten and eleven years old, were killed at Croke Park. There was panic and pandemonium. Some people were even trampled to death, trying to run away."

"Does Eamonn know yet?" Bert asked, wondering if he would he be carrying orders tomorrow for retaliation in the West.

"He was fit to be tied. He couldn't sit still so I sent him off to see Seán."

Bert sat down suddenly, all his breath leaving him in a hot wave.

"It can't go on," he said. "There must be a better way."

"We all know fine well what the better way is," said Mairéad.

"We need a political solution. A pact, like the Versailles Treaty."

"Don't you know well, Bert, that the English will sweet talk their way to an agreement that suits nobody but themselves. It has happened too many times before. Look at all those Home Rule bills. Not worth the paper they were written on. What we have now is only a pretense at self-government. The English think if they let us play at it we will be content. Enough is enough, Bert. They only understand one thing. We have to make them feel pain. Enough pain to make it not worth their while to stay."

"Isn't that a bit naïve?" asked Bert.

"They fought in the Great War. They hurled men over the edge of trenches into the teeth of machine gun fire. Thousands and thousands of them. What pain threshold do we need to hit, for them to walk away from Ireland after hundreds of years? We are an irritation to them and nothing more."

Mairéad's eyes filled with tears and she turned away.

"We can't stop believing in ourselves now."

He shared her feeling of desperation. Eamonn came back from Seán's house looking exhausted. None of them had an appetite for dinner.

"We had more news while I was there. They killed three of Collins' lads in Dublin Castle. 'Shot while trying to escape' is the story. I met one of them, Peadar Clancy, up in Dublin once. He was a good man. I didn't know the others. They were being held for the spy shootings. There was talk of torture."

He pushed an uneaten potato across his plate with the edge of his knife.

"I'll have to go up to Dublin in the next few days, love."

Mairéad nodded, and a tear fell onto the congealed bacon fat on her plate.

The uncertain flickering of candles on draughty parlour window sills did not arouse in Bert the usual sense of anticipation of the good things of Christmas as he cycled past. How many of those homes were empty of men who would not dare to return? No matter how strongly the flame drew them, enticing them to share just one cold night under a warm roof with food in their stomachs and their children singing Christmas carols, they would not risk being burnt out by the Tans or the Auxies, the new and even more deadly force that had supplemented the RIC since the autumn. Bert's legs were leaden, not only with the cold and the abrasive rub of the wet woollen trousers against his thighs, but with despair. He would spend Christmas day with Paddy, Noreen and Paddy's mother, who was very frail. They were some substitute for his own family, but he wished he could be at home in the kitchen at Saltwell Road playing cards to pass the time until Midnight Mass. His mother would have her hair up, and a freshly pressed dress smelling of lavender, and his father would have his Sunday shirt buttoned up, a tightly knotted tie, his shoes polished and even his moustache somehow looking shiny for this special night. They wouldn't be worrying tonight about the knock of a rifle butt against the door or listening out for unusual sounds in the street. Nearly a month had passed since Eamonn went on the run and the strain was telling on Mairéad, for all her declarations that fighting tooth and nail was the only answer. Eamonn had come back from Dublin with orders to form a flying column. It was the only way to respond to the new martial law. The courts-martial were doling out death sentences to men for just being in possession of arms.

"I wouldn't bring it on you, love," Bert heard Eamonn say, before he left.

The walls of the house were thin and Bert couldn't help hearing the pleading in Mairéad's lowered voice.

"They don't know anything about you, Eamonn. You've been so careful these last few months they wouldn't suspect a thing."

"They know me well, *a ghrá*. I'm a marked man and I was lucky the last time to get away with only a broken leg. I won't let them burn the house down and make you homeless."

Mairéad's sobs were audible through the bedroom wall.

"What will I do without you?"

"You'll be grand. Seán will mind you. He'll come over to you every day, and you'll have Bert to keep you company, some evenings."

"When will I see you?"

"I don't know, love. We'll just have to see what happens. Isn't it better that you don't see me this way than me being interned and God knows what happening to me? I'll be out under the sky with lads who I know and I trust and everything will be grand."

"What will I tell the Tans if they come to the house?"

"Tell them I went over to England to do some work for an uncle of mine, since times are so hard here."

They hadn't seen him since, although Mairéad had had a few messages that he was safe. A rash of ambushes on Army patrols and raids on RIC barracks were credited to Eamonn's unit, and Bert could not imagine when he might be able to return home.

CHAPTER 26

Máirtín Feeney was standing in his customary position in front of the blazing fire blocking the heat from the rest of the room.

"Is it afraid, you are?" he growled at Bert.

This time Bert was not warmed by the rosy glow of Máirtín Feeney's approval. Garlands of ivy and bunches of red-berried holly hung from the huge gilt mirror behind the big man, framing his florid face as he spat out the question. Ina had discreetly withdrawn when her father dismissed her with a nod of his head.

"No, I'm not afraid at all," said Bert, his chin lifting as it had when his father addressed him as a boy.

He had asked himself the same question. He glimpsed his reflection in the glass, a head taller than his portly interrogator, an arrogant tilt to his head. Bert looked down at his feet. He had paused often in recent days and stared at his reflection in the shaving mirror, wondering if he really was a coward. Leo had proven himself in battle. As an infantry man living like a rat in the trenches he overcame his fear, put behind him all the horrors he had witnessed and fought valiantly right until the end. Even then he had struggled back, wounded, to report to a commanding officer he despised. What courageous things had Bert ever done? He had nightmares for weeks after reading Leo's diary and was so frightened of being conscripted to the infantry and sent to the trenches he had volunteered for the Royal Naval Reserves. Then he was demobbed before he even finished his Naval training. All he had ever done for the Volunteers was carry messages and the one time he had carried a gun he had managed to lose it. Now he was telling Máirtín Feeney he didn't even want to be a courier any more.

"What is it, so? You have the perfect cover story and you are very useful to us, especially now when we have to keep in touch with so many flying columns."

"I don't believe that these tactics are the best ones to defeat the English," said Bert.

Ina's father snorted, "Well, you should know, I suppose."

Bert just stopped himself from responding. He took a deep breath.

"My brother Leo wrote a very moving diary about his time in France," he began, watching the older man's face for any signs of impatience.

"He wrote about how hard it was to kill other human beings just because they were wearing a different uniform."

"This is not the same at all," said Ina's father, turning his back on Bert to look into the fire.

"The war in Europe was fought for the sake of political alliances. This war we're fighting is for our very existence."

"There are men being killed every day on both sides, and families being burned out of their homes. There are no lines of demarcation, no rules of engagement, just random, needless killing. I don't want to be a part of it anymore."

"It is not random, needless killing. Any killing we are doing is just punishment for their atrocities. They're not even under any semblance of control by their own officers."

"We are in danger of reducing ourselves to their level, of losing our humanity, because we are so blinded by our rage."

"That's very eloquent Bert, but if we don't fight to the bitter end another generation of Irish children will be born into this miserable situation and grow up wondering why nothing was done about it."

"I want to do something about it. I just don't believe that violence is the answer. Look at how the world is changing after the war. Europe is taking a different shape. Empires are crumbling. We can negotiate our independence."

"Negotiate with the English? Do you read your history books, Bert? Hasn't it been tried, and failed?"

"History is being written now Mairtin, and we have a chance to shape it."

"So, you'll be standing as our next Irish Parliamentary Party TD then, will you?"

"You don't understand..."

"No, you are right, I do not understand," the big man said, swivelling around to face Bert again.

"Then we shall have to agree to differ," said Bert, looking back at him defiantly.

"I wonder what Michael Power would think if he could hear you talking like this."

Máirtín Feeney relished the wince he saw on Bert's face.

"I might write and tell him that our finest courier in the West has decided he is too good for us and won't be helping us any longer."

"That's not at all why..."

"Actions speak louder than words, young man. Off with you."

He dismissed Bert with a wave of his hand. Bert strode across the room and opened the tall drawing room door. He caught a glimpse of Ina's skirt disappearing through the kitchen door.

"Good evening to you, Sir," he said to Máirtín Feeney's broad back and closed the door quietly behind him.

Ina immediately rushed out.

"Is everything all right?" she asked.

"I'm afraid everything may be very far from all right," said Bert, holding her two tiny hands in his and looking into her eyes.

"I've made a decision to leave the Volunteers."

She took a sharp breath.

"But why?"

"I've explained it all to your father at great length and he is very angry. I want an independent Ireland as much as the next man, but I want the killing to stop."

"He will probably forbid me to see you again," Ina said, unable to meet his eye.

"I know, my darling. I've been grappling with this for months. If we are meant to be together for the rest of our lives I want you to be with me because of who I really am, not because of someone I am pretending to be to please your father."

"What about to please me?" she asked, looking up, her pale eyes swimming with tears.

"I don't believe that you would truly love a man who was responsible for the killing of others, when there is another way."

"I love my father. Are you asking me to choose between you?"

"I could never do that, Ina, *a ghrá*. I hope your father may find a way to accept me."

"Twice he has relented and let us see each other. I'm afraid he won't do it a third time," she said, a tear escaping.

He squeezed her hands before releasing them.

"I have nothing to offer you now, Ina. I could spend years in this limbo, performing endless Herculean tasks to prove my worth to your father and still have nothing to offer you. Something has to change. When it does, I will come back."

Ina's trembling smile warmed him. He turned away while he still had the strength and walked down the path, waving as the gate clicked closed behind him. The fair halo of her hair glowed in the lantern light and she lifted one hand to wave.

CHAPTER 27

The house at Saltwell Road had shrunk. Even the road seemed shorter as Bert walked down it, lopsided with hefting his suitcase. The houses huddled more closely together, whispering about his return. In his childhood every brass door knocker shone brightly and every front step gleamed from weekly scrubbing. White curtains billowed at open windows. Now the overwhelming colour that greeted him was grey. Even the sky was pulled down over the street like a grey woolly cap on an old wrinkly forehead. Bert whistled, trying to dispel the gloom. Instead of having happy homecoming thoughts he felt slightly apprehensive. Perhaps he should have written to warn them he was coming. His mother would have wanted to cook his favourite dinner and dust his room. Papa didn't like surprises. Should he knock at the front door, or just go around to the back? Why was he even hesitating? He turned into the alley.

A tall boy with dark hair was kicking a ball rhythmically against the brick wall, humming. Bert touched each gate with the tips of his fingers as he passed, idly wondering if a new family had moved into the road. The boy turned, and he beamed with delight.

"Bertie, Bertie, you came home!"

He ran towards Bert and barrelled into him, hugging him fiercely. Bert dropped his suitcase and the catch broke, spilling his clothes out onto the wet cobbles.

"Oh, sorry Bertie, I help you!" the boy cried, picking things up and shoving them haphazardly back into the case.

"Conor, you've grown so much I hardly knew you," Bert said, bending down so they were at eye level. "That was great kicking you were doing just now."

Conor stopped his frenetic activity, and blushed. "I do it ev'ry day. I knew you'd come home one day," he said.

Bert nodded enthusiastically.

"Not like Leo. He won't come home, never, will he?"

Conor shook his head solemnly as if repeating lines he had learned by rote. Later, Bert watched as Conor hefted the coal bucket and carried it into the yard. He had the same bruise, just above his sock line that had marked Bert's own leg for so long. His mother laid the table. She wouldn't let Bert lift a finger, and he felt like a welcome but distant family guest. New linoleum adorned the floor and there was a fresh oilcloth on the table. Bert felt as out of place in the familiar room as the gigantic Alice after she had followed the white rabbit underground and drunk the irresistible magic potion.

Mama moved as if she was in a dream and had not much to say. She had smiled when Bert came into the kitchen, but not fussed over him. She had recently been bed bound for several weeks with a severe bout of influenza and Bert had felt drawn to come home after receiving a letter from Louise. He sipped tea from the best china that was only taken out for special occasions. His mother had put a towel on the end of his old bed, and that gesture of hospitality had struck him as the most odd. He was not expected to share the worn and faded family towels now, but was singled out with a new, flower embroidered towel of his own. Conor bustled past and filled the coal scuttle, whistling through the gaps in his teeth.

"I'n strong now, Bert," he said proudly.

Then suddenly he had to put the bucket down while a chesty cough racked his body.

"You're extra strong because you have to be the man in the house now," said Bert.

He looked up and saw his father standing in the doorway.

"Papa's a man. I an a boy," said Conor, breathlessly, pointing at his heaving chest.

"That's true," said Bert, standing to shake his father's hand.

"Hello, son. Welcome home," his father said gruffly.

He placed his other hand over Bert's and shook it and the old warmth was in his look, from the time before he lost his Oxford scholar for a son.

"Boys are coming for tea," said Conor self-importantly.

"Which boys?" asked Bert.

"Tom and Kevin boys," said Conor, looking at Bert as if he had a screw loose.

"Oh, Eileen's boys," Bert replied, nodding.

He was curious to see his sister with her own family. She and Joe had wasted no time. His father asked all about his work and his mother asked roundabout questions about whether he had any interest in a girl. Conor soon lost interest in the adult conversation and went back out into the yard.

"Why can't Uncle Bert speak properly?" Four year old Tom asked later, as they finished the meal.

"Tom, that's ever so rude," his mother reprimanded him.

Louise explained, "Uncle Bertie went to Ireland and got himself an Irish accent."

She winked at her brother. Bert could not be cross with her. She was still living at home, a surrogate mother to Conor, bearing most of the burden of the housework as well as going out to work. His mother and sisters exchanged anecdotes about neighbours and their children and Bert felt out of step with the new rhythm of his family.

"It's funny but when I'm in Ireland, people keep telling me I have an English accent," he said. "Sometimes I wonder myself, am I one thing, or another?"

Try as he might, he could not imagine Ina sitting at this table even if it were laid with the white linen cloth and the best china cups. Did that mean he had to choose between these two worlds or could he straddle both? If he had to make a choice, where would he decide to plant his feet? The boys wriggled off their chairs and ran outside to play. Eileen and Louise soon followed. His mother looked worn out. His father puffed quietly on the pipe, and there was a kind of comfort in the companionable silence.

That night Bert lay in his narrow bed and stared at the familiar crack in the ceiling. He had to decide what to do next. Ina seemed unattainable. There might not be a job for Bert to go back to. People were being attacked and places ransacked just because they were connected with the Irish language. Stiofan Bairead, the Treasurer of the Gaelic League, had been arrested and charged with keeping arms at his office – the very place where Bert was interviewed. The Gaelic League had not been an illegal organisation for over a year now but the soldiers did not care for such niceties and Bert's well-rehearsed St Cuthbert's 'old boy' act might no longer protect him. At midnight, still unable to sleep, Bert heard the door of his parents' room opening. He sat up. Conor was coughing; a deep rattling sound. His mother tiptoed downstairs and Bert pulled on a dressing gown and followed her. She was filling the kettle.

"Can you stoke up the range, Bert? We need to get some steam into that boy's chest. He is completely congested."

Louise appeared, her hair dishevelled.

"No, darling, go back to bed, you have to go to work in the morning. I'll mind him."

Her mother pushed her gently back towards the stairs.

Louise was shaking her head. "It sounds like the croup, Mama."

"Please, darling, go back to bed now, before you get cold too," her mother gently scolded.

The kettle finally boiled. Bert strode up the stairs while his mother fetched a damp cloth and a bowl and gently pushed open the bedroom door. His father was standing over the boy gently stroking his forehead which was slick with sweat. Conor's eyes were rolling in his head and every bout of coughing seemed to shake his whole frame. His teeth were chattering even though there were blankets piled on

173

top of him. His mother stood with the steaming bowl and Bert tried to sit him up to inhale the steam. The boy's body was limp and his skin was clammy now. He seemed not to even have the strength to hold up his head.

"Will you go for the doctor?" his mother asked quietly.

Bert pulled on his boots and ran through the silent streets to the old doctor's house in Bensham Road. He knocked furiously at the front door. A window slid up and a night capped head leaned out. Bert tried not to shout and wake the whole street.

"Sorry to disturb you Doctor, but Conor is very ill. We think it might be the croup."

The doctor nodded, waved one hand and slid down the window. Less than a minute later the front door opened and he stepped out, his bulky leather bag in one hand.

"He's had a weak chest from birth, that poor boy," he said as they hurried through the streets. "It's one of the conditions that often afflicts the Mongoloid children, God love them."

Doctor Hilliard was a matter-of-fact, professional man Bert had known all his life and he had not meant to be cruel but Bert could not help remembering Audley's stinging comment when they were boys. 'They don't live long, it's God's way.'

His knuckles tingled with the memory. The Doctor led the way up the stairs. There was hardly any room left to stand in the tiny box room but Bert could not bear to go too far away. He peered around the door frame. Mama was kneeling on the floor beside the bed, holding Conor's limp hand. He was ominously quiet now, not even coughing. She looked up at the Doctor and he gently took her shoulders.

"Stand up, Mrs. O'Brien, please, so that I may examine the boy."

She stood up and moved to the foot of the bed. Tears streamed down her cheeks. Bert touched her elbow and she turned and tried a brave smile but it turned to a grimace. Bert could hear his father pacing up and down in the other bedroom. Louise was huddled beside him on the landing, her arms crossed and fear in her eyes. It was when he saw her face that Bert realised what was happening. She knew better than all of them what death looked like. The Doctor, having taken Conor's pulse and felt his forehead, shook his head.

"You might want to say your prayers," he said gently.

Bert knelt down first at the side of the bed and his mother sobbed, stepping into her own bedroom. Bert took his brother's hand and squeezed it. Louise sat on the edge of the bed and stroked Conor's head. Conor's eyelids flickered and he opened them briefly. A beautiful smile crossed his face.

"I'n goin' to see Jesus an' Mary an' the angels," he said.

Bert nodded.

"An' Leo?"

"Give our love to Leo," Bert said gently.

Conor's hand slackened and he closed his eyes. Papa took his turn by the bed, holding Conor's hand as it cooled, and Bert went to comfort his mother.

"I never showed him how much I loved him," she wailed.

"He knew you loved him, Mama, of course he did," Bert crooned.

He stroked her curved back where she lay curled up on her bed.

"I let Louise mind him. I wasn't myself, from the day I fell pregnant with him; something wasn't right. Even inside me he felt different to all the rest of you."

She raised a tear stained face to him. He was embarrassed and looked away.

"He was such a happy, loving little fellow," she said, fresh tears falling. "I sometimes found it hard to even give him a kiss at night. Not because I didn't love him, but because I was afraid to love him too much. He was always so *grateful* that it made me feel even worse."

Bert sat in silence. This must be how priests felt when people unburdened their darkest thoughts in the confessional. He was stunned. He had only ever seen Conor through his own eyes, his affectionate, funny little brother, full of determination playing football, and full of mischief at the dinner table.

"I knew I'd lose him young and I was trying to steel myself. Why, oh why didn't I just give him all the love I could while he was here?"

She twisted her skirt in her hands. Papa came in and nodded to Bert to leave and sat beside his wife on the bed.

Louise took charge of the practicalities. Through the wall at night Bert could hear the soothing rumble of his father's voice for hours and hours, punctuated by his mother's sobbing. After the funeral, the house was eerily quiet.

"Will you stay here now?" Louise asked one evening as they sat at the fire.

"Papa wants me to apply to study at Oxford again. As his last remaining son, I don't want to disappoint him."

"What do you want to do, yourself?" she asked. "You cannot live your life for him. You have to live it for yourself."

"He seems to have forgotten his own urge to go home and he can't understand what draws me back to Ireland."

Papa had even gone so far as to tell Bert that he was duty bound to go to Oxford, otherwise they had all wasted the last twenty years of their lives in England. In a fit of pique which he now regretted, Bert told his father that Dublin was almost unrecognisable, with barricades and wire fences around City Hall and burned out factory buildings everywhere. Many of the houses had been destroyed and in places like Balbriggan there were no habitable buildings left intact. It was no longer the beautiful capital city his father had left and it would be much better for Papa to keep his fond memories than to go back and face the grim reality of the present. He had seen tears in his father's eyes, and only then relented.

"Papa, you made a choice to come and live in England. It hasn't been so bad, surely? You enjoy your work at Guinness and they value you. Eileen has a lovely little family. Louise is doing a good job as a nurse. We've lost Leo and Conor but we might have lost them to the influenza or something else entirely if we had been living in Dublin. Aren't you glad to have a son who wants to be a good Irishman and go back home?"

His light-hearted tone had fallen on stone deaf ears.

Bert spent the next few weeks grappling with his conflicting loyalties. He avidly followed the Irish news in the daily papers. Regular newsreels shown in the cinema reassured the great British public that the 'Irish situation' would soon be under control. Seán O'Farrell wrote to Bert in great glee to tell him that news footage of the RIC capturing a Volunteer flying column in rural County Kerry was completely fictitious. It had been so carelessly constructed that audiences had spotted a Dublin landmark in the background. Bert's letter to The Times in London exposing the newsreel as a hoax was published and the next day his father brought a copy of the newspaper home from the office.

"Mr Hathaway drew it to my attention," he said, putting the folded paper on the kitchen table, with a ring drawn around Bert's letter.

Bert smiled wryly.

"You are really a man of words, aren't you, Bert?"

"It's all I've ever wanted to be."

"That's why I wanted you to have the University education. But you must do whatever you think is right."

Bert stood up and they embraced. His father cleared his throat and sat beside the fire.

"I think I will go back on the boat next week," said Bert and his father nodded, absent- mindedly poking at the bowl of his empty pipe.

Louise and his father had already left for work, and his mother stood on tiptoe to kiss his cheek. She cupped his face in her hand and her green eyes swam with unshed tears.

"Maybe one day we'll meet this lovely Ina of yours?"

Bert was choking on the lump in his throat. He lifted his suitcase and his mother held the front door open for him. The suitcase was heavy with cake and a new sweater his mother had feverishly knitted, working late into the night to finish it. When he looked back he imagined the stout, dark haired figure of Conor standing beside her holding on to her skirts with one hand and waving frantically with the other. Bert lifted his hand and waved goodbye to both of them.

CHAPTER 28

Ina's lace mantilla lifted slightly in the warm spring breeze as she stepped out of the church, her eyes avidly seeking him out, her hand resting lightly in the crook of her father's arm. Bert was standing to one side of the steps adjusting the bicycle clips around his ankles. Anyone watching him would wonder at the precision with which he had been re-adjusting them for almost five minutes now. Máirtín Feeney had obviously waited until the rest of the congregation had left the church and now stood vigorously shaking the priest's hand, a smile playing across his lips. His eyes were as quick as his daughter's to find Bert's huddled form. Only the slightest inclination of his head acknowledged Bert, who smiled and stepped forward, deciding to brave it out despite the slightly incongruous tapering of his trouser legs. Ina stifled a nervous giggle. Bert's hair had grown. It was sticking up like a chimney sweep's brush, although he had combed it with water just before coming into Mass. He flattened it absent-mindedly with his left hand while holding out the other to shake Máirtín Feeney's. She had to admire his temerity. Her father's arm stiffened, clamping her hand against his side so that she could not step away from him.

"Good morning, good morning, and a very happy Easter to you," Bert said, his lopsided grin lighting up his face as he saw Ina's blush.

He behaved as if the two men were the best of friends and stood making small talk for several minutes, carefully including Ina in the conversation but not allowing a single inappropriate glance to escape in her direction. Máirtín Feeney was well known for keeping a straight face but Ina could see the strain playing across his forehead and in the pounding at his temple. They were signs she had learned to read in childhood and did not auger well.

She tugged at his arm, trying to catch Bert's eye as she said, "Father, we are due at the O'Malley's for Easter dinner. It would be rude to be late."

"Yes of course, we must get going."

He did not bother to say farewell to Bert but turned sharply on his heel, swinging Ina in his wake and Bert was left standing there, looking after them. He wondered if Ina was doing a line with one of the O'Malleys and if that would explain both her blush and her eagerness to escape. He turned sadly back to the bicycle to find the priest still standing on the steps, although the rest of the congregation had vanished away, salivating at the prospect of their roast Easter lamb. The priest smiled benignly.

"Good day to you, Father, and Happy Easter," Bert said, steering the bicycle towards the gate.

"Come here to me, young man," said the priest. "I have something for you."

His Kerry accent was sometimes difficult for Bert to decipher but he had warmed to the older man in the last few weeks since his return from England. He preached peace from the pulpit when many other priests were waging war. Bert turned the bicycle awkwardly on the gravel path and Father Grogan came down the steps, slipping a small envelope from the wide sleeve of his cassock and holding it out. Bert's heart sank. He had carried many such envelopes from Máirtín Feeney to various towns around the county – the seal was unmistakable. The priest was smiling conspiratorially as Bert slit the envelope open and gleefully recognised Ina's hand. He quickly folded the letter again, embarrassed.

"Miss Feeney asked me to pass it on to you," said the priest.

"Thank you very much, Father. She must have been very quick to slip that to you while Mr Feeney wasn't looking!"

"Yes indeed," said the priest, winking.

"Happy Easter to you, and may God bless you."

Bert smiled and waved as he cycled up the road, knowing he would not have the willpower to last all the way back to Paddy and Noreen's house before reading the letter. He succumbed at his favourite spot just outside the town and crossed the field to sit by the river. The breeze had died down and although the air was cold, bright sunshine lit the rippling water. He allowed himself to be mesmerised by the play of the light on the water for a while before taking the letter out of his pocket.

* * *

Balla House, Dunmore
16th April 1921

My Dear Bert
I think it is unlikely we will have an opportunity to speak openly after Mass, and my father has instructed Brendan and even Bríd, the maid, not to carry any

letters for me that he has not seen first. I will ask Father Grogan to be the messenger and hope this reaches you safely.

We had some terrible news the day before yesterday. Michael Power has been arrested and is being held at the barracks in Athenry. We think he was trying to make his way home to Carraroe. The Black and Tans are burning families out of their homes on the slightest suspicion of Volunteer support and the whole area around Limerick and Ennis is a war zone. As you know, these farcical military courts impose the death penalty on the slightest pretext. I hope that his end is quick and that he is not subjected to torture before they shoot him or hang him. We have no news of Annie or Tomás, or even if they were travelling together. Brendan is gone to see what he can find out and might bring us some news when he comes back on Easter Monday. In the meantime Bert, all we can do is pray and we both know that Michael is a great man and he'll go straight to heaven, which is one consolation. I miss you terribly.

Yours truly,
Ina

Bert leapt off the rock, his foot slipping into the shallows in his haste to be upright. He shook the water off and galloped across the boggy field, rehearsing the best route to Athenry in his mind. How long would it take him to get there? He turned the bicycle and rode ferociously back into town, speeding through the silent streets as the waft of roasting meat and cabbage carried from some of the houses. The strains of Chopin reached his ears as he passed the Presbytery. Father Grogan was a great man for listening to the gramophone.

By one o'clock Bert was cycling through Tuam, his stomach rumbling now, and his mouth parched. There was very little activity outside the barracks. Bert quickly turned into the lane behind the safe house where he had often delivered messages. He dismounted and put the bicycle into a bush, then crept down the lane keeping his head low behind the garden hedges until he reached number twenty three. It had been almost six months since he had reason to come here. The curtains were drawn over the windows so he could not see who was inside before knocking quietly at the shabby, peeling back door.

"Who is it?" a timid woman's voice called.

He put his mouth as close as he could to the keyhole.

"Bert O'Brien," he muttered.

The door opened suddenly and he almost fell inside. A strong hand grabbed the collar of his coat and pulled him roughly across the room before he had a chance to regain his balance. The barrel of a gun pressed into the tender skin at his temple.

"What kind of nerve have you, turning up out of the blue like that?" a rough voice asked him.

Bert looked up to see Brendan standing in front of him, grinning in his simple way but making no effort to intervene. There was no sign of a woman.

Bert shrugged off the hand that held him and stood up straight.

"I'm on my way to Athenry. Michael Power needs help."

Brendan looked slightly surprised and then nodded. There was a loud guffaw of laughter from the other man who was nearly as tall as Bert, with a narrow, bearded face and long muscular arms in a grubby undershirt. He had high cheekbones and cold blue eyes and his sandy hair was tousled with sleeping rough.

"Does he indeed? And what kind of help did you think you could give him?" the man sneered.

"Who are you?" Bert asked, undaunted by his uncouth manners.

"Who am *I*?" the man asked.

The likes of Brendan deferred to him without question and he wasn't used to young spalpeens like the one in front of him, challenging his authority.

"*Níl orm freagairt ar bith do dhuine ar bith ach amháin do Éamon Ó Fearáil.* I need answer to no-body but Eamonn O'Farrell."

"Is Eamonn here?" Bert asked excitedly.

He hadn't seen him since last November.

"It's none of your concern who is here or not here," the man said after a brief flicker of doubt in his eye.

"Are you a spy? Do you know what we do with spies?"

The man's upper lip curled, showing pale anaemic gums and rotten teeth.

He put his face close to Bert's, and his foul breath made Bert gag.

"*Do you?*"

Bert shook his head, unwilling to take another breath so that he could speak.

"We cover them in tar and tie them up onto a pole in Main Street, so everyone can see what we do to traitors."

He hissed the last syllable.

Bert had had enough.

"If Eamonn is here, I would like to speak to him."

"Oh, would you now, and have you brought your calling card, so I can put it on a silver platter and take it in to him and announce you?"

It had been a while since anyone had mocked his English accent, but Bert was unmoved.

He turned to Brendan.

"Brendan, there's a good lad, is Eamonn here, tell me?"

Brendan nodded, pointing upstairs before the other man could intervene.

"He's asleep," said Brendan.

"Does he know about Michael Power?" Bert asked.

"I only got here a few minutes before you. I didn't tell him yet. I didn't want to disturb him."

Brendan looked sheepish.

"Brendan, every minute counts! They will probably shoot Michael Power tomorrow. We have to get him out!" Bert said urgently, completely ignoring the other man.

"Brendan, you big eejit, why didn't you tell me that before?"

The man leapt to his feet and went up the stairs two at a time.

Brendan shrugged.

"I couldn't get a word in edgeways, Bert. You can see the way he is."

"I'm glad you're here, Brendan." Bert said.

Then he whispered, "Who is he?"

"One of Eamonn's lads. I think he has a screw loose," Brendan murmured.

"He behaves like that with everyone. His name is Liam Greaney. He's from Oughterard I think. They're like that, himself and Eamonn."

Brendan held up two fingers, tightly intertwined. Eamonn came racing down the stairs after Liam, his face wet with the water he had splashed on to wake himself up.

"Bert, how the devil are you?"

Eamonn took him in a bear hug, squeezing the breath out of him.

"Grand. You're not looking so great yourself," Bert replied, scanning Eamonn's three day old stubble and red rimmed eyes.

"I'm alive anyhow and that's the main thing," said Eamonn, pumping Bert's hand.

"This fella is a good one, Liam. Don't be hard on him, he's one of us."

Liam would not meet Bert's eye.

"So, Bert, what's this news I hear about Michael Power?"

"They arrested him and he's in the barracks at Athenry," Bert said.

"Do you know any more about it, Brendan?" Eamonn asked.

Brendan reported that Máirtín Feeney had had a message that Michael Power was picked up on Friday night outside Athenry and a gun was found on him.

"They must have surprised him, so. That's not like him at all. Any news of the family?"

Brendan shook his head.

"We'll have to get him out tonight. Who's with me?" Eamonn asked.

Three heads nodded in agreement.

"Have we four bicycles between us?"

More nods.

"We'll leave one by one, over the next hour. Bert, you go first. We'll meet at five o'clock at the Flanagan's barn. It's just as you come into the town of Athenry on the right hand side – you can't miss it. There's a big red gate and a fine oak tree to one side of it."

Bert was on his bicycle again before remembering the hunger that had made him stop at the safe house. He cycled hard, wanting to have time for a rest in the barn and maybe to find an egg or something to eat before the others arrived. The adrenalin coursing through him made him light headed and it would be a long night. He had no idea what Eamonn was planning but Bert had complete faith in his abilities. Before the night was out, Michael Power would be free.

It was dark inside the barn and the dust made Bert want to cough but he lay still, listening to his heartbeat slowing, trying to calm his racing thoughts. He might die tonight or be arrested and thrown into a cell. He peered out through a crack between the stones of the barn wall and watched the last rays of the milky sunlight disappear behind a scrubby hawthorn bush. Would that unremarkable sunset be his last?

He lay back on the sweet-smelling hay staring at the wooden beams of the roof that were barely visible in the gloom. It didn't seem to matter that this might be his last night alive. Now that his body was quiet his thoughts were eerily calm. He hoped that Leo had found this calm while he was lying somewhere wounded, wondering that very same thing – will this be my last few hours alive? Would Leo have wished to change the words in his diary or would they have stood true in the face of imminent death? Did he die happy, knowing he was fighting for what was right? Bert had never really thought about dying. If tonight were to be his last there were no words written anywhere to reassure his family that he had died happy, fighting for what was right. Should he have kept Leo's diary a secret?

The day that Audley had come to the house in Saltwell Road would always be etched in Bert's mind, one of those turning points in life that only later assume their real significance. Bert had been alone in the house with Papa at work and Mama visiting a sick old lady at the other end of the parish. Conor was at Eileen's house. Bert had just stoked up the fire in the range as Mama had requested, so there would be enough heat in the oven to bake bread when she came home. Bert was studying at the kitchen table when a knock at the front door surprised him. Anyone who knew them well would come to the back door and the rent was not due until Friday. He opened the door expecting to find a travelling salesman selling funeral insurance or furniture on tick. He was shocked to see Audley standing there, taller than Bert remembered, his uniform neatly pressed, with polished buttons and his waxed moustache standing to attention, as he was. Audley was just as surprised to see Bert and the oft rehearsed words of condolence for Leo's parents never came to his lips.

"You!" he said as though he was accusing Bert of a crime.

"Audley, come in," said Bert graciously.

He opened the door wide and wished he had lit the parlour fire so that he could show Audley in there.

"The kitchen is warmer, if you'd like to go straight through," he said.

He closed the front door and followed Audley along the passage, which suddenly seemed narrow, ashamed of the shabby paintwork and patched linoleum. Audley stood awkwardly in the kitchen, holding his peaked uniform cap in front of him with two hands.

"Sit down, Audley. I am alone in the house. Can I offer you some tea?"

"No, thank you, O'Brien. I shan't stay long."

Bert could sense Audley's discomfiture as he glanced sideways at the Sacred Heart picture above the mantelpiece.

"How can I help you?" Bert asked.

He had obviously come with a message of some kind but seemed unable to deliver it. Audley reached into the pocket of his army tunic and withdrew a small parcel. He put it on the kitchen table. Bert sat down opposite him and they both stared at it for some time before Audley spoke. He spoke man to man and when he had finished Bert took a deep breath and looked at the parcel again, wondering if he should throw it straight in the fire.

"I have agonised about what to do for the best," said Audley.

Bert was tempted to say that if Audley hadn't read Leo's diary in the first place, he would not have had the dilemma, and could have simply sent it on with Leo's other personal effects without knowing the contents.

"I know you'll wonder how a gentleman could have read another man's private diary." Bert simply sat silently waiting for Audley to go on.

"I have a confession to make. I was curious about what your brother might have written about me."

Bert nodded. That was understandable.

"When I read the diary, I was very moved. Your brother had a very compelling turn of phrase... like you, I suppose."

Bert refused to meet his eye, to accept the premise that this man could offer an olive branch, however tenuously.

"I wrote the letter of condolence to your parents and I kept it for a day and a night before sending it because I didn't know whether I should include the diary. I thought it would distress them."

Bert felt his throat constricting as he stared at the innocuous parcel on the table. What could Leo have written in this diary to move the stone heart of a man like Audley?

"I decided to keep the diary and to deliver it to them in person if I survived the war. I hoped to find a way of explaining it, of softening the blow. Now that I am sitting in front of you I find myself unable to do that, or indeed to justify my actions. As an only child I cannot imagine what it must be like to lose a brother. I have seen enough men die to know that losing a friend or fellow officer is painful enough. Your brother was a brave man. I sent him out with a special reconnaissance party to establish the exact position of a new German trench. Leo was the only man to return. The Germans somehow knew they were coming and lay in wait for them in a forward fox hole. They slit my men's throats."

His Adam's apple bobbed as he gulped.

"But not Leo's?"

"Yes, his too. They left him for dead. He crawled back across no man's land. It took hours. Dawn was breaking when he slid over the sandbags and fell into the trench."

Audley's eyes briefly met Bert's and then he looked down. Bert pounded the table, and Audley's head shot up, alarmed.

"Do not, do not dare to expiate your guilt by telling me how my brother died!" Bert shouted, tears streaming down his face.

They were tears of anger that Audley of all people should see his grief.

"No, O'Brien, please, let me finish!" Audley begged, holding up his hands in supplication.

"Your brother. Leo. He drew a map. He managed to summon enough strength to draw a map of the trench location. We used it. We took the trench!"

The last statement was made with such emphasis, such triumphalism that Bert was stunned briefly into silence. Audley was nodding vigorously as though to a child who has finally understood the complexities of multiplication.

"He died for a map?"

"A very important map. It was the first step in breaking through the German lines."

"I see you have been promoted," Bert said, nodding at the three stars on Audley's sleeve.

Audley nodded, beaming. Did he think they were the best of friends now that he had unburdened himself?

"You had a 'good war?'"

Audley had the grace to squirm.

"Perhaps it is for the best that I should have found you here alone and that you should read the diary and decide if you wish to share it with your parents. You are a man of principle, and you will know the right thing to do."

He stood up abruptly, pushing his chair back and pulling his cap on by the peak. He stretched out his hand to shake Bert's. In his eyes Bert could see no trace of the vicious and cruel boy he had known. He met the look and returned the firm handshake and led Audley to the front door again.

"Good luck, Bert," Audley said.

He stood and saluted before he strode down the road.

If Bert died tonight and his parents had his effects returned to them they would open the parcel with his few clothes, his photograph of the family, his embroidered handkerchief from Ina, and Leo's little brown diary. His Mama and Papa would have the double grief of losing Bert and then reading the diary and losing Leo all over again. They would lose the optimistic, brave and daring Leo who had left the house in his uniform that day in 1916, whistling happily. They would lose the Leo who had written those cheerful letters from the trenches, reminiscing about Mama's beef stew and thanking her for sending cake. They would know that aguish and despair and loneliness and grief had filled Leo's last days. They would finally know how futile it had all been. Bert dashed away a tear from his eye and promised himself that if he survived tonight he would destroy Leo's diary as his brother had always intended. There was a low whistle outside and Brendan came quietly into the barn, calling his name.

Eamonn had devised a plan while he was cycling along and he explained it as they sat huddled in the dark, afraid to show a light through the cracks in the walls. He knew the layout of the Barracks and thought they could enter by a back door which faced onto a lane behind the main street. He had already arranged for two men to meet them there, one of them the local publican who regularly delivered stout to the Barracks and often picked up useful intelligence for the Volunteers.

"For a Protestant, he's a sound man," said Eamonn.

"He'll knock at the back door with a barrel of porter and once they open it we'll come out from behind the wall and overwhelm them. There's only three of them on duty – they're spread very thin these days."

Bert's heart was pounding now and although he hadn't eaten he felt his bowels heaving. The others were calm and focussed so he forced himself to listen and when the time came to leave the barn he was glad of the fresh, cold air on his face. A frost was settling, coating everything in a light coat of white. Once in the town he found the place where he was to hide easily enough, relieved to have the job of lookout. All was quiet by eight o'clock and his breath plumed as the air cooled. He muffled his mouth with a scarf, not knowing how alert the sentry might be. He could hear the tuneless singing of the Publican and the rattle of the small cart he was using to wheel the barrel of stout down the street. Bert peered out from his hiding place behind the high wall around a builder's yard and watched as the Publican turned in the gate and went around the back of the Barracks. He was joined by another man, his tall, rangy shadow merging with the Publican's. Bert gripped his hurley so tightly that his hands ached in the cold air. He kept his eyes on the main street and craned his neck to hear the slightest sound – the knock on the door carried in the night air followed by the laughter of the Publican as he joked with the man on duty. There was a muffled yelp and the sound of scuffling boots and the quick slam of a heavy door. Silence descended again.

The windows of the Barracks were boarded up so there was no clue from light or shadow about what might be happening inside. Bert dreaded the sound of a motor or the clipped tones of English officers coming to inspect the Barracks. Not a sound emerged from any of the houses or even from the public house. It seemed as though hours went by in the strained silence before there was more scuffling and suddenly the huddled forms of three men emerged from behind the Barracks. Eamonn gave a whistle and waved his arm at Bert and then they were all scurrying down the street. Bert had taken a single step towards the place where his bicycle was hidden when he caught a movement out of the side of his eye. A dark shape flitted behind the building next door to the Barracks, as if to follow the men. Bert ran silently across the moonlit street and flattened his back against the wall of the building opposite. Holding his breath, he edged towards the corner. A gate clanged shut and there was a whispered curse, an English accent, less than a yard from where Bert stood.

There was no time to think. Bert launched himself from behind the wall, swinging his raised hurley. It connected with a grisly thump with the nose of a uniformed RIC man as he stepped towards the road. His gun fell from his grasp and his knees crumpled. He landed face first, his reactions too slow to put out his hands. Bert looked down, shocked by the spreading pool of blood that encircled the insensible man's head, dark against the icy road. He dropped the hurley and ran to retrieve his bicycle. Then he doubled back and picked up the gun, shoving it in his trouser pocket. He pulled down the scarf, sickened by inhaling his own hot metallic breath, not caring that his identity was no longer hidden. He pedalled hard, ignoring the danger of slipping on the ice, desperate to put some distance between himself and the dark pool of blood. A few miles out of town the others were waiting impatiently, huddled in the gateway to a field, out of immediate view of the road.

"Come on, Bert. What took you so long?"

They mounted without waiting for an answer and cycled for miles before finally stopping at midnight, the full moon high and clear in the cloudless sky.

"Well, that's another Easter Monday that I will hold dear in my heart forever," said Michael Power, his round face glowing like a second moon in the low roofed cow byre they had occupied. He turned his beaming smile on Bert.

"It's good to see you again, Bert O' Brien."

They shook hands. Bert was shivering uncontrollably and his teeth were chattering.

"Where will you go now?"

He wondered what it was like to be a marked man, unable to show his face in daylight.

"I'll keep going to Carraroe. Annie and Tomás are gone ahead of me, thank God. I was thinking I'd lift a few rifles from the big house outside Athenry – one of the stable lads told me the gun room was easy to break into, and he was to meet me outside and show me. But the RIC boyos were hiding in the grounds and as soon as I came out of the cover of the woods, they had me. Whether it was a trap or just bad luck I'll never know, but wasn't I the lucky fella to have you as friends?"

He shook every man's hand again and everyone was quiet. Bert remembered the evenings when Michael had held court in his cottage, always seeming to say everything that needed to be said.

"You might have a use for this," he said, holding up the gun.

"Holy Mary, Mother of God, where did you get that from?" Brendan asked breathlessly. He was looking around as if Bert could have picked it up from the straw.

"There was an RIC man following you. I relieved him of it," Bert said.
Michael slapped him so hard on the back he coughed.

"I left him a hurley instead."
Michael's laugh was so loud that Eamonn had to jump on him and push his face into the straw until he quietened down.

"I knew we'd make a real Volunteer out of you, Herbert Vincent O'Brien," said Michael, spitting out bits of straw.

They stayed for an hour, sharing a loaf of brown bread and gulping down warm milk from the cow which was surprisingly accommodating about being milked in the middle of the night. Brendan and Bert rode together, glad of the moon and the stillness. The dawn chorus was tuning up as Bert wearily climbed his loft ladder, hoping for an hour of rest before Noreen would stir. He lay on the mattress and held Ina's handkerchief to his lips, imagining that it still smelt of her. He dared to hope that Brendan would make a good report of him to Máirtín Feeney. His legs were twitching and he felt the blood pumping around his body. He could imagine the flow of it through his heart and lungs and then out to each fingertip and down to his toes. He stroked the brown leather cover of Leo's diary. There was no need to destroy it now. The sickening thud of the hurley against the RIC man's nose still reverberated in his hands although when he held them up in front of his face there was not even a tremor.

Noreen's manner was chilly when Bert came down the ladder, woken from a light doze by the sounds of her morning routine.

"I'm sorry I didn't get back for my dinner yesterday," he said when she put a dish of porridge in front of him with a loud clunk on the wooden table.
This was becoming a habit.

"I suppose you got invited to the Feeney's and you couldn't say no," she said, sullenly. He shook his head vigorously.

"No, Noreen, honestly, they hardly stopped to talk to me after Mass. It was something else entirely."

"I'm sure it was more important than coming home for your lovely Easter dinner," she sniffed.

She poured tea from the black bottomed teapot into his cup.

"Michael Power was taken into the barracks at Athenry. They would have shot him this morning. We had to go and rescue him," said Bert.

She froze, her mouth open, the china jug of milk held in one hand. She leaned on the table with the other like a ship listing into a strong wind.

Paddy came through the front door just then.

"Well, Bert, it's not often we see Noreen lost for words. It must have been a good excuse you trotted out!"

Noreen finally took a breath.

"I declare to God, Bert, you put the heart crossways in me!"

She sat down, milk sloshing from the jug.

"Is he all right? Are you all right?"

She craned her neck, looking at him from all angles to find wounds or bruises on him.

"He's fine, and I'm fine, thank God," said Bert.

He was suddenly overwhelmed with the significance of it all, now that it was over.

"How on earth did you do it?" Noreen asked.

She pointed at the teapot indicating that Paddy should help himself. It was the first time in their marriage and he was slightly taken aback. He poured a cup and put the teapot back on the hearth and covered it with the green knitted cosy his mother had made them for Christmas. Bert recounted the events, leaving out the bit about the hurley. The RIC man was probably eating his breakfast now with nothing worse than a bruised head and a broken nose. Paddy laughed again.

"Well, aren't you the dark horse?"

Noreen was rubbing her hands with glee.

"I didn't actually *do* anything," said Bert tentatively, testing his own resolve.

"That's not the point," said Paddy, "and anyway, you did do something. Who knows how long Brendan would have sat there, wondering when to wake up Eamonn? If you hadn't been so quick to get them all going the whole undertaking would have failed."

"Being a look out doesn't really count for much," said Bert.

"You need your wits about you in these situations and Brendan, as grand a lad as he is, hasn't many wits about him – you were the one who made all the difference," said Noreen.

Her chest swelled with an adoptive mother's pride. Bert had to look away as Paddy poured a generous dollop of dark red plum jam into the middle of his porridge. Noreen treated herself to the second cup of tea she usually saved until after she had cleared up.

"When are you back to the lessons?"

"Thursday," said Bert, whose thoughts were running along the same lines.

"Ina might not be there, but I'm going into the school during the day to hear the children's *Buntús* recitals next week."

"It will only be a matter of time, now," Noreen said, sighing happily. Finding the right person to marry was the key to everyone's happiness. Even miserable oul' Máirtín Feeney knew that much.

"Bert, you might need to give some thought to how you could earn a decent living to support a family," she said thoughtfully.

Bert took the last spoonful of his cold porridge and swigged down his tea.

"It's all I've been thinking about since I came back."

He caught the indulgent, conspiratorial look that passed between Noreen and Paddy.

CHAPTER 29

July 1921

Mairéad put the *Freeman's Journal* in front of Bert on the kitchen table. "The Truce is all over the papers today."

The back door was open and the sounds of neighbourhood children laughing and running around in the late sunshine after their tea brought back memories of the lane behind the house at Saltwell Road. Mairéad's garden was a colourful chaos of dahlias and chrysanthemums, and the heady smell of exotic white lilies occasionally drifted inside. His mother would have loved such luxurious foliage in her own back yard but it always seemed to be full of clutter – old bits of wood that Papa thought might come in useful, half-completed go-carts made with old pram wheels and even a rusting iron bedstead that should have been given to the rag and bone man long ago.

Bert looked at the headlines and read aloud from the lead article.

"*'Ireland's four delegates are well chosen. Mr de Valera, Mr Griffith, Mr Austin Stack and Mr Burton represent at once the intelligence, the fighting spirit, and the self-sacrifice of Sinn Fein. What they put their hands to, the country will countersign'*.

Do you think it will be safe for Eamonn to come home, now?" he asked.

"It seems more real, now that it's in the papers," she said.

"I couldn't believe it when Seán told me the ceasefire orders had come through from the Headquarters. I thought it might be some kind of Dublin Castle trick to flush the men out of hiding and then arrest them all."

"Even the English would not be devious enough to come up with that plan," Bert said. "But they seem to have finally realised that they won't bully us into submission. De Valera did the right thing to refuse to talk to them until a truce was agreed."

"It's the first time they've conceded that the *Dáil* is worthy of negotiating with, anyhow. That's progress in the right direction."

"They must have been kicking themselves, with King Edward one minute making his speech in Belfast saying that the strife should end and the future of Ireland was in the hands of the people and then De Valera, our democratically elected representative, being arrested by the King's army the very same day. They had to eat humble pie and let him out again."

"I, for one, am ready for peace."

Mairéad sat down opposite him and put her face in her hands.

"I miss Eamonn, Bert."

"I can't imagine how you cope with the situation so well. How long have you and Eamonn been married?"

"Twenty seven years, this year," she said, sighing. "We weren't even twenty when we got married. We're the same age – only a month between us. He's getting too old for this – I'll be delighted if he doesn't have to spend another winter out sleeping in fields and barns. I know I said we should fight to the death, but I'm worn out with it."

"It says here that a delegation has been sent to London continue the negotiations," Bert read out some of the article.

"Please God they will put an end to all the killing soon," Mairéad said, staring out at the lengthening shadows in the garden.

"Did you see the bit where it says Griffith is leading the delegation? I wonder why De Valera isn't going?" Bert asked, and then read on.

"He's saying he's the President of Ireland and as the head of state he will only negotiate with King Edward."

"That's arrogance for you," said Mairéad, smiling.

"I wonder if there's another reason for it," reflected Bert.

"What do you mean?" Mairéad said distractedly.

She was still thinking about Eamonn.

"Well, if for any reason the negotiations fail, Dev could dissociate himself from them."

"Or, if you look at it another way, he's holding himself back so he can come in at the last minute and save the day," said Mairéad.

"Either way, whatever his motivation, it seems to be a self-interested rather than statesman-like attitude to take, wouldn't you say?" asked Bert.

Mairéad almost laughed. For a young fella, Bert could sound so pompous sometimes.

"From what Eamonn tells me about him, he is a man who doesn't have many doubts. He probably thinks we could win if we just kept on fighting – we would wear the English down in the end."

"Well Turkey was made a republic this year, even if they're still fighting with the Greeks about where exactly the borders are, and Mongolia declared itself independent of China. The world is changing. The English will ultimately have to accept that, but the question is, how much more bloodshed do we need to have?"

"That's a very profound conversation you're having," a voice came from the kitchen door.

Mairéad jumped up and was across the room and enfolded in Eamonn's arms almost before Bert looked up from the newspaper.

"It's great to see you, altogether."

Eamonn smiled broadly across the room at Bert while gently stroking Mairéad's hair.

Bert stood up and shook Eamonn's hand.

"It's great to see you looking so hale and hearty, considering what you've been through recently. I think I'll go out for a stroll now and leave you two in peace."

Bert ignored their protests and went out, closing the front door gently behind him. He felt empty inside. He should be jubilant that a truce had been agreed – all over Europe and the Middle East, national borders were being negotiated. The British had their fingers in so many pies that surely they would welcome an opportunity to resolve the situation in Ireland as soon as possible? The difficulty would be reaching agreement about Northern Ireland. It wasn't as easy as just drawing the lines on a map which they seemed to be so fond of doing, deciding which pieces of pre-war empires should be shared out where.

He was walking through the town with his head down, his hands behind his back, completely oblivious to his surroundings and trying to pin down the reasons for the empty feeling inside him when there was a shout from across the road.

"Hiy, Bert!"

He looked up and Seán was crossing towards him, smiling and looking oddly like a penguin with his dark swept back hair, rotund body and dapper walk.

"Is it true? Is he home?"

Bert nodded and Seán didn't even stop to talk but ran towards Eamonn's house.

So much for privacy for the reunited man and wife thought Bert, wryly. Then it hit him. Her instinct to run into his arms, his embrace, their wholeness as they stood together. Bert yearned for the certainty of that kind of love. Ina was still way beyond his reach, even though her father's hostility had recently been less marked. Bert suspected that Máirtín Feeney's reservations revolved more around his financial wherewithal than his republican credentials. He could try to get a junior clerical job in a solicitor's office or a shop but how long might it take for him to be earning enough to justify a proposal of marriage? No, he needed to find a job with decent prospects, so he could support a family.

Mairéad had suggested coyly that Máirtín Feeney might consider passing his business interests on to a son in law since he had no sons in a position take it over. Bert had absolutely no interest in the building business. He would find a way to provide for Ina by himself, without being beholden to anybody.

The next months were strangely dream-like. Bert cycled along the same familiar roads but instead of anxiously craning his neck to see if there was a road block around the next corner he just surveyed the gently rolling hills, enjoying the ride. Over the long, sunny summer freckles appeared on the bridge of his nose and Ina teased him that he looked more like a naughty school boy than a teacher. He would self-consciously flatten his bristly hair and straighten his jacket, making her laugh even more. They were allowed a few minutes to chat after Mass and one Sunday Bert had even escorted her home. Máirtín Feeney was waiting on the front door step when they arrived so Bert did not linger but waved breezily before mounting his bicycle and pedalling home to Paddy and Noreen's. Whenever he remembered that special bicycle ride from Kilkeely to Dunmore after the dance, Ina's hair tickling his chin, her narrow shoulders enfolded between his outstretched arms on the handlebars and the light scent of her skin filling his nostrils as they swooped through the silent dark night, he despaired. After that auspicious start, it seemed as if the romance had been going in reverse and he would have to do something radical to change its direction, before he was driven demented.

The Autumn passed with occasional news about the negotiations in London. Michael Collins was getting all the credit for the good progress that was being made, and there was optimism that an agreement would be reached before the winter. Eamonn was restless. He found it difficult to adjust to life at home after six months in the flying column, constantly on the alert, sleeping rough, finding food wherever it was on offer, and making friends with new people who thought the same way as he did, and weren't afraid to take a few risks for the sake of Ireland. Mairéad confided in Bert that Eamonn's sole purpose in life had been fighting for so long that it would nearly be an anti-climax if an agreement was signed.

"He's only restless because nothing is certain yet. Once we all know where we stand, he'll go back to normal, I'm sure," said Bert to console her one night.

Eamonn was late coming back from Seán's house and Mairéad was worrying that they might be up to no good.

"He should be concentrating on the business, now that he's home. We've used up all our savings," she said.

It was the first time Bert had ever heard Mairéad express any doubts about her husband.

"Maybe I could help with the business?" he suggested.

He immediately regretted the suggestion. A clerk's wage in an agricultural feed business would be no better than one elsewhere and the work would certainly be no more interesting than Máirtín Feeney's building business. Perhaps his father had been right – he should not have turned down the opportunity to take his degree. Coming down from Oxford this year, he could have walked through so many open doors – into the law, insurance, or any number of other professions, with introductions to the right people in the right circles, wearing the right tie, of course. He would be as good as any man to court Ina. But if he had gone down that road he never would have met Ina. Eamonn breezed in just after midnight.

"You're looking very serious, the two of you," he said, bringing in the cold November air.

Mairéad shrugged and rattled the poker in the grate to settle the embers for the night. Eamonn looked at Bert, raising one eyebrow in a question. Bert didn't know what to say so he bade them both goodnight and went upstairs.

He was never quite sure how vocal he should be about his opinions these days. Paddy and Noreen were adamant that the Truce was worthwhile and optimistic that whatever was agreed in London would be better than what had gone before. Eamonn and Seán, and to some extent Mairéad, were more worried about the rumours that the English would renege on the spirit of the negotiations and might even be stringing the discussions out to gain time to regroup and send in more troops. Opinions in his classes were split too. Now the standard of their Irish was high enough to have debates on the subjects of independence, empire and statehood. Bert enjoyed listening to the heated discussions but rarely interjected with his own opinions. He was still an outsider and an Englishman, albeit an acceptable one.

December came and a deep frost settled on the land. Cattle were brought in to shelter and sheep were given extra hay. The brittle grass snapped under his feet as Bert leaned on a frost rimed gate one cold bright morning and ate his bread. He contemplated the tussocky fields that stretched out in front of him. The boggy brown soil near the gate was pockmarked with hoof marks, some hosting tiny frozen pools. Everything lay still and dormant. The ragged cawing of a crow was the only sign of life. The sun crept above the hedge as Bert gulped down a mouthful of cold buttermilk from the can he carried on the handlebar and he shivered in distaste. There were some things he would never get used to. He inhaled the stillness in a single cold breath and mounted his bicycle again. He felt the sun rising higher over his shoulder, the fresh golden light sweeping the frosted tips from the grass ahead of him to the east and he laughed out loud in the silent morning, suddenly filled with optimism.

He remembered that euphoric feeling three days later as he sat at the fire with Mairéad, Eamonn and Seán, raising a glass of stout in celebration. Collins and Griffiths had pulled it off – the Treaty had been signed. Mairéad kept leaning over to put her head on Eamonn's shoulder as if reminding herself that he would not need to run again, that they could spend every evening at the fireside together.

"We'll have Christmas together this year, anyhow," she said contentedly.

Seán could not resist adding a note of realism to their celebration.

"It won't go down well everywhere," he said.

"They're already saying that Michael Collins is a traitor and that he should never have agreed to the six counties staying with Britain."

"I think it's true, what the man said himself, 'This agreement gives us the freedom to achieve freedom,'" said Eamonn.

"I want a Republic as much as the next man, and the whole country in it, but I think Michael Collins did the best he could. Lloyd George was threatening a 'real and terrible war' on us if the Treaty wasn't signed."

"That's blackmail," muttered Bert.

Mairéad sighed. "I couldn't have coped with you going off fighting again, Eamonn," she said.

"I know it sounds selfish, but we can get on with our lives now. We've won the first battle."

"Mind you, the Treaty still has to be ratified by the *Dáil*," said Seán.

"But it has been signed!" said Bert.

"De Valera is claiming he never gave authority to the plenipotentiaries to actually sign the Treaty. They were supposed to come back to the *Dáil* with a draft agreement."

Seán was waving a copy of the Irish Independent, lines scored through the daily report of the *Dáil* debate.

"Why didn't he go to London himself then?" said Mairéad indignantly.

Then she nodded towards Bert.

"Bert was right. Dev kept himself one step removed so he could shout 'foul' when it didn't go completely his way."

"It's not over yet, lads," said Seán, shaking his head.

Mairéad waved her hand at him.

"You're full of doom and gloom, over there in the corner. Let's enjoy the one bit of good news we've had in a while, and we'll see what happens."

Christmas greetings were only briefly exchanged by the members of the congregation as they poured out of ten o'clock Mass on Christmas day, superseded by the immediacy of the debate about the sermon. Father Grogan had excelled himself.

"He must have spent a good while writing that sermon," said Máirtín Feeney to Tomás O'Malley as they shouldered out through the crush of people lining up to shake the priest's hand.

His old friend shook his head.

"Priests should stick to the teachings of Our Lord and steer clear of politics, in my opinion," he said.

Tomás O'Malley pointedly walked off down the main street without wishing Father Grogan a Happy Christmas. In principle, Máirtín Feeney couldn't agree with him more, but on this occasion Máirtín concurred with everything the priest had said. There was a time for fighting and a time for peace. While it wasn't perfect, the terms of the Treaty were the best that could be got by the best men to get them and the people of Ireland should support it. They could all start afresh in the new year of 1922, committed to peace and to the success and prosperity of the Free State.

Bert was relieved when he saw the look on Ina's fathers face. He had watched Tomás O'Malley's thunderous expression as the priest's sermon had unfolded and his heart had sunk. Tomás and Máirtín had been friends since their National School days and they rarely disagreed. Máirtín's expression, as always, was difficult to read but if Máirtín Feeney was anti-Treaty, Bert could wave goodbye to any hope of courting Ina. When they knelt for the Eucharistic Prayer, Bert rested his forehead on his hands, leaning on the pew in front of him, praying hard that Máirtín would be persuaded by the priest's words. Ina teased him later, saying his eyebrows had looked as if they were knitted together, he was frowning so hard. He smiled.

"You should have been paying attention to your prayers, instead of looking at me."

"I was concentrating on my prayers," she said coquettishly.

She quickly glanced around to make sure her father was still engaged in conversation.

Bert held out his arm.

"Do you think I would be permitted to escort you home today?"

Ina tentatively placed her hand on his sleeve and looked for her father's approval. He was talking to Father Grogan and pumping his hand, congratulating him on a great sermon. He nodded jovially towards her and Bert felt included in his smile, so they stepped together through the church gates. A few people nodded, and Paddy waved theatrically from across the road. Bert could almost imagine a future when he might do this every Sunday, his beautiful wife on his arm, basking in the approval of the neighbours.

"What do you think of the Treaty?" Bert asked as they walked through the town.

"That's a very serious topic for Christmas morning," Ina laughed.

"Well if Father Grogan thinks it's suitable material for a sermon, who are we to disagree?" he said.

"It's hard to believe it's five and a half years since I leaned out the window of the dormitory at school and saw the green flag flying on the top of the GPO," said Ina.

"We've come a long way," said Bert, "but I wonder how many people will think we still haven't come far enough?"

"Brendan has left us," Ina said sadly.

"Why on earth would he leave after all these years? Has he ever worked for anybody else?" asked Bert.

"He doesn't agree with the Treaty. Whether it's ratified by the *Dáil* or not he says he can't work for someone who settles for half measures. Imagine anyone describing my father as a man of half measures! Brendan left yesterday, and he says he's not coming back after the holidays."

"Where will he go?" asked Bert.

"He said he'd go to Connemara to see if he could do anything for Michael Power."

"Michael Power won't have any work for him – their land holding is tiny, maybe only three small stony fields," said Bert.

"There's no work to do in the winter, anyway. Michael and Annie will be trying to eke out the little they have until the spring."

"Perhaps he'll come back with his tail between his legs, after Christmas," said Ina. "Father would have him back, he's a great worker."

Bert wondered what Michael Power would make of the Treaty. It seemed that lifelong friends and even brothers were taking different sides – there was no way of predicting which way he would go.

The delicious aroma of roasting goose greeted them at the front door when Ina opened it.

"Maybe next year, we'll be eating our Christmas lunch together," said Bert, kissing her politely on the cheek, knowing that there would be several pairs of eyes watching from windows across the street, and that Bríd the maid might well be spying from behind the kitchen door.

"That would be lovely," Ina said wistfully.

She put her pale, fine boned hand on the rough, dark tweed of his coat as she looked up at him.

"Happy Christmas," he said cheerfully, and turned away before she could see the desperation in his eyes.

"*Nollaig Shona!*" she replied.

She stood holding the door open until he went out of sight. Bert didn't turn around to wave. Out of the side of his eye he could see curtains twitching and one front door stood open a tiny crack until he passed, when it closed with a gentle click. He smiled. You would think they would have more interesting things to think about on Christmas day. His Mama had written to say that they would miss having him home and he was feeling a bit guilty. He could have gone on the boat train himself instead of just sending another plump Irish turkey to fulfil his familial obligations.

Paddy and Noreen were in great form. Although neither of their sons had been able to travel home for Christmas they treated Bert as their own and as soon as Bert came in the door, Paddy started joking.

"I said to Noreen not to set a place for you at the table, that you'd probably have a better class of an invitation that you couldn't refuse," he said.

Bert smiled.

"I won't make the mistake of not coming home for my dinner, after the last time I missed my Sunday dinner."

Noreen flapped a tea cloth at him.

"I was only cross that time because it was a waste of the lovely leg of Easter lamb. It doesn't taste the same when it's cold."

Paddy winked at Bert as Noreen turned her back to keep an eye on the roasting bird.

"Will you have a glass of something?" he asked.

He held up his own almost empty glass of stout.

CHAPTER 30

Bert had always disliked the month of January with its blustering winds and cold, biting showers of rain. There was no sign yet of the days lengthening. The clouds hung dark and low, and dripping ash and sycamore trees stood sentinel over sodden, dormant fields. Life was at a standstill. Eamonn was struggling to rebuild his business and his heart wasn't in it. Many of Bert's students had stopped coming to the classes, as if the declaration of the Free State three weeks ago had suddenly made redundant any attempt to revive the Irish language. Bert was beginning to wonder if his own high-flown ideals about national identity and language had merely been an excuse not to fight. Ironically, now that there was complete freedom to teach Irish without the fear of road blocks and RIC searches, the task had lost its lustre. No longer the heroic hedge-school master rebelling against a tyrannical regime, he had been demoted to the status of an ordinary citizen, teaching the national language for a pittance to a swiftly reducing number of less motivated students. He cycled into Ballinasloe, his coat weighed down with rain, rivulets of water tracking down to the toes of his boots and onto the road, his face numb, and his nose running.

The only consolation was the promise of a chair beside the fire in Mairéad and Eamonn's house and a plate of stew. He salivated at the thought and finished the last few yards of the journey with a lighter heart. He knocked on the front door and shook himself to shed some of the moisture on the step. He was looking down at his feet when the door opened and his eyes crossed to the threshold then climbed up, taking in a new pair of dry boots, creased wool trousers and a single breasted green jacket with harp embossed brass buttons, large square pockets and a stout brown belt. Finally, his gaze rested on the round, grinning face of Eamonn. Bert stumbled forward over the step as Eamonn grabbed the handlebars and pulled the bicycle into the hall.

"What do you think?" asked Eamonn, his chest puffed out like a pigeon in the spring.

He tried to turn but caught his leg on the pedal of the bicycle and tutted with irritation. "Come in here to the warm kitchen, and get those wet things off you," he said, leading the way down the passage.

Bert shrugged off his heavy coat and followed, holding it out in front of him. Mairéad took it as he entered the kitchen, her pursed lips and the slight frown on her usually open face not needing any words.

"Take off those boots and let me put them in front of the fire," she said sternly.

Bert felt as though he had done something wrong.

"Sorry to make such a mess on your floor," he said, not knowing what else to say.

"What do you think?" Eamonn insisted.

He turned so that Bert could see the flap at the back of the jacket. Eamonn picked up a soft green peaked army cap from the kitchen table and pulled it on.

"I'm amazed," said Bert.

He was remembering vividly Patrick Leahy standing tall in Michael Power's tiny cottage kitchen in 1916, as proud in his makeshift Volunteer uniform as a man could be.

"Michael Collins wrote to me personally," said Eamonn.

"He said he wanted the best of men in the new Free State Army."

Behind her husband, Bert could see Mairéad shaking her head as she draped his sodden coat over the back of a wooden ladder-back chair and turned it towards the fire. A thin steam rose from it. She stuffed newspaper into the toes of Bert's boots and stood them on the hearth. Every movement was leaden and for the first time since Bert had known her, she spoke not a word for several minutes.

Although Bert had not asked, Eamonn seemed determined to give him all the details of his appointment.

"The Free State won't happen by itself. We need an army to keep law and order. I was wasting away in that office, calculating how many sacks of feed I had in stock and wondering when I would be paid for the ones I sold."

There was a note of apology in his voice and he half turned to include Mairéad in the conversation, although she pointedly avoided his eye.

"Where will you be stationed?" Bert asked.

He was wondering if Mairéad's upset was because her husband would be far away.

"Here in town, in the old RIC barracks. They've cleared it out. I have an office and a few men will live above in the upstairs rooms. But I'll be able to come home at night."

He turned again to Mairéad, his hesitant smile met by a scowl.

"So, you will be more of a police officer than a soldier?" Bert asked, hoping that the analogy might appease Mairéad.

"Indeed, keeping the peace," said Eamonn smugly.

"Only until a new police force is set up," spat Mairéad.

"And then what? Who will you be fighting, in this Free State Army of yours?"

It was his turn to be silent. Bert had never heard Mairéad use anything but endearments and a loving tone with her husband, so he sat silently too, while she continued.

"You'll be fighting your own countrymen, that's who!" she shouted.

"We all know fine well that De Valera took a lot of men with him when he refused to be part of the provisional government. Where do you think all those men will be? Sitting at home by their fires waiting to see how things work out? Those men were as passionate about the Republic as you were – do you think they'll turn around now and accept things as they are?"

She pointed towards the front door.

"They're out there right now, holding meetings, planning raids, all the things you did yourself only a few months ago. They won't rest. They've said as much."

"Would you prefer me to be out there with them, so?" Eamonn asked, his eyes appealing to her.

"Indeed not. What's wrong with just being an ordinary person, selling cattle feed and making a living? The animals need to be fed, the farmers need to farm, the teachers need to teach..." she included Bert in the wave of her arm.

"I can't do it, *a ghrá*," he said.

He was looking down at his feet as though he needed the reminder of the fine new boots to bolster his courage in the face of her anger.

"That's what I don't understand," she said, sighing.

She flapped her apron and sat down on one of the chairs near the fire. The anger was all gone. She was a defeated woman, her arguments falling on deaf ears. Bert had planned to get their counsel about whether to continue teaching or look for other work. He decided to save the conversation for a better time, and they passed quite a pleasant evening after Eamonn had taken off his uniform and hung it up and Mairéad could pretend for a few hours that he was just an ordinary man rather than an officer in the new Free State National Army.

"We have few enough *Timiri*," Seán said sadly, shaking his head when Bert told him he was considering his position.

"I know you have to make a decent living, but we can't afford to pay you any more money. God knows, we're struggling to do that out of the funds – and with people thinking that the job is done and there's no need for the Gaelic League any more, it's less money we'll have, instead of more."

Bert was torn. Seán's passion for the language was contagious and now that he was sitting in the parlour of Seán's house drinking his porter, all the doubts that had assailed him for months on the miserable cold cycle ride from Dunmore to

Ballinasloe seemed to fade into insignificance. For this man, Treaty or no Treaty, Free State or Republic, he had a single-minded purpose – to get people, all the people, speaking Irish. He had spent his whole adult life working for the Gaelic League, setting up the branches in the West, attending the meetings, organising the speakers, co-ordinating the *Timiri*, stretching every penny as far as it would go.

"I don't feel as if I've made enough of a difference," said Bert, wondering if Seán would think him arrogant.

Seán smiled.

"When Eamonn and I were young lads, we'd talk about what we would do when we grew up. We'd lie back on the top of the hay wagon looking up at the sky and imagine the great deeds we would do. Eamonn was always cut out to be a fighter even though he's a bit of a dreamer too and all I ever wanted to do was to teach people. I even thought I might be a Jesuit when I was thirteen."

He laughed.

"That didn't last long, I can tell you!"

"That sounds like my brother Leo and me, but we were lying on our beds in a dark little bedroom, rather than out in the fresh air," Bert said.

He could see Leo's face, his green eyes alight with wild ideas - of travelling to Australia, of adventures in America, of fighting in a great war.

"What happened to him?" asked Seán.

He realised how little he really knew of this young *Timire* and his family in England.

Bert looked away.

"He died."

He knew that Seán would not ask any more questions. Would it have been easier to talk about Leo if he had died in bed of the influenza in 1918 instead of dying in a trench in France? Seán put his hand on Bert's shoulder.

"I'm sorry," he said, imagining what it would have been like if he had lost Eamonn.

"What do you think of Eamonn's new occupation?" asked Bert, partly to change the subject and partly out of curiosity.

"He could easily have gone the other way. Michael Collins got in at the right moment and flattered his ego."

"What would you have done if he took De Valera's side?" Bert asked.

Seán looked up at the ceiling, rolling his eyes as if trying to imagine the unimaginable.

"I honestly don't know, Bert," he said.

"Would you try to change his mind?"

Seán laughed.

"He might be my little brother, but I never held any sway with him. It would only make him go his own way, further and faster, if he thought I was trying to change his mind. He was always like that, from when he was a small fella."

"I don't know where I stand, any more," said Bert.

Seán looked surprised.

"What do you mean?"

"Well, if I had taken an oath in the *Dáil* to serve the Republic, I don't think I could have agreed to the Treaty because of the oath of allegiance to the King."

"Yes?"

"Well, I took the oath as a Volunteer, but I also think that the Treaty terms were the best we could get, and it was right to sign it."

"So, you do know where you stand then," said Seán, looking relieved.

"I suppose so, but I am just one man. I don't have the responsibility of trying to lead the country. How will De Valera and Collins ever be reconciled?

"They won't be, Bert. And that's the dangerous part. We are not finished fighting yet, by any manner or means."

He cracked the top off another bottle of stout and poured it out between their two glasses, looking over his shoulder guiltily.

"Vera doesn't like it when I have one over the odds," he said conspiratorially, and then leaned back in the rocking chair and stretched out his legs on the rug in front of the fire.

"I'll make it my *deoch an dorais*," said Bert, sipping the bitter porter and glancing up at the clock on the tiled mantelpiece.

The ubiquitous Sacred Heart of Jesus picture that hung above the fire was almost identical to the one at home and he felt again the twinge of guilt that picture always stirred in him. He should be doing more, and he should be doing better, but he was never quite sure of *what* he should be doing more or doing better.

CHAPTER 31

June 1922

Mairéad collapsed onto Bert's chest before he was even in the door.

"He's gone to Dublin," she sobbed.

Bert held her shoulders and eased her back into the house.

"He got orders the night before last, to go up with reinforcements. He went off in the middle of the night, with no time even for a cup of tea to warm him," she said sadly.

"I knew it would come to this! Didn't I say to him, Bert, in front of you that day in the middle of the winter when you came in soaking wet, and he was showing off his fancy new uniform. Didn't I say then, that he would end up fighting his own?"

Bert sat down heavily at the kitchen table.

"They said in the paper."

She waved her hand in the general direction of the folded newspaper on the seat of her fireside chair.

"Michael Collins got big guns from the English. From the British, would you credit it? And they have them lined up outside the Four Courts, ready to fire in on top of their own countrymen."

She twisted her apron between her hands and paced up and down, so distracted she didn't even offer Bert a drink or a bite to eat after his journey.

"It might all blow over very quickly," Bert soothed her.

"The Republicans don't have many guns or much ammunition. They are not very well organised either," he added lamely.

"I don't care who wins," said Mairéad. "I just want him to come home alive. Why did he have to join in? Why in the name of God could he not just…"

Bert interrupted.

"Mairéad, he's only doing what he thinks is right. Don't be angry with him."

"How can I not be angry with him? What if he gets himself killed?"

Bert stood beside her.

"You never got this worried when he went away before. Why are you worrying so much now?"

She looked up at him, her dark eyes swimming.

"Because I believed in what he was fighting for, before. He had God and the angels watching over him, then."

"And he doesn't, now?" he asked gently.

"I don't know, anymore. Is it right that brothers and friends are killing each other over the difference between a Free State and a Republic?"

"I don't know either, Mairéad," said Bert, sitting back down.

"But the country voted, and we elected our representatives. Michael Collins won. What can we do now but hope and pray that De Valera and Rory O'Connor and Cathal Brugha will come around to the idea that we have to make the best of the Treaty that's been signed?"

"I don't think it's that simple," said Mairéad.

"I can see their point. I wouldn't take an oath of allegiance to the king of England myself, so I can hardly expect those men to take it."

"I think Collins has the right idea. We can't wipe out hundreds of years of history in one go, and we've come so far in the last few years, we have to hold on to the ground we've gained."

"Bert, you know me and Eamonn well. I grew up with Eamonn down the road. I swam in the river with him when I was six. I learned my sums with him and I walked out with him when I was only a girl. I had my first kiss with him. He's the only man I ever loved. I married him and I've loved him all these years. We've raised our family. We always agree with each other, and never a cross word between us."

Bert turned away when he saw her dashing away the tears in her eyes.

"God knows, I have fed and given hiding to men for so long now, they all blur into one. When Eamonn was wearing his own shirt and trousers with only a hurley over his shoulder I sent him off, as proud an Irish woman and a wife as I could be. But when I open my eyes and see that green uniform hanging on the front of the wardrobe it breaks my heart. When he puts it on I lose Eamonn and get another man, like a changeling put there by the little people. He looks the same but there's something different in his eyes. I don't know who he is, anymore."

"He's the same man, Mairéad. We're in difficult times, when it's hard to know which side is the right one. He's fighting for the same dream. He's chosen his side and he's not afraid to do what he has to do to win the fight."

"Even if it means killing his own friends?"

"This is the real test. Isn't there something in the Bible about enemies and friends? Whoever is not my friend is my enemy? There's no middle ground any more. But instead of thinking about friends and enemies, let's say it's people looking to the future and people looking to the past. We've had enough of looking to the past. We have to build the future."

"You'll be joining the Free Staters, at this rate." Mairéad said flatly.

Bert was quiet. The clock ticked loudly on the shelf. The turf crumbled in the hearth and gently fell into ash. Bert roused himself.

"Do you remember me telling you about Brendan, who used to work for Máirtín Feeney?"

"Yes, wasn't he the fella who went to Athenry with you, that time, to get Michael Power out?"

"The very one. He was arrested yesterday trying to break into the Feeney's house."

"No, I don't believe it!" she declared.

"What in the name of God was he doing that for?"

"Máirtín Feeney has a few hunting guns and apparently Brendan had it in mind to liberate them and bring them back to Michael Power."

"And was it Máirtín Feeney who handed him over to be arrested?" she asked, imagining the drama and temporarily distracted from her own woes, just as Bert had intended.

"Brendan knew where the key to the back door was kept, under a flat stone in the yard out the back, so he just walked in. He knocked something off the kitchen table in the dark and Ina's father heard it and came down."

"And Máirtín Feeney wouldn't just let him off?"

"No. Ina said he thought about it but he was angry that Brendan had abused his trust. He said if Brendan had broken in as an 'honest to goodness burglar' and stolen the guns he could have forgiven him more easily."

Mairéad laughed.

"What are we reduced to, when we start thinking like that?" she asked, returning to her apron twisting.

"What will happen to Brendan, now?"

"Well, he'll be put in prison anyway. He might be shot."

"Arragh, Bert, what are we coming to?" Mairéad wailed.

She ran her fingers through her hair. What if Eamonn was ordered to shoot one of his own countrymen in cold blood? Eamonn came home that night. Bert heard the commotion at the front door and peered out of his bedroom to see Mairéad briefly embracing him as he entered the hall followed by four other men in Free State Army uniforms. She took her husband's coat when he shrugged it off his shoulders and quietly ushered the other men into the kitchen.

Bert felt like a coward as he lay under the blankets hearing the occasional bellow of laughter and raised voices. It was easier to pretend to be asleep than to face a roomful of loud, boasting men. He pictured Mairéad playing the dutiful wife, feeding them and making tea and finding spare blankets and building up the fire for the night. Would she stay silent, or would she have her say? Bert tossed and turned and when he finally fell asleep he had a dream. It began with him smoking a cigarette with Leo, companionably sitting on the top of a tower, their breath rising in the cold Christmas night, and ended with a scream as he turned to see Leo's head exploding in fire. He shot awake and sat up, sweating. The door creaked open and Mairéad's dishevelled head poked in.

"Are you all right, *a ghrá*?" she asked.

Bert shook his head, momentarily confused. She sat on the edge of the bed. He rubbed his head vigorously and came to his senses.

"Sorry, did I shout?" he asked, and she nodded.

Then he remembered the men downstairs. What would they think of him, a *garsún* having bad dreams, with his surrogate Mammy coming to see if he was all right? He was gruff in his dismissal of her and was already regretting it as the door quietly clicked closed and Mairéad stepped lightly across the hall to her own room.

Male voices woke him in the morning and he swung his legs out of bed and had a quick wash at the basin before pulling on his trousers and shirt. He wished he hadn't left his boots by the fire last night. He padded down the stairs in his socks and braced himself to enter the kitchen. The room was full of their green jackets and brown belts and their boots and the smell of sleep and sweat and their rough, jocular camaraderie. He nodded and made his way to the fireplace to retrieve his boots, feeling slightly ashamed. He had slept on a comfortable ticking mattress and had his own water for washing while these men had shared the hard floor and a few bowls of shaving water between them.

Two stood eating hunks of bread, another bent over the kitchen table to shave in a cracked mirror balanced against the milk jug. A fourth man stood in the back doorway smoking a cigarette, exhaling into the early morning air. Their rifles stood leaning against the wall, a pile of fabric ammunition belts lying casually on the floor beside them. Bert watched his own soft white hands tying his boot laces. Not one of the men even acknowledged him. Within five minutes they were shouldering each other as they went out into the hall, thanking Mairéad, shouting farewell to Eamonn who was still upstairs, and then they were gone. Mairéad came back into the kitchen, tutting at the crumbs on the floor, and the rough bundle of blankets pushed into the corner. Silently she swept, folded and tidied until there was no trace of them left. Mairéad and Bert did not exchange a word. He watched her performing the familiar chores, his elbows leaning on his knees, his chin in his hands, and she moved about the room, thinking her own thoughts. She filled the kettle and put it on the stove, kneaded another batch of soda bread and put it in the oven, set the table with crockery for three.

"They're going West, with General MacKeon," she said finally when all was ready and the sounds of Eamonn stirring came from overhead.

"What happened in Dublin?" he asked.

"They cleared the Republicans out of the Four Courts. Cathal Brúgha got shot," she said.

"Did he die?" Bert asked.

"Died of his wounds," she said.

Bert dropped his head.

"A great man. He wouldn't surrender. He came out of the Gresham hotel firing two guns and they shot him down."

"How could they shoot him down, just like that?" he asked.

"Eamonn said they were all shouting for him to surrender but he wouldn't. He was one of the last ones out. He died in the hospital."

"Is the fighting over now?" Bert asked.

She shook her head, tears in her eyes. Eamonn could be heard stamping down the stairs. He burst into the kitchen.

"Do I need to worry about you two spending so much time together talking?" he joked. Mairéad looked up at him with what Bert could only describe as venom in her eyes.

"I was only joking," he said.

"I heard you sneaking out of his bedroom last night. If I was a jealous man..."

"It's hardly the time for jokes, Eamonn," she said sullenly.

She went to take the bread out of the oven. Bert tried to bolt down his breakfast so he could leave them to talk. Mairéad put her hand on his arm.

"Bert, don't be worrying about rushing off. Eamonn and me have said all that we need to say to each other."

Eamonn tried to laugh it off but Mairéad kept her head down, chewing every mouthful with deliberate slowness, her head only lifting when she refilled their tea, or passed the blackberry jam.

Bert excused himself and went upstairs. Despite the closed bedroom door he could hear the shouting, then Eamonn's boots on the stairs, first clambering up them two at a time, then a brief shuffle as he put on his uniform jacket and cap in the bedroom next door, then thumping down the stairs again and straight out the front door. Bert heard an engine revving and glimpsed the square bonnet of an armoured car through the fanlight of the front door as he came down the stairs. Then the engine gunned, there was a rallying shout, and the men were gone.

Bert was glad to leave for Tuam although he felt sorry for Mairéad when he left her alone. Saving the turf was the topic of conversation at the dinner table when

Bert arrived at Paddy and Noreen's that evening, more tired than usual after his bicycle ride because of his broken night's sleep.

"Bert, you look exhausted," said Noreen.

She put a plate of floury potatoes down in front of him that reminded him of his very first meal in this house, when he had been watched by twenty pairs of eyes, eagerly awaiting their first lesson. It seemed a long time ago now.

"I had a bad dream last night, about Leo, and I couldn't get back to sleep," he said.

"I wonder what made you have that?" asked Noreen.

"Four Free Staters slept on the kitchen floor last night," said Bert, and Paddy's ears pricked up.

"Eamonn was home?"

Bert nodded, his mouth full.

"Briefly. They were on their way from Dublin, going west, but Mairéad didn't say how far they were going."

"What were they doing, up in Dublin?"

"The Four Courts was taken. Cathal Brugha was shot."

"Ahh, no, God rest his soul," said Paddy.

He and Noreen crossed themselves.

"May he rest in peace," said Noreen.

"I wonder will he have a state funeral?" asked Paddy.

"Hardly, a ghrá," said Noreen.

"Well, he was a TD in the Dáil for four years and a long-time Volunteer. They can't take that away from him just because he didn't want the Treaty," said Paddy.

"Isn't it a crying shame that they're killing each other now, the very fellas that won independence for us," said Noreen sadly.

"Will nobody talk sense into them?"

"Speaking of fellas needing sense, I'm worried about Michael Power," said Paddy. He leaned over towards Bert as if the walls had ears, even in his own house. Bert lifted his eyebrow.

"There's fierce fighting going on in Limerick, altogether. Brendan was supposed to bring those guns from Dunmore down to Michael and his lads in Limerick."

"I hope to God Eamonn and his men are not sent down to Limerick," Bert declared. "They were in one of those armoured cars the Black and Tans used to use."

"God forgive me for saying it, but they're nearly as bad as those other fellas," said Noreen, blessing herself.

"Mairéad is very upset with Eamonn," said Bert, then felt disloyal, and wished he hadn't opened his mouth.

"Although, to be fair, somebody has to keep law and order," said Paddy ruminatively.

"I never thought I'd see the day when I was glad our own two boys were gone to America!" said Noreen emphatically, taking their plates to the sink.

Paddy nodded and a puff of smoke rose from his pipe as he sucked it contentedly, and was drawn away towards the chimney.

One late summer evening, Bert was sitting on the step of Paddy's front door, thinking. Seán O'Farrell was optimistic that the severely diminished numbers attending the Irish classes would grow again, once the fighting in the country settled down. Bert was not so sure.

He heard rapid footsteps approaching on the sun baked road. He glanced up but saw no-body and thought he must have imagined the sound. Suddenly he felt an iron grip on his shoulder. Before he had a chance to look up he found himself standing and being steered through the half door into the gloomy interior of the house. Paddy and Noreen were at a Novena Mass for peace and would not be back for a few hours. His eyes adjusted to the gloom and took in broad shoulders, tousled dark hair, and a wide grin that could not be mistaken.

"*Herbert Vincent O Briain, tá cuma breá breáthacht ort,* Herbert Vincent O'Brien, you're looking well," said Michael Power, pumping his hand as he had at their very first meeting so long ago.

"*Ní féidir liom an rud céanna a rá fútsa.* I can't say the same for you. You're not looking so great at all," said Bert, looking him up and down.

Michael's jacket was ripped and the collar was grimy. A thin, grey shirt hung from his shoulders, and his trousers sagged at the muddied knees.

"I'm grand, and as the wolf said to Red Riding Hood, 'All the better for seeing you, my dear.'"

Michael had adopted the slightly mocking tone he used to tease Bert as a boy.

"You're a long way from Limerick," said Bert, wondering if Michael was alone.

"The Free Staters flushed us out – we were outnumbered so we left the town to them and got out while we could. We burned the Barracks and took as much as we could carry."

Michael had developed a twitch in his leg so he looked as though he might take flight at any moment.

"Are you on your own?" Bert asked.

He leaned out the door half expecting to see a trail of followers coming down the lane.

"No, we split up, so we'd be harder to spot."

"What about Annie, and Tomás? Are they well?"

Michael shook his head.

"Tomás was killed by a mine. It went off when he and a few lads were blowing the bridge into Limerick."

"I'm so sorry," said Bert.

He put his hand on Michael's arm. He had lost both of his children now.

"It must be very difficult to keep going?"

Michael was looking at the floor.

"If only I had Annie, but I've lost her as well."

"What happened to her? How did she get killed?"

"She didn't. When Tomás was killed, she was like a woman possessed. She screamed blue murder and pulled her hair out. She was...I didn't even know who she was anymore."

Michael's eyes went out of focus and his voice cracked. Bert nudged him towards the fireplace.

"Sit down, Michael. You are exhausted."

Michael turned obediently and sat heavily in Paddy's rocking chair. He was still not looking at Bert as he continued murmuring.

"She went home to be with her own family. Just for a rest. They put her in the district asylum."

Bert was shocked.

"Can you not get her out?"

Michael was silent.

"You don't want to get her out?"

"She needs a rest, Bert. When she got the news about Tomás, she tried to kill me. She picked up a bread knife, and she ran at me with it, screaming that it was all my fault. It would always have come to this – he was killed because of me."

Great sobs racked him as he sat, his broad shoulders hunched, his elbows on his knees.

"I feel like I'm going mad myself, some days, Bert," he said finally.

He wiped his nose on his sleeve and sniffed loudly. Even cowed by grief and tiredness, his charisma filled the dim room. Bert stared at him. Only ten years before, Michael was a man in his prime, the muscles of his arms bulging through his shirt sleeves, his big shoulders used to carrying heavy weights, his wrists strong from striking at the coal face with a pick. Now he was a wasted shadow with yellowing nails and teeth, his hair thin and grey, his shrivelled face showing all the wear and tear of living rough. What would the life of an outlaw do to the gentle, softly spoken Annie, with her precious children constantly hungry and in danger? With Tomás gone, maybe she had lost any reason to carry on pretending it was a normal life.

Bert hesitated to offer his bed to Michael. What if Paddy and Noreen wanted to have nothing to do with him? Michael looked up and the light in those deep, blue eyes was not extinguished yet.

"Why don't you go upstairs and sleep?" Bert suggested, pointing to the ladder.

Michael staggered towards the ladder, suddenly weakened by the prospect of sleep after three days on the run without any rest.

"I'll just have a bit of a sleep and then we can talk," his voice slurred as he climbed the ladder.

Bert stood at the bottom, ready to steady him if he slipped.

Paddy and Noreen came in the door an hour later, talking animatedly about one of their neighbours. Bert put his finger to his lips to silence them, pointing with his other hand to the ladder leading to his loft bed. He whispered.

"We have a visitor."

Noreen put her hands on her hips. First, to be silenced in her own home, and now to be told she had a visitor, by another visitor? She was just about to open her mouth to protest, when Paddy put his hand on her arm.

"Father Grogan gave us a great sermon," said Paddy, steering Noreen towards her chair. She took a deep breath and when she had straightened her skirts around her, she sat looking expectantly at Bert.

"So, who is the mystery visitor?"

She managed to keep her tone light.

"Michael Power," said Bert, watching their faces closely.

"And what possessed him to come here?" asked Noreen.

Had Bert had had the cheek to invite him?

"I don't know. We only had a brief conversation. He was falling on his feet, so I told him to get some rest," said Bert.

"Quite right, too," said Paddy, poking tobacco into his pipe.

The pure, shrill call of a blackbird came through the open door, and there was a rare moment of silence in the house, while Noreen framed her thoughts.

"His son Tomás was killed by a mine, and Annie is in the district asylum in Galway," said Bert.

Noreen blessed herself.

"The poor man. Is he on his own?"

Bert nodded. Noreen suddenly jumped up.

"I'll heat up some water for him. He'll want a bath and a decent dinner in him."

Michael stayed for a week, sharing Bert's bed.

On Saturday morning, while they were eating breakfast, he said, "Noreen, I want to say that apart from my own Annie, God help her in her troubles, no-one has ever minded me so well. I'll go on my way today, not to outstay my welcome."

"Indeed, you're more than welcome, and you can stay longer, if it suits you," said Noreen, her bosom heaving with the pleasure of a good deed.

"There's work to be done, and I would be shirking if I didn't do it," declared Michael, looking at Bert.

They had gone fishing the day before, sitting peaceably side by side on the river bank, their improvised rods and lines surprisingly effective. Bert basked in the forgotten pleasure of Michael's exclusive company.

"How long do you think the fighting will go on?" Bert asked him, after sitting silently for almost half an hour, gently tickling the surface of the dark water with Michael's beautifully crafted flies, tied out of duck feathers.

Michael shrugged.

"It's hard to know, Bert. We can't hold the towns anymore. The Free Staters have all the ammunition and equipment that the British ever had. They always win whenever we try to stay still and hold a position. But we're still good at fighting the old way, keeping ourselves moving, hitting on targets, flying off again before we're caught."

"What do you hope to achieve?"

Bert wondered if he had been too blunt, when Michael was silent for a while.

He cleared his throat, intending to clarify his question, and Michael took the cue to finally answer.

"Do you know what? I'm not entirely sure. It's not as clear as it was when we were just trying to get the English out."

"That's what I've been trying to grapple with," said Bert.

They settled into silence again. A bumble bee droned past, its heavy rear end drawing it towards the earth like a magnet. Michael flicked his wrist to make the fly dance.

"All I know is, the Volunteers took an oath to fight for the Republic. We haven't got it yet, so we keep on fighting."

"But you're fighting Irishmen now," said Bert. "You could end up shooting Eamonn O'Farrell, for God's sake."

Michael spat into the water.

"Don't I know that, all too well? The worst thing is that Free Staters know all the safe houses and the paths over the mountains and where we hide our weapons as well as we do ourselves. I don't know how long we'll be able to keep going."

"So why do you keep fighting, then?" asked Bert.

Michael shook his head.

"Bert, I've been fighting so long now that I don't know how to do anything else. I've no son to hand over the few acres in Carraroe to. I've no wife to go home to. I'll just keep on fighting until the end."

"That's not a good reason to keep fighting." said Bert.

"Michael Collins believes we can achieve full independence, in due course. We might have to travel a bit of a winding road to get there, but we will get there."

"Do you really believe that man anymore?" said Michael, scornfully.

"He gave away the six counties. How can he say that he's for a united Ireland, when he did that?"

"He didn't do it lightly, Michael. It was inevitable, once partition came in, that the six counties would be lost. The Boundary Commission are supposed to take the local populations into account."

"I'm not prepared to accept that. That's like saying the British have been here for seven hundred years, what's another few years, or the sharing out of a few counties, between friends?"

"No, it's not like that at all. It's being practical. We can be full of ideals, but we have to be practical too. People want peace now. They want to settle down and have a normal life again. The Treaty has given us that opportunity. We should take it."

Michael looked at him sadly.

"You'll be all right, Bert. You'll get a job as a National Schoolteacher and marry Ina Feeney and have children with her, and turn into one of the ordinary people who never think beyond the day to day, and forget the blood that has been shed..."

He stopped, his face flushed. His eyes were glittering. Bert was shaking his head sadly.

"Bert, you have just reminded me what I am fighting for, and I thank you for that. Tomorrow I'll be on my way. There's work to be done, and it won't get done with me filling my belly and staying warm and safe, and thinking that's all there is to it."

"I didn't really say anything," said Bert.

"That's exactly it. This goes beyond words. You can tell yourself that there's no real difference between a Free State and a Republic, but you'll only be lying to yourself. I might not have Tomás anymore, but I want to be able to look myself in the eye. I will not give up until we have a Republic."

They caught no fish.

CHAPTER 32

After Michael went off, wobbling up the lane on an old rusty bicycle Paddy had given him, Bert sat on the doorstep in the late afternoon sunlight. The sheepdog flopped down beside him and sighed. Bees droned in the woodbine. Bert had not been paid since June. The Gaelic League was short of money. The donations had dried up, with everybody trying to make ends meet. Bert patted the dog's warm head and he opened one eye and settled his nose more firmly on his paws. A line of ants marched past him, unnoticed.

The stillness was shattered by a car, roaring up the Dunmore road. Instead of passing by at the top of the *boreen*, it slowed and turned towards the house. Bert stood up and looked over the stone wall. It was Máirtín Feeney's car. He went to the gate. Ina stepped out of the car, her face ashen.

"Michael Collins has been shot!"

Bert suddenly wanted to sit down again, and he leaned against the stone gatepost.

"Is he dead?"

She nodded. "He was on a tour of inspection in West Cork – his home county! It was an ambush by the Republicans."

This would be a disaster. There was nobody as strong as Collins, who stood for the Treaty. His charisma and his commitment carried the people along with him. Without him, the Free State Army and the new Civic Guard might run amok. Bert bent down to see who was driving the car. Pat O'Malley sat behind the wheel. Bert looked quickly at Ina.

Her face was guileless.

"Father asked Pat to drive me out here, to tell you."

She waved carelessly at the car. What had prompted Máirtín Feeney to do such a thing?

"Father says if you have time, could you come and see him?"

Bert stepped into the house and grabbed his jacket off the back of the kitchen chair and in two bounds was back at her side. She climbed into the car. He reached for the handle of the passenger door and then hesitated. By joining her in the back seat he would confirm Pat O'Malley's status as a chauffeur. He slid in beside Ina, her thigh only inches from his, her bare arm brushing his sleeve. He caught Pat O'Malley's eye in the rear-view mirror and lifted his chin slightly. The back of the other man's neck flushed red.

Máirtín Feeney was pacing up and down in the office above his builder's yard, vigorously chewing on the stem of his pipe. He heard the car and sat behind the desk. Ina thanked Pat. He smiled at her and half bowed. He strode away down Castle Street, only the vigour of his step giving away the turmoil inside him. Bert followed Ina up the narrow stairs, his nostrils filled with the smell of freshly sawn wood and turpentine. The office was spartan with a bare wooden floor, groaning shelves full of accounting ledgers and a single large mahogany desk that must have been lifted through the window with a crane. It would never have come up the stairs. On it lay a scattering of papers and a fountain pen in a stand beside a pot of ink. A typewriter stood on a small table at one end of the room, a dusty sheet of paper scrolled half way into it, and a single key jammed down. Dust motes floated in a shaft of sunlight that shone through a single window overlooking the yard. The sound of men shouting and the rhythmic buzz of a two-man saw rose from beneath. Máirtín Feeney stood up as they entered and came towards Bert, his hand outstretched.

"Bert, terrible news, altogether," he said.

A tiny jewelled string of spittle was hanging from the pipe he held tightly in his other fist. Bert shook the older man's hand, frowning in a way that he hoped looked wise and knowing, but without any idea why he had been summoned.

"We'll need every sensible man to keep his head about him," said Máirtín.

Bert nodded his agreement.

"Michael Collins was the voice of reason. Without him, who knows what will happen."

"Do you think DeValera was responsible?" Bert asked.

Máirtín shook his head.

"I don't think he'd go that far, but there's a man out there who did. They say it was a sniper shot."

He picked up a newspaper from the desk and waved it at Bert.

"You know what that means, don't you? Probably it was a man who was trained in the British Army – that's ironic, isn't it?"

He started pacing again. Ina gave a tiny shrug when Bert looked to her for guidance. Why was he here?

"I think it's time every man showed for once and all what he stands for," Máirtín Feeney declared, stabbing the air with his pipe.

What was coming?

"Michael Collins paid the ultimate price for what he believed in. Would you agree?"

Bert gulped and said, "Yes."

After his conversation with Michael Power a few days before, he wasn't sure what he believed in, anymore.

"We can't let him die for nothing."

Ina's hands were involuntarily twisting around each other and she looked anxiously between the two men.

"We'll have to make difficult decisions about who are our true friends, and who are not, would you agree?"

"I would," Bert mumbled.

"I want to go up to Dublin to the funeral, tomorrow," Máirtín said, abruptly turning towards them again.

"I don't want Ina left on her own in the house."

"I wouldn't be on my own, father. Bríd is here all the time."

"She wouldn't be much good in a crisis, a ghrá," he said softly.

He dropped his voice even further.

"I wouldn't be surprised if she was more inclined to the Republican side, anyhow," he said.

Ina agreed, but she didn't want to concede the point about her personal safety. She tried to keep her tone respectful.

"She's hardly going to take a lighted torch to the place if you're away for one night."

Bert could hardly believe his ears.

"She certainly won't if you have someone here protecting you."

"Are you asking me to stay at the house, sir?"

"I am, Bert. I trust you."

"Thank you, sir."

Why hadn't Pat O'Malley been selected for the honour? He was good enough to drive Ina around the countryside, but not good enough to act as her bodyguard?

"Although we'll have to take suitable precautions," Máirtín Feeney said, vigorously clearing his throat.

Bert suppressed a smile. Ina's reputation was only slightly less important than her safety.

"I thought you could come to our house for dinner and stay the night. I will leave for Dublin at about midnight, so as to get there for the early hours of the morning."

Bert agreed to the plan and walked out of the office in a daze, musing the other possible outcomes of the conversation about every man showing which side he was on. For a little while there, he had been expecting Máirtín Feeney to ask him to murder someone to prove his loyalty to Michael Collins. What else might Máirtín Feeney have asked, to test Bert's loyalty? He shuddered. There was no doubt about it. Michael Power was on the 'wrong side' now.

"To what do I owe the pleasure of a visit in the middle of the week?" Father Grogan asked expansively.

He pushed his chair back from the dining table after a hefty dinner of lamb stew and potatoes. Bert pointed to a chair, asking for permission to sit down. The priest nodded.

"Of course, sit yourself down. Mrs O'Shea, will you add another cup to the tea tray for Mr O'Brien here, please?"

The housekeeper nodded as she cleared the priest's dinner plate. Bert did not want to make his request in front of her. She was Bríd's mother, and it would take no time for the news to get back to her daughter. The priest was intrigued but he had enough discretion to wait. They talked about the weather until Mrs O'Shea appeared with the tea tray, laid out the crockery, fiddled around with the teaspoons, took the lacy cover off the milk jug, and stood back to admire her work.

"Thanks very much, Mrs O'Shea", the priest said, giving her a look that brooked no more delaying tactics.

"You're very welcome, indeed," she said and bustled out.

There was no guarantee she wouldn't listen at the door. Bríd didn't pick that up from the wind. Bert cleared his throat.

"I'd like a character reference from you, Father," he said.

The priest smiled. "How long have I known you?"

"Nearly two years, Father. I know you haven't seen me at Mass every week, but that's only because I was going to Mass in Ballinasloe, at the beginning."

"Before you met a certain Miss Feeney and got a good reason to come to my church," the priest teased.

Bert said nothing.

"What do you need the reference for? Are you looking for a new job?"

"Yes."

Bert craned his neck to see if the dining room door was ajar. It was closed.

"Why have you such a guilty look on your face?" Father Grogan asked.

"I want to join the Civic Guard," Bert murmured.

"Do you indeed?"

The priest sat forward and put his hands on his knees.

"And what class of a man are they looking for, in the Civic Guard?"

Bert handed him the recruiting leaflet.

"Well, you're above five foot nine, and you're in good health, physical and mental. You're not married... yet!"

He looked up at Bert. Bert wouldn't rise to the priest's teasing.

"How old are you?"

"I just had my twenty third birthday."

"So, you just need a character reference from your priest. You'll pass the writing and arithmetic tests, with flying colours, I'm sure."

He continued to read the requirements.

"So, who would you say was your Commanding Officer in the Volunteers?"

"Eamonn O'Farrell," said Bert, still unsure how he would track him down.

"Wouldn't it be easier to ask Máirtín Feeney to write something for you?"

Bert coughed. "We've had our ups and downs with regard to my service in the Volunteers."

The priest sighed. "He's a tough man, Bert, but he has a good heart."

"I know. But I still don't want to be beholden to him for a reference."

"I understand. Call in tomorrow and I will have something for you. I hope it goes well for you."

They stood and shook hands. Bert was relieved to see no sign of Mrs O'Shea in the hall as he left.

CHAPTER 33

February 1923

Ina passed the pew where Bert was standing, his hands fidgeting with his cap while he waited for the congregation to disperse. Various people nodded as they passed, and a few of the women gave him sideways smiles. Everyone in Dunmore was talking about him and Ina. Paddy and Noreen were already out of the church, standing on the steps. Ina's finely crocheted lace mantilla barely touched her shoulders and emphasised her delicate features, her refined cheekbones. Bert slipped out into the aisle behind her, his hand resting lightly on the small of her back as he followed her out. He quickly withdrew it when they reached the door of the church and he took his turn to shake Father Grogan's hand. Máirtín Feeney paused to talk to a neighbour and let his daughter escape into the daylight with Bert, a drop of holy water glittering briefly on her forehead as she turned to smile at Bert in the spring sunshine.

"This is a nice surprise," she said.

"I didn't think they'd give you any time off at all."

"They only gave me the weekend," he said, returning her smile.

"No uniform yet?"

"They're not very organised," he murmured.

"Have you made many friends?"

They strolled towards her house, knowing that her father would soon follow behind. A light breeze ruffled her fair hair. She shivered. Then she folded the mantilla and put it in her handbag.

"No friends yet, but I've made some enemies," he said sadly.

"Why on earth do you say that?" she asked.

"The training officers are all from the British army or the old RIC," he said.

"Yes, I suppose that's to be expected, since they were the ones with all the experience."

"They've been given higher ranks than other recruits, and some of the men are not happy about that. They say it should be a fresh start, with everyone having the same chance of promotion."

"That's fair, I suppose," mused Ina.

"When I finish my training, I'll be promoted to Sergeant straight away," he said, finally sharing the good news he had been bursting to tell.

"Oh Bert, that's fantastic!"

Then her face fell. "Is that why you've made enemies?"

"I think so."

"Do they think you're getting the English treatment?"

"That would be ironic, when I'm one of the very few who can speak Irish. I'll be sent to the West. Mind you, the West could be anywhere from Donegal to Bandon."

"That's better than Dublin, or Wexford," she said.

"I don't care where I am, until I've saved enough money to ask your father if I can marry you," he said fervently.

Ina laughed.

"You would say yes, wouldn't you?" he asked, suddenly wondering if Pat O'Malley was still loitering in the wings.

"Is that a proposal?" she asked, looking uncharacteristically coy.

Before he could open his mouth, she went on, "Because when the time is right to make a proposal, I would hope it would be slightly more romantic."
There was no sarcasm in her tone, and her eyes were laughing.

Bert smiled. "I'll bear that in mind."

He was invited for lunch, and spent a pleasant afternoon playing backgammon with Máirtín Feeney, glancing away from the board every few minutes to watch Ina, who was sitting by the tall window embroidering a table cloth, the fine white linen spread over her knees like a bridal gown. At four o'clock, as the light was beginning to fade, Bríd came in with a tea tray and Bert could hardly believe he was expected to eat more food. Ina poured the tea into fine china cups and the nervous shake in Bríd's hand showed how infrequently they were used. Bríd tried to curtsey as she handed Bert his cup, which wobbled dangerously on the saucer. He leaned forward to take it from her.

"Thank you, Bríd," he said gently.

She bobbed and stumbled back to the tray. Why did he make her so nervous? If she knew that Bert was just as unfamiliar as she with the grandeur of the house, she might not tremble quite so much every time she laid eyes on him. Ina winked, and he did not understand until later when they were parting. Ina whispered to him as they stood in the hall, the door to the sitting room ajar so that her father could see them, and the door to the kitchen ajar so that Bríd could hear them.

"You know that Bríd has a soft spot for you, don't you?" she giggled.

She took a risk and caressed his cheek with her hand. Bert was astonished.

"Really?"

"That's why she always trips over herself when you are around."

Bert could see over Ina's shoulder that her father was dozing by the fire, his head nodding. He took Ina by the shoulders, and kissed her hard on the lips, and she trembled under his hands like a captive bird. He stood back.

"I really want you to marry me," he said fiercely.

She looked up at him, two bright spots in her cheeks.

"I really want you to ask me nicely," she said.

She kissed him quickly on the cheek before opening the front door.

She said loud enough for Bríd to hear, "Good bye Bert, and safe travelling back to Dublin. I look forward to your letters."

Máirtín Feeney stirred in his armchair and Bert took her fingers gently in his big hand. He squeezed them and looked into her eyes.

"I'll write soon."

He raised his voice and waved at her father.

"Goodbye, sir, thank you again for the fine lunch."

He received only a nod in return. Would he ever soften the heart of that stern old man? Ina squeezed into the porch with him and they stole another kiss, this one tender and sweet. He stepped out onto the path, determined that the next time he set foot in that house he would propose properly to Ina, and seek her father's permission to marry as soon as possible.

* * *

Garda Síochána HQ
Phoenix Park
Dublin

9th November 1923

Dear Ina

The bad news is that I am being sent to Skibbereen and will be leaving the day after tomorrow, so there will be no time to visit you before I go. The county of Cork is rife with Republican activities and badly needs us. I am taking a Sergeant and two

Gardaí and we have to find a suitable place when we get there to establish a Garda Station. The old RIC barracks was burned down last year and nothing has been done to restore it. We have been issued with blankets, tin mugs and cutlery, and a station log book and paper, but little else. The full uniforms are not ready even yet, so we have to wear our own trousers with the blue tunic jacket. It sometimes feels as though the men in HQ are making it up as they go along. I wonder would it be different if Michael Collins were still alive?

You would have laughed to see me yesterday, cycling down the Quays to Phoenix Park with several other men, not once, but twenty times, on different bicycles! Ship Street was evacuated and there were three hundred bicycles to transport to the new stores. They bought lots of bicycles, intending that we should buy them as a condition of our service, but so many men have refused that there are a lot of bicycles with no homes! The townspeople of Skibbereen might not take their new Superintendent too seriously if they had seen me yesterday, pedalling along with my hands in the air, laughing like a boy on a day off from school!

I felt optimistic, speeding along by the Liffey, which for once did not smell like a mediaeval midden. The only sad sight was the poor broken domes of the Four Courts. I tried to imagine it as an egg that had hatched, so that a new Ireland could emerge. We *Gardaí Síochána* can make a difference in this new Ireland of ours, armed with the 'moral authority' that Commissioner Staines claims is more powerful than weapons. I hope this letter finds you in good form and good health, and I will write again as soon as I know my new address.

Yours truly
Bert.

The rain eased just as the train pulled into Cork station and the four men stretched and shook themselves. Bert took a deep breath. Once again, a single metal step down to the platform would take him into a new life. The others stood, waiting to follow his lead. All the men were several years older than him. The Sergeant had the slightly self-conscious stoop and head tilt of a tall man who has spent his whole life bending down to hear what people are saying. His washed out blue eyes and the grey pallor of his face, topped with wispy strands of sandy hair created the impression that he might dissolve into the air at any moment. This gave him a great advantage in blending into the background when he chose. He had been promoted quickly because of his astute judgement and quiet confidence.

Bert pulled his jacket down and squared his shoulders. The men had used the journey to ask him less than subtle questions about his time in the Volunteers, trying to understand what made him so special. His promotion to Superintendent had been as much a surprise to himself as to his peers but he would not be drawn into a long-winded justification. He remembered Máirtín Feeney's advice, cloaked in all his favourite clichés.

"Don't get too familiar with the men. Keep your cards close to your chest. They'll be looking out for your soft spots. Trust no-body until they prove themselves to you."

Bert doubted that he would put his men through quite as many trials as Máirtín Feeney had given him. He lifted his holdall from the rack and the others followed suit. As soon as they set foot on the platform a porter came charging towards them with a trolley, hailing them loudly.

"Here it is, Sirs. I have it all here for you! Seamus Heaney is outside waiting for you. Will I show you where to go?"

Two bicycles were balanced precariously on top of the trunks and boxes and the short, squat porter struggled to keep everything in place.

"Wait, let's take the bicycles off and wheel them," Bert said, waving to the Guards.

They stepped forward with alacrity and heaved the bicycles off the pile. The porter nodded, talking constantly.

"Isn't it great to see ye all, bringing us some law and order. That's what's needed, and no doubt."

He looked them up and down as a proud parent would inspect his children and only showed a flicker of surprise to see the great variety of trousers and footwear they displayed. Bert had to tune into the Cork accent with the tight, narrow sounding vowels so different from the broad, round sounds of Galway and Roscommon. He strode after the porter who was already disappearing through the main door out onto the street, where a few horses and carts and a single motor car awaited the arrival of the train passengers.

The porter hailed one man, who brought his cart forward, tipped his hat and then scratched his head when he saw how much luggage would have to be loaded on the cart.

"These two men will cycle behind," said Bert, as he swung up onto the seat beside the driver.

The Sergeant organised the loading and within minutes they were passing through the blackened and bruised city of Cork.

A FINE YOUNG MAN

* * *

Heaney's
Main Street
Skibbereen
Co Cork

12th November 1923

Dearest Ina

I am writing after my first day here. We travelled by train to Cork and a man named Seamus Heaney met us with a horse and cart and took us to Skibbereen. He is renting us two rooms above his public house! We must have made an amusing sight for the locals when we arrived, like blow-ins from another land. Our uniform jackets are very creased already and look as if we have been wearing them for years. The quality of the fabric is poor. When we are settled I will requisition more so that we can maintain some semblance of a disciplined peace keeping force.

I am sure that Mr Heaney would prefer to see us in the old Barracks at the other end of Main Street but we surveyed them today and they are badly burned out and some of the roof beams are missing. We are unlikely to occupy those premises in the foreseeable future.

We ate very well this evening. A local woman brought a tasty mutton stew and it was reassuring to be so welcomed here, when most people might see us as a mixed blessing. We are all sleeping in the same room so I must extinguish the light and bid you good night.

Yours truly

Bert

The creaking of the makeshift wooden beds had become a familiar counterpoint to the babble of conversation from the Lounge Bar beneath, with an occasional raised voice or banging door as the evening wore on. Bert lay on the bed with his hands behind his head. Sergeant Duggan was on duty tonight and would shortly return from his night patrol and chivvy the last lingering drinkers to leave. Heaney said he liked having the excuse of the Gardaí upstairs to clear the house at a respectable hour, but he walked a very fine line. Bert had overheard him muttering to one protesting local that the rooms above had been commandeered by the Gardaí and he had no choice in the matter.

Bert couldn't really relax until Duggan was back safely. He had decided in the early days that they would only inspire confidence if they displayed it, so they made lone patrols rather than walking in pairs. The men had agreed, despite the risk of ambush, and so far, the tactic had been effective. The noise levels below were rising now in their usual pattern, as Seamus Heaney banged on a glass and called for his patrons to drink up. The door opened and slammed a few times, loud voices moved off down Main Street and the low murmur of the intransigent late drinkers continued.

A sudden shout and the sound of smashing glass made Bert sit up and grab his over-shirt. Sergeant Duggan should be back by now. He pulled on his jacket and trousers and slipped on his boots. The shouting continued, and Bert could hear Seamus Heaney's soothing tones. Bert imagined him frantically pointing at the ceiling and raising his eyebrows to warn of the impending disaster of the Gardaí getting involved. Bert cleared his throat as he stooped to pass through the low entrance into the bar. The door into the street slammed as he came in and the eyes of the remaining three drinkers swivelled as one, from the door to where he stood.

He strode through the bar, saying firmly, "Gentlemen, please leave the premises at once. Mr Heaney called the last drink at least half an hour ago."

He pushed open the street door to see two young men thrashing around on the road, punching and kicking each other with great ferocity. Sergeant Duggan arrived panting from running down the street, having seen the men bursting out through the door. Bert leaned into the fracas and grabbed the collar of one man and Sergeant Duggan grabbed the other. They held them up like a pair of wiry terriers, still punching the air and swearing at each other. Their freckled faces, long noses and red hair declared them brothers.

"What has you two trying to kill each other?" asked Duggan so quietly that they stopped shouting to listen to him.

"He's a traitor," cried the one in Bert's grasp as Bert lowered him to his feet and he stood glowering at his brother.

"It was good enough for Michael Collins, so it's good enough for me," replied the other, spitting out a tooth and wiping blood from his lips.

"Free Stater, traitor," said the other with the mocking, sing-song tone of a thwarted child.

Bert sighed. They had nowhere to put these men to cool their heads and sleep off the drink. The nearest gaol was in Cork and the Gardaí had no means of transporting the men. The other drinkers had come out and were standing in a semi-circle, watching silently. Garda Naughtan came strolling around the corner, whistling after a visit to his girl on his night off duty.

He quickly assessed the situation and asked, "Sir, will I send these men home or do you need to question them?"

"Send them home," said Bert.

He was grateful to reduce the number of witnesses to their fundamental lack of power.

"We were better off with the old RIC," one old man muttered as he shuffled off, waving his walking stick emphatically.

"At least they let a man have a peaceful pint in the pub."

"Aren't you here to bring peace to the place, and root out the Irregulars, not to be bothering law abiding citizens having a drink?" shouted another, shaking a fist.

Bert marched the young men inside and made them shake hands. After they had been sent home with a warning not to breach the peace again, he sat at one of the small tables and watched as Seamus Heaney put the bar across the door and tidied behind the counter.

"You're doing a grand job," Heaney said consolingly.

"Can I get you a small night cap?"

Bert had allowed his shoulders to slump and his chin to rest on his hands. He stood up abruptly.

"No, thank you. I'll say good night."

He climbed the stairs wearily.

* * *

12th December
Skibbereen

Dearest Ina

It is very cold here and the bed without a mattress is hard, so I am not sleeping well. The only good thing about not sleeping at night is that it gives me more time to think about you. I stared out through the skylight last night and imagined you were looking at the same stars. I wonder if the distance of half the length of Ireland makes any difference to your view of the constellations? It seems like a long way to me, and I don't know when we will see each other. I will not have any leave until the Spring. Perhaps during the Easter holidays, when you have a few days off work too, I could travel to Dunmore.

We might have a new stove delivered next week, if it isn't hijacked on the way down from Dublin like the last one. Why don't Headquarters let us buy provisions from the local people? It would put us in a better light with them, and we wouldn't have to worry about things disappearing en route.

Garda Naughtan wants to get married already. We've only been here four weeks and he has met a girl from the town and claims to be in love. Who am I to contradict him? When you have met the right woman, there is no doubt about it. They hope to get married in the summer. Perhaps the country will be a bit more settled by then. I have to go on duty now, having lingered over this letter and a cup of tea for longer than my due.

I send my thoughts and kisses,

Bert

Bert sat in the gloom of the late afternoon, staring at the letter he had just received from Máirtín Feeney. Brendan had been condemned to death for possession of firearms. The letter, dated the sixth of December, weighed heavy in his hand. By now Brendan would be dead. The Free State was just as ruthless in meting out its justice as the British ever had been. How could the men who had sat in a court room and condemned him to death be so sure that Brendan deserved to die? When had the beautiful ideals of the Republic become so sullied that her former champions now killed each other with such alacrity? He looked down at himself. By donning this creased blue jacket, had Bert merely perpetuated his self delusion and avoided the fight again? Those red-haired brothers had taken different sides in this struggle. Why did one brother see the potential of the Free State to lead to ultimate independence, and other see only the barriers?

Garda Naughtan had told Bert that his biggest fear was the late night knock of a rifle butt at the door. He said he wasn't afraid for his own safety, but only feared that he would betray his sworn duty to 'protect the property of the State.'

The Commissioner regularly circulated reports of Gardaí in isolated stations standing up to 'cowardly armed raiders.' The Gardaí had very little worth stealing. The real purpose of the raids was intimidation. The old Volunteer tactic of frightening the RIC out of their barracks was failing with the Garda Síochána. The psychology was different now. The guardians of the peace were not an occupying force, unwelcome to the people. They were from among the people themselves, although care had been taken to place Guards away from their home towns where they might be compromised in their duty. Bert fervently hoped that the Commissioner would hold firm on the policy of an unarmed force – there was a rumour that guns would be issued if these raids continued.

CHAPTER 34

The creaking rowing boat touched on the pebbly shore and Naughtan, the lanky, fresh faced Garda who was the son of a fisherman deftly stepped ashore to hold the boat steady for his Superintendent. Bert climbed out and stood up, straightening his jacket. The shingle crunched under their feet as they crossed the narrow beach. They didn't speak to the boatman who was now standing deferentially by the prow, the mooring rope in his hands.

A thin waft of smoke rose straight from a chimney just over a small rise in the centre of the island. Not even a tiny gust of breeze disturbed the tranquillity. A shrill whistle from the direction of the beach suddenly cut through the air and Bert slapped his thigh in frustration. He strode through the long, reedy grass with Garda Naughtan gasping as he tried to keep up. A squat thatched cottage came into view, huddled in the lee of the rise, the greying whitewash and tattered curtains at the window reminding Bert of an elderly lady, past her prime. On the right stood another stone building with no glass in the windows and a cracked wooden door hanging off its hinges. From inside came the clatter of pots and the sound of muttered curses. The young man turned to Bert for permission to go ahead, the heat of the chase burning in his cheeks. Bert shook his head.

"*Ná bíodh imní ort, a mhic.* Don't worry, lad. There's no place for them to run to."

He immediately regretted the words when he saw the crestfallen expression of his eager acolyte.

"*Lean ar aghaidh!* Go on, then."

The Garda squared his shoulders, took a deep breath and ran towards the outhouse, calling out, "*Is cuma cad atá tú ag déanamh ansin, tar amach...* Whatever you're doing in there, come out where we can see you!"

After a short pause a tall, bearded man emerged, stooping to pass through the low door. His shirt hung loose outside his trousers and he was wiping his hands on an old rag, affecting casual disinterest. He touched his cap with his left hand, acknowledging Bert who was standing outside the door of the cottage, but he completely ignored young Garda Naughtan who was no more than three feet away from him.

"*Dia dhuit*," he said to Bert. "*Céardd atá uait?* What do you want?"

Bert waited to see how Naughtan would handle the situation.

"*Ba mhaith linn scrúdú grinn a dhéanamh ar chró na mbó.* We want to conduct a detailed search of the cow byre." he said, after clearing his throat nervously.

"*Cinnte is féidir libh, agus fáilte romhaibh.* You can, and welcome," said the man.

He waved his arm in the direction of the sagging door. He was still not looking at Naughtan. This Superintendent had a reputation for taking no nonsense but you never knew the measure of a man until you could look him in the eye. He licked his upper lip nervously. Garda Naughtan would be no problem. He was engaged to be married to one of the O'Neill girls. The girl's father owed Dunphy a few bob. A quiet word in that direction should work fine. But this other tall fella with the clear blue eyes standing so still on the doorstep just watching his every move like a fox would watch a rabbit - he was a different matter altogether.

Garda Naughtan bent down and entered the gloomy outbuilding and Bert could hear him moving things around, rustling in the hay and a loud clatter as he knocked something over. Dunphy didn't move a muscle even when they heard the crash inside. After a few minutes, Garda Naughtan emerged, his face flushed and his hair tousled. He shook his head at Bert, looking disappointed. Bert noticed a tiny twitch at the corner of Dunphy's mouth.

He asked, "Can we go into the house?"

"You can indeed. My mother will make you a cup of tea," Dunphy said.

"We'll follow you in," said Bert.

Garda Naughtan whispered, "There was nothing there, Sir. Only a few enamel buckets for mixing up animal feed and a bit of hose and string. No sign of any weapons. I even looked for a trapdoor under the hay. Nothing."

Bert indicated that he should be quiet, and they stepped over the threshold into the cottage. An old woman was sitting perched by the fire, knitting. She peered at them.

"*Dia dhuit, a Bhean Uí Dhuibhne.*" said Bert respectfully, removing his cap.

Garda Naughtan followed suit, standing one step behind him. Her son was standing on the other side of the fire ostentatiously warming his hands even though the weather was mild. The old woman smiled a toothless smile and waved them to two wooden chairs.

"*Dia 's Muire daoibh,*" she said.

Bert glanced around the cottage which was sparsely furnished and was without a curtained alcove, cupboard, or storage trunk which might conceal anything. The wooden table was scrubbed, and a small cracked jug in the middle of it contained a bunch of dried heather. Shelves on either side of the fireplace held crockery, an iron, and a loaf of bread wrapped in a cloth. A butter churn stood beside the old woman's seat. She didn't move from her place, but nodded absently, and returned to her knitting.

"She's having a bad day, today," said her son quietly.

She started rocking from side to side and singing tunelessly, completely ignoring them.

"Is it just yourselves, living here?" asked Bert, looking up to the rafters.

Nothing was hanging there, no herbs drying out, or a salted ham. There was a general air of neglect. There was very obviously no house-proud wife, just this middle-aged bachelor and his ailing mother. Bert had noticed a few sheep grazing in the field behind the house, and some chickens were scratching around the yard, but otherwise it seemed a barren place. Garda Naughtan nervously cleared his throat again. They were obviously not going to be offered tea and there was no need to search the place – everything was visible from where they stood. Dunphy said not a word.

"Thank you very much for your time, Mister Dunphy. Sorry to have disturbed you in your work."

Bert turned to leave.

"Not at all, you're very welcome, any time."

He grinned over at his mother. She didn't lift her eyes from the knitting but continued to sway and hum tunelessly. Garda Naughtan led the way and as they crossed the yard he tried to frame his question in a way that wouldn't sound stupid. Was it possible that the informant who had told them there were weapons concealed in the shed had just wanted to cause trouble for his island neighbour?

Suddenly Bert swung around and re-crossed the yard in three giant strides. He bent to look in the window. The old woman was standing up, waving her finger and scolding her son who was staring at the floor. Where she had been sitting there was a wooden barrel resembling the one on the butter churn and on top if it was her abandoned knitting. Out of the side of her eye she glimpsed Bert's face looking through the window and she leapt across the room, picked up the knitting and sat on the barrel again, spreading her skirts around her. When he knocked and walked in, she was humming again. Bert walked up to her.

"*Seas suas, le do thoil?* Stand up, please Mrs Dunphy?"

She feigned surprise to see him again and smiled inanely. He didn't move so she shrugged, looked venomously at her son and stood up, her long black skirts swishing around her ankles. Bert took hold of the five gallon barrel and swivelled it from side to side, feeling the liquid sloshing. He stepped over to the butter churn and lifted the lid. Inside was a heavy pottery crock in the shape of a large ink bottle.

"You haven't any cows on the island, so I was wondering why you would be making butter," he said.

Garda Naughtan, who was standing on the threshold, exhaled in astonishment. The clean sharp smell of poitín rose from the crock as Bert lifted it out of the churn and opened it.

"We'll have to take you across to the Garda station, I'm sorry to say," said Bert to the old woman.

She looked sheepishly at him. Her son cursed under his breath.

"You can't be taking an old woman and put her in jail," he said indignantly.

"Are you taking responsibility?" Bert asked, turning towards him.

"I am. It's my doing. She was only trying to protect me," Dunphy said between gritted teeth.

The woman said nothing, but as her son stepped out into the sunshine she let out a wail of frustration. Garda Naughtan rolled the barrel to the door and hefted it onto his shoulder. He carried it down to the boat without a rest and returned for the crock. It was standing empty by the door and the tang of poitín rose from the dirt in the yard as a wet trickle passed his feet.

"It's gone, anyhow," the woman said defiantly.

"The Guards are not having it, that's for sure."

He returned to the boat with the copper coil and copper pipe that had been hidden in the butter churn with the crock. Dunphy was sitting slumped on the seat in the stern, staring gloomily out over the water and ignoring Bert and the boatman.

They crossed the water in silence until Dunphy asked, "What made you come out to us?"

Bert did not reply.

"I suppose it was Jack Lydon, the divil, wanting to ingratiate himself with you early on," Dunphy muttered.

Garda Naughtan's eyebrows went up and Bert made a mental note to teach him how to play poker. Bert looked towards the shore, inhaling the tang of sea water churned by the oars, rolling with the gentle rocking motion as the boatman made each stroke. A lifelong fisherman, he deftly navigated them around rocks and through the shallow places and finally they came ashore at Baltimore. The Sergeant looked up when they came into the room.

"Liam Dunphy, is it yourself that's in it, again?"

The man stood, sullenly waiting to be charged.

"That's double the fine, so, for your second offence. Twenty four pounds."

The Sergeant was sitting at the rickety table they used as a desk, writing in the charge book and smiling as benignly as if he was recording a grocery bill.

"Double?" Dunphy spluttered. "Where am I going to find twenty four pounds?"

"Aren't you just here on behalf of your mother?" asked Bert, catching the Sergeant's eye.

"Has Mrs Dunphy been charged previously for possessing an illegal still?" he asked.

The Sergeant smiled.

"No, indeed not, she's an upright citizen with an unblemished record. Am I to record her name against the offence and to indicate that her son will pay the fine of twelve pounds on her behalf?"

Bert was already on the way down the stairs and pretended not to hear.

CHAPTER 35

Heaney's
Main Street
Skibbereen

15th January 1924

Dearest Ina

I hope this finds you well. I was very sad to read the letter from your father about Brendan being shot. He was a faithful Republican and it is a great tragedy that we have lost him. Unfortunately, we all know that his bravery exceeded his wits and without your father's steady guiding hand, he probably took one risk too many.

I hope that this 'war' will end soon so that we may be together. I could not expose you to the dangers and discomfort of our present conditions. We have less space here for each man than the prisoners in Kilmainham Gaol. The only difference is that we return to sleep here every night by choice! It is no wonder they would only recruit unmarried men.

I am sure there will be better days ahead. I noticed a snowdrop under a tree today. There is hope. Spring always comes, and perhaps by the summer, the fighting will be over.

Yours truly,
Bert

As Bert signed the letter there was a timid knock at the door.
He called out, "Come in."
After a moment when there was no response he stood up and opened the door. A small boy was standing there, his red knees sticking out of his shorts and hand with bitten fingernails held up as if ready to knock again. Bert could barely see his eyes through a tousled fringe of mousey hair.

"Please can you come to see Sister Angela at the convent?" he stammered, gulping as he spoke.

"Of course. I wonder what that is all about?"

The boy didn't think it was his place to enter into a conversation with the tall fella in charge of the Guards so he scampered down the stairs, turning at the bottom to make sure Bert was following. Bert took up his hat and followed the boy along Main Street. The lad jogged ahead, humming to prevent any opportunity for questioning and when they reached the Convent gate he tugged at the bell and ran away without a word or a backward glance.

A Novice in a white habit answered the gate with lowered eyes and showed Bert into a parlour murmuring that Sister Angela would be with him shortly. He never saw her face. The room was furnished sparsely but elegantly with two upright chairs flanking a gracious fireplace in which a freshly lit fire roared. A highly polished mahogany side table stood against one wall, adorned by a grand arrangement of dried grasses and flowers. A brown leather upholstered button-studded sofa gleamed softly in the ray of afternoon sunlight that crossed the room. A statue of the Madonna with child stood in the centre of the marble mantelpiece looking benevolently down at the place where Bert was sitting. He found it more disconcerting than the distant stare of Jesus from the wall of his childhood kitchen and after quickly glancing at the door he changed to sit in the other chair, feeling slightly ridiculous. Sister Angela glided silently into the room and crossed the parquet floor to shake his hand. He stood up and tried to make himself smaller in the way he had seen Sergeant Duggan do, to appear less intimidating.

"Good afternoon, Sister, it is very nice to meet you," he said.

She nodded, indicating that he should sit down. While the narrowness of her face was accentuated by the wimple and there was not even a wisp of hair to soften her forehead, the warmth in her dark brown eyes was unmistakeable. The Novice returned with a tea tray. Homemade biscuits, fresh out of the oven, steamed gently on the plate. She poured tea and Bert accepted a biscuit.

"I have been noticing the difference you've made in our small town," Sister Angela said forthrightly.

Bert thanked her. He must have looked slightly bemused because she started to elaborate.

"There is much less noise late at night on Main Street."
He nodded. Discouraging late night drinking would hardly transform the country but it was a starting point.

"And the poitín stills have been a scourge for many years. The poitín is responsible for many an evil deed. We haven't had law and order for so long now that it is a blessed relief to some of us to see you working so hard for us."

Bert was pleased, but he didn't really have time to sit around drinking tea and chatting with the nuns.

"You and your men must be very cramped, above in those rooms?" she asked.

The lift of her dark eyebrow was oddly framed by the wimple and veil.

"It is sometimes difficult, Sister," he replied. "But the old Barracks is too dilapidated to repair and there are no other premises available. There is no money to spare either. Our colleagues around the country are all facing the same problem."

"The Convent was recently bequeathed a small shop with several rooms. I was wondering if you could make use of it?"

"We certainly could, Sister Angela. It is very generous of you to think of us."

"Well, as I say, we have noticed that there is a general feeling of law and order returning to our community. If we can be of assistance in this way we would be delighted to draw up an agreement with you for the use of the building."

Bert was tempted to whistle as he returned to their makeshift accommodation after viewing the palatial new premises. The old draper's shop had a serving counter and space for people to wait, a tiny office and even separate rooms for the men to sleep in. There was a functioning stove as well as a fireplace, and a coat of whitewash would make it look like new.

The Gardaí huddled around the last embers of the fire, postponing the moment when they would have to move away from the hearth to lie down and get some rest. The new station would be ready by the end of the week. They were eagerly looking forward to the extra space and privacy.

Suddenly there was a loud hammering at the door. Bert caught the eye of each of the men before standing up to answer. He looked out onto the landing. It was full of men. The front man shouldered past, pushing at Bert's chest with the butt of a rifle. He stood silently while six or seven more men filed in and Bert focussed on each face, memorising every detail. No-one said a word. It was as if they were enacting a pre-scripted drama. The Gardaí were all standing now as if called to attention, but with their arms folded.

The Irregulars looked around in vain for anything to remove. The room was bare but for the stools the Guards had been sitting on and the four narrow wooden beds with their newly acquired mattresses. Their peremptory search did not reveal the station log book, concealed in a gap underneath the floorboards.

"Take off your jackets," shouted the leader, leaning into Garda Naughtan's face. Spittle sprayed Naughtan's cheek. He used the back of his hand to wipe it off and two of the men raised their rifles nervously. He slowly wiped his cheek and folded his arms again.

"Off. Take them off!" shouted another man.

He looked from one face to the next but didn't find a flicker of uncertainty in their gazes as they stood silently defying him. The smell of sweat and the sour breath of poor nourishment combined with too much poitín filled the room. The invaders fidgeted and the Gardaí stood like rocks.

"If it wasn't for our orders I would take great pleasure in lining them up and shooting them one by one," muttered one of the Irregulars.

"Would you ever shut your mouth," hissed another.

"*Imigh libh amach as seo...* Get out of here, we have nothing here worth taking but our lives. We would willingly give them to protect the people of Skibbereen. Would you take them?" Bert shouted at them in Irish.

He could see that most of them didn't understand a word. The leader jerked his rifle towards the door. They filed out, shamefaced and empty handed. In less than a minute, they were gone. Garda Naugthan whooped with delight and Bert reprimanded him.

"They'll hear you. If you make them feel they have lost this battle they'll have to come back to prove they're in charge."

They sat up for another hour, unable to sleep. Bert sent a message to Superintendent O'Duffy in Bandon the next morning. He appealed for the immediate issue of full uniforms. His men deserved better. They had stood firm, unwilling to surrender their jackets, the only symbol of their authority.

✳ ✳ ✳

Heaney's Drapery
Main Street
Skibbereen

23rd February 1924

Dearest Ina
You will notice little difference in the address, but we have moved! Our new station and accommodation are in a former drapery shop, bequeathed by 'Old Mr Heaney,' an elderly relative of our former landlord, to the Sisters of Mercy, who have kindly allowed us to use it as our new Garda station.

This week brought two welcome arrivals. The first was a parcel with the promised uniforms, including new belts and I could see my own pride reflected in the men's faces as we stood admiring each other. The second arrival was a new journal called *Iris na Garda,* Voice of the Guards. The minister for Home Affairs, Kevin O'Higgins contributed a most inspiring article. He said that democracy is the only barrier between mankind and anarchy. The *Garda Síochána* are in the fullest and truest sense, servants of the people and guardians of their peace, and we are set to become the finest police service in the world.

From a bad beginning, this week has turned out to be a watershed for me. I have no more doubts. I have not only a new uniform, but a new determination to succeed. I am counting the days until I see you.

Yours always
Bert

CHAPTER 36

April 1924

D affodils danced in the front garden as Bert strode up the path, enjoying the sound of his freshly heeled and polished boots striking on the gravel. He lifted the knocker on the black front door, his heart pounding. How long would he have to wait before he could speak to Ina alone? Before the roaring lion head had made contact with its brass pillow the door opened and Ina was standing there. She was wearing a dress he hadn't seen before and her hair was pinned up, showing off her long, delicate neck. He stood admiring her and realised after a moment that they hadn't spoken and that she was staring at him too. He ran his fingers through his hair nervously, and she laughed.

"You look so handsome!" she said.

He made a face, pretending to be hurt at her surprise.

"Come in!" she laughed.

She led him through the hall to the sitting room where the fire had been lit unusually early. There was no sign of her father and Bert could not believe that the moment had already come. Now that it was here he felt his stomach loosen and an inexplicable catch in his throat.

"You can take your cap off," Ina said, patting the couch beside the fire.

"Oh, I am sorry," he said, coughing to clear his throat.

"What on earth is the matter with you?" she asked gently.

She was wondering why he had chosen to sit in her father's chair, opposite her. Bert looked around nervously to make sure Bríd wasn't hovering in the doorway. There was no sound but the crackling of the kindling in the fireplace.

"Ina, I thought I would have more time to frame my thoughts," he started.

"Your thoughts?" she asked.

Her head was tilted to one side like a robin on a twig. She was not going to make this any easier for him.

"Would you do me the honour of becoming my wife?" he asked, half sliding out of the low chair onto one knee.

She giggled at the awkwardness of this big man, half kneeling, resplendent in his dark blue uniform, his hair gleaming with unaccustomed oil, looking so beseechingly at her.

"I would," she said, blushing.

His smile made her heart turn over.

"Thank you."

He stumbled to his feet then promptly sat down and took her hands in his, stretching across the hearth, looking into her eyes.

"It will not be easy in the beginning because we will have to be apart for some time yet, but peace will come and then we can have a safe and happy life together."

Ina nodded. She loved this new humility in him.

"I thought perhaps in the Summer?" he asked.

The door opened suddenly. Bert dropped her hands and they both sat up straight. Her father bustled into the room.

"Bert, is it yourself that's in it? How well you look, in your fine uniform!"

He shook Bert's hand heartily.

"I'll just have a quick word with Bríd about the dinner," Ina said.

She slipped out, closing the door quietly behind her. Bríd was just scurrying into the kitchen. Ina wondered how she could move so fast when she was eavesdropping but take so long to do her jobs. Bríd was filling the kettle at the sink.

"Will I make some tea, Miss?" she asked obsequiously.

"Yes please, Bríd. And Mr O'Brien will be staying for dinner."

"Yes, Miss," Bríd said, struggling to suppress a giggle.

Ina hovered nervously in the hall for a few moments before going back into the sitting room. Bert and her father were standing in front of the fire, shoulder to shoulder, each with a shot of whiskey in the best Waterford Crystal tumblers. Bert towered over her father, his shoulders seeming even broader in the dark uniform jacket. His hair was already rebelling and bristling up into the familiar brush on top of his head.

"Well, young lady, I have agreed to your young man's proposal," her father said. "Although I will be left on my own in my old age, with you down in Skibbereen or wherever they send him next."

"I don't anticipate taking Ina anywhere near Skibbereen with the county of Cork in its current state," said Bert pompously.

"She'll be the wife of a *Garda*, albeit a Superintendent, so she'll have to go where she's told," said her father.

"I'll make sure she's safe, wherever she is," said Bert.

Ina smiled. It looked as though she had fulfilled the age-old tendency of women to marry men like their fathers.

"Did Bert tell you we were thinking of the Summer?" asked Ina. "I would want to finish this year's teaching."

Her father nodded and sipped his whiskey.

"Yes indeed."

His face fell.

"It's a pity your mother isn't alive to see this day. A girl should have her Mammy to help with organising everything. I'll do my best, but I might ask your aunty Maureen..."

"Father's youngest sister," Ina explained for Bert's benefit.

"...to come and stay with us for a month or two, to help you with all the preparations."

"Thank you, Father, I think that is a lovely idea," said Ina.

"Would you like some tea?"

Bríd came in just then with her left ear burning red from pressing it against the door. She set the tray down on the table. Ina was the only one who partook of the tea. The men had another generous shot of whiskey to toast the happy couple.

They stood in front of the laurel hedge, suddenly uncomfortable with each other and the photographer laughed raucously.

"Stand closer; you are man and wife now, we won't say a thing!"

Ina smiled tentatively. Bert put his arm around her waist. There was no-body else in the garden. Ina's father was busy playing host to all the neighbours and his business associates, showing off the fine furniture and crockery and glassware that hadn't really been used since his own wife had died. What need did they have of it when it was just himself and Ina in the house? The French doors were thrown open to the soft summer air and the sounds of laughter and gramophone music carried out onto the lawn. Ina spread her hand on Bert's chest, displaying the simple gold band. He smiled down at her. She was like a swan, full of elegance and grace but fierce and strong when she needed to be.

His mother had immediately taken a liking to Ina when they met in the days leading up the wedding. They spent hours together walking and chatting over cups of tea. Bert had not seen his mother so animated for years. Papa was restless, out of his routine and uncomfortable in Máirtín Feeney's ebullient and ostentatiously prosperous company. Máirtín Feeney was trying his best but could not restrain his domineering manner or withhold his strongly expressed opinions. Papa had withdrawn into his shell and looked like a condemned man serving his sentence, just waiting for the big day to pass so that he could go home.

A few days before the wedding Bert found his father alone and asked what he thought of the new Ireland.

"You were right, Bertie. I was very upset when we were passing through Dublin. It's like a different city altogether, and as sad as I am to say it, Newcastle feels more like home to me now."

"How were Regina and Grace?" Bert asked.

"They were in good health, although of course the house was destroyed. That was another thing that upset me. Seeing the gap in the houses and only an empty space where our house used to be."

This was the first Bert had heard of it.

"Where are they living?"

"Their brother took them in. He has no family himself, so he had room for them."

"I feel terrible. I should have stayed in touch. They were very good to me when I first came over."

His father nodded.

"They were asking for you," he said, stroking his moustache.

His mother came in and overheard the exchange.

"They were grand, Bert. Don't be feeling guilty. They were grand. You can't be minding everyone."

On the eve of the wedding Bert and Ina strolled through Dunmore, deliberately parading for the eyes behind every curtain.

"I'm tempted to kiss you on the lips in front of them all," he said, turning to face her.

"Don't you dare!"

"What would you do?" he teased.

"I'd find a way to shame you in return," she said, with a glint in her eye.

"I'd better not risk it, then," he said, "It's taken long enough for me to get to this stage, only a few hours away from our wedding. I daren't risk annoying you now!"

"I'm glad you appreciate your position, Superintendent O'Brien," she said, "I think you'll go far."

"Do you think I neglect my family?" he asked, frankly.

She nodded.

"I think my father gets more letters from Gerald in Africa than you ever send to your parents."

"I have very little in common with them any more," he said ruminatively.

"Every time I see them I feel as if I've changed and they have stayed the same. I've left them behind."

"Maybe that's how it happens in every generation," she said.

"Gerald is a priest. He'll always be the son of Máirtín Feeney and never be anyone else's father or grandfather. Maybe because of that he has a stronger sense of his duty as a son."

"It's a funny word, isn't it? Duty. It sounds so noble. But it's a two-sided coin. Leo thought he was doing his citizen's duty by fighting in the war but he betrayed his duty as a son just by joining up. Eamonn betrayed Mairéad when he put his duty to his beloved Ireland ahead of his love for her."

"I think we all do our duty to the love we hold dearest," Ina said.

They turned back down Castle Street so that he could take her home to Balla House for the last time.

CHAPTER 37

The latest *Fógra Tóraigh* was lying on Bert's desk. He sighed. He wondered if any of his men would take the time to read it and memorise the details. Only last week he had tested them and they failed miserably. Although he had made Ina laugh when he told her the story, it was infuriating. The weekly notice contained descriptions of men who were wanted for murder or burglary or suspected terrorism and included their physical details, where they had last been seen and any known facts about them. Last Wednesday, Garda Murray had come into the station and said there was a suspicious looking man having a pint in the snug in one of the public houses in Oughterard. Bert had asked him if the stranger met any of the descriptions in the *Fógra Tóraigh*, at which the Guard had shrugged, as if it was a matter of indifference to him.

Bert had summoned all the Guards who were on duty and lined them up. He called out the names of the wanted men and asked each of the Guards in turn to give a physical description. They mumbled and struggled, remembering some random details but nothing useful. Finally, he had come to young Garda Welsh, for whom he had an inexplicable soft spot.

He gave him the last name on the list, "Freeman Reese, wanted for murder."

Garda Welsh gulped nervously, his Adam's apple riding up his skinny neck and a flush making the spots on his face even more vivid.

"Five foot eight inches, fair hair, fresh complexion," he said.

Bert was incandescent.

"*Is fear gorm é!* He's a black man!" he shouted.

As if the place was full of black men. What kind of a fool would run away from London and come to hide out in Ireland where he would stand out like a sore thumb? Bert had declared angrily that the wanted man, probably the only black man in the whole of the country, could probably have walked into the Garda station to ask for directions to Spiddal and have them all running around to help him and then going home to tell their wives they had seen a real, live black man.

Now, he sat behind his desk and dispiritedly flicked through the week's notices. Since the IRA had been declared illegal after the recent rash of bombings in England there were more and more names appearing on the notices. Some of the names he recognised from years ago. Most of the recent IRA activity was happening in Dublin and up near the border, but it paid to be vigilant. Only last week they had raided a house out near Oughterard and found an illegal weapon. Garda Welsh had arrested the man of the house, Tomás Ó Liodáin, and brought him into the Garda station for questioning.

"Not a word of English to this fella, now," said Bert, as they entered the interview room.

"Why not?" the younger man asked.

"He's a *Gaelgóir*. He thinks in Irish. We need to get inside his head."

"*Cé thé a bfhuil tú?*" he asked Ó Liodáin, who was slumped on a wooden chair, staring at his boots.

"I could be better," the man replied.

"What happened, that you ended up with a gun hidden in your house, with the times that are in it?" Bert asked gently, continuing in Irish.

He looked into Ó Liodáin's eyes. There was no defiance, no guilt, only fear. Was he protecting someone?

"How old is your son?" he asked.

The man's eyes widened.

"He turned fifteen last month," he said, looking down again.

"Does he do a bit of poaching?" Bert asked.

Ó Liodáin looked up, pleading for understanding.

"Only the odd time. We lost five acres of potatoes to the blight this year. I know it's wrong, but when the children are hungry, you do rash things."

"Where did he get the gun?"

"He says he found it. I didn't ask any more questions. I thought it was better not to know."

"And what do you think, now?" Bert asked.

"I was stupid. I should have made him take it back. I should have made him work for his food somewhere, instead of..."

"What's done is done. We need to know where he found the gun."

Ó Liodáin muttered, "I can find out for you."

"Bring him in and we'll ask him ourselves. He needs a fright, to understand how serious this is."

The father nodded furiously.

"Bring him in yourself tomorrow morning and we'll talk to him," said Bert, pushing his chair back.

"I can go?" he looked confused.

"Go home and bring him back tomorrow with you."

Bert left the interview room and returned to his paperwork. He drew a sharp breath. The name he dreaded seeing, above all names, was there in black and white. Michael Power was wanted for membership of the IRA and for suspected involvement in an armed raid on a Post Office. The man must be nearly sixty by now.

Bert had not thought of Michael for many years. Occasionally when he took a day off to go fishing on Lough Corrib Bert would remember those early years; how he had worshipped the blue eyed, smiling Connemara man full of passion and patriotism. He sighed. Ó Liodáin passed the window outside and touched his cap. The Sergeant came in with a mug of tea.

"Mr Ó Liodáin sends his regards."

He slid a five pound note across the desk.

Bert stared at the grimy note and said icily, without looking up, "I would strongly suggest that you get your lazy legs under you and run after that man as fast as they will carry you, to return his lost property."

"Yes, Sir," said the Sergeant.

He was gone before Bert took the first hot, refreshing sip of tea. He slid open his desk drawer and took out an oaten biscuit from the tin that Ina filled for him every Monday morning.

Bert was silent as they passed through Spiddal and Inverin the next day, with Garda Welsh at the wheel and Sergeant Tobin in the back seat. To their left across Galway Bay the purple hills of Clare stood out like a dark bruise against a pale white sky and Bert wondered how long it would be before Garda Welsh trotted out the joke that had become a ritual whenever they went out west on the coast road. He just couldn't face it today.

"The mountains are very clear, aren't they?"

Bert would agree, and Garda Welsh would grin.

"You know what they say around here, don't you? If you can see them clearly it's going to rain and if you can't see them at all it's raining already!"

Bert would laugh politely, and Garda Welsh's smile would last for a mile or two. Maybe he would have the wit to stay quiet.

Bert felt like a man going to the gallows. His mouth was dry and there was a knot in his stomach. He hadn't eaten any breakfast, even when Ina had urged him to be sensible. His early morning cup of tea scalded his throat when he gulped it down, eager to get going but finding every reason to delay; looking for his wallet, polishing his shoes, even offering to help with the children. Ina calmly presented him with bread and cheese in a brown paper bag, took hold of his two arms and turned him towards the front door. She pushed him firmly, her small hands surprisingly strong.

"Go, Bert. I can hear the car. They're waiting for you. God Bless."

All along the road, out past Bearna and Furbo they were hailed; with a pitchfork waved from a field of freshly cut hay, a raised cap outside the hotel in Spiddal, a flourish of a whip from the seat of a pony trap. Bert waved back but felt none of the warmth he usually took from their greetings. People might have been thinking as the car went past how unusual it was for three Gardaí to travel together. Two men were sufficient for the routine inspections in Spiddal and Clifden. Only a murder would justify three. His men knew they were going to Carraroe to carry out an arrest.

The young Ó Liodáin had not taken long to tell Bert the whole story. The father was devastated. The boy had not found the gun but had been given it and told to hide it and wait for instructions. He sat behind the table at the Garda station, his legs twitching nervously, the freckles standing out against his pale skin, his pupils dilated. He described the man.

"He said he would let me know when I was needed. He said there was important jobs to do and I would get training. There's a place in Letterfrack where they do the training."

"What kind of training?" Bert asked.

"In the name of God, Seán, what were you thinking?" his father wailed.

"I don't know," the boy sobbed.

"Wait, wait. Don't say another word."

Ó Liodáin put his hand up in front of his son's face and looked desperately at Bert.

"They kill informants. Don't make him tell you any more."

"How was he going to get in touch with you?" Bert continued, implacable.

The boy froze and refused to speak another word. But he had already said enough.

They passed the crossroads to Rossaveal, turning away from the sea, and the landscape changed. Long grass rippled in the summer breeze like another golden sea and small dark blue lakes were frilled by tiny white waves. Bog cotton nodded. They passed a man saving turf, who raised his cap. His donkey waited, slack-kneed, in the shafts of an old cart. A small turf fire burned under a kettle and a child sat on her hunkers waiting for it to boil. Two boys were footing turf and didn't even look up at the sound of the car engine.

"There's nothing finer than the cup of tea you have when you're out saving turf," said Sergeant Tobin, smacking his lips.

Bert's stomach rumbled. He should really eat the bread and cheese, but he gagged at the thought of it. He opened the passenger window a crack to let in some fresh air. Only another ten minutes to go. The two men had picked up on his mood and were silent as they drove the last few miles, the road curving towards the sea again, the heady tang of seaweed coming in through Bert's window.

"Do you know the house, Sir?" asked Garda Welsh, slowing as they entered the village.

A group of children on their school holidays and not yet burdened with any chores were skipping along the road, singing. Bert gave terse directions and in less than a minute the car pulled up outside a cottage. The door was shut, but through the small windows they could see some movement in the gloomy interior.

"Broad shouldered, blue eyes, fair complexion, six foot four," murmured Garda Welsh as they stepped out of the car.

Bert knocked. The door opened. The man's eyes widened slightly and he rubbed his wet face with his hands and then wiped them down his trousers.

"Herbert Vincent O'Brien," said the man, smiling wryly. "*An bhfuil aon iasc agat?* Have you any fish with you?"

Will you come back to the Garda station with us?" Bert asked in English.

"Did you need three of you for such an old man as myself?"

The Guards stood on either side of him and he walked, moving slightly stiffly, to the car. They put Michael Power in the back seat and the Sergeant looked to Bert, who nodded and climbed in the back too. The car started up.

"*Tá mé tuirseach, a Bhert. Tháinig mé abhaile faoi choine sos beag ar feadh tamaillín beag.* I am tired, Bert. I came home to rest for a little while."

Bert was fighting back tears.

"*Tá brón orm.* I'm sorry."

EPILOGUE

September 1939

The big car drove up Taylor's Hill, through the tunnel of tall chestnut and sycamore trees whose branches met above the road. There was still heat in the sun even this late in the day, unusual in September. Bert wiped a bead of sweat from his forehead. Two veiled nuns emerged from the Sisters of Mercy Convent, engrossed in a serious conversation. They didn't acknowledge the passing car. A blackbird declared the end of a sweltering, humid day and Bert looked forward to a little nip of whiskey before his dinner to celebrate his promotion to Chief Superintendent, confirmed in writing today.

Ina would smile and put her hand on his arm and tell him it was well deserved but she understood the bitter sweetness of it. She was still his rock and his anchor, the mother of his seven children, and another one on the way. She had walked every step of the journey beside him, from Bandon to a brief sojourn in Bray, before happily returning to their beloved west of Ireland, first to Letterkenny, and then to Galway. The children were thriving under her loving guidance.

Bert was glad he had asked Garda Welsh to drive him home today, so he could arrive in his full glory. Conor and Fintan would come running out to say hello to Garda Welsh. They had a soft spot for him, too.

As the car crested the hill, Bert could see the two boys there, perched on the gate pillars, their pale, skinny legs dangling beneath grey flannel shorts. His heart lifted. They were too old for sitting on the pillars scuffing the white paint with their boots, but this time he would say nothing. They were waiting for him.

As soon as the fourteen-year-old Conor saw his father, he stood up, tall and lanky on the top of the pillar, his dark hair tousled, his eyes gleaming with excitement.

He shouted, "Daddy, the English declared war with Germany!"

A FINE YOUNG MAN

Sharon Mulrooney

Acknowledgements

This is truly a work of fiction, inspired by some of the anecdotes my Dad heard from my grandfather as they fished on Loch Corrib in the late nineteen fifties, when the stories were still quite fresh. In my research, both into family history and into the real events of the time, I learned a lot about how the telling of a story changes the truth of it, little by little, until sometimes even the people who lived through it would not know it was theirs. My wish in telling it this way is to capture the essence of the times, to reveal the dilemmas and to illustrate the courage it sometimes takes to simply live an ordinary life when your country is in conflict.

Thank you to Ciarán Mac Guill for his help with the first drafts of the Irish; any errors or missing *fadas* after editing are mine! Thanks to the many different Irish teachers I had as a child; we lived in three of the Provinces, so my rusty Irish is a mix of Connaught, Leinster and Munster varieties.

A heartfelt *Go raibh míle maith agat* to Peadar Mac Fhlannchadha of Conradh na Gaeilge for his amazing support with the Connaught Irish, and his advice on some of my first draft anachronisms – voles, marts and GAA under 21s!

Thank you, Jane Onslow for your diplomatic feedback about typos and babbling brooks. Print on demand rocks!

Thank you to Michael Burdett for his thorough research and finding the perfect picture for my Fine Young Man. The Guinness Archive was a treasure trove of documents including employment records of my great grandfather and my great uncle, 'a son of employee'. The National Archives of Ireland and the Garda Síochána museum were also great sources of information, including my grandfather's application to be a guard in 1924 and copies of the magazine 'Iris na Garda.'

Thanks to the diligent work of the War Graves Commission I was able to visit my great uncle Leo's grave in Arras, a moving and humbling experience.

Thank you, Colin for encouraging me to tell the story and not to let it lie, and for encouraging and supporting me in everything I do.

And Da, thanks for retelling the stories so we can pass them on.

30692064R00153

Printed in Poland
by Amazon Fulfillment
Poland Sp. z o.o., Wrocław